CELG

W9-DGP-734

ALL SHE
*L*EFT
*B*EHIND

Center Point
Large Print

Also by Jane Kirkpatrick and available from
Center Point Large Print:

The Memory Weaver
This Road We Traveled

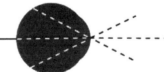

**This Large Print Book carries the
Seal of Approval of N.A.V.H.**

ALL SHE
*L*EFT
*B*EHIND

JANE KIRKPATRICK

CENTER POINT LARGE PRINT
THORNDIKE, MAINE

This Center Point Large Print edition
is published in the year 2017 by arrangement with
Revell, a division of Baker Publishing Group.

Copyright © 2017 by Jane Kirkpatrick.

All rights reserved.

This book is a work of historical fiction based
closely on real people and events. Details that
cannot be historically verified are purely
products of the author's imagination.

The text of this Large Print edition is unabridged.
In other aspects, this book may vary
from the original edition.
Printed in the United States of America
on permanent paper.
Set in 16-point Times New Roman type.

ISBN: 978-1-68324-542-1

Library of Congress Cataloging-in-Publication Data

Names: Kirkpatrick, Jane, 1946– author.
Title: All she left behind / Jane Kirkpatrick.
Description: Center Point Large Print edition. | Thorndike, Maine :
    Center Point Large Print, 2017.
Identifiers: LCCN 2017031109 | ISBN 9781683245421
    (hardcover : alk. paper)
Subjects: LCSH: Oregon Territory—History—Fiction. | Large type
books. |GSAFD: Christian fiction.
Classification: LCC PS3561.I712 A78 2017b | DDC 813/.54—dc23
LC record available at https://lccn.loc.gov/2017031109

For Jerry

If I were to wish for anything, I should not wish for wealth and power, but for the passionate sense of the potential, for the eye which, ever young and ardent, sees the possible. Pleasure disappoints, possibility never.

—Søren Kierkegaard,
Either/Or: A Fragment of Life

The impeded stream is the one that sings.

—Wendell Berry

Cast of Characters

Jennie Pickett: early Oregon citizen
Charles Pickett: Jennie's husband, assistant
    superintendent of Oregon State Prison
Douglas Pickett: son of Jennie and Charles
Baby Ariyah: deceased daughter of the Picketts
Lucinda Sloan: Jennie's sister and housemate
Joseph Sloan: Jennie's brother-in-law, Charles
    Pickett's boss as superintendent of OSP
Nellie and Mary: Sloan children
*****Ariyah Cole:** Jennie's best friend
*****Alexandro:** Ariyah and Peleg's son
Jacob and Mary Lichtenthaler: Jennie's
    parents (farmers and legislators)
George Lichtenthaler: Jennie's brother
    (botanist)
David "DW" Lichtenthaler: Jennie's brother
    (lawyer and judge)
Fergus Lichtenthaler: Jennie's brother, butcher
    and later policeman in Portland
William Lichtenthaler: Jennie's brother, farmer
    near Salem
Mathias and Rebecca: Jennie's siblings,
    deceased
Josiah Parrish: early missionary, blacksmith,

Indian agent, benefactor of Blind and Deaf school, Trustee of Willamette University

Elizabeth: first wife of Josiah Parrish, benefactor of orphanage

Norman Parrish (wife Henrietta): child of Josiah and Elizabeth

Samuel Parrish: child of Josiah and Elizabeth

Charles Winn Parrish (wife Annie): child of Josiah and Elizabeth

Lamberson (deceased): child of Josiah and Elizabeth

Charley Chen: Chinese cook

*Lizzie: maid and nanny of Josiah and Jennie

Callie Charlton: (child is Lenora) colleague and fellow student with Jennie

Mary Sawtelle: Jennie's doctor

*Character not based on historical person

ALL SHE
L EFT
B EHIND

Prologue

L ove came later, when his words reached out to catch her as she fell, offering a cushion of comfort that held her and began the healing before she even knew the depth of ache and loss she carried. "Dreams delayed are not always dreams destroyed," he told her. That truth brought healing to her life.

But her story begins long before that day, on her wedding day, when Jane "Jennie" Lichtenthaler took Charles Pickett to be her wedded husband. Their vows were spoken at her sister's Hillsboro home, Washington County, Oregon, a state just celebrating its first birthday. A judge presided, even though her father was a pastor and could have officiated. It was five o'clock in the afternoon, March 27, 1860.

Later, each guest brought a lantern to the wedding dance and set it along the boardwalk, the shards of light a path the hopeful couple would follow into the Tualatin Hotel. Charles and Jennie slipped through the Oregon mist, the lantern lights shining on her slippers, sprinkling liquid diamonds onto almost auburn hair. The last to arrive, as was the custom, they laughed beneath the hotel's canopy covering the entrance. March, a month of new beginnings, is often marked by rain in the Willamette Valley. Jennie settled her hooped skirts, brushed water drops of weather from the yellow-dyed linen, and straightened the waist bow, as large as her husband's fist. He stood behind to smooth the ribbons cascading down Jennie's back, his hands then gentle at her bare shoulders, his fingers a tingle on her skin. "Ready?" he whispered in her ear.

At seventeen, she thought she was.

She nodded. Charles kissed her cheek, commented on her dimples, and they stepped through the doorway into the promise of their new lives, greeted by the music, laughter, and good wishes. Cheers went up and someone struck a tambourine to thrill the fiddlers into a faster jig, which Charles took as a sign to swing Jennie onto the cornmeal-covered floor. He swirled his bride as she caught glimpses of her father's smile, her mother's tears upon her cheeks. Ariyah, Jennie's friend and wedding witness, waved her gloved fingers as they danced by. Jennie's brothers and sisters clapped and stomped their feet to the fiddle and tambourine. The strong face of Josiah Parrish, the reverend and Indian agent, graced the crowd as they swished across the oak floor, his silver beard the only sign of age, belying the stories of the courage associated with a much younger man. He was a friend of Jennie's parents; his wife a generous soul whose dress of red stood out among the many darker cloths much easier to acquire in this far western place. Jennie leaned her head back and she let her husband lead her. Each guest blurred into a room of goodwill carrying present and future prayers for happiness.

Then Charles lost his footing.

Jennie blamed the cornmeal.

His arms flailed as though a skater on ice and he slipped from her perspiring fingers. She reached but they couldn't grasp each other. Charles fell backward. In the slow arc of disaster, she heard the crack of his head against the hardwood floor, his moan into sudden silence as the fiddlers saw the fall unfold and lowered their bows.

Jennie bent over him. "Charles? Charles?"

His eyes rolled away and he lay quiet. Someone gentled Jennie aside, but she saw Charles return, his eyes open, try to focus. The crowd helped sit him up. Charles rubbed his head.

"Is there a doctor here?" someone shouted.

"I'm fine." He listed, woozy. Joseph Sloan, Charles's new brother-in-law (and boss), clapped his back as others stood him up, brushed off his dark pants of the cornmeal, and flicked the grains from white blousy sleeves. He'd removed his coat with the dancing heat. Others urged Charles toward his new wife and she reached for his hand. He grabbed and held it.

"Are you all right?" She shouted in his ear to be heard above the music that had begun again.

His answer was to hold her elbow, turn her out toward the crowd, and bellow, "It's the father's dance with the bride." Her father moved forward as her husband handed Jennie off. One of her twin brothers took her mother's hand to dance. To Jennie, Charles said, "I need fresh air. Don't feel so good. Be back soon, promise." He rubbed his neck and Joseph Sloan walked out beside him, steadying him.

Is that blood on the back of his head?

Her father began the now much slower waltz as Jennie twisted, trying to watch the two men disappear outside. "He'll be fine. Just took a little spill."

She nodded, tried to let the music slow her racing pulse. She didn't tell her father what she'd seen that quickened her heart: something in Charles Pickett's countenance had changed.

Chapter 1
Sharing All That Matters

Six Years Later

Spring in the Willamette Valley is rain-soaked grasses pierced by early blooms. " 'And then my heart with pleasure fills and dances with the daffodils.' " Jennie Pickett quoted Wordsworth to her almost-three-year-old boy, Douglas, as they walked toward Pringle Creek in Salem. The short, white-petaled wildflowers dotted the fields, colorful essentials breaking the soil and the winter malaise and the pall from President Lincoln's assassination the year before.

In a rare respite, Jennie and Douglas followed the path toward the tributary of the Willamette. Jennie spoke the word in her head, *Will-AM-it,* a pronunciation people said didn't match with its spelling. But spelling had never been Jennie's gift. Mother and son walked beside the mighty river, watched the commerce of ferry crossings, steamships, and small river craft gliding on its surface.

Dougie was never one to settle easily, and Jennie gripped him tighter at his urge to pull away, caught his emerald eyes that matched her own. "If we're very quiet when we reach the creek, we'll see a surprise. You can look through the brass and glass. Would you like that?" That slowed his resistance, and he reached around to grab at the quilt draped over his mother's arm, the telescope safe beneath it.

"You let me?"

"Yes. Careful." He matched his pace to hers, skipping but still letting himself be held. They stopped to look at beetle tracks in the sand, listened as a hawk screeched in the distance. Jennie was pleased she'd left her hoops at home, as she could feel her son press against her side, his closeness warm and welcome through her blue-dyed linen skirt.

They reached the shoreline and Dougie nestled among the willows, then stood, wiggling as a child does. Jennie patted the quilt, urging him to sit, to lie on bellies side-by-side. For a moment a thread on the nine-patch gained his interest. Then he sat up and lifted the quilt to seek what bugs or twigs beneath it might need his scant attention.

The Schyrle brass and glass lay beside Jennie, the draws already out so she could quickly put the eyepiece to her face and then to his when the time was right. She debated about a practice look, decided against it. Like all almost-three-year-old boys, he could be a scamp about other people's things. She still taught boundaries and borders, yours and mine and others' being concepts in formation. A warm breeze brushed her cheeks.

Jennie had witnessed the promised "surprise" three times now. On the first occasion, she'd been uncertain of what she'd really seen and didn't have the Schyrle Jennie's brother George had brought all the way from France. The next time, she intentionally carried the telescoping glass, and like a prayer answered, the "surprise" happened again, an intersection she claimed of Divine presence into her fretful days, a gift to move her another step through the grieving of a great loss. That day, she hoped it would happen again so she could share it with her son.

"Lie beside me." She patted the spread quilt. The viewing spot beside the creek was hidden from the water but close enough they could see the ripples, hear the impeded stream gurgling around tree falls and rocks. She whispered, "There, you see?"

"See what, Mama?"

"Shhh. The fox. We'll see if he does what he's done before. That's the surprise."

"I see foxes. Daddy shows me." He pushed away from her, rose on his knees, scanned with his eyes, looked for the Schyrle, then turned back to the creek.

Jennie lifted the brass and glass and allowed the practice view. She helped him hold the telescope as she sat behind him. "Look at that rock there. You'll have to close one eye." She leaned around to see his face.

He squeezed both eyes shut, opened each, tried again. Jennie hid her smile.

"Pretend you want to wink at me. I've seen you do that."

He giggled, then put his own finger to his lips, remembering to be quiet. He tried again and this time he closed the eye not against the lens.

She held the wooden barrel for him. "Can you see the rock?" He nodded, which took the lens from his eye. "Try again."

"I see, Mama." His voice held excitement. "E-nor-mous."

"Yes. It does look big through the glass. Now when the fox comes by, if he does, look at his head. This fox plans and we can see him doing it if we're very patient and wait." A warmth filled her stomach, so pleased she was by her son following her direction. He often didn't, listening more to his father and his aunt and uncle than to her—even his cousins and the boarders who lived with them held his attention better. Today, he held the Schyrle, a precious instrument. An artist had painted a calla lily on the smooth wooden barrel.

Birds sang into the silence as Dougie swung the Schyrle back and forth through the air like a confused symphony conductor.

20

"Careful." They wouldn't be able to stay much longer.

With her hand she stopped Dougie's thrusting. She pointed as the animal trotted along the opposite bank that narrowed the waterway. One could see the rusty-red fur with the naked eye, but seeing the surprise required the Schyrle. She modeled stillness, then softly, "Can you see the fox?"

"Yes, Mama." He mimicked whispering.

"Good boy. Watch what he does."

The fox had stopped at a willow and did what she'd seen him do before: he tugged at tufts of wool that passing sheep had left behind. The creak of willow canes as he mouthed the wool snapped in the still air. Again and again, he pulled at wooly bits until he had a mouthful. Then the fox plunged into the creek, his muzzle still a foam of grayish-looking fur. His head and the top of his back cut a chevron in the water.

"What's he doing, Mama?"

"Look through the brass and glass." He turned back. "Point it at his head. See?" He nodded, moving the telescope, and she chided herself for asking him questions he felt compelled to answer.

As the slow current carried the fox along—they were so close—small black dots leapt from the fox's head and nose and dropped onto the bits of wool in the fox's mouth. The animal then released small tufts into the water. Laden with fleas and bugs, the islands of wool floated away from him. "Keep following with the Schyrle. I hope you can see the little black things jumping from his head to the little boats of wool he spits out."

Dougie sat spellbound, watching as the cleansing continued until the fox swam around a bend, out of sight. Unbidden tears formed in her eyes. She wasn't certain if the tears came from the delight at witnessing this natural event with her son or at some unknown emotion moving in to fill grief's leaving.

Dougie turned his head and she took the Schyrle from him. He smiled. "What was that, Mama?"

"That fox found a way to get rid of unwanted visitors to his fur."

He frowned, then tucked his chin in thought.

"Those little black things bouncing from the fox's head were fleas and ticks, creatures that trouble him. They jump onto his fur when he's not looking, but he knows they're there."

She collapsed the telescope back into the barrel, clipped the lens cover over the end. They stood. She considered asking Dougie to hold the Schyrle while she folded the quilt but didn't want to test his good behavior. She put it down, draped the quilt over her arm, then lifted the lens, noting Dougie's still-confused face.

"He gathers wool from the willows and then lets the wool trick those little beasts into leaving his fur. They think they're hopping onto another sentient being instead of onto little wool boats that will carry them away."

"Sent-tent?"

"Sen-tee-ent." She sounded the word out and hugged her son. "The fox is a warm being with breath and blood and heart. It can feel pain and even plays at times. I've seen that fox jump up on all four feet and hop around. We are feeling, sentient beings too. We have that in common with animals. That fox tricked those bothersome things into floating away from him." She lifted a bit of lint from Dougie's short pants.

"I run ahead, Mama."

"Yes. But be careful."

She bent down to kiss his cheek as he startled forward toward his next adventure. But then he turned his face, popping warm lips on her cheek instead as he scampered away. She folded the quilt, cast a last glance at the daffodils, touching her fingers where Dougie had planted that rare kiss. A second surprise.

She walked the path back to her sister's home, keeping Dougie in sight, breathing in the scent of spring, allowing the light breeze to lift strands of hair from her bonnet-less head. Dougie disappeared behind the house and would likely untie the dog, who barked his own impatience at not being allowed to go with them. Inside, the world would be in full motion.

A steamboat whistle shrieked in the distance as Jennie ascended the wooden steps. Would the cargo boat have brought her latest shipment, unloading it at Pringle Creek before the boat headed to Eugene? She hated waiting for cargo from San Francisco. There'd been lung illness each summer in the Salem village, and Jennie did her best to keep her family healthy. The oils and aromatics she ordered helped cleanse the house and heal bodies.

It came to her then as she opened the door that the fox was not only clever, but that he was a self-healer, one who didn't wait for something or someone else to solve his discomfort of ticks and fleas that irritated his days. He'd found release with a little help from the sheep who wandered past and left their wool. Had he thought it through somehow? Was it the gift of instinct? Who knew? What mattered was that it worked and he had cleverly healed himself. Perhaps all sentient beings had that capacity. There was a lesson there. Jennie just had to learn it.

Chapter 2
From Loss to Repair

Lucinda lifted her eyes from her work to greet Jennie. "There you are. I wondered what happened to you two."

"We took a little hike." Jennie hurried past, up the stairs, and put the quilt back into the trunk, laid the Schyrle onto it, then rushed back down.

"Nellie cried looking for you." The child sucked a thumb as she stood beside her mother. "Mary wondered too."

I should have taken the girls with us. "I'm sorry. We walked by the creek. This fox came by. Have I told you about that?" She lifted her apron from the kitchen hook, dropped it over her head, then wrapped the strings around her still-tender middle. Tender from the birth—and death—of her baby.

Lucinda wiped her forehead of the dampness worked up while she kneaded the bread dough before her. A second pang of guilt rose up: Jennie shouldn't have been off playing with her son while Lucinda worked so hard. But they all labored.

Charles and Joseph Sloan had worked to

25

build the two-story clapboard house they lived in. Though it had three bedrooms, it was nonetheless crowded with the Sloans, Picketts, and new boarders. The three single men shared one room and the two sisters and their families found scant privacy in the other two bedrooms. At times it felt like they were still on the wagon train that brought them from Illinois to Oregon, exposing them to new people finding their places in a moving menagerie of hope elbowed by discomfort. Jennie was only ten when she traveled the Oregon Trail with the "Missionary Train," but she remembered the strangeness of so many new people and the habit her parents had of inviting others to their fires. Her sister collected strays too, and more than once Jennie wondered if she wasn't one of them, arriving at Lucinda's hearth when she was fifteen, perhaps having worn her own parents out.

The boarders left each morning, securing work as bricklayers, fashioning harnesses, or helping widows plant their beans and peas. They brought home happy stories from their labor. Joseph and Charles brought their work home too, but their talk didn't contribute to an enlightened atmosphere. Joseph was the superintendent of the Oregon State Prison, containing those convicted or feebleminded; and Charles was his assistant. The county spent twice the money on dealing with the legal system as on building roads, a disparity Charles and Joseph thought appropriate until a horse became mired in muck while taking a prisoner from court to jail. They didn't share Jennie's view—that everything was interconnected, roads and criminals two threads to the weave of humanity.

Charles and Joseph spoke of control and punishment, sometimes making fun of the feebleminded, which made Jennie sad and, worse, guilty that she didn't speak up to defend them. They never pondered about how people came to be the way they were, unable to think clearly or making choices that landed them in prison.

"You're soft, Jennie," Joseph pronounced once when she braved the confab at the table to bring up an alternative to the opinion that their prisoners were worthless men.

"Justice and mercy both are required of us," Jennie said.

Charles snickered into his soup bowl.

Joseph pointed his fork, jabbing a bite of duck toward her. "You can't heal everything, Jennie Pickett. Your oils might be good for children and docile women but not for those with hardened hearts."

Charles kept his blue eyes to his bowl, not wanting to disagree with his boss. She supposed she was fortunate Charles didn't say out loud what he growled about in their room: how his hard-earned money ought not be spent on oils

27

and aromatics, lavender and licorice root. But they were her passion, healing not an effort to her but rather her greatest joy.

Jennie shook her head of the memory. She sighed, patted her apron that smelled of lavender soap she'd made. She continued telling Lucinda about the fox, reaching for the rolling pin. "This fox—I assume it's the same one each time—trots along and takes sheep's wool from the willows and, with a mouthful, jumps into the water." Lucinda's brow furrowed, so Jennie sped up her telling. "As he floats along, he releases tufts, but only after the bugs and whatnot from his fur have hopped onto the wool. They disappear and he's free of them. It's a cleansing ritual. Self-healing. Quite fascinating to witness."

"You got close enough to see that?"

"My eyes are good. And I had my Schyrle."

"I wasn't questioning you." Lucinda reached her hand across the table to touch Jennie's as she pressed the rolling pin on the dough.

"I know that. Everything urges my . . . defensiveness, I'd guess I'd call it. Then I turn to weepy." Her eyes watered, unbidden.

"Your wounds are still fresh." Lucinda spoke with a mothering tone. "How sweet you got to see something like that fox. I suppose the sheep scrape against the willows?"

Jennie nodded. "Maybe Reverend Parrish's Merino ewes are leaving wool behind. I wonder if I could pluck enough to spin some of that fine wool for a shawl."

"And deprive your fox?" Lucinda laughed.

"And deprive my fox." Jennie smiled, wiped her eyes with the edge of the apron. It smelled of sunshine too. Why the sight of the daffodils and fox brought such comfort she didn't know. Perhaps a sign that she'd now start thinking of happier, healing things.

Jennie had named their baby Ariyah after her best friend. The word in Italian meant "musical" and in Greek it suggested "pure." She liked the sound of the word, and its meaning even more, asking her friend to write it down so she could memorize the letters. Pure music. It was perfect for a child born without blemish and whom Jennie had sung songs to while the infant grew within.

Charles had crafted the coffin, suggested Jennie line it with silk. They buried her in November, the ground rarely freezing in the Willamette Valley, so she could be laid to rest in a steady drizzle. The child was rarely mentioned now—doing so upset Charles. But Ariyah was seldom far from Jennie's mind.

After the death, Charles's evenings took on the pattern of disappearing with Joseph, both returning late. He brushed aside Jennie's need to speak of Baby Ariyah, creating a widening space between them.

The evening of the fox sighting, Jennie had intended to share that happy memory, but Charles was in one of his moods, offering one-word answers to questions about his day. She put Dougie to bed and didn't mention the fox. She spoke her evening prayers, whispering Ariyah's name.

"The baby didn't require a name." He spoke into the darkness as they lay side by side in their featherbed.

"Not name her?" This was a new complaint. His grieving took a twisted turn. "God gave names to everything he made. We always name the things we love. The people we love."

She could feel Charles massage his neck in the darkness, but earlier he'd denied he had a headache when Jennie asked if he might like a rub of periwinkle to his temples.

"We have a son named Douglas," he said. "That's what matters now. Your mourning brings gloom to the entire household. I don't look forward to coming home to such. So stop it." He rolled to his side, pulling the cover over his shoulder, leaving her shivering in the March night.

He'd been so kind, so tender in their courting. Flowers pleased her, especially daffodils, and he often picked them growing wild. His look into her eyes had sent trills of passion through her in those days before his fall.

"Perhaps it's all the people under one roof that brings our trouble. And the harsh discussions of prisoners that keep joy from the atmosphere." She hesitated then. "Or the scent of liquor that follows Sloan home." She knew she had just raised the tension, but then plunged into the abyss of lingering loss. "She might have lived if you'd gone straight for the doctor and returned before—"

A quick jerk, his shoulder whacked against her face. "Enough or I'll give you something to whine about!" He had never struck her, though he had said things that hurt as much.

Does he not know he's split my lip?

Threatening now, hissing. Spittle hit her face. "You put two and two together to make it my fault? You can't remember the sequence to starching my shirts without a disaster but wrap blame around a stick to make it a cudgel to beat me with?" She couldn't see his face. He gripped her shoulders. She curled into herself. "You're so swift to find fault with me when it was your body that defiled the child."

His words sliced. She was too stunned to speak.

"I don't want to hear another word about 'A-rye-ahhhh.' Sounds like what you say to a doctor with a tongue depressor stuck in your throat."

What does a tongue depressor have to do with our deceased child? Was it the shock of his threatening her or one of those times when she didn't understand his sarcasm?

She rolled out of bed as he turned away. A shaking hand lit the candle, carried it down the steps to the kitchen shelf where she kept her herbs and oils. Charles called them snake oils, no better than those peddled by the Hebrews in their carts. But Jennie put them to good use and sometimes earned their cost back. She opened the vial of eucalyptus and inhaled, hoping it would calm her pounding heart.

At least the herbs and oils gave a way to pay Lucinda back for all she did for Jennie and her family. She often rubbed peppermint oil onto Lucinda's sore muscles, treated her nieces' cuts.

She sat at the table, waiting for dawn, a shawl wrapped around her shoulders, praying for guidance. Her lip grew fat as she bit against it.

How had she come to marry a man so different from her father or brothers? Oh, Charles was interested in business and public life, had been a petitioner to create a new county from Washington County where her parents lived, and he urged improvement on the Tualatin River to advance commerce and transportation. Her family was all concerned with civic duty and responsibility to others, and she'd seen that in Charles and welcomed it. Her brother David Lichtenthaler—DW—was the first Republican elected as county clerk in Marion County and two years previous had been appointed county judge for the new Union County in the far east of the state. Jennie was young, just fifteen when they'd met, with dreams she never shared with Charles, dreams that couldn't be now.

She was susceptible to the wiles of an older man able to take care of her, she supposed, one with a honeyed tongue, quoting poetry and prose and lines from sermons, who dwelled on her "beauty" and didn't take note of her flaws. Perhaps her family saw him as one who would look after her, given her deficiencies so important to a well-read family. Reading was a challenge to Jennie's brain. No one seemed to know why.

Charles was well-read. Jennie was lovesick. Her parents didn't object. On their wedding day her father did bless the marriage with Scripture and a prayer following Judge Wilcox's pronouncement.

No, she had not misread Charles. Their union was a knot tied tight like that of rawhide, meant never to be broken. But that knot did need oiling, often, to keep it from fraying. That was what she was doing now, sitting alone in the kitchen, watching the sun come up, putting oil on her lip and creating a story of protection, of how she'd stepped on a rake and the handle had struck her in the face. It would explain the bruising on her cheek too. And who would question Jennie Pickett doing something so inept as letting a rake she'd failed to put away come back to haunt her. "Oh, that Jennie," her siblings would say as they shook their heads, familiar with her faults.

Maybe that was a reason disciplining Dougie proved a strain: his oafish efforts at expression of frustration reminded her of her own challenging childhood.

Once, not long after Ariyah's birth and death, her sister said something about Dougie being a blessed trial. She took it as a comment on her mothering.

"Maybe he misses Baby Ariyah too," Jennie defended.

Lucinda scoffed. Their mother was there, visiting, her knitting needles clicking. She looked over at Lucinda.

"He does," Jennie insisted. "He asked me one day what happened to the baby in my belly, what I'd done with it. I told her she'd gone to be with God. He asked me then if he was next."

For all their goodness and experience with child-rearing and tending grandchildren, neither of them believed that small children noted the passing of another, had wonderings about life and death, even while they lacked the words to speak their thoughts. For so long, Jennie had lacked words to express herself. She still struggled. But one thing she knew: a death becomes the hub of a wheel and family members its spokes.

They move around it for a very long time. It was Jennie's dream to prevent the deaths, illnesses, and sufferings of others, especially for women and children, and when she couldn't, to change that hub.

Chapter 3
Something Changed

Before dawn, Charles came down the steps. He saw Jennie sitting there. She braced herself.

"I . . . I can't believe I did that, Jennie. I don't know what came over me. I can't even describe it. I'm—I'm sorry."

Relief flooded. "It won't stay puffy for long. I should have chosen a better time to speak."

He ran both hands through his hair that fell below his ears. "I guess my head, it hurt more than I realized, and when you said about the doctor—"

"I shouldn't have brought it up. It's over. It's just that I miss her so."

He pulled the chair next to his wife, put his arm around her, rubbed her narrow shoulders. "A doctor might not have made any difference. It was one of those things. The midwife said that." Jennie held still. "But I still wish I hadn't failed you that night. Not sure what brought it on."

"You're a good man, Charles Pickett." She held his hand, then rose to stoke the cook fire.

"I want that to be true. Maybe just not so much talk about . . . ," he hesitated, "Ariyah. She's of the past. And we're future people—possibility people. We're going places."

"Are we?"

"Yes, we are."

But he didn't say where.

The solution came to her because of George's interest in science and his fortuitous arrival that next afternoon. Jennie didn't believe in coincidences, but rather accepted that a larger hand turns the world and humans were small parts within it. Charles and Joseph had gone off to work, as had the boarders. Lucinda had said nothing of Jennie's lip, so perhaps it wasn't as noticeable as she'd thought. Dougie asked if a bug had bitten her. "It could be." An explanation better than her rake story.

George gave both sisters bear hugs, and he lifted Jennie and swung her around. "Still light as a snowflake," he said, one eyebrow raised as he looked at her lip. They sat at the table now, Lucinda taking a rare moment to drink tea. Eleven years older than Jennie and twin to DW, George loved solving problems—in a laboratory or in a botanist's field. He told tales of his travels, sharing the good news of efforts in the south to recover from the war, lamenting still the death of their brother and of President Lincoln. "He could have led the healing of this country's wounds," he said.

"Speaking of healing." Jennie cleared her throat. "How could I make my own oils instead of having to purchase them? I have to wait a long time for things to arrive from Boston or San Francisco. And I'm not sure if the oils and aromatics are pure or have lost their essence in the long journey around the Horn."

George looked over the top of his spectacles. "I can make you a distillery." He tugged at his tie. He always wore a suit, wool pants, and coat, brocaded vest, and tie. "Will Charles approve?"

Jennie touched her lip. *Did Lucinda hear us in the night? Is that why she hasn't asked?*

"A distillery is a still and it could be used for moonshine too," George said. "I know he signed the anti-saloon petition."

"It can be used for good. Could we make it together?"

"Of course." He hesitated. "But it'll take longer if you help." He winked.

Jennie punched his shoulder, glad he hadn't pursued his Charles question.

George was big and burly, with bright brown eyes flecked with gold. He knew of her problems, not with Charles, but the other things, Jennie's poor reading and writing skills, her seeming lack of understanding of jokes. But they shared a love of earth and plants.

George even kept specimens and performed experiments. He had studied chemistry and botany in Illinois before traveling west. Oregon proved to be a placeholder in his wandering life.

"Go ahead then. How would we begin?" Jennie persisted.

Lucinda gave her opinion while bringing hot tea to the table as the children chattered outside, getting along. "You have enough to do without putting time into distilling plants, Jennie."

"I hoard the oils now because I don't know how soon I can replace them. I skimp. The homeopathic book you read to me says one has to start with small dosages and observe. It's different for each patient. Remember that terrible infection from the neighbor girl who stepped on the rusty axe head? With more lavender and thyme, perhaps she wouldn't have suffered so long."

Lucinda considered her words.

"And I could sell them or even seek payment when I gave a treatment, not just a trade. It could help the household."

"They'll require extra time to distill, time we don't have. Dougie needs your attention." She'd picked up her crochet hook. Her hands were seldom idle even while she drank tea with a brother and sister.

Warmth rose up Jennie's neck. She needed Lucinda and Joseph, was grateful to them. She didn't want to be a burden, and the distillery, it could be her way out. Their way to a different place. If they had their own home, all would be better. Fewer tensions, Dougie with his own room. "I'll get up earlier."

George twisted the wooden server in the honey pot, let the amber liquid sink into his steaming teacup. "Which oils do you want to have more of and why?"

Jennie sat up straighter. What a blessing to have a conversation with someone who didn't belittle her interests nor turn her thoughts to guilt over not doing enough. "Rosemary and chamomile."

"Interesting."

"For liver cleansing," she added. Then, "I thought it might discourage the use of liquor and help those trying to overcome that terrible thirst."

She glanced at Lucinda, whose eyes were on her crocheting but who appeared to be listening. "We need the prohibition law passed, that's all," Lucinda said.

"Now, Sister," George said, "it's possible the citizenry won't ever approve that legislation, and healing alternatives might be warranted. I think Jennie's idea has merit."

"We encounter no one with such problems." Lucinda rose, checked the fire. A pile of sheets and shirts awaited well-heated irons.

"But others do," Jennie said. "The streets reek of yeasty smells."

"And prisons are full of men struggling with the effects of drink," George said. "So your husbands certainly experience the impact."

"It doesn't touch us here," Lucinda said, her fingers a blur on her crochet hook.

Jennie stared at her. Did she really not smell the liquor coming out through her husband's pores? Was Lucinda blind to the red eyes and slurred words over the supper table now and then? And what of the long hours away, and the claim that the "authorities" were taking more out of his weekly earnings and that she would need to be more frugal with her household expenses. Charles had similar complaints. "How can you ignore—"

"I don't want to talk about it." She plopped her needle project into the basket at her feet, walked outside. She called the children to come in and have a biscuit while Jennie and George exchanged looks. Dougie rushed to George and leaned against his side. Even a three-year-old recognized the safety of a fine uncle who listened intently about rabbits in the chicken yard.

Lucinda had changed the conversation but not the facts.

"Go ahead and make the distillery yourself," Jennie told George as he mounted his horse to leave, tea dispatched not with talk of drink or laws but with children and George's latest wanderings. "You can explain the parts and process to me when it's finished," she said. "I don't want to waste any more time."

Chapter 4
Finding the Essence

Jennie pondered Lucinda's reluctance to face facts, not yet willing to face her own. Like most women with children in this state, Lucinda was dependent upon the man she married. Women were at the largess of fathers and brothers, husbands and sons, to take care of them. It had been the way of things since Adam and Eve. But when rum—or an injury or old age or the lust for gold—kept a man from doing his duty to his family, a woman might be left destitute, unable to pay for medicine for her children or suffering from infections of childbirth, still required to take in laundry, tailor clothes by candlelight, welcome boarders even if their presence interfered with daily life.

Children, too, Jennie thought, were engaged too early with household tasks and chores, forcing them to think their births were welcomed for the extra hands they'd someday bring to the tasks of living rather than the mere joy of their creation. Jennie's parents had left no such thoughts to linger in their offspring's minds: Jennie and her siblings were loved as they said God loved, loved before they knew those smiling faces, loved each of them already.

But the Lichtenthalers did not drink, so their minds and hearts were not impaired by liquored thinking. Jennie had never tasted brew, and she was certain Lucinda hadn't either. But even she who sometimes missed the meanings of glances or subtle words, even she could see that Joseph Sloan had a problem. Her usually clear-headed sister could not.

Both Charles and Joseph arrived home later than usual that evening. Charles's tired hands shook at the washbasin as he prepared to clean up. They were in the bedroom and it was before supper.

"George came by today." Jennie brought fresh water for the pitcher.

Charles wiped his face with the towel. "Where's he been off to?"

"Here and there. We spoke more of a task I put to him."

"And that is?" Charles spoke through a towel drying his face.

"He's going to build me a distillery so I can make my own oils and ointments. I can stop having them ordered. It'll save us money and—"

"A still, you say. I wonder what your father might think of that."

"Papa? Why should he say anything. It's for

my plants. I'll be able to use them more freely and know when they're harvested and have purer oils. I can treat people more effectively. And I can set aside the money so one day—" Jennie took a breath. "So one day we can have our own home. I think we'd have more peace then, the three of us. Don't you?"

Charles looked at her in the mirror over the washstand. A more handsome man did not exist in the territory. Clear, lake-blue eyes like jewels in a sculpted crown. A dark mustache, cheekbones like a rock edge, full lips that, when warm against her throat, caused her limbs to shiver. "Who do you want to treat?"

"The cuts and bruises of children. Coughs and colds. Spider bites. Remember how that basil soothed your wasp sting? I think you fell in love with me that day."

He smiled. *Is a side of his face droopier . . . ?* Jennie continued, "Some plants bring on breast milk for babies, and others, like periwinkle, can help headaches. I'd combine what I know of oils and herbs and offer more healing ointments that way." She hesitated. Moving forward required risk. "Some oils cleanse the liver, for those who consume too many spirits, maybe even calm the hunger that takes a man to drink."

His lake-blue eyes narrowed.

Her heart beat faster. "It's Joseph I'm worried about. And your prisoners."

Charles wiped his beardless face, holding her green eyes in the mirror as he tossed the towel aside. "Keep a man from drink, you say."

"It's possible. I'd like to try."

He turned around to face her, his shoulders lifted, hands at his hips, elbows pointing left and right. He was physically strong, a necessity for managing prisoners. For the first time, Jennie noticed the beginnings of a belly peering over his duck pants waistband. "What does George think it would take to make the still?"

He's going to have a serious conversation with me! "Brass tubing or rubber, a large crock to catch the oils, another for the waste. A place to heat the plants. Ideally, I'll grow my own."

"You'll need a drying shed of some kind if you do that."

"Yes. That's right." Joy bubbled up. Could this be something she and her husband would share? Charles did deserve to live outside the shadow of his boss. "And a smaller hut where I can build a fire and distill my lavender and rosemary and all the others. Could you . . . would you help build it?"

"And when not in use, such a still would find itself suitable use for corn or barley."

"There's no healing from corn. Barley eases stomachaches. Oh . . ."

"So you say. I'll have to thank your dear brother when the time is right."

"It's for herbs, healing plants." Jennie held her fingertips to her lips, her hands as though in prayer. "I want to sell them. I'll need to keep them pure. We couldn't contaminate the distillery with—"

"If it has other uses, we'd be fools not to take advantage."

"But he's making it for me." Her heart plunged like a butter churn, thumping faster.

"I am still the head of the household. You'll do as I say."

Her capacity to anticipate and keep discipline over her tongue took flight. "No. Sloan is the head of this household and he has a liquor problem and I won't let my still feed that."

With one stride Charles reached her, grabbed her arms, shook her, his breath hot against her face. *Are those spirits on his breath?* "In this room, I am the head of my family. In this house, in this town, in this land, I am the head of you."

He tossed her back with such force, she hit the side of the oak dresser. It felt as though a mule had struck. She gasped but did not cry out. *A broken rib.* He'd never been such a volcano, now twice in one week? What was she doing to him? And then the flash of *Einsicht*: it was liquor

47

driving this wedge between them, not anything she had done.

"Supper must be ready. I'll tell Lucinda you'll be down shortly."

"You say." He sat on the chair and reached for a copy of the *National Police Gazette*, scanning its pages that held lurid stories of crimes, criminals, and arrests.

He'd say she stumbled and she had. She'd been as blind as Lucinda. But she could see now, though physical pain cut down what she could do with her improved vision.

"What on earth happened?" Lucinda tugged the strips of cloth around Jennie's ribs.

She thought about tightening her corset so her sister need not know, but her wincing would alert her sister. It was after supper, and Joseph and Charles had left, saying there was a required meeting back at the prison. Discoloration spread across Jennie's side.

"You're becoming clumsy of late. First that split lip and now this."

Lucinda deserved the truth. "It was Charles. I disagreed with him."

Lucinda pulled back, her hands still on the bandages. Jennie smelled wild onion on her breath. Her voice held softness. "It's not a woman's place to challenge her husband. I'd think you'd know that."

"Oh, Lucinda. Mama and Papa disagreed about things, but Papa never laid a hand on Mama. Not ever. And I'd wager our brothers never put a finger of harm against their wives either."

"Charles is very patient with you. We all are."

"I know . . . I'm slow about some things. But I don't think anyone deserves to be struck, not even a child needing discipline. And I'm no child." Jennie stopped Lucinda's hand, held it. "He'd been drinking, Lucinda. My husband had liquor on his breath."

"Nonsense. The men don't do that." She pulled away.

"Lucinda. Joseph drinks too."

"Have you seen him? No. He works hard. He drinks sarsaparilla. A beer now and then when the water gets contaminated, but not hard liquor. He told me so. It's one of the worries at that place, keeping water available for the men, preventing people who visit from bringing in liquor and"—she lowered her voice—"cocaine. But no, he doesn't drink. And I don't believe Charles does either. You upset him. And then you stumbled. That's all."

How did one disagree with someone so certain, a perspective filtered by her love for her husband but one that put blinders on her eyes? Or perhaps Lucinda couldn't see a way out if she acknowledged what was true. But Jennie could.

If they had their own home, Charles would be all right. This new behavior—and Jennie was certain it was new—could be pruned. What would thrive would be a flourishing family. She'd show Lucinda how things could change and then maybe her sister could face facts.

Charles didn't come home that night, returning after work the next day, eyes cast down, contrite. They ate a quiet supper and later, in their bedroom with Dougie playing outside with his slingshot, sunset yet to come, Charles said, "I've done it again, haven't I?"

"Where did you and Joseph stay the night?"

"The barn." She hadn't heard them out there. "I don't know what's happening to me, Jennie. It's like I've got a volcano inside and I never know when it's going to explode. I take the liquor, I do." He hung his head in his hands, elbows on his knees. "It calms me, kills the headaches. But then, I don't seem to have a way to take just enough. I thirst for more and then there's no more calm."

"Would you try black currant seeds? It could help your thirst."

"I don't know. I don't know." He lay down on the bed then, his hand over his brow. "I can't remember things I used to. I keep thinking someone's behind me when they're not. Crazy thinking. So I take a snort, and for a while, I'm sharp again. And I tell myself I won't repeat that. Never do it again. Not lash out at you. Not rough up a prisoner. Not tip liquor to my lips. But then I do."

"We have nothing to lose by trying the black currant. I've read of its use."

"You've found books about that?"

"George loaned me a tome on oriental medicine."

"Take you years to read through one, wouldn't it." His words stung, and she wondered if he felt deceived by marrying a woman not always quick in her thoughts. But she didn't apologize. What was, was. She'd make room for a cure of currants.

Building the drying shed became a family affair like the raising of a barn. Joseph had approved the structure; George and her father pounded nails instead of pegs. DW and William and their families came by to work, and even Charles helped set the ridge beam. Her sisters-in-law and Lucinda baked fresh bread, and Jennie found herself singing as she brought out trays of cold ham, venison, and cheeses to the table set beneath the pines. These people, her family, did this for her. Charles likely only wanted access to the still, but she hoped he'd see her family's contribution to this effort as legitimizing her plan, a goal that would help them leave one day to find their own home, build a drying shed on their property.

How easily she slipped back into fanciful thinking.

Children and dogs rushed around the builders. Jennie's mother brought peach pies and cobblers, and Jennie's brother William and his wife and children carried pails of cream the women whipped to top the desserts. They couldn't stay long, as their cows needed milking twice a day. It wasn't exactly a barn raising but similar, with its satisfying outcome.

Jennie treasured the frame structure that had a fireplace at one end and lengths of rope so she could attach lavender or belladonna from the rafters. She'd be careful with the latter as it contained poison; but used correctly, it could help a new mother with painful breastfeeding or a child's ear infections or even relieve boils. For drying roots, her brothers built shelves with little troughs so air could circulate around them but keep the tubers from rolling off onto the swept dirt floor. Now they awaited the arrival of the distillery.

George brought the contraption out on a fine August afternoon, shiny and complete. He'd alerted her father and William, who stood ready to help. Her garden flourished, and before long Jennie would be harvesting pumpkins and beans. And from the herb quarter, lavender and violet. This Willamette Valley soil allowed nearly anything to grow. She could almost plant pennies and harvest dollars.

The distillery would lodge at the far end of the drying shed.

It was a Saturday and Charles had been splitting wood for winter's use. He'd struck the axe into a log round before entering, sweat beaded on the dark hair of his forearms. "It probably could have used a separate building. Joseph and I talked about that, just haven't gotten it put up yet."

Jennie had heard nothing of these discussions.

"We built the drying shed large enough to house the distillery," George countered.

"Well, things change, don't they? Just unload it here for now. I'll assemble it later. No need to trouble yourself further, Brother." He leaned against the center column of the shed, arms crossed.

George looked at Jennie and shrugged. "My work here is finished then. Until you complete yours, Charley. I'll come back and set it up. Do you have a sassafras, Sister? Let's let the man to his work."

"I'm sure Joseph and I can manage the distillery. But you've done a fine job with it. Many thanks." Charles slapped George on the back.

George stiffened.

"I'd like it set up now. In the shed." Jennie

made herself sound firm. "Later, when you've had time to build a separate structure, we could move it but it's here now. It has a place. It was built for this."

Her father chimed in. "It won't take long to set up, Charley."

George patted the container like it was a friendly horse. He signaled Jennie's father and William to help him lift the tubes and glass onto the metal shelf he'd set into the fireplace. "It's too bad we don't have one of Bunsen's burning devices," he grunted. "Much more efficient."

Jennie moved closer to her husband, who stood with hands on his hips, chastened by her family's listening to her request instead of his. "They want to help," she said. "And it would be good to see if it works while George is here so he can fix it if needed." Dougie leaned against her knees and she pointed for him to watch what the men were doing. "They aren't trying to defy you," she told her husband quietly.

"You say."

Charles spun around then and headed toward the house, the shadow of the tree leaves like stripes across his back. Dougie broke from her hold and trotted after his father. She was torn between the happiness of her idea moving forward, her family's loving support, and an ache for choosing that over soothing her husband, watching her son seek after him. She was selfish and yet felt affirmed that what she did, she did for Charles and Dougie too.

She watched the installation, the distillery's twists and curls of tubing were a metaphor for her life. Even the essencier, the part that separated the treasured oils from the waste, reflected her efforts to sort out what mattered from the unessential that could tangle up her days.

Chapter 5
The Alchemy of Hope

Because of Jennie's inability to read as others in her family did—swift and without effort—she'd thought for many years that she had no real abilities, that instead her brain was as mixed up as the hog's mash. Mathias, a favorite brother, who had died in 1861 during the Terrible War, had been her patient teacher, helping her link the scratching on a page to names for letters and then matching them to sounds. It was her sister Rebecca—who died the year that Dougie was born—who taught her how to write. To print, actually, in big block letters, as in cursive she reversed the *b* and *d*. She still struggled with both reading and script. Before her parents pulled her from the humiliation of school, she'd had to stand in front of others and read fresh and unfamiliar words, an effort that caused her heart to pound and breath escape her lungs as she listened to the snickering of schoolmates. Though once Jennie memorized material, she could stand before a crowd and declaim whole paragraphs of words.

Her father was a pastor, George a scientist,

DW a teacher and lawyer. Lucinda ran a household and a boarding business that took thought and action. Girls didn't go on to school, and certainly not those for whom reading was such a trial. But her family's presence told her they trusted her ways with oils and herbs. They might not know of her longing to understand better how people became ill or how they healed. Nor had she ever said that if she'd been trained, perhaps she might have saved her own baby.

She watched the distillery be set up, her thoughts going to Ariyah's birth and death, thoughts rushing through a memory tunnel the way the Schyrle brought distant objects into closer focus. Women and children needed access to a university-trained woman physician. Maybe one day she'd have a daughter who would be that healer.

Jennie took a deep breath. Her ribs still hurt from Charles's shove.

"I don't think I knew that Charley wanted to build a separate building," her father said. "I hope he isn't too discombobulated. One really should see if the thing works."

"Oh, it'll work, all right." George had few doubts of anything in life. In that, he was like Charles, or at least as Charles had been before his wedding-night fall.

Her father handed George the glass tubing he connected to the tin-lined copper pot he'd had made. He'd fashioned a brass coil that snaked from the kettle into a large tub of water, both containers sitting almost side by side. "The spring water here is quite cold, so that's good. You have to cool the steam to liquid to get the oils. The steam will travel through the coils. Do you have plants ready? As soon as this water starts to boil, we'll be adding them."

"Lavender." Jennie spoke with pride. Half the flowers on the stems had withered when she'd harvested them the previous week, so they were perfect. "I'm going to start with lavender."

"That'll do."

She gathered the plants, holding them gently so her own body oils wouldn't contaminate them. She watched every detail of her brother's actions. They waited for the water to boil and spoke of land law changes; the sermon Pastor Parrish had given that Sunday. Her father remembered Mathias and his going off to war, and Rebecca's love of novels brought her into this occasion. She'd died of typhus. Joseph came out and watched, entering into the conversation. Jennie looked for Charles, wishing he'd join them too, but he didn't. Hopefully he was watching Dougie. She felt a twinge of guilt that she hadn't wondered earlier where her son was, but he'd followed his father inside. He'd be fine.

Finally, George stepped back to remove the cover. Jennie placed handfuls of what she'd dried into the copper pot. George secured the lid that sported a hole where the tubing rose straight up and then angled toward the cooling tub coils. The copper pot sat over the flames. As the fire heated her plants, steam rose up into the cooling tub. Inside, it coiled like a snake and came out the side near the bottom of the water cooling tub. The area around the opening had been caulked as tight as a newly framed log cabin so it wouldn't leak. Whatever oils would appear would then pour into a beaker that had two openings. "A glass receptacle works best," George said.

"The essencier," Jennie said.

"Right. It'll separate oils from waste."

"How much will it make?" The scent was strong.

"That depends. The oils are found inside the plant's oil glands and the tiny hairs and even the veins."

"Like our own veins," Jennie said.

"Like that, I believe. If you were very careful when you harvested them, you might get a few more ounces than if you weren't. I suspect there's a method to it, just as there is to being in a laboratory, like that Bunsen finding an antidote to arsenic. Alchemy is an art."

"An antidote to arsenic?" Joseph expressed interest.

George told them more and Jennie asked to borrow the paper that had informed her brother. It would take her a time to read it, but there were many accidental deaths from arsenic and strychnine that settlers used to manage rats and mice. To find something that would halt a terrible death seemed miraculous.

"You may as well go inside," George said. "It's just a waiting game now." He shooed them toward the door. "Mama's pie is baking and the little girls' arms are tired of whipping up the cream William brought. I'll watch the flames."

"I'll stay here with you." Jennie imagined repeating this process with rosemary and violets and peppermint too. She didn't need notes. She'd memorized what George had done. But she also wanted to go through the cleanup process.

"Best you check in with your husband." Her father put his arm around Jennie's shoulder and pushed her toward the house.

"He—he'll be fine."

Her father frowned. She felt the pressure on her shoulder. Her small stature made it easy for even those who loved her to push her in their direction.

"Yes. I'd better face the music."

Charles wasn't in the main room of the house.

"Upstairs." Lucinda pointed with her chin while she plopped whipped cream onto slices of pie. "Tell Douglas the pie's ready." Mary and Nellie licked their fingers of the cream. "I suspect he's ready for something sweet. Did everything work all right with the still?"

"Yes. It seems to. I'll have lavender oil in a few hours. Isn't that grand?" Jennie pulled an apron over her head, the movement sending a lavender scent into the warm room.

Jennie started to tell them about the arsenic antidote George had mentioned, but her mother looked over the top of her spectacles in that way she had of expressing her displeasure at Jennie's hesitation.

"Jane Jennie Lichtenthaler Pickett, you'd best—"

"Alright. I'm going upstairs." She felt like a recalcitrant child, yet why should she? She was a grown woman, a mother of two—one living— and a wife who worked hard to take care of her family and contribute. A man didn't always have to be pampered, did he? Compromise was part of the language of a marriage or ought to be. And this distillery was as close to Jennie's dream of being a real healer that she would ever have. With it, she could not only meet her family's needs, but she could help others. Couldn't she have just one afternoon to celebrate without having to soothe her husband's wounded spirit?

She took a deep breath, shortened with the jab of pain that came as she climbed the stairs. She pushed open the door. With Charles, it was always something.

Chapter 6
Certainty

Charles curled on the bed. Dougie sat on his trundle bed, simply staring. *Odd.* "Dougie, there's pie downstairs." He didn't move. She turned to Charles. "Pie is ready. Will you come down?"

Neither of them stirred. She bent over Charles, lowered his arm from his face. He rolled over, revealing a brown bottle he cradled to his chest. She smelled the spirits. He snored.

Jennie stumbled backward, making sense of what she saw. He was drunk, had to be. While Dougie was under his care.

My son! "Dougie?"

He looked up at her, eyes glazed.

"Douglas. Come to Mama."

He mewed like a kitten and lifted his arms. As she picked him up, she smelled the vile scent of spirits on his breath. A child! Her husband had defiled their child.

She carried him down the stairs, him on her hip pressing against her ribs; her other hand on the wall to balance, gasping as she entered the kitchen.

"What is it?" Lucinda said. "What's wrong with him?"

"He's . . . I smell liquor. Charles is . . . out. Snoring." Tears burned behind her nose. "I—how could he? I don't know how much he's taken."

"Maybe Dougie just spilled it on himself." Lucinda, offering an option that didn't pierce with pain.

She had to think. Pretending would not help. "Chamomile. If we can get him to drink it. Maybe violet root. I've some crushed in a tin in the drying shed. It's marked."

"I'll get it." Lucinda lifted her skirts and ran.

Her father took Dougie from her arms. He stroked his grandson's shoulders, rubbed his thin little arms. "There, there now." Dougie burped. His eyes stayed open, but they did not focus. Still, he smiled, giving hope that he would be all right with time—and an expectorant to empty his stomach. Alcohol poisoning was as dangerous as arsenic.

"How could Charles . . . I can't condone consumption like that, not for him and certainly not for a child." She blinked back tears.

"Dougie might have gotten into it after—well, after Charles slept. It could happen to anyone," Joseph said.

She wished Lucinda were present to listen to her husband's defense of her abusive, neglectful-of-his-son, drunk-upstairs husband. "I can't believe you'd defend what he did to a child."

"He made a mistake, but we all do at some point in our lives. Even you, Perfect Jennie Pickett."

"Here now, there's no call for that," Jennie's father said.

Jennie touched her father's arm to calm him. She frowned. Joseph's mocking made no sense. She had never claimed to be perfect, far from it. Why would he even suggest such a thing. Unless her certainty about the vileness of alcohol was what he ascribed as her "perfection." She was certain of that: alcohol was the perfect, heinous brew and she did perfectly condemn its use.

Lucinda returned with the root and Jennie crushed a small amount with calomel. Her little finger shook as she placed the mash on her son's lips. "Lick your lips, Douglas." Dougie pushed away, but his grandfather held him as Jennie urged yet a greater swipe with his tongue. At his grandfather's urging, the boy licked, then chewed, then swallowed again.

"Feel bad, Paw-Paw."

Her mother handed Jennie a bowl. *Let the impurities leave him.*

Dougie found the edge and vomited.

Gratitude mixed with fury at Charles raged through her, along with guilt at not having watched her son; with letting herself enjoy the possibilities of the new distillery; with having trusted Charles.

"We should get him to a doctor to bleed him," her mother said.

"No, no bleeding. It weakens the body." Jennie knew that much about modern medicine. "But we should take him anyway, make sure we haven't missed something."

She scurried then, grabbing a quilt to wrap him in.

George had come in. It was decided he would carry him and Jennie ride a second horse.

Dougie cried now. Were there bruises? Had he consumed something else? "Let the doctor check him," her father reassured. At least this family offered hands she could hold in times of trial. They rode off, leaving her husband behind.

Evening had come upon them while she prayed for her son, for herself. Dougie vomited again.

"Oh George, I'm so sorry." She pressed her horse up beside him. George's red vest was splashed with brown.

"It's nothing, Sister."

"There, through those trees." She pointed to the path.

The doctor wasn't that one whom Charles had dragged back too late the night Ariyah was born.

"You did well with the expectorant applied." He spoke to George, though Jennie had told him about the herbs she'd used.

"Speak to his mother. She's the one who treated him."

"I'm sure you offered direction."

George shook his head.

"I suppose he grabbed an unwatched stein, did he?"

"We don't rightly know. His father was watching him, but he's currently . . . indisposed and not able to convey to us the circumstances of his son's condition."

"And his father would be—"

"Charley Pickett. Works at the prison."

"Ah, yes. With Sloan." He pulled Dougie's lower eyelid down, looked at both pupils. "I think he'll sleep now. Wake him every hour and have him drink water." He put his stethoscope against her son's chest. "Heartbeat steady. Looks like he'll come through it. Waking and water and food in the morning. He'll be hungry."

They spoke good-byes, and this time George handed Dougie up to Jennie so she could hold him in her arms as they plodded toward home.

Home. She thought of what she could do, where they could go. She'd been so certain the distillery was the answer. But now, being alone with Charles and Douglas made no sense at all.

Or did it?

If she could get Charles away from Joseph, at least after hours, free of the prison talk; if she could be alone with him and Dougie, maybe they could still make a way as a family. She decided then: she would find a home, one that might even have a small drying shed where she could set up the distillery. She'd get Charles to help, let him be more a part of things. That was why he'd made the poor choice. He hadn't meant to lose control like he had. He'd be sorry and ashamed.

She shared her plan with her father when they got back. He'd waited up for them, checked on the essencier while they were gone. Her father bedded down in the main room too, where Jennie could watch her son whose clothes she changed. She'd wake him every hour. Her mother slept on the small day cot, Dougie beside her. George took his bedroll to the drying shed where he said he'd monitor the distillery as the lavender oil finished dripping into the beaker.

"We'd need a small place," Jennie said as she fluffed up a feather comforter for her father's use. "Not far from the prison so Charles can keep his job. We could rent or maybe find an abandoned cabin, take it over." There were many tumbling-down structures left behind by those lured by the '62 gold strike in Canyon City farther east.

"Would Charles agree?"

"I'll make my case that his temper and his drinking are—"

"Temper? What's that about?"

"He—it's only happened twice. I . . . provoked him. He didn't mean it. He sometimes grabs me to get my attention. You know how I don't always understand. He doesn't intend to hurt me."

Her father frowned. "This drinking has happened before?"

"His—his temperament is hampered by us living with his boss, Lucinda, and the girls. Dougie and me. And the boarders. Joseph, as both relative and a superior, it's too much for him. It's as though he's never free of that prison."

"I don't like what happened today." He shook his head. "Don't pretend, Jane." He called her by her given name only when he was deeply concerned.

"I won't, Papa." She kept her voice light. "I don't think I am. No. Today . . . it must be the pressures and perhaps how excluded he felt when I insisted we set up the distillery without him. I didn't handle it well. I should have been more attentive to his feelings."

"A man who uses his family as an excuse for his own moral demise doesn't speak well of his future or his family's. You remember that."

"I'll try."

"And there is no excuse for his not protecting Douglas. That's unforgivable. I'll speak to him myself about that."

"No, Papa. This is my trial." She pulled the covers over her son. "I'll deal with him and Dougie. I will."

Jennie called up the stairs when Joseph and Lucinda and the girls came down for the morning meal. No one answered. She walked up, dreading what she'd find. Charles wasn't there. He must have risen early and threaded his way through the sleeping people on the floor, as she'd heard nothing and no one else woke either. His uniform no longer hung on the hook and she was surprised at her relief. Until that moment she had worried he might leave out of humiliation for what he'd done and she might not ever find him. What if he didn't come home?

Back outside, she checked on the oil, then woke Dougie and fed him, finished sending her parents and George off as Joseph and the boarders left for work.

Dougie talked with his cousins, seemed unaffected by what had happened. "Where's Papa?"

"At work, I imagine. We'll see him later."

"Why don't you take him for a walk," Lucinda suggested. "Get some fresh air in him."

Jennie should have thought of that. "Would you like to visit Aunt Ariyah?"

"All right." The boy was docile as a lamb

despite his sleep being interrupted every hour. "Carry me, Mama? Like last night?"

Her ribs still hurt. "Oh, no, you're a big boy. Last night was special and I had your grandpa's horse to help me hold you. Your uncle George too."

"All right." He let her take his hand and they made their way to Ariyah's. Jennie had known this vivacious woman since their school days. She'd never teased Jennie when she'd struggled with her words, could make her laugh. She dressed and cooked with a flair. Ariyah lived with her parents, a happy arrangement. Jennie heard piano music as they turned up the path to the stone steps. *That's new.* The ship from San Francisco must have brought the instrument. She hadn't even known that Ariyah could play. Jennie chastised herself, always so wrapped up within her own world, her own wonderings. What else had been going on in Ariyah's world that Jennie had missed?

She knocked on the door. Someone played a Bach concerto. Jennie could almost hear the violins and cellos as she'd heard them played in a big church back in Chicago before they'd headed west. She let herself get lost inside the music, stepping across the tops of the notes, whisking her from worry and uncertainty to momentary pleasure. Even Dougie held her hand and listened. It would be his first time to hear piano music of any kind. How lovely that Bach introduced him.

"Ariyah, I had no idea," Jennie told her friend when she opened the door. "You have a piano and you play."

"My new beau ordered it in." The music began again. "And he's the one making music."

She motioned them to follow her, a blonde twist with black combs climbed up the back of her head. She stood nearly six feet tall. Striking. Her beau played beautifully. When they entered the spacious room with natural light falling on the dark piano wood, he stopped and rose, smiling at Ariyah as though they were alone in the room.

How Jennie longed for that look of devotion to be on her husband's face; prayed for its return.

Ariyah introduced them to Peleg, her beau, his dark eyes and olive skin spoke to his Spanish heritage.

"How wonderful to hear piano music once again," Jennie said. "I'd forgotten how much comfort it could bring."

"Peleg seemed to know it was just what I needed too," Ariyah offered.

"Love seeks to see always with fresh eyes," Peleg said with a thick accent. "It is so, is it not, my Ariyah?"

"Fresh eyes, yes. And fresh ears too."

She put her arm around Jennie's waist, led

Dougie to the second piano stool as Peleg sat back down. "Put your hand here."

Dougie looked to Jennie for confirmation. She nodded.

"We give a little lesson, *si*?" And the kind man placed his hands over Dougie's and plunked a simple tune.

Her son looked up and smiled. "I play, Mama."

"Yes, you do."

Music might be a way to reach her son. People responded to different ways of mending. She considered telling Ariyah what had transpired in recent days but didn't. She didn't want her friend judging Charles. And she didn't want to watch Ariyah's eyes grow sad with Jennie's news. She'd keep the pain to herself and find a way to bring Charles to a restorative place. Wasn't that what families did for each other?

Chapter 7

Pearls of Wonder

That evening, with the call of geese overhead, Jennie arrived home with Charles already there. She invited Charles to walk with her.

"Where to?"

"Just the drying shed."

She felt relief at seeing the distillery unharmed. She picked up the beaker of lavender oil. "Here it is. Our nest egg." She'd need to clean the tubs and coils before beginning another distillation. She told Charles how she'd have to do it. "It's quite a process, but I want the purest of oils."

"I'm sure you do." He leaned against the center beam, scratched his back there. "So what did you want to talk about? The thing with Dougie. Look." His eyes scanned the rafters, he blinked. Dust motes danced in the slanted sunset pouring through the open door. "That wasn't my fault. I fell asleep, and he, well, he consumed what was left in the bottle."

She didn't point out that Charles had been holding the empty bottle in his arms. This was no time to confront him about that.

"Dougie came through it," she said. "I should have had him with me in the shed."

"Yes. You should have." Her husband was more than willing to let her shoulder the blame.

Jennie took a deep breath. "Joseph and Lucinda are most gracious. But with them, the girls, the boarders, us, there are too many people mixing together day and night. Sometimes I can't think straight."

"You don't think straight anyway." He said it to tease, but it punched her confidence. The people who knew one best could also slice the deepest.

She set the beaker down, pulled her shawl closer around her shoulders as the evening cooled the day. "I propose that no one thinks straight with so many competing voices. What if we were to find our own place? You, me, and Douglas. Close enough for you to walk or ride to work. I could distill my plants and make a little extra that way."

He stood quiet, giving no indication of what her suggestion might mean to him. Then, "And I can simply stay on being an assistant superintendent."

"Yes." His acidic tone surprised her. "Don't you like what you do?"

"Would you?"

She hadn't thought that he wasn't happy at the prison. He'd taken the job with regular pay when he had injured his hand while working on a new

75

building in town, before they were married. The job offer had been timely, he'd always said. And his working and living with the Sloans was how they'd met. She'd always thought him pleased with a steady job.

The truth was, she didn't know what he might wish to do instead. She hadn't paid attention to his dreams, even though she lamented how little he attended to hers. Maybe he held back his own hopes as she had hers, each fearing the other wouldn't care.

"How would you prefer to spend your time?"

He walked over to the distillery, bent down to look at the coils. Jennie held her breath, felt as anxious as when Dougie got too close to something fragile, like the brass and glass. "Buy land and sell it," he continued. "That's what this country is, people moving in, making buys. I got here too late to get in on the free land, but I can buy up and resell." He turned to her. "If I had a stake."

Birds chattered near the ridge beam, building nests it appeared.

"I—I didn't know you had any interest in real estate."

"That's why I petitioned for improvements on the Tualatin River. Land increases in value if there's reliable transportation, a way to get goods to market. I keep my eyes open all the time about things like that."

"You've thought about this."

"Of course I have. But with no stake"—he rubbed his fingers together as though they held coins dribbling through them—"no land." His hands dropped to his sides.

"Could we take out a loan? Ariyah's father owns the bank. Your income could be the collateral. Or we might save a portion of your wages, set it aside for investing."

"Not if we live by ourselves. My salary will soon be eaten up and your little adventure with oils won't bring in enough to buy onions, let alone a fine orchard somewhere."

"I'll grow onions, not buy them."

"You say."

Conversing with him wasn't unlike negotiating with Douglas at times. She tried again. "I know we've had our trials, Charles." She thought of their baby but didn't say her name. "I do think we'd be better on our own, without people listening even when they don't want to."

He ran his fingers along the coils.

"What about asking my father for a loan?" Jennie said.

"No. I won't be indebted to your family. No."

She was pleased with his response. She didn't want to be beholden to them either. "Would you consider moving out from Lucinda and Joseph's in the meantime? If we can find an inexpensive place. You could start your land acquisition adventure by finding an abandoned cabin. For the three of us."

"I can look, but we'd do better staying right here. You have help with Dougie and we save money. Like you suggested. But I'll look. Consider it."

The scent of lavender still filled the shed. It soothed her as it always did.

He reached for her then, and while she stiffened initially, he made no move of pressure. He was gentle and pulled her into a warm kiss, then held her face with both hands. "I never meant to hurt you, Jennie. Nor Douglas. I don't know what's happening to me."

"I know." Her eyes began to tear. "It's all the demands. It'll be better when we have our own home. I'm certain of it." She kissed him back and sank into cautious comfort in his arms.

The Sloan home sat in the middle of a block of houses on dirt streets with boardwalks to keep slippered feet from spring and winter mud. Cobblestones marked the busier commercial areas. Most residences were composed of two-story clapboard houses with small sheds or barns behind and room for a cow or goat or chickens, a buggy or wagon, and a horse or mule. William graciously provided the Sloan household with milk. Lucinda's girls gathered eggs from their chicken coop. An alley ran behind the houses that backed onto similar barns and garden areas with cabins facing the other street.

It was on the street behind them where the request came for someone to help an elderly woman suffering from malarial fever, the woman having taken the train across the Panama Isthmus some years previous. These occasional requests for Jennie's "doctoring," as she thought of it, brought in a few coins, but mostly people paid in butter or eggs or vegetable harvests. In a place of their own, they might actually have little cash to manage, only Charles's salary. Otherwise, the currency was still trade, even though the region had Beaver coins minted until Governor Lane said doing so was unconstitutional. But they could manage with Charles's income and what she could bring in.

Jennie used quinine, sparingly as it was expensive. Sulfate of cinchona was less costly but harder on the stomach for treating malarial fevers. She'd visited Mrs. Staat before, but malaria fever had a way of returning.

Her daughter led Jennie into the room, and she set her carpetbag with medicines and oils on the sideboard in the Staats' bedroom. Doctoring brought healers into intimate places, and Jennie tried not to pay attention to the things people surrounded themselves with in their bedchambers.

"Did you use all the quinine I left you?"

"I did, Miss Jennie. I did as you said. And felt better for a time, I did. But then it comes back, it does." Mrs. Staat, a squat woman when she stood, lay now barely taking up half of the length of the bed.

"We just have to keep fighting it." Jennie dipped a clean cloth into the water bowl and began to wash the woman's face and neck to help hold the fevers down. Mrs. Staat shivered. "We'll get you through this season." Jennie smiled and gave the woman the spoonful of quinine. "A little glycerin on those lips will make you feel better too."

"How's that boy? And that handsome husband of yours?" Mrs. Staat was one to want to take attention from herself when she could, even when her body trembled with intermittent fevers.

"Both fine, thank you for asking." Jennie looked at her pocket watch and held her wrist to take the woman's pulse. It was fast but steady. She patted her hand, tucked it under the nine-patch covering her. "We are looking for a place of our own. If you hear of anything, not too expensive nor too far from where Charles works, you let me know."

"There's an empty cabin on the lot where I work," her daughter offered. She sat on the far side of her mother's bed. "I do the cleaning for the people and they once had live-in servants."

She leaned over and whispered, "Might even have been slaves. They used the small house."

"Where is it?"

"On Third Street. I can ask if they would rent it."

"Yes. Thank you."

"What do I owe you today, for the quinine, Miss Jennie?"

"If you find us a place we've been seeking to call home, then not a thing today, Mrs. Staat. Not a thing."

Jennie visited the property mentioned, but it wasn't suitable. Too small, too dilapidated. But looking at it was an impetus to seek out more possibilities. Charles was always so tired after work and he often volunteered for extra hours, so Jennie made it her mission to find the perfect place. She and Dougie walked the back streets, looking at places that might work, finding the time with her son restful. Working toward something was more invigorating than merely moving away from discomfort. And the fresh air helped too.

October arrived with a dusting of snow shivering the lilac bushes to the right of the back door of one empty house she found. The lilacs' presence said that a woman had lived there once, not only an old settler now gone off to find gold, but someone who valued fragrance and beauty. Daffodil stems lined the path to a small shed that sat at the back of a yard cluttered with blackberry vines and black currants. Charles could build a small heating shed for the distillery. *I can distill the currant seeds. Excellent for bone aches, facial blemishes, and excessive alcohol use.* Charles could construct a table, and plenty of stumps dotted the entire town and would serve as chairs without backs once they were rolled in. They'd make a rope bed and Charles could make a wooden bed for Dougie.

The shed itself would be suitable. A lean-to stall on one side could house a horse. Or maybe a cow. There'd be room for a couple of chickens and for hanging plants from the rafters, once they repaired the holes in the shake roof. Jennie imagined cooking at the fireplace for her small family. A pang of discomfort struck then, loss hitting still-aching ribs as she thought about Baby Ariyah and about leaving her sister.

She'd face Lucinda when the time came, telling her of their plans to leave. She suspected Lucinda knew something was happening as Jennie and Dougie took those daily walks. Jennie knew she'd be disappointed, but perhaps their absence would force her to face Joseph's problem with liquor.

Charles approved the cabin when she showed him where it was on the map and they'd walked to it. He'd gone to the courthouse the next day to see who owned it. Jennie didn't want to be a squatter, forced to move out should the original owner return. Charles said the papers needed some tending. The previous inhabitant had been a squatter, and no one was sure who the original owner ever was. Those confusions had happened as land laws changed from the time Oregon was a territory until becoming a state a few years previous. He'd keep at it until the title could be cleared. "It's good experience for when I start my business. But it'll take a little cash for a lawyer and such."

Jennie had been setting funds aside from her sale of oils and a portion of Charles's salary. But she was aware of a gnawing in her stomach when she handed the money to him.

Still, joy found its way inside her. Perhaps it was the Advent season or maybe it was the idea that soon, by spring perhaps, she'd have her own home. Her dishes would grace the table, her savories bring scents to the meals she prepared for her family. Charles would be the master of his home and Jennie the mistress of her kitchen and her oils. Maybe they'd plan another child.

They celebrated Christmas that year of 1866 by attending the Methodist church services. Once again, her father preached. Later they traveled to William's farm outside Salem; visited with their parents, now living but a few miles away.

No liquor appeared to mar Joseph's nor Charles's good nature. No arguments. Just a celebratory time of love, forgiveness, and new beginnings told through the story of a baby and God's presence within him. They gave each other homemade gifts.

But then on Christmas night, Charles said he had a special present for her.

"You already gave me a new sewing box." They spent the evening at William's farm and were in the bedroom with the others already sleeping or having gone home. Dougie played with his wagon and two wooden horses that his grandfather had carved for him. The scent of evergreens looped on every flat surface kept the Christmas spirit in each room. Jennie's hoops swirled as she turned to face him.

"No, stay there. Close your eyes."

She felt something cool drape around her neck, settle at her throat. She reached up. *Pearls.*

"You shouldn't have."

"You say. Open your eyes." Charles grinned. "I've wanted to do that since the day we married."

"They're beautiful." She watched her reflection in the mirror. "But we need the money for our move, to make it on our own. For investments. They must have cost a fortune." She fingered them, smooth as baby's cheeks.

"I made a good deal." His voice held a pout in it.

"You should say thank you, Mama." Douglas listened, even though she hadn't realized it.

"Of course. You're right, Dougie. They're lovely. Thank you."

"He kept the secret, didn't you, Boy?"

Douglas nodded, returned to his wagon play.

So the men in her life had held a secret, one meant to bring her joy. But pearls were costly. Where had Charles gotten the money?

Chapter 8
Departures of a Certain Sort

New Year's, 1867. A fat doe on porcelain legs stared at her as Jennie headed toward the quiet of the drying shed where the distillery had continued to do its work. It darted away as she opened the door. She began to think of "last times." The "last time" she'd bring in wood to Lucinda's home. The "last time" she'd distill rosemary in this drying shed. *The last time I'll be in the room where baby Ariyah died.* Going back in memory moved her forward, helped her say good-bye.

Lucinda and Joseph seemed to know that change was in the wind. The men came home each day from work without any evidence of spirits, the tension that had once urged her to seek another place to live had dissipated like steam. If anything, they all laughed more and told stories. The men stopping sharing horrible things their prisoners had done, relating instead funny incidents featuring the cook or one of the delivery drivers. Charles even acted out a few scenarios. The children giggled, even little sober-faced Dougie. Maybe they didn't have to move after all? Why was it that once a decision had been made, hesitation came to call. Perhaps it was the mind's reluctance to make a major change.

February came with rain and spits of snow and wind. They'd set March as moving month, but the roof still needed repairs. Charles had worked on it, at least that was where he said he'd been. They lay in the bedroom curled beneath the down comforter. Charles whispered, the lantern flickering with the draft.

"I've found someone to give me a stake." His blue eyes looked black in the lamplight.

"Who?"

"It came to me. Like a bolt of lightning. On Christmas Day. I'll ask the Reverend."

Her mind tangled. "Reverend?"

"Reverend Parrish, your father's friend. He gave land for the Willamette University and he's helping fund it. And a few days ago, the *Weekly Enterprise* reported that his wife donated ten acres to the Oregon Children's Aid Society, and last week that she gave another ten acres to the future orphan home. They are land-rich people, those Parrishes. And generous."

"I doubt poor pastors and part-time Indian agents have much to call their own. My father certainly doesn't."

"You say. Parrish's wife does, then. Did,

until she gave away twenty acres like that." He snapped his fingers. "They had to have been here in 1850 when they could claim 320 acres, both husband and wife, and the woman got to keep the land in her name." Jennie and Charles had married too late to take advantage of Oregon's allowing women to receive government property in their own name. Her mother owned private land, but that didn't mean she had cash on hand to loan to someone else.

"They may not have cash."

"Look, Jennie." He got up on one elbow. "Parrish has to have money he needs to invest. And I'm the perfect investment." Charles kissed her nose as punctuation, laid back down.

"Have you spoken to him?"

"Not yet. I figured you should come along. He must be a bit of a bleeding heart, pastoring and all, plus working with Indians like he does. I've heard he's a natural diplomat with those heathens."

Jennie frowned at the word he'd chosen to refer to the bands of people displaced by all the settlers.

"And his wife giving away land for children's causes, they're both generous souls." He folded his hands over his chest. "You can play on his emotional side. A young wife and mother, wanting to help her husband get a good start in life, move out from the malaise of doing public work in a prison, a man who wants to make it on his own. You're living in a small house hardly habitable. But working through it for your husband. And your boy. Grieving the loss of a baby." Jennie winced. "And her husband wants to make good for her too. I think it's a stalwart plan."

"You say."

"But don't wear your pearls."

"It breaks my heart." Lucinda put all her weight into the hot irons that smoothed the sheets, then folded them over her arm.

"Mine too." Jennie took the linens and with quilts and other bedding, put them into the trunk Charles hauled down from the attic. They'd told the Sloans of their plans after the evening meal. Her nieces took it the best, asking if they could come and visit soon.

"Then why go if your heart is broken? Haven't you been happy here? I apologize for being demanding at times."

"You aren't." Jennie stopped and sat beside her. "I think it's time we did things on our own, with Charles and I forming a family life outside of his work. Imagine what it would be like to have a supervisor all day and then come home and live in his house. I mean, if he did have a disagreement at the prison, he'd have to evaluate whether Joseph would be upset there and at home."

"Joseph is very fair."

"I'm not saying he isn't. But—"

"Things have been so good here. I don't know what I'll do without you."

Jennie held her tongue, didn't share her pangs of worry over how their presence might have kept Lucinda's own family pot from boiling over. "I won't be that far away. We can still butcher hogs together and stitch and I'll share my oils. You know that."

Lucinda cried now, soft shakes of her shoulders.

Jennie put her arms around her and held her. "I'll always be there for you and for the girls. I will. We will. It's just that—"

"I've looked after you, Jennie. We've lived together our whole lives."

"I guess we have."

"You needed me."

"I did. And now I need you in a new way. To wish me well as I take this next step for my family."

"Who will discipline Dougie?"

Jennie kept her voice light. "I'll have to, won't I? And I will. That boy means the world to me and I wouldn't do anything I thought would harm him. You've been a good teacher."

"Will you be . . . safe with Charles?"

"Charles has apologized. And I should have

been watching Dougie that day. I was distracted with the distillery. I'm as much to blame as Charles."

Lucinda wiped at her eyes with the edge of her apron.

Jennie's glasses had steamed up too with tears. "Let's not go backward. We're looking forward. It's going to be all right. You and Joseph will be fine."

"I'm not worried about us." She stiffened, then stood. "Let me clean your eyeglass lenses. They're cloudy as pea soup."

They were settled in their new home by the first of March, the promise of spring like a fresh breeze pushed aside the web they'd been under for so long. Charles said their move would be good evidence for when they approached Reverend Parrish. He hadn't let go of that plan. His attitude was one of energy. He built the drying shed and the Sloans helped move the distillery into it one day in April. Charles helped clear a plot for Jennie's plants, shored up the lean-to, and led home a cow. He didn't seem to mind walking to work. She'd never seen him this . . . *engaged* is the word she called it. She didn't begrudge him an occasional time after work with Joseph, as he never came home with the scent of brew on his breath. It was the calmest period of their lives, an interlude reminding her of Divine gifts of uplifted spirits promising strength to draw on when the turmoil returns.

"I'll care for him, Mama."

"I'm not sure a porcupine baby is a good playmate, Dougie."

He held the helpless thing in his tiny palm. Dougie had already named the little animal "Quilton," a blend of quilt and quills, the latter soft as lamb, arched over Quilton's small back. Jennie didn't think Charles would approve, but he surprised her.

"He needs a pal. Sloans kept that dog of theirs, but it rarely got off the chain and never could be trusted to run with a boy. This'll be good for Douglas."

The day proved eventful for Jennie too.

"Today," Charles said, "I've arranged for us to meet with Reverend Parrish."

"But I've made soap and I've got to get a cage of some sort ready for the porcupine." The May day wore flouncy clouds and waved warm air through the clothes she'd hung on the line. Square molds of soap covered the table in the drying shed, the scent of lavender strong.

Charles laughed and swung her around. "Put that little porcupine in a crate, comb Dougie's hair, and plant a hat on your head and you'll be fine. You don't want to look too perfect. We're appealing to his good nature, remember. And his wife's." He swatted at her behind. "Hurry up now."

She did as bid, exchanged her drab wrapper for more festive hoops and skirts, dabbed rose water on her neck, then called to Dougie from the back porch. Charles held out clean pants for Dougie to put on.

"No. I want to stay here with Quilton."

"We'll get a sweet later. Come on for now. Papa says."

"I learned today that his wife isn't feeling well." Charles said it as though he reported on the weather.

"Mrs. Parrish?" Jennie stopped dabbing a wet cloth on a stain on her skirt as Charles adjusted his son's galluses over his small shoulders. "We shouldn't intrude then, Charles. This isn't a good time."

"Best time is when people are vulnerable. We can't delay. We need to dance while the music plays. More people are coming west and they'll need land. I'm the one to sell it to them, but I have to own it first. Hurry along. They're waiting for us."

She didn't like his comment about vulnerability, felt more uneasy about asking for money. She went out of obedience to her husband.

Chapter 9
Charming

"The Parrishes are expecting you?" It was a question, not a statement. A young woman—the maid, Jennie supposed—had opened the door. Behind her was a portrait-lined hall. Jennie gripped Dougie's hand tighter as she spied glass vases with roses gracing side tables they'd have to walk beside. An open door at the end of a long hallway allowed a breeze to flow in and provided a view of an expansive formal garden where stone birdbaths dotted the green like lily pads on a pond. There was also a pond. Charles was right: this man might have been a poor pastor once and an Indian agent who was not regularly paid (according to the newspaper), but he did have resources. Or his wife did.

Jennie answered the maid. "Yes. My husband has an appointment and—"

"Not specifically today, no. But the Reverend said for us to stop by sometime." Charles poured out his charm.

Jennie glared. *No appointment?* They were intruders on a Saturday morning. If the Reverend was preaching somewhere the next day he'd be busy working on his sermon. That was how it was for Jennie's father, and visiting at such a time was disrespectful.

"We can come later," Jennie said. She held Douglas's hand and started to turn, careful to keep her hoopskirt from knocking against the sculpture of a draped Greek woman holding a bowl in which a rose floated. The flower was the size of her own hair comb but much more beautiful. First roses of the season often are. Someone here loved flowers.

"Why don't you let him know that Jennie Lichtenthaler Pickett is here with her family to see the Reverend. Go ahead." Charles urged the maid away with his hat he'd removed.

The maid left to do what Charles suggested.

"Let's leave," Jennie said.

"No."

"We've intruded, Charles, we should—"

"Welcome, Picketts." The big man had moved on cat's paws, entering the hall without a sound as they'd argued. His hair was dark and thick, trimmed around his ears, and his beard was a silvery white. He had blue eyes, the color of sky right after a summer storm. Kind eyes. To Dougie he said, "You must be Mr. Pickett. I don't believe we've met." He knelt down and reached out his hand.

Dougie sought permission and Jennie nodded.

She'd never seen a grown man squat down to shake a child's hand.

"Pleased to make your acquaintance, Mr. Pickett."

Dougie laughed and kept pumping Mr. Parrish's hand.

"Minnie, let's see if Chen can rustle up some cookies for this young man. Is it all right if he goes with her? Our cook's quite gifted when it comes to cookies."

"Of course," Charles answered, though the question had been posed to Jennie.

Mr. Parrish transferred his gaze back to Dougie. He stood without pressing his palms against his thighs and smiled, passed Dougie's hand onto Minnie's, who walked with him to the kitchen. Mr. Parrish motioned for them to enter the parlor on the right. Her heart beat a little faster, hoping Douglas would be on his best behavior. Cookies increased that likelihood.

"Now then, what can I do for you? It's been years—maybe since your wedding—that I've had the pleasure." He shook Charles's hand, directed them to sit on a red velvet settee.

Charles rubbed his hand across the fine material, and Mr. Parrish told the story of having it sent around the Horn. "Quite an undertaking for a settee, but it belonged to the Winns, Mrs. Parrish's family, and when her father died, it was left to her. Of course she longed for it. I could bring it here, and so I did. It's what one does for family." He raised his palms together, as if to say "I had no choice."

"We're here because of family," Charles began. "We have a proposition for you. An investment you might make. Go ahead, Jennie, tell him."

Oh, she knew he'd want her to speak, as she had some sort of relationship with Mr. Parrish as a preacher like her father, but still, to talk of money before first finding out how his wife faired, that was rude. "I wonder, first, about the health of Mrs. Parrish. We hear she suffers."

He nodded and the after-storm blue eyes clouded over. "She does. No one seems to have any way to stop the deterioration. So we keep her comfortable. I was gone for five months. I came back as soon as she took a turn."

"I'm sorry," Jennie said. "Unexplained illness is the most difficult. It's like living through a flood and then having the water never recede. Everything has a new level of vulnerability around it."

"Yes. That's exactly what it's like." He looked at Jennie, who saw respect or perhaps surprise in his eyes. He bowed his head, clasped his hands together as though in prayer.

Charles frowned, used his hands to urge Jennie forward. She shook her head.

Minnie entered then with tea and cookies.

"Shall I pour?" Jennie offered as Minnie set the tray down on the table.

Mr. Parrish accepted Jennie's offer. The scent of mint lifted from the porcelain pot. It mingled with the roses in the cut-glass vases set around the room. A slight breeze moved the ribbons hanging from her straw hat and tickled her neck. The three sipped in silence. Then, "I wonder if Mrs. Parrish might like a brief visit. I'd be pleased to thank her in person for the lovely honey she sent us after the wedding."

Mr. Parrish hesitated, then said, "I think she'd like that. Let me see if she's up to it."

He left the room.

"Just talk about the loan. I didn't bring you along to dally."

"I'm not. It's disrespectful not to pay attention to the lives of people we're hoping to have a commercial relationship with."

Charles sat up straight. "Oh, you're playing them. I get it. Softening them up for—"

"She says she'd love to have you come in, Mrs. Pickett." Mr. Parrish had returned on those cat-paw feet. She hoped he hadn't heard what Charles had said or even her comments about the loan. Jennie didn't look at Charles but stood and allowed herself to be taken to a room that might have been a dining room at one time, as it was across from the kitchen. It was now a large bedroom. Perhaps so that Mrs. Parrish didn't

98

need to climb the stairs. Another settee, not red velvet but green, owned the wall opposite the windows that reached from ceiling to the floor. Sunlight poured into the room and landed like the end of a rainbow on a figure so small she looked childlike among the comforters and quilts.

"Mrs. Pickett." She reached out her hand as she spoke Jennie's name with effort-filled breath.

"Jennie. Please call me Jennie." She reminded Jennie of her sister Rebecca, who had died of typhus, that terrible disease. Mrs. Parrish's eyes remained clear, and she motioned for Jennie to sit next to her. Mr. Parrish faded away. It was only this ailing woman who drew Jennie's attention. "You've had a time of it."

"Oh yes. That's a good way to say it. 'A time of it.' One can imagine what the time was like."

Jennie smiled, and nodded agreement.

"My time has been good, filled with such joys. A loving family. A kind and faithful husband. We've been blessed. And you? I've not seen you since the wedding. You're well? Your parents are well?"

The woman's gentle resignation of what awaited her, carrying the weight of it without resentment nor evidence of fear, took Jennie's thoughts to her child. Jennie considered telling her about Baby Ariyah and her great loss, but she answered her question instead. "My parents are well. And I am. We are. We have a child now.

Douglas. He's in scamping cookies from your cook."

She smiled, coughed. Jennie stood to hand her the glass beside the bed and helped her drink. She wore a flounced cap that framed her oval face, and Jennie's fingers against her neck felt like she gentled a newborn's.

"Chen makes the best cookies. I've had little hunger for such of late."

"Your doctor has given you aromatics and herbs?"

"Oh, all that's available has been done."

Her lips looked dry and cracked, so Jennie didn't think everything was being done. "I have some glycerin. It might help your dry lips feel better." *I'll bring her my blend of cinnamon, garlic, cloves, and eucalyptus for her cough.*

"That would be lovely."

Jennie reached inside her reticule and brought out the tin. "Let me wash my hands before I put it on." The rose-decorated bowl and pitcher on the washstand held fresh water. The mirror above revealed Jennie's hat askew. She straightened it, then rewashed her hands. In the mirror, she saw Mrs. Parrish close her eyes. "Here we are." Jennie brought her fingers to the paste and spread it on the ailing woman's lips. Her eyes watered at the touch. So did Jennie's, so grateful to bring comfort.

"Thank you." She dabbed at her eyes with

a handkerchief she pulled from her sleeve. "It does feel better." She sighed, coughed. "I don't know why every little thing seems to make me want to cry. I'm really in little pain and Josiah is so good to me. Minnie as well. And my boys, all grown now, so I've not to worry over them. I think Charles Winn is about your age." She patted Jennie's hand. "Endings were always beginnings for me, but this ending . . ." Her voice trailed off.

"My sister Rebecca shed many tears with her typhus. Tears must be a way to chink the cracks in our hearts with liquid love."

"Liquid love. I like that." Her eyes fluttered. She was tired.

"Thank you for letting me visit with you. I need to check on Douglas. I'll leave the glycerin. Perhaps Minnie can put it on for you."

"Oh, Josiah will do that. He loves to touch me." Jennie thought she might have blushed, but it was difficult to tell. "Thank you. Come back. Any time." She waved a weak hand, closed her eyes, adding as Jennie left, "It's still a new beginning, isn't it? Just one we have to take alone." Then she began to softly snore.

The kitchen sat across from Mrs. Parrish's room, and Jennie heard Dougie chattering with Minnie, she thought, but the response came from an accented voice. The Chinese cook. All sounded well, so she returned to the parlor before

Dougie could spy her, wondering if there was anything more she could do for Mrs. Parrish.

"There you are. We were about to come and get you," Charles said. "Wouldn't want to tire Mrs. Parrish out now, would we."

"She's resting. She seemed to like the visit."

"A woman's touch is always welcome, I suspect." Mr. Parrish turned back toward Charles as Jennie lifted her hoop to sit beside him. She smoothed her purple-dyed linen skirt. "Now that Charles and I have solved the problems of the world—including getting the anti-liquor laws passed—what was it the two of you wished to discuss with me?"

That Charles would have talked about the anti-liquor laws amazed her, but then it shouldn't have. Chameleon that he could be—as charming people often are—he would have found a way to see Mr. Parrish's preferences opposing liquor and suggested he agreed with it. "Go ahead, Jennie."

A flare of irritation escaped her eyes as she looked at Charles.

"We've come seeking a loan, Reverend Parrish. It's a terrible thing to discuss commerce with someone who has his own trials, but here we are, hat in hand." She motioned to Charles, who was kneading the edge of his bowler hat, crown down as though they were begging. Which they were. Her tone or the words caused him to stop the finger twisting and turn the hat crown up. "Charles has a good job at the prison working as an assistant to my brother-in-law. But we'd like very much to one day purchase our own property, have a small farm where I could grow my herbs and plants, and Charles could spend less time with people who have criminal intent."

"Many are imprisoned by their addictions," Mr. Parrish said.

Charles started to speak, but Jennie interrupted. "I agree. And that's one reason why we seek a loan, so that Charles can spend more time with those not impaired by drink or laudanum or morphine. He'd like to use the funds to invest in property that he'd improve and then resell. Our capital city is growing here, now that the war is over. You've seen so many changes since you arrived in . . . what year?"

"We left New York in '39. Arrived here in '40."

"It would take us a while, but Charles is a good carpenter and farmer and we are young and healthy and could improve properties. But we need a stake. Like the miners who head into Canyon City to find gold. Land would be our gold."

"How much are you seeking?"

Charles said, "Five hundred dollars."

Jennie gasped. That wasn't what he'd said.

They'd agreed on one hundred dollars; more than enough, in fact. Why had he surged ahead to ask for such an impossible amount? Jennie couldn't imagine Mr. Parrish loaning that much.

"I'd need to think about it." *He isn't turning us down outright?* "Elizabeth and I like to encourage young families in our state. But that is a large amount of capital, especially here. You'll soon discover that assets aren't always in currency."

"We understand," Jennie said. "Please take all the time you need to consider our request. Or an alternative." She narrowed her eyes at Charles and he sat back, his lips tight.

"Let's speak on Monday. I like to discuss things with Mrs. Parrish. I'm sure we can do something to assist."

Dougie bounded down the hall at that moment, all smiles, and it seemed the perfect time to depart. Jennie stood, taking Dougie's hand and pulling him into her skirts. "And were you a good boy?"

"Quite the little charmer," Minnie said. Jennie couldn't tell if it was a compliment or not.

"We should be going. Charles has promised to help me with the love apples we've planted. Tomatoes, I believe they call them now. They seem to be doing well, but we need to transplant them."

Charles stood then. "We'll stop by Monday—to

answer any questions you might have." That last he said hurriedly before Jennie could stop him.

"That'll be fine. Two o'clock. And be sure to bring young Pickett too. Chen always has more cookies."

Chapter 10

The Passionate Sense of the Potential

"Mama, not so tight."

She loosened her grip on her son. "Five hundred dollars. What were you thinking?" Trees drifted white blossoms on them. Birds chattered and squirrels with long tails ran up the fir tree trunks. Pink azaleas spread between picket fences, but Jennie barely noticed. "How could you ask for so much?"

"He's good for it. Did you see the sculptures? And the vases themselves would bring in a hundred."

"I—this is not what we're about, Charles. Is it? We had a plan—"

He hugged her to his side, bent down and lifted Dougie, who squealed his delight. "They like you. He likes Dougie here. He'll make the loan. Oh, maybe not for five hundred but half, I imagine. We can move so much faster that way. Don't be so fragile."

Fragile. It was a good way to put how she felt. Her stomach hurt. In that moment, she wished they still lived with Lucinda so she could discuss this afternoon as soon as they got home. But she'd chosen to have her family on their own. She had to find a way to deal with the disappointments or worries alone too. They walked past Ariyah's home and heard piano music drifting through the window. Maybe she'd visit tomorrow after their second appointment and get Ariyah's thoughts on what had just happened. Jennie's family didn't need to know.

"I apologize for my husband's not being here," Jennie told Reverend Parrish on Monday. "He had additional duties, at work. He suggested I come alone. How is Mrs. Parrish today?"

"As well as can be expected. She appreciated the glycerin." He had the warmest smile that went right up to his eyes.

She held Dougie's hand, wishing she'd asked Ariyah to watch him while Charles skipped out. That wasn't fair. He had received a request from Joseph to come to the prison at dawn. Of course he had to comply.

"I have a Quilton." Dougie spoke to Mr. Parrish, who once again knelt down to his level.

"And what is a quilton, Mr. Pickett?"

Douglas looked around as though seeking his father.

"You're Mr. Pickett too," Jennie told him.

"I am?"

She nodded. "Tell Mr. Parrish about Quilton."

"He's my pork-a-pine. He eats leaves I find for him, doesn't he, Mama? And he holds his tin cup when he wants milk."

Mr. Parrish smiled and stood, patting Douglas on his back as Jennie nodded agreement. "You'll have to introduce us sometime. I've never seen a pet porcupine."

A Chinese man Jennie assumed to be Chen appeared. Douglas's eyes lit up. "Cookies, Mama?"

"Of course." Her son went willingly with the small man, who quick-stepped down the hall, his single braid bouncing on his back. To Mr. Parrish she said, "You've won the heart of my son."

"Cookies can do that." He took the seat across from her. "I do have a few questions about the loan request."

She swallowed, dreading the conversation about finance, even while aware of less anxiety than the day before, when Charles had been along. "I hope I can answer them." She wondered if she should make the case that she and Charles had discussed it overnight and really only needed one hundred dollars and then tell Charles that's the amount Mr. Parrish would loan. But she didn't, not ready to tell a lie nor live with the consequences of upsetting her husband in the process.

"We'll need to work out an interest arrangement," Jennie said, anticipating.

"Elizabeth and I feel it isn't right to charge family interest."

"But we aren't—"

He raised his palm to silence her. "Perhaps an exchange of labor now and then could suffice."

"I could look after Mrs. Parrish. I'd be honored."

"You mentioned Charles is a carpenter."

Jennie nodded. It was one of Charles's strengths.

"We have need of some repairs. So if labor is exchanged for interest, let me say that Mrs. Parrish and I felt that we could release two hundred fifty dollars now and the remaining in three months when I've sold some of the lambs. Would that be agreeable?"

"Yes. Of course. I—we—that's very generous of you. All of it is very generous."

"I'll have papers drawn up with terms of repayment and Charles can sign them. We'll ask you to sign them as well. Elizabeth and I believe that women ought to have a say in things legal and financial. We're impressed that both of you came for the initial discussion. Oregon's decision to allow a woman to own land in her own name is a great step forward for America, we believe."

"Yes. Indeed."

Jennie felt unbalanced with his goodness. Charles had been right in insisting she come along. He'd been right about asking for that amount of money, and now they had been given an even greater gift in Mr. Parrish's interest arrangement: labor in return. What more could she receive?

He spoke then about her parents, expressed how he admired her father's ministry and his public service. Jennie accepted his compliments and offered to visit with Mrs. Parrish, if she might be of help.

"She's resting now. But perhaps you'd care for a walk in the garden?"

"Yes. Oh, that would be lovely."

He described the variety of roses he'd planted, spoke of herbs he'd nurtured at the suggestion of some of the Indian healers he encountered in his work as Indian agent. "The healers share their skills among the tribes. I've learned about pasqueflower the Blackfeet use, and of course elderberry."

"For treatment of poisons, as an expectorant."

"Indeed." He looked at Jennie with new respect. "The Tillamook," he continued, "use dogwood root tea, should one run out of quinine, for malaria."

He learned from his Indian contacts, didn't just go there to tell them what to do.

Near the garden house, rhododendrons she'd

seen growing wild beneath forest firs prospered in this place. Beyond the borders of the garden, white fluffs she realized were sheep dotted the rolling green fields. She remembered her wily swimming fox. A chipmunk with yellow stripes poked its head from the rock wall surrounding a pond, and Jennie found herself babbling on about the distillery and her plants and her wish to use them to heal people. They paused in front of a wooden bench that overlooked a topiary. The entire landscape reminded her of pictures of an English garden she'd seen in a book. Sparrows washed themselves at the stone birdbaths, and some sort of ivy promising a purple bloom wove its way up a trellis.

"I'd say your healing plants are an extension of your own gifts," he said.

"It's only the plants. I—I once thought of becoming a doctor, oh ages ago, but those are fanciful thoughts." *Why did I share that?*

"You're young. That Danish philosopher Kierkegaard said he'd give up wealth and power for the 'passionate sense of the potential, for the eye which, ever young and ardent, sees the possibilities.' "

"I like that." She asked him to repeat the quote and wrapped the words in memory.

He motioned her toward a wrought-iron bench with a rose design in the back, and Jennie lifted her single hoop to sit. A blacksmith had worked overtime creating that treasure. "I was referring to your natural healing arts," Mr. Parrish continued. "Elizabeth said your presence gave her peace, a gentle respite that eased her breathing."

"Did it? I'm so glad she felt better. I've brought an aromatic for her. I didn't want to tire her."

"On the contrary."

Dougie ran out then, with Chen behind him, looking frazzled with a reddish stain on his white apron. "Boy like rhubarb but not know how to wait for sauce to arrive in bowl."

Jennie started to apologize, but Mr. Parrish stood and gestured for Dougie to sit between them. Douglas kicked his feet up and down.

"Was the rhubarb good?" Mr. Parrish asked.

Dougie nodded.

"Excellent. Thank you, Chen. We were just finishing here."

The cook bowed twice and walked quick-quick back toward the house. The manor, was how Jennie saw it.

She took Dougie's hand, stood, and curtsied to Mr. Parrish. The yellow ribbons of her straw hat draped loosely at her bodice and they swished as she bent. "My son . . . I'm so sorry."

"Think nothing of it."

Douglas hadn't embarrassed himself any worse than she had, sharing a dream with this man. At least she hadn't confessed to how reluctant she was to leave the peace of this garden.

• • •

Charles's eyes carried a glazed look, which he explained resulted from the demands of the day. A sweet scent Jennie couldn't name rose from his mustache when he kissed her. He combed it absently with his fingers when he talked now. "How did it go?"

"Better than I expected. He'll loan us the full amount, providing half after we sign the papers and the other half in three months. I . . . was stunned. It's so much money. He wants quarterly payments."

"He sees the possibilities. That's the youth in him."

Jennie laughed. "The youth in him? He must be fifty." She thought of her father. "Maybe older."

"It's his mind, Jennie, that's what's young. What interest did he demand? I said no more than 2 percent. Were you able to negotiate to that?"

"No interest. He wants you to do some carpentry work for them. Repairs on the garden house or maybe the barn. I don't know, really."

"No interest? How did the man ever get so wealthy not charging interest?"

"He said we were like family." She remembered something biblically about taking care of family, about not burdening them with additional costs attached to a financial assistance. "Maybe he hasn't made many loans."

"We have ourselves a future, Jennie Pickett. Let's drink to that!"

She frowned.

"Sassafras, of course." He laughed, but it felt forced. He kissed her then, the gesture fleeting as a butterfly landing on a petal, soon moving on to other sweeter things.

Chapter 11
Peplum

And so it began, their new entrepreneurial life. Charles busied himself at the clerk's office, looking for donation land claims up for sale. He bought a fine horse and buggy ("Every businessman needs a steed and carriage. How else will customers accept my good judgment?"). He drove it on weekends and, as the summer continued, in the evenings too. He bought new suits tailored for his physique and insisted Jennie go to the dressmaker for additional frocks. And hats. And reticules, even though outside pockets were fashionable—and more practical. He evaded questions of how he'd paid for the pearls and how much money was left. He wanted Lucinda and the girls to have new clothes, to spread his largess, but Joseph declined the offer. Charles bought new short pants and suspenders for Dougie and a bow tie he insisted the boy wear to church. Dougie tore it off as soon as they stepped into the carriage to return home. Charles insisted they pay George for the distillery, have no obligation "so it's totally ours." He insisted on calling cards for Jennie and had business cards made up at the printer.

Pickett and Son

Land Acquisitions and Dream Attainment

Jennie urged restraint. He had yet to buy a piece of property and sell it at a profit. All he'd spent had gone into what she called "peplum," like little flounces on women's dress jackets that made things look bigger and perhaps finer and fancier than they were, that brought the eye to a slender waist while ignoring the larger bustle behind.

"Everything has to look prosperous" was his retort.

Charles sometimes took Dougie with him on a Saturday or Sunday afternoon and the boy loved the buggy rides. Jennie would have liked to join them as a family but was not invited. Still, it pleased her to see her husband and son doing good things together. And selfishly, their absence gave her time with the essencier without the worry over Douglas. She lost herself in her efforts, setting aside the worry of her husband's rate of spending without seeing results from his "dream attainment."

"He's enthusiastic," she told Ariyah on an afternoon. "All dreamers have to have that blind passion, I suppose. But I'm not seeing much from all his effort. It worries me a little."

"Peleg says men need to experience their impact on the world. Women less so."

"Do you think that's true?" Jennie thought of the satisfaction derived from seeing her oils or herbal pastes bringing comfort to a mother. Healing was her passion, and yet it failed to fill her with the enthusiasm of the kind that drove her husband.

Ariyah plunked on the piano and the two sat on separate round stools in front of it. She stopped to look at Jennie.

"Women have children to show their impact on the world. That's what Peleg says."

"But what about women who don't have children, or whose children . . . die or turn out to not be good people in the end? Surely a woman still wants to know her life has meaning, even if she fails at something so significant."

Ariyah turned back, played a few notes, squinted at the music sheet. "It's supposed to be those keys and those sounds. I think I hit them, though maybe not perfect." She let her hands fall into her lap. "We don't control the outcome of another's life I don't think. We do the best we can but just as with your plants—you provide good soil, you fertilize, you stake them before it looks as though they'll need it, bring fresh water. Still, it's the sunshine that makes the difference, the very thing you don't control. We can only do what we can do."

"You're a philosopher, Ariyah."

"I'm also an engaged woman."

"And I didn't even notice!" Jennie looked for a ring. "That's wonderful!"

Ariyah giggled and leaned in to Jennie. "It's perfect. And I'll have the most unique engagement ring ever. Voilà!" She spread her hands across the keys. "He said he wanted to buy me a ring, but I like the idea that the promise of our marriage will be kept in music." She patted Jennie's hand, held her friend's eyes. "Don't worry about Charles. He's venturing into something new."

"We're in this together, but it feels as though something's missing between us." Not unlike the jokes she never understood: she could hear the words but miss the subtle point that made others laugh and left her in the dark.

"It's my first major transaction. Of course I had to celebrate a little. It would have been rude not to." It was late on an August evening and Jennie smelled alcohol on his breath. "We've made enough on this one to buy you your own buggy and I've paid for the pearls. I've put the order in. That's why I'm so late. Don't put a damper on this day, Jennie."

Dougie looked up from his new wooden horses

he'd shown his mother. She frowned at Charles. "He already has wooden horses."

"These are quality. He has to learn how to handle nice things."

Quilton scratched in his box. The porcupine still kept his quills laid flat even when Douglas dallied filling his water bowl. The rodent expressed agitation as voices grew louder. Jennie wondered later if Quilton anticipated the tension that came next, the way horses race around a field, tails to the air, before a thunderstorm crests the horizon.

"The spending, Charles. It concerns me."

"Everything concerns you."

"You haven't done any carpentry work for the Parrishes and they're about to loan us the second half. We have a quarterly payment due. We need to keep the bargain. We don't need another buggy. We have yours and—"

"I try to do nice things for you and what do you do?" He stumbled backward. "You thwart me at every turn."

"I'm not. I—I'm worried."

"You have no faith in me." She thought of what Ariyah had said.

"I'm proud that you've made the first sale. I am. It's just that . . ."

He looked around as though he'd mislaid something, his eyes settled on Dougie. "Come on, Douglas. Leave the toys. Let's give your mother time to appreciate what she has and what she's about to have." Dougie dropped the horses and followed his father out without a word of protest.

The quiet left behind with the slammed door felt like the heat preceding a summer storm.

Why didn't she wait before confronting him, especially when he smelled of spirits? Instead of his inebriation making her hold her tongue, it loosened it. She should follow them, rescue Dougie. But Dougie's presence might encourage his father's better judgment. *Will it?*

Everything was a decision.

She fed Quilton, fixed herself some tea, remembered Scripture: "Let us not grow weary in doing good, for in due season, we shall reap, if we do not lose heart."

Her mind skittered to noises within the household, hoping for sounds of her husband and son returning. They did not. She ate a biscuit. Watched the day melt into sunset. Slept the night in the chair. She did not dream.

The new clock Charles had bought that stood sentry in the living area struck six when she heard the horse whinny and pulled the curtain back to sunrise and her husband in the carriage.

Dougie wasn't there—What on earth could he have done with Dougie? But then her son's head bobbed up, allowing her full fury she could direct at Charles. "Thank goodness." Her words stirred Quilton, but the porcupine would have to wait for breakfast. She grabbed her shawl and rushed out.

She'd prayed that if he wasn't sober she wouldn't say anything until he was. There was no sense arguing with someone influenced by strong drink.

Then weak spirited as she was, she violated the vow.

Charles missed the step as he slid from the carriage, grabbing the handhold to balance himself.

"Charles, are you—drunk?"

"Oh, she's so smart this woman. Drunk? No, celebrated. Help me unharness this thing, woman. You drove me to be out so late, so no lectures."

"I drove you? How dare you—"

"Mama, my tummy hurts."

"I don't doubt it. Have you eaten?" She reached for Dougie. "What have you done to him?"

"Miss Priscilla gives me giggly candy. I don't feel so good, Mama."

"Miss Priscilla? Who is—"

"I got him." Charles lifted Dougie from her. "Come on, boy. We'll get you some laudanum."

"No. Charles. Please. I'll take him." Charles had already swung Dougie onto his shoulder, wobbling toward the house. "Saleratus, not laudanum. Please. It's in the white tin."

She shook as she led the horse toward the barn. *I should follow them in.* The horse wasn't hot, so they hadn't been far away. Who was "Miss

Priscilla"? And what had gone on? She headed inside.

Dougie cried and ran to her. Charles had sprawled on the settee, his lanky legs hanging over the narrow seat. His eyes were closed.

"Did Daddy give you some white powder for your tummy?"

Dougie shook his head no. "Tummy hurts." His eyes weren't dilated. He had no bruises she could see. She couldn't name the scent from his breath.

She scurried to the cabinet with cooking spices. The tin of saleratus used to raise bread dough had not been moved. She opened it and put a small spoonful into a glass of water. Dougie drank it down. She hoped the leavening agent would soak up some of the stomach acid caused by, what had he said, "giggly candy"?

"Better?" He nodded and she settled Dougie in his trundle bed. No fever. He drank water but didn't gulp it. "Try to sleep. You've been up a long time."

"I saw Mary and Nellie."

"Did you? You went to Aunt Lucinda's. Was Miss Priscilla there with her candy?"

He shook his head. "Papa and Uncle argued. Miss Priscilla lives in a bi-i-i-ig house." He yawned. "I like giggle candy. Papa likes it too." Dougie lay in his trundle bed and then closed his eyes, immediately asleep.

Fury like a fire burned inside her. What kind of "candy" had her child been exposed to? And his own father had allowed it to happen. Just as before, only this time he'd given Dougie whatever it was, not merely "allowed" him to drink from the bottle while Charles slept in his stupor.

"Wake up, Charles!" She shook him. "You wake up and tell me right now what's gone on."

He moaned and rolled over, his neck in an odd position. He'd have a headache when he awoke. It would serve him right. "Charles!" Nothing. And then she heard an inner voice remind her of that earlier vow: *Don't argue with a drunk.* She would have to wait to expectorate her anger.

She unharnessed the patient horse, cooled him with the curry-comb, fed and watered the gelding, then let him out to the small paddock where he shook his chestnut mane and pranced around, then came to the fence to nuzzle her. Maybe for human touch too. He was there to do his duty and then receive reward for it. Green moss grew on the top rails except where the horse had rubbed, leaning across for a pat on his nose. He whinnied low as she caressed the velvet.

"What do I do with this . . . outrage that's burning in my stomach?" Surely holding such anger was a sin. And one was supposed to confess sins and then be given a route to freedom or at least another path away from self-righteous rage.

She left the horse eating, went inside. Her knitting needles passed the time. What would Joseph say about his assistant superintendent not showing up for work? She checked on Dougie now and then. He snored, so she knew he breathed all right. He looked peaceful in his sleep, so she didn't consider another humiliating trip to that doctor.

The clock struck twelve times, waking Dougie. When she asked if he was hungry, he nodded yes and she sliced a piece of ham for him and spread butter on bread to make a sandwich. She ate one too and finished it as Charles awoke.

He groaned. "What time is it?"

"Almost one in the afternoon."

"I really slept." He sat up and shook his head. "Uh . . . I didn't, that is, I didn't hurt . . . ?"

"Physically, no. I'll fix you a sandwich so you can work a part of your shift at least."

He leaned back, his arm across his forehead and his eyes. "Ah, Jennie. It'll be all right, so I don't want you to sputter now when I tell you this, but Joseph fired me."

"What? After you go in to work for him at dawn? After all you've done through the years for him? No. We need that stability, Charles. We need—"

"I can turn it into a good thing. I'll have more selling time. I can't be trying to do this evenings or the day of rest. People are uncomfortable speaking of buying and selling on the Sabbath. And I have to consider time to do the carpentry for Parrish. You even mentioned that. My not working at the prison will make that easier."

"But they've made the loan with the understanding that you had a job and could make repayments. Now you—"

"We will. With the one transaction I've got a quarter of the payment already."

"But now we'll need to live on that. Maybe Joseph will take you back."

"He won't." He sat up. "Don't you worry. I'll work for Parrish this afternoon."

"It's already afternoon."

"You worry overmuch." He yawned, closed his eyes, and was asleep within seconds.

Once a woman had come to her for something to ease burns. She confessed to throwing hot coffee at her husband as he slept off too much brew. She expressed great remorse but at the time had been furious that he had simply slept through her deep, profound, and futile expression of frustration and fear. They had stayed together, her husband saying he deserved the pain she inflicted, a tit for tat. At the time, she thought the interaction belonged to the lower classes, but at that moment, as Charles snored, it was all she could do to let him sleep and pour the hot tea water into the pot.

Charles took his tools and the buggy to the Parrishes the next morning where he spent the day, and he said he was too tired to talk when he got home. She tried not to interrogate Dougie, but when on Tuesday Charles walked to "pick up the new buggy and horse" over her objections, she drove their existing buggy toward Liberty Street with Dougie along. Brick buildings lined the commercial center, and at a cross street, Dougie pointed and said, "Miss Priscilla's house. Down there." How did he remember that? Her cheeks felt warm and her stomach lurched. She knew of *that* area.

She flicked the reins on the horse's back and he picked up to a trot, moving at a good clip down that street. "That one." Her son pointed to a two-story house with a wide porch back among the firs and behind a white picket fence. The shrubbery was well trimmed.

Even though she knew of the work those women did, Jennie had always felt compassion for them. Now and then one had come seeking herbal treatments for their intimate rashes. She wished she felt more confident using pasqueflower. A trained doctor would know better what to do. The plant looked like a buttercup and Indians back in Illinois used it to speed childbirth—and to treat syphilis. But it also dangerously slowed the heart. Though she had the treatment, she had turned the woman away, suggesting she speak with a doctor who would have more options.

"Those willing to treat us are difficult to find," the woman had said. Jennie didn't doubt it. Men caused the problem but didn't like to participate in the solution.

Miss Priscilla is behind that door.

Jennie tried to think kind thoughts. She understood how easily a woman abandoned by a husband or abused by a father or beau could fall into such work. Alcohol took its firm finger and wrote on the lives of women and children, even if they didn't imbibe. That her husband would expose their son to that. Surely not because he . . . perhaps someone there was the person who had bought the land Charles had sold. Maybe Charles being there was innocent, land being exchanged and a little celebratory drink, as he had claimed. Didn't the proprietor of the house—the Madam, she was called—often have money she needed to invest? Yes, that was it. Charles might have only stopped for a moment. He'd visited the Sloans long enough to have an argument, hadn't he said? And to get fired. Charles spoke of not being drunk but "celebratory."

But that didn't explain nor excuse Douglas's condition. She turned the horse at the end of the street, heading toward Pringle Creek.

A steamboat whistle perked the horse's ears forward, then back, paying attention. Maybe the fox would come by and remind her that he knew how to heal himself.

She would have to deal with Charles, whether he wanted to talk about it or not. She just didn't know when or how or if she could accept whatever answer he offered. DW, her attorney brother, had advised her once to never ask a question unless she already knew the answer. That might work in law but not in life.

Chapter 12
Rivers Gouging Canyons

Ariyah arrived the next morning full of nuptial talk. "We're going to marry in the parlor. I hope your father will officiate. And you'll be my matron of honor. You will, won't you?"

"If it means honoring you and honoring marriage, yes!" She chose not to flatten her friend's enthusiasm with the realities of what marriage sometimes brought.

"My parents are so happy. Peleg's even paying for my wedding dress. It's going to be a deep madder red, the hue Vermeer used in his palette. Maroon is such a sunrise color, don't you agree?" Jennie nodded. "And we'll serve Norwegian Omelettes."

"Something exotic, I suspect." Jennie served her friend tea, only a little embarrassed at their frugal furnishings. Ariyah didn't seem to notice.

"They're little cakes Peleg said Thomas Jefferson served with iced cream inside a pastry and meringue baked on top. The cakes will look like our Mt. Jefferson." She pointed with her chin toward the east where that white peak rose up as if pushed out of the rolling green fields and forests. "Peleg says they'll be our 'Alaskas' but not Seward's Folly. He's quite distressed that Congress authorized that purchase. Our Alaskas will be the toast of the town, not the joke of it." She stopped talking. "What's the matter? You're so quiet."

Shame is a powerful silencer. "It's—it's nothing. Tell me what I'm to wear, what color? And what materials. Oh, and goodness, when is this grand event happening?"

"Two o'clock on the twenty-first. I've even arranged for someone to watch over the children so you'll have nothing to worry about with Douglas. I know how you worry." She patted Jennie's hand.

At the moment, Dougie shouted like a buckaroo, riding his hobby horse outside. The women watched as he swirled a rope, hoping to lasso the butter churn on the porch.

"Peleg is composing a piano piece for me that he'll play. I think that's so romantic, don't you? I'm getting flowers from that fabulous garden of the Parrishes. He offered. Or rather, Mrs. Parrish did through her husband, when she heard of our engagement. Peleg had some business with Reverend Parrish when he first arrived. Something about sheep, I think. The roses are gone, but the gladiolas should be beautiful." Ariyah stood, her dress a swirl of blue. She clasped Jennie's hands and pulled her up, spreading their arms as she looked down at Jennie's short frame. "Let's see those dimples. Perfect! I'm using the seamstress on Center Street. She'll design something to show off your tiny waist and that creamy skin and those emerald eyes. A buttercup yellow, I think." She sighed. "How I envy those eyes."

"That seamstress, she's . . . expensive."

"Don't fret. I'll pay for it, Jennie. Or rather, Peleg will."

"Oh, no. I was just thinking about the new millinery shop. She's hoping to make a go of it, a small business, widowed. I'm sensitive these days to women who take a risk like that. I wonder if we could—"

"You're a collector of lost souls, Jennie." She held her friend's eyes with warmth. "It's one reason why I love you so." She smiled and adjusted her hair clip. "All right. We'll use your milliner for hats and ribbons and chemises and my dressmaker for our gowns. This'll be such fun." She swirled herself around, then grabbed Jennie in a hug. "I like your new home, Jennie." She smelled of rose water. "Both our lives have a new melody written over the score of love."

The music she described fit her life, and Jennie wouldn't do anything to silence it for her friend.

Lucinda kissed Jennie on both cheeks, then turned to Douglas. "We don't see you often enough. Douglas, you've grown. Such a big man you are."

"I see you sooner."

Lucinda frowned. "Oh, you mean earlier. Yes, you did, with your papa."

Dougie put his hands on his hips, his elbows out the way Charles stood when he hoped to look impressive. "I'm a buckaroo."

"Did you bring your horse along?"

Dougie shook his head, his shoulders dropped.

"Maybe Nellie and Mary will help you find one to play with today. They're in the backyard. You know where that is." He headed out and Lucinda turned to Jennie. "How are . . . things?"

"A bit wobbly. Charles being fired has certainly complicated things. But that happens, I guess." With her fingernail, Jennie picked at a dried piece of pastry stuck to the deep grain of Lucinda's oak table edge. Her sister placed her palm over Jennie's to stop her mindless picking.

"He wasn't fired, Jennie. Is that what he told you?" She sighed. "And you believed him?"

"He wasn't?"

"Oh, Sister. I'm so sorry. I didn't mean to sound harsh." Lucinda reached to hold Jennie with one arm, rubbing gently. "We didn't know what to say, actually. He up and told us he was quitting."

Married people often said "we" and "us"

as though the "I" of a partnership needed to disappear in order for the marriage to work. Jennie didn't belong to much of a "we" anymore. She'd been saying "my son" rather than "our son" for some time. Had it been a subtle awareness that her heart knew of the disruption before her head did?

"It's not your fault." Jennie dabbed at her eyes with a handkerchief pulled from her reticule. It smelled of peppermint. Her fingers lingered on the beaded purse. *Something I must sell.*

"What will you do?"

"He's—well, you know, we got this loan from Reverend Parrish. Both Parrishes."

"We thought there must be something more than this land purchase and resale."

"He's using it—things are booming here. He—he needs more time to devote to it. And he can do carpentry on the side now that he's not working at the prison."

"You're all right with his decision then."

"I'm saying what he said." Jennie looked away, couldn't bear the compassion of her sister's eyes. "I'm terrified. He—he took Dougie with him last weekend and they didn't come home all night. And when they did, he was . . . impaired. And Dougie was . . . different. He's been better since it's the three of us. Dougie said he'd gotten giggly candy, whatever that is." She couldn't tell her about Miss Priscilla. "I need to find work,

Lucinda. We need something steady coming in. And there's a payment due on the loan."

"But the loan can tide you over."

"He's gone through the money, Lucinda. Almost all of the two hundred fifty dollars, with so little to show for it." She picked up the beaded purse, her hands shook when she set it down. "We're to acquire the next two hundred fifty at the end of the month."

"Oh, Jennie, how is that possible?"

"Some of it is all the accoutrements he said were necessary to look profitable so others would take him seriously, that he knew what he was doing. But two carriages, a big gelding, and a fine mare, his expensive clothes, the greater upkeep feeding two horses. This." She lifted her skirts with both fingertips. "Insisting on expensive clothes for me and Dougie. Speaking of which, I'd better check on Douglas." Jennie stood.

"I don't know what to say."

"There's nothing to be said. I can try to sell more oils and herbs. I can promote myself more, as someone who treats minor scrapes and bruises, but I'm not trained. I don't want doctors starting rumors about me or people calling me a charlatan. It's going to be difficult enough to keep the rumors about Charles down."

"Maybe people will think he's doing so well he doesn't have to work for the state anymore."

"Maybe. But he'll have to stop his spending

habits or I won't be able to pay the bills and then complaints won't be rumors, they'll be facts."

The sisters walked outside, elbow wrapped in elbow in a weave of love and safety. Douglas chased the girls swirling his lasso.

"Douglas, it's time for us to go. Would you like to walk home past the creek, see if that old fox comes by?"

Douglas stopped. "You don't have the brass and glass. I couldn't see without that, Mama."

He was right, of course. A special lens and light were critical to seeing the smaller, important things in life that are often overlooked.

"Look, Jennie." It was the week before Ariyah's wedding, well into September and the turning of leaves. Days had passed without Jennie confronting Charles, who sat now on their settee while Jennie settled her straw hat on her head before the hall mirror. "It's time we talked."

"Now? Ariyah's expecting me for a fitting." She looked at the clock that struck every quarter hour.

"Just sit."

"Charles, no."

He'd been wary or racing of late, frenzied at times, or morose. He spoke of land, money, and men he had deals with, the ups and downs of commerce, while showing no empathy for their personal financial strain. They lived parallel lives.

Jennie assumed this was another announcement of what new acquisition he'd made and it could wait. She picked up her reticule. "You watch Douglas. I won't be gone long."

He was at her side in a flash, grabbed her elbow, and turned her to face him. "You listen to what I'm going to do for you, Jennie Pickett. It might be the one decent thing I've done in my whole life, so don't stop me from telling you."

Her pulse quickened, her heart sensed danger before her head. "That's pretty ominous." Her hands felt damp inside her gloves.

"The truth is . . ." He took a deep breath. "We're getting divorced. You'll be free of my decisions." *What is he saying?*

Ariyah would have to wait.

He raced on. "I already acquired the second half of the loan from the Parrishes, several days ago. I didn't tell you, and yes, it's already gone. I made some bad buys, paying cash and finding out later the so-called owner didn't have deed to the land. And the man that did wasn't interested in selling. I've sued . . . but that's more money to the lawyer, and as he said to me, 'How stupid can you be, man, to not check out the deed.' But he's well known, the guy who took advantage of me. I thought I was . . . maybe I took a shortcut."

She didn't ask him if he'd been imbibing at the time. "You'll have to get your job back. Plead with Joseph." She offered sense to his senselessness, stepped over the word *divorce*. At last he was telling her, being honest.

Charles shook his head.

"Then find another job. We can pay it back. I— maybe I can sit with Mrs. Parrish. Dougie likes it there. He'd be able to come with me. Or maybe we can move back in with Lucinda and Joseph. We can sell things." She ran the gloves through her hands. "The second carriage at least. People make mistakes. It doesn't mean the end of things, Charles."

He shook his head. "I haven't told you the worst of it. Dougie, that night, at Miss Priscilla's, I gave Dougie—"

"I knew that. I could tell. But you're sorry. You are. I know because you're confessing this."

"And Miss Priscilla gave me something."

Syphilis. She waited for him to say it. He didn't. Instead he said, "Cocaine. She gave me cocaine. Well, I bought it, of course. And I—" He turned away from her. "I gave some to Dougie."

Breathe. She tried to speak, but the words choked inside her throat.

"I'm a bad influence, Jennie. I see that now." He'd collapsed onto the settee, held his head, spoke to the floor. "I've put you both at risk. Miss Priscilla's wiles are not the first time for me, but it was the first time I let cocaine enter my son." He looked up, combed his mustache with his fingers, bachelor-button eyes clouded over, but he hadn't been imbibing, at least Jennie didn't think so. "It's a vile, enticing siren. Odysseus could not have resisted it and neither can I, Jennie." He breathed deeply.

She was grateful Dougie played outside. She could hear him chattering to his wooden animals, unaware of how his life would change.

Charles's confession, his divorce solution, cut like a river gouges a canyon, deep and long. But it also meant there was a bottom, the canyon floor. And they could ride that river out. They could stay on top of the water. Truth would be the boat to ride on.

"We can manage this," Jennie said.

"You say."

"I do say. God is with us in this, I feel it."

"Wish he'd prevented it in the first place."

"It isn't like that, Charles. Your telling me of what you've done is a start." She could forgive him, she was sure she could.

He took a deep breath. "I'm divorcing you, Jennie. For your sake and for Douglas's. I actually saw a lawyer back in June. Right after we got the loan. It's settled."

She was a canoe bobbing on a turbulent stream, paddles long lost to the depths.

"I don't understand. Women who are divorced, they have—"

"Some women, that's true. Some women have difficulty. Might be ostracized. But you come from a good family. They'll support you. And as I am divorcing you, that'll be better for you. I didn't contest custody. That says you had no choice." He straightened his shoulders. "You can live with your parents."

Her mind spun like a leaf in a whirlpool. She couldn't think straight.

"I—I will not be a burden to my family. We—I'll have to find employment of some kind. I'll take in laundry. I'll—this is ridiculous." She stood, wiping her hands on her skirt. "We can begin again. That's what we'll do."

"I'll never give it up, Jennie. It's like a fever with me. The cocaine, the whiskey. Don't put your head in the sand, woman. I'm giving you a way out."

"There are herbs. I have oils meant to help with that. I'm a healer. Please let me heal this, us. It's possible to—"

"No. It. Isn't. Jennie, stop seeing a . . . a possibility. I become the bad man because I am. You and Dougie get on with your life safe from me." His voice cracked and Jennie saw tears squeeze at the corners of his eyes. She dropped before him, her skirts sighing onto the floor. She took his hands in hers. She felt his shoulders shake and she pulled him into her. But she knew in that moment, her love and forgiveness was not enough. He had yet to forgive himself. Perhaps he never would.

If he'd been saying these things while drinking, she could understand it: irrational thoughts, weeping. But he wasn't drunk.

"The worst thing right now is that you think you are addicted to spirits. And that we owe money. But often the worst becomes the best thing." Jennie took a deep breath. "We start over. You stop drinking, one hour at a time. You keep busy. We keep our commitments to the Parrishes, but we live like normal people." She calmed her voice, kept hold of his hands. "We'll sell the carriages. I'll find work. You'll get a job—"

He lifted his eyes, resigned. "Jennie. It's done. Over. I've divorced you. You have no say in it. The courts won't even let you. Dougie remains with you, away from me. That's the end of this discussion." He stood, then headed for the door. She sank to the side, looked up at him from in front of the settee. "I have nothing more to say. Except you'd better treat yourself for venereal infections."

And then he was gone.

Chapter 13
Each Ending a Beginning

She told Ariyah that she and Charles were having marital discord and asked to be relieved of standing beside her as her matron of honor. How could she witness in public when her own marriage had disintegrated like a love letter left outside in the Willamette Valley rain?

"Oh, Jennie, I will miss having you there beside me. You'll still sign as witness though? It's a short ceremony."

"I'd start crying and ruin things. This is your day." Jennie hugged her friend, held her. "It needs to be filled with happiness."

"Everyone cries at weddings." The women wiped at damp eyes. "You'll there, that's what matters. And you'll wear the dress, yes?"

Jennie nodded. After the wedding, she'd rework it and sell it to help pay off the debt.

Jennie and Douglas slipped into the ceremony on a September day, and she prayed for God's blessing and a long life of love for Peleg and Ariyah, prayed for wisdom and answers.

Ariyah's home was decorated with gladiolas and greens from the Parrish gardens. The

Parrishes were there, among the happy attendees. Mrs. Parrish clung to her husband's arm for support; she carried a cane. Her mustard-colored dress enhanced dark blue eyes that sparkled, promising a recovery. Jennie said as much to her and she smiled.

"I'm regaining my vigor in time for the rainy season to begin." Her voice was breathy and close up Jennie could see by her eyes that she still suffered.

Mr. Parrish patted her hand laced through his. "She insisted we come. We take what we can get, right, Pet?"

His intimate name for her in this public place surprised Jennie and she could tell he hadn't realized he'd said it. They had eyes only for each other and Jennie felt an ache inside for what she'd missed—would be missing.

"Where is Mr. Pickett today?"

"Here," Dougie answered. He'd found the Parrishes in the crowd just as she had.

Mr. Parrish looked down at him, and with his arm not occupied with Mrs. Parrish, he reached out to shake Dougie's hand. "So you are."

Dougie beamed and moved his small paw up and down, as though he pumped the well handle.

"My mistake. We look forward to seeing you again soon at Mr. Chen's kitchen, don't we, Elizabeth?"

"Tell Mr. and Mrs. Parrish you'd like that." Jennie urged his good behavior.

"Can we go tomorrow?" Dougie looked up to laughter as Jennie said, "Perhaps Monday might be more agreeable."

She needed to see the Parrishes and tell them some of what had transpired, but there was still so much uncertainty. Did Charles intend making payments? Would he contribute to her support? Could she stop the proceedings of the divorce?

"Monday it is. I'll have Chen bake extras."

"It's so good to see you out and about, Mrs. Parrish."

"Elizabeth, please."

A breathy voice. She wondered if she had a lung disease or was simply weak from having come through a demanding ailment.

"Elizabeth." Jennie curtsied. Something about her demeanor invited respect. "We'll come by midday on Monday."

They both nodded, then Mr. Parrish walked his wife away. Jennie was grateful neither had commented on Charles's absence.

Her father wasn't so subtle. "Where's Pickett? I hear he isn't working at the prison anymore."

"Hello, Daddy. He's . . . occupied, with new ventures."

"Is he now? And how are you doing, Dougie?" He lifted the boy into his arms, exaggerating the effort. "Won't be long and I won't be able to do this, you're getting so big."

"Don't drop me."

"Got a good grip on you. Soon, you'll be carrying me." He rubbed Dougie's nose with his own. Dougie leaned his head into his grandfather's neck.

"I can carry Quilton, but not you, Paw-Paw."

"Quilton? Have I met Quilton?" He frowned. "Who is this Quilton fellow?"

"He's a por-co-pine."

"A porcupine. Well. Something innovative. Like father, like son, eh?" He winked at Jennie. "What does Quilton do with his quills?"

Douglas looked thoughtful as he held onto his grandfather's neck, his small fingers gripping. "They sleep on him. He holds his bowl up for milk in the morning, doesn't he, Mama?"

"He does do that. It's the cutest thing to see."

"I'll stop by one day to gawk. Oh, there's the bride signaling me." He set Dougie down and Dougie hugged his legs before running off toward the table covered with food and where other short-pants-and-gallus-clad boys plucked away at Norwegian Omelettes. "I've got to make this marriage official." He started away, then turned back. "You don't look well, Jane. Eyes are puffy. Everything all right?"

"Fine, Daddy," she lied. "All the gladiolas, I suspect."

"Never knew them to bother you."

"I'm getting older, more things irritate."

"Getting older. You're twenty-three. Still a child." His eyes were filled with such compassion she nearly told him everything.

"Go do your duty." She patted his shoulder.

"You have to sign as a witness. Come along." He took her elbow, waved to Ariyah across the room that they were on their way.

It pleased her that her father knew her age, though that day she felt much older than twenty-three.

A narrow staircase that challenged women's wire hoops led to Ariyah's third-floor ballroom, where hired servers had already carried trays of sweet treats and apple punch up the stairs. No alcohol. Jennie let the music comfort, reluctant to end the day escaping from her uncertain world. When an unknown gentleman bowed before her asking for a dance, she knew it was time to leave. They never should have come up to the dance floor without an escort. Tongues would wag. She found Douglas as he pushed a bigger boy who pushed back. "Time to leave," she said.

He sulked, and as they reached the staircase, he raced down and out the door before she'd barely settled her hoopskirts to whisper across the landing. A servant helped her with her cape taken from the coat closet, and Jennie caught up with her son, who was hiding behind a potted plant. She gripped his hand. "Let's go home."

He pulled.

"Maybe Papa's back." That calmed him and they marched in the early twilight, dodging oak leaves scattered on the path.

The evening laid its quilt on the shrubs they passed, muffling bird sounds, so only the click of their shoes broke the silence. In the yard, Jennie noticed that both buggies were gone, and she hoped Charles had taken them to sell. But that also meant he likely wasn't home.

"Where is everything?" His little voice expressed surprise.

"I . . . I don't know." She scanned the room. No tables or chairs, no beds, no doughboy, no paintings, no mirror. A single oil lamp sat on the floor next to an open trunk where her clothes and Dougie's spilled out. Quilton occupied his cage beside it. The rodent's toenails scratched as he pulled himself up on the tin slats and made a plaintive cry.

Douglas stomped toward Quilton's cage, took the animal out, and stroked the quills.

"You made Papa mad and he took everything— except me. Why didn't he take me?"

"I did not make your father angry. I—" She swirled in the room, unable to believe her eyes. *How could I have missed Charles's anger?* Only outrage or disdain would lead him to do this, strip their home of not only himself but everyday things. Why?

"My horses!" Dougie ran into the only other room, came back out, frantic. It must be empty too. He rummaged in the trunk, the only place to look. Jennie's hands shook.

"Your hobby horse might still be in the barn," Jennie said. "Let's go look there."

"You sold my horses!"

"I didn't. I—"

Even then she didn't want to blame Charles. She fought back tears. The night Charles had left, she cried, but knowing she needed to look presentable for the wedding, she'd put slices of cucumber on her eyes at sunrise, going over all that Charles had said, wondering what she might do that could change his mind. The slices were on the floor where the bed had once been.

"Let's go look in the barn."

"No. Don't want your help."

He ran out to the yard, disappeared inside the building. She let him, her head swirling, breath coming short. *The distillery.* She picked up her skirt and rushed into the drying shed. The plants bobbed their heads, most harvested already. Bottles of oils sat undisturbed. She spoke a silent prayer of gratitude. But the distillery was gone.

Dougie pranced out of the barn on his hobby horse beneath the full moon. For the moment, placated. Jennie stepped into the barn. It, too, was empty of even the nicker of a horse.

Back in the house, Jennie walked toward the flat-topped trunk with the name PICKETT stenciled on the side. The words had faded and Charles had told her he'd brought it with him from Virginia. She realized how little she really knew of him when they married. A carpenter. A state employee. A charmer. But where had he really come from? She lifted Dougie's shirts and pants, stacked them in the open lid, until she had everything out. Or thought she did.

At the bottom of the trunk lay two blankets, folded, cradling a narrow piece of paper tied with a blue ribbon. It was a trifold official-looking document.

JANE E. PICKETT. With shaking hands, she opened it. She read and reread. *Am I reading this correctly?* Charles had been granted a divorce, giving full custody of Douglas to her. All back in July. The 29th, to be exact. She'd been a divorced woman since July? How could she not have known?

Chapter 14
When Change Comes Calling

Early Sunday morning Jennie built a fire and heated up water in the caldron left hanging on the andiron. She found a tin of old tea in the loft, perhaps left by the previous owner. She fixed some for herself, taking the cup from the well outside while she prayed for clarity. She had missed so many signs, the way she failed to grasp her husband's jokes. Her hopefulness clouded her vision the way a breath can veil a lens. "Help me see," she whispered. "Help me know."

None of this made sense. Bewildered. Bereft. Betrayed. She searched for words to describe what she felt. *Powerless.* Yes, that was it. She'd been stripped of confidence, insight, purpose. She slept in a wooden boat caught in an eddy. Tears began. She shook them off. Despite the shame of it, she would talk with DW, her lawyer brother. He would help her figure this out. But now, she and Dougie needed food.

She slipped out of the house and walked the half block or so to a neighbor who had eggs she traded oils for. Thank goodness she had a credit with her.

"So early, Mrs. Pickett!" She still wore her nightcap, the flounce framing her chubby face.

"Yes. I didn't realize I was out of eggs and I wanted them before my . . . family woke up."

She waved Jenny on toward the chicken coop, where Jennie reached beneath a cooing hen, carefully pulling out two warm eggs in her hand. She hurried back to rouse Dougie, who like her had slept poorly on the wood floor. "Have a little tea."

"Hungry, Mama. I am very hungry." He lengthened the word "very," and her own stomach ached for this child who had yet to experience the real hunger he would face unless she could get his father back. She had no interest in eating but knew she must. "I'll fix you a big egg. We'll boil them today, in the pot. All right?"

He nodded and thankfully didn't ask where the frying pan had gone. "Where is Papa?"

"I don't know for certain." She watched the pot of water boil, put the cover on, then removed it from the heat. She waited what seemed to be around three minutes—she couldn't find her watch. She closed the trunk and sat on it now while Dougie sat cross-legged on the floor, eating his egg from the single teacup they had shared.

"Why isn't Papa here?"

"I don't know that either."

"Can we go to Miss Pricilla's? Maybe he forgot something there."

"Maybe he did. I—we'll see. Let's hurry now or we'll be late for church."

"He left because he's mad at you, Mama."

"I—I don't think that's true, Douglas. I love your father very much. He's confused, that's all." *Should I argue with a child?*

"He's mad at you."

Should I ask him why? No, a child should not be asked to witness. "He might be. I'll talk to him and find out." She kept her voice light.

"He's mad at me." He lowered his head and his lower lip pooched out.

"No, Dougie." She reached for him, her hand stroked his hair, his little-boy neck. Wetness pressed against her breast and she knew he cried. "You did nothing wrong."

"I did!" He jerked back like a startled deer not sure how to get out of the path of danger. She opened her arms to him, but he turned his back and cried alone. She stood, touched his shoulder lightly, the action turning him into her skirts, grasping at her legs as though he stood at the edge of a terrible height.

"Oh, Douglas. You're a good boy. This is a grown-up problem. We'll get it worked out. But you are loved by your father and by me. More than anything on earth." She wiped his face and nose with her handkerchief. "And God loves you most of all. Come on, let's go find a leaf or two and some twigs for Quilton. He must be hungry, don't you think?"

Douglas nodded, and hand in hand they headed outside.

They walked to the Methodist church and Jennie was comforted by the dahlias in bloom in yards they passed. Flowers brightened the world, then faded, feeding the soil, their host plants resting through the winter and in the spring, would rise again. She had to remember that cycle, remember that after the dying and the resting came the growing again.

Once at the brick building, she nodded to people as they found their pew, grateful that her father wasn't preaching, as he occasionally did. She didn't want to face her family. *Divorced.* Her mind wandered as people entered. They needed to find a place to stay or somehow refurnish where they were. *Divorced.* At some point she'd have to tell her family. Or they'd read it in the paper. If only she could meet with Charles, they could get through this impasse. All marriages hit ruts; people learned how to straddle them and go on. When would he file those papers? When would her status appear in the *Spectator*? Should she speak with Miss Priscilla? No, her brother first. He would tell her what she could do, give her back a smidgeon of control.

The Parrishes entered. Elizabeth looked stronger still. Perhaps it was the malaise of summer put to rest, the cool nights now taking out the bugs and mosquitoes that brought on summer ague, illnesses, and death. Her improvement meant the Parrishes would have no need of a caregiver for Elizabeth. And besides, she had daughters-in-law who would have been preferred caretakers. Their youngest son, Charles Winn, had married Annie Robb that fall, so all the Parrish sons would likely soon be bringing their children for visits. When they did, they'd be sharing grandchildren, not a sad little boy who longed for his papa.

She reached out of habit for her pearls. She'd worn them to Ariyah's wedding. That was her next step: sell the jewelry and buy food and a bed. She and Douglas could sleep together for a time—time she wouldn't have to tell her parents and siblings about what happened and time to try to talk sense to Charles.

"I've dried raspberry leaves and they make a good tea," Jennie told Ariyah. "A female tonic. Good for reproductive health."

"I'm healthy." Ariyah glowed with new marital bliss.

They walked along a path beside Mill Creek, Douglas scrambling before them riding his hobby horse, going nowhere, just friends together.

"The berries make a fine tea as well. Maybe you could tell others. I'd be happy to supply them." Jennie thought more of income now, appalled at how quickly her love of healing with oils and aromatics had sunk to mere commerce.

"Let's stop on the way back and have some," Ariyah said.

"I'll bring it to your home."

"Jennie Pickett, are you keeping me from your house?" She bumped Jennie's hip with her own.

"No. No, not really. I just thought maybe Peleg would play the wedding song he composed for you. I'd love to hear it again."

"I'm sure he'd be pleased to." They walked in silence then. "Jennie, these past weeks since I've been married, is something wrong? More trouble with Charles?"

"You're seeing through the eyes of a married woman." Jennie kept her voice light. "How have you had time to notice a change in me?"

She pulled her shawl closer against a sudden chill. Not sharing the challenges of her life with her best friend felt like a betrayal, but she couldn't expose herself. No one was granted a divorce in the state except for moral failures. The only thing that saved Jennie was having custody. Usually the father got that privilege, even if the divorce was granted because of his "moral failure."

Jennie's lawyer brother had not been optimistic that anything could change. Jennie rubbed the nubby wool like the shawl she'd worn that day in her brother's Portland office.

She had pulled off her shawl, flung it over the back of his office chair. "But it says here . . ." She pointed to the document, read with hesitation. " 'When the divorce is granted on account of misconduct of the husband, he has then forfeited his right to the property and the woman should be endowed with his lands.' "

"Does Charles have lands?"

"I—he made purchases for reselling. I don't know the status of those. Or even of our home."

"I'll see what I can find out. Were there . . . signs of problems?" He didn't look at Jennie as he asked the question, the papers taking his attention.

"There was . . . drinking. Cocaine. An infidelity." Shame washed over her.

"Father told me about the night Charles failed to tend to Douglas. Maybe, Sister, he did you a favor, letting you go, granting Douglas safe harbor."

He lifted his eyes to hers, so full of concern.

"You don't have to explain to anyone why your marriage failed, Jennie. He's done it for you. The divorce is granted to you, yet you didn't have to prove it in court. He's accepted blame in that sense."

"Do you see him, ever? Hear anything from his friends, from Joseph?"

DW shook his head. "And another thing to your advantage. So far the divorce filing hasn't appeared in the paper. The editorials they print with those announcements often beg litigation. Yesterday with the posting of the Hutchinson divorce, the editor wrote, 'If daughters would be more careful in their selection of their friends, there would be fewer divorces and desertions, seductions and heartbreaks in this wide world and we might therefore have a great deal more of sunshine and less of shadow.' Is it the paper's business to make such comments? I think not."

"They make it the woman's fault for having chosen friends poorly." As if her choice of friends had anything to do with Charles's desertion.

"But meanwhile"—his voice became lawyerly—"you and Douglas can't stay on in an empty house. You'll come live with us."

"No. Not yet." Shame and isolation helped Jennie tell herself half-truths.

She had heeded some of her brother's advice, drank his tea that day, taken her woolen shawl, and left.

"Jennie?" Ariyah grabbed her arm, tugged on the soft wool.

She was back, walking with a friend.

"Where'd your mind go? You're chilled." She hugged the wool to Jennie's neck. Jennie looked for Douglas. He was still in sight. "I'm sorry, Ariyah. I really am." *How long did I give time to the past at the expense of the present?* "It's easier if I bring the tea to you. Then you'll have it when friends stop by. I've wild strawberry too. Serves the same purpose."

"Are you trying to get me with child?" She grinned.

"I hope to be a godmother one day."

She nodded and they walked again, joy piercing her heart with the thought of Ariyah having a child.

"Dougie and I visited the forest for berries. You should have seen my shoes, all muddy. Dougie was a mess." Jennie laughed, hoping she would not pursue troubling issues.

"That's another thing. You're always out gathering herbs. I thought your distillery would help you refine your work, allow you to have oils and not rely on wild plants."

"It's the season," Jennie said. "Things have changed." She didn't tell her that they picked up branches and hauled them back for firewood on those forest forays or that she'd dismantled the drying tables to burn the oak to keep them warm. That she no longer had a distillery. Nor of the growing anxiety of how they'd weather the winter on their own.

She knew that before winter came in force, they'd have to do something different. She'd sold the pearls and made a small payment to the Parrishes, avoiding seeing them by leaving the envelope—with cash and a note—with Minnie when she answered the door. With the remaining funds she'd purchased a bed, table, and two chairs and bought food and a cabinet to act as a pantry. And everywhere she went, every time she walked beside Salem's brick buildings, looked in an alley, or listened outside a saloon, she hoped she'd hear Charles's voice or he'd stumble into her and she could hold him through this disastrous time and change his mind. But she never did. It was as though this city had consumed him.

In mid-October, Jennie dressed in her yellow linen to look her best, then walked to Miss Priscilla's. She'd asked Ariyah to watch Dougie for a few hours and made her way to the house with a wide porch and a gardener tending the lush shrubbery, preparing it for winter. His black face smiled up at her and she saw pity in his eyes.

Does he think I'm coming here to . . . work? She hadn't thought of that. Jennie's face grew warm.

"I'd like to speak to a Miss Priscilla, if I might." She used her most dignified voice toward the woman who answered the door. "I'm looking for my husband." She said it loud enough so the gardener would hear and only later wondered why. The maid's skin was the color of good earth.

"May I tell her who's callin'?"

"Mrs. Charles Pickett."

"She indisposed right now. Maybe you leave your card and—"

A petite woman wearing a pink dress over a mountain of petticoats approached from a side room. "I'll see Mrs. Pickett, Emma."

"Yes, Miz Priscilla." The maid pulled open the door and Jennie followed Miss Priscilla inside, sat when she was directed. Miss Priscilla took a seat across from her, covering what appeared to be a colorful cross-stitched scene of barns and horses beneath a blue sky. She rested both elbows on the curved arms of the wide chair. Her posture said "confident," but her blinking suggested something else.

"What can I do for you, Mrs. Pickett?"

"You can tell me where my husband is."

"That, sadly, I do not know, though it is my understanding that he is no longer your husband."

Her childlike voice cut deep. "Charles told you that?"

She nodded. "While you may not believe me, I tried to dissuade him. I urged him to stop his pursuit of liquor and powder and—"

"Adultery."

She nodded. Her cheeks took on color. Was she younger than Jennie?

"You will sit there and tell me that you did nothing to bring about his downfall in this— this place?" Jennie spread her arms to take in the opulently furnished room. "Fresh flowers in expensive vases does not give legitimacy to what goes on here, to what disasters befall both your clients and . . . and . . . and . . . other young women in ruin."

"Charles said you were a moralizing woman."

"Moralizing?" Jennie blinked away tears. He had spoken to this woman of her, of their lives. The betrayal seared almost as much as his abandonment. "I came to ask if you know where he might be." She softened her words. It had been easier to shout at this woman than at her own husband, where the blame belonged. "His son misses him and assumes he's responsible for his departure. If you can't help me, perhaps you could consider a small boy who wonders about his father."

"The very reason I urged him to work things through. But liquor, as you may know, can take over a man, or woman for that matter." She looked down, then back at Jennie. She had a very small mouth and tiny white teeth that sat like piano keys on her lower lip. "But he said that was the very reason he needed to go away, that he could not resist whiskey, nor the white powder, and that he could not drag you into that life, neither you nor your son. He divorced you out of his care for you and to keep Douglas and you from exposure to those substances. I did not introduce him to those, despite what you might think."

She hated that she used her son's name, as though she was familiar with him. "But you served those vile substances here."

"People bring it in. They sell it."

"You did this to my son."

She shook her head. "Not the powder, no. But he did consume a bit of rum. I called it giggly candy. That was poor of me, I admit. But I needed time to try to talk sense into your husband, and your son demanded all his attention. I had the best of intentions."

Jennie snorted at that, a most unladylike response. "My husband gave him cocaine." Miss Priscilla's eyes grew large. Jennie didn't stop. "There are oils and aromatics known to help curb the desire. Are you aware of those? And offering rum to a child, for whatever reason, is . . . is . . . despicable. And letting cocaine powder lie around."

"Spoken like a good mother." She picked at her bodice, raised her eyes, woman to woman. "I don't blame you for being angry with me. It's easier than being angry with our men or ourselves. We women are powerless against so many forces. That's why I chose this profession. Here I control certain things and I can support myself. A doctor visits or we go to him. We have no disease here. Being abandoned as you are will be harder for women like you. Harder to admit that there is little you can do to change the world of men."

"I don't need to change the world of men," Jennie said, aware of an *Einsicht*, an insight, as she stared at this woman. "I need to change myself."

Chapter 15

Momentum

The senior Lichtenthalers lived in Marion County, but several miles from Salem. Her father paid the wagon driver, helped unload the trunk, then held Jennie while she told her story through tear-filled eyes. The humiliation was like a heavy cloak that scratched and weighed her spirits down. But humiliation lives next door to vulnerability, and in that neighborhood, one can find new direction. Years later she would come to believe that new beginnings can only grow out of the confusion of uncertainties and how life can spin one around like a top. Trusting she wasn't alone in those turning places became a strength she learned to draw on.

"You did the right thing in coming here," her mother said. She patted the cap over her tight gray curls. "We've been worried sick not hearing from you. It's easier to start over when you have family beside you."

Starting over. Her mother had started over when they'd left Pennsylvania, traveling by covered wagons to Illinois, and then began again when Jennie was almost ten and they headed

163

west to Oregon. She'd faced an empty cradle, as had Jennie, and grieved lost hopes, outliving two other children she had come to know as adults. Miss Priscilla was wrong that women had no power; they did. Women could clarify their hopes and dreams and have the courage to act on those, trusting that they weren't alone in the trials. And they could ask new questions and increase their compassion for each other and for themselves.

"There's time to think of what next. Rest now." Her mother smiled. "Come along, Douglas. Introduce me to Quilton. What does that little rodent eat?"

She watched her mother lead her son away, and for the first time since Charles had left, Jennie felt that Douglas was truly safe. And so was she. *Why did I wait so long?*

"We'll go to the fair this week," her father said over a supper of ham and bean soup flavored with carrots pulled from the earth. "You'll come with us."

"No. I think Mama's right. I need rest."

Her father nodded. "We'll take Dougie and give you the day."

Her parents never plopped blame at her feet and they didn't demean Charles. Perhaps they understood that any bad words about Douglas's father would somehow get tangled inside Douglas's views about himself.

Jennie meandered through their harvested

garden, tugging at old pumpkin vines, letting the scents and feel of earthy things bring her nurture. She prayed and even wrote in a small book Lucinda had given her, telling her that writing could heal. Jennie had blushed, remembering how hard it was for her to write. "When reading and writing are filled with effort, I suspect repair is going on," Lucinda had said. Alone with birdsong and Quilton's chewing, words did bring her comfort. *I will seek sunshine, let the shadows disappear. Maybe they will not do so on their own, but I will one day write a new ending to this story of missteps and betrayal.*

But what next? Would a doctor have her as a nurse? Should she have George build her another distillery? One thing was certain, she must give up the dream, the possibility that one day she could be a trained physician. If she couldn't heal those she loved, she had no right to seek the pleasures of possibilities.

"Reverend Parrish spoke at the fair." Her parents returned, filling her in on who won awards for their swine and their goats, who had made pioneering speeches.

"He was urged to say a few words as one of the oldest residents on the prairie," her father continued. "He extolled the virtues of the settlers, always granting credit to others as he is wont to do."

"I didn't realize he'd been in the region for twenty-seven years," her mother said. She stirred the stew Jennie had started, nodded her approval.

"A stalwart soul, that Parrish," her father said to no one in particular as he chewed on his pipe stem. He rarely put tobacco in the bowl.

They ate a good supper. Douglas chattered of all he'd seen, while Jennie washed the dishes and put them away.

"He's a nice man," Jennie said with a nudge of guilt about how she'd ever pay him back. She'd still not told her parents of that outstanding debt.

"He asked after you, and Charles."

"Did he?"

"Said he hadn't seen Charles at the prison of late."

"He—why would Mr. Parrish be at the prison?"

"He's preached to the inmates there for years. Didn't you know that? Chides a few of the rest of us pastors to do likewise. It is a gratifying ministry, I have to say, bringing the Word to such men who think they're nothing more than slugs."

Jennie thought she knew how they felt, at least a bit.

"And since each pastor has one or two from our own congregations who are imprisoned now and again, it eases them back into the community and the pew once they get out. Parrish started the ministry, from what I heard, in '54 when the prison moved to Salem."

Her father droned on about prisons while she tried to grasp all Mr. Parrish must have known about them before they ever came to ask for the loan. Would he have been aware of Charles's quitting? No, he made the loan before Charles surprised her with his news. Charles had already been buying and using up the funds by then. Mr. Parrish had not asked for a dime from her yet, unlike the carriage owners who had asked for their payments and the other creditors who wanted their horses, settees, or land investments back.

"He is a good man," Jennie said.

Jennie's father stood and called after Douglas, who had disappeared outside, but she didn't go after him. Her son was four years old, and in the few days they'd been with her father, he'd told Jennie that if she didn't quit hovering over Douglas, he'd end up a "b'hoy"—a boy lacking common sense. "No one needs a ruffian created by being over-mama-ed." Dougie's birthday hadn't been much of a celebration with his father absent and their sparsely furnished home. She'd tried to let him go unattended more, but she also worried over him, indulged him. It was good to have her father as a buffer, even if it sometimes felt like criticism.

"He asked after your health."

"Who?" Her mind had wandered. "Oh, Reverend Parrish did?"

"I told him you were doing well, considering."

Her stomach lurched. "You didn't tell him—does he know that Charles and I are—" She couldn't say the word.

"He read it in the paper, Janie. I hadn't seen it, but Parrish quoted the reporter's added-on comment at the posting: 'Charley couldn't give up the run.' R-u-n."

"It was a typeface error," her mother piped in. "Should have said 'rum,' of course."

Jennie laughed. They both looked at her as though she was daft. But what else could she do? One more humiliation now posted in the press with commentary added on. Words that took their place beside her own stumbling as she'd done for years. She'd worked so hard to overcome how those letters came together on a page. "Yes, my husband couldn't give up the run. More truth than error in that as he's run off and I might never find out where."

The leaves were dribbling off the oaks and aspen, the chilly rains succumbing to the possibility of a clear, warm October day. Jennie watched the rider approach and recognized Mr. Parrish. He sat a horse well. For weeks she'd put off calling on him about the loan. Now he was coming to see her. She hadn't made any more payments, had not yet found an income.

Mr. Parrish settled onto the porch with Jennie.

Her mother hummed in the house, saying she'd bring out tea.

"Years ago I lived here on French Prairie ministering to the Indians, learning from them more than anything. Remarkable people with the same ups and downs as our race." Parrish's eyebrows were thick, white frames over deep blue eyes. Gray threads whispered through his dark hair. His silver beard and mustache were trimmed. His broad smile filled the lower portion of his long face. A handsome face, especially for one as old as Jennie assumed he was.

"I haven't had much contact with natives," Jennie said. She watched Douglas help her father put winnowed wheat into a bag they'd take to the mill for grinding. Douglas seemed eager to assist. The bag, made from the canvas that once covered their cross-country family wagon, was nearly as tall as Douglas.

"When the French Canadians retired from Hudson's Bay Company, many brought their wives here from other tribes, and they stayed on this fine prairie, mixing languages and customs. Madame Marie Dorion was one. Have you ever heard of her?"

Jennie shook her head.

"Came with the Astor Expedition. Settled here with her third husband after surviving horrendous tragedy—and keeping her two rambunctious sons alive."

Jennie wondered if he wanted to speak with her of territorial history or if this was a subject he warmed to and simply wanted to share.

"She was a remarkable woman. Buried beneath the altar in the Catholic church. Even the priests are buried in the cemetery, so that was quite a coup." He smiled and so did Jennie, understanding his humor better than she did Charles's. There seemed no malice in it. He didn't make fun at others' expense.

A raven cawed and a whirlwind of cool air lifted the napkin covering the wicker tea table. There wouldn't be many more days for sitting on a porch, and even in late October, one usually didn't remain outside past sunset when the coolness seeped into one's bones or rains dropped from the burdened skies.

"I guess you know about my . . . situation," Jennie said, taking the lead. "I will make good on our loan. I don't know how yet, but I will."

Jennie stood to take the tea tray from her mother. *What had she heard?* Jennie really wanted to get the conversation of her debt over with without her mother knowing it even existed.

Mr. Parrish stood, giving her mother his seat and pulling her father's rocking chair toward the gathering. "I feel a bit guilty sitting here drinking tea while Jacob works the fields," he said, lowering himself into the cushion. His knees pushed out like elbows akimbo, and he reached for the teapot and began to pour. He had long legs. She'd noticed when he arrived that he moved like a mountain lion to dismount, with sureness and grace. His tea-pouring hands were steady.

"Oh, Jacob loves being out there," her mother said, responding to Mr. Parrish's comments about her father working the fields. "It's his respite from the courthouse goings-on. And we've so enjoyed Douglas being here, and our Jane." She leaned in to pat Jennie's hand.

"My parents have spoiled us both."

"That's what healing takes," Mr. Parrish said. "Much gentle giving, like holding a baby over a baptismal bowl, a place of perfect peace, and future hope."

"You sound like my friend Ariyah. Everything is 'perfect' with her," Jennie said. "I'm so happy for her and her Peleg."

" 'Perfect love casts out all fear.' Perfect doesn't mean without mistakes, it means 'complete.' "

"Does it?" her mother asked. "How very interesting. We love words, don't we, Jennie?"

"We do, much as they can escape my management of most of them."

"But you do manage herbs and oils well." Mr. Parrish had removed his hat and it lay, crown down, beside him on the porch floor. He'd finished his tea and leaned back into the chair, his long arms brushing the top of his hat.

"I do, though my distillery isn't . . . available right now."

Jennie sipped the tea and brushed the crumbs from the cakes her mother served. She heard Douglas laugh from the field and saw that they approached. Before they reached the porch, Mr. Parrish spoke.

"Mrs. Parrish has taken on the ague again."

"So many people here suffer from that," her mother commented.

"The cooler nights aren't helping?" October was to Jennie the ideal weather, with the warming days, cool evenings, and rain skulking the mountaintops looking for ways to unload their burden. "Does she cough?"

"Some, yes. But mostly she has labored breathing. Clearing her lungs is difficult."

"You have a good doctor, I'm sure." Jennie leaned into the conversation.

"Yes. But I'd like someone more attuned to her, someone familiar with homeopathic care. I've even asked a few of my native healers to bring in their scents and potions. Could you work with both medical and native healers?"

Work with them? "Both have merit, but I don't know what you mean, really, by 'working with them.' "

"I'd like to hire you for Elizabeth's care. I can pay you or in lieu of—"

"Mother, I wonder if you could get another cup for Daddy and a glass for Douglas? They're on their way."

"Oh, certainly." She rose and rushed out.

"My parents don't know that I owe you a substantial amount of money, Mr. Parrish. That's why I interrupted you. I didn't mean to be rude."

He bowed his head. "It was my error. I should have waited to speak to you in private. What I meant to propose was that you might work toward the loan payment, or perhaps not, using the money as you see fit now that you are . . . alone . . . to reestablish yourself. I'm truly sorry about the divorce. No marriage ever intends to end in dissolution. It's always painful to see dreams put out to sea."

"Adrift. Yes, that's how I've felt. And ashamed for my husband's actions and my own, that I didn't see him changing. Well, I did, but I thought if we lived alone, if we had our own little family, that he'd, well, that he would find his direction. I hoped the loan would help, but I didn't know he'd taken so much out so quickly." She rushed her words. "So much I didn't know." She thought of Miss Priscilla. "Please forgive my rambling."

"Nothing to forgive." He sat without speaking, the silence welcome. Then, "Please consider our offer of employment, Elizabeth's and mine."

173

"I'm honored."

Mr. Parrish suggested she bring Douglas with her.

"I might not want to do that, at least at first. I'd want to give Mrs. Parrish—Elizabeth—all my attention." He nodded. "Douglas has had so many shocks and changes. It might be good for him to remain here. I'll speak to my parents about it."

"About what will you speak to us?" Jennie's father stepped up onto the peeled logs of the porch landing, swinging Douglas up with one hand. Mr. Parrish stood, and as though they'd practiced, grabbed Douglas from the air as her father released him, setting Douglas on the far side of the rocking chair.

"I'm flying like a bird, Mama. See?"

"Yes, I do see. Now that your feet touch ground, go wash your hands and join us for cakes."

"Need to feed Quilton first." He scampered off.

"I've asked to employ Mrs. Pickett as a nurse," Mr. Parrish told her father. "And suggested that she bring Douglas with her."

Jennie said, "I thought giving Douglas more time with you might be better than bringing him with me, at first."

"He can stay right here, Jennie. Besides, the Parrishes might not like a porcupine in their household, and I doubt Douglas would go too far without Quilton."

"We can accommodate the rodent," Mr. Parrish

said. "Whatever Mrs. Pickett thinks will work best."

Every time he said "Mrs. Pickett," her skin prickled. She wasn't Mrs. Pickett anymore. Her husband had rejected her, sent her packing, as they say, or rather, he'd packed. He left her destitute, dependent on family and friends, weighted down with debt and maybe an illness, though she'd seen no signs as yet. She didn't think she needed to bear his name forever, but it was part of Douglas's name too. She couldn't really shed it.

"Mrs. Pickett would be my mother-in-law, if I had one. I think having my employer call me 'Jennie' would be a good place to start, Mr. Parrish." She nodded her head to him.

"Josiah," he corrected. "And Elizabeth has already directed you to call her by her Christian name. We can discuss the terms of your employment, if you'd care to walk." He didn't pick up his hat, but he stood, all six feet of him.

Douglas came out onto the porch with Quilton in his arms.

"We're going for a walk. Do you want to join us, Douglas?"

"No."

"No, what?" her mother prodded him.

"No, thank you, Mama." He stroked the animal and sat with his back against the wall, feeding Quilton one of her mother's cakes the animal held in his human-like hands. She was grateful her son had a friend of sorts, even though it was a rodent. Douglas looked up at her and smiled.

Mr. Parrish—Josiah—motioned with his hand for her to precede him down the steps. And in that pause of an October afternoon, Jennie began to see the possibilities of her new life.

Chapter 16
It Happens

The weather changed, turned rainy and cold with skiffs of snow melting on the mosses that blanketed shake roofs. Thanksgiving gave them pumpkins and squash from rich black earth. Her employment had begun the week after Mr. Parrish visited. Jennie stayed at the Parrishes' through the week, visiting Douglas on the weekends while Mr. Parrish—Josiah—took over Elizabeth's care. Douglas thrived. Perhaps his rash behaviors had been a consequence of the strain of his parents' rash behaviors.

Several children from the orphanage that Elizabeth had helped found came by and sang to her in December. Jennie had bundled her up with a hot stone at her feet and quilts warmed at the fire while she sat in the parlor on her beloved settee. Members of the Ladies Christian Commission for Marion County visited. Elizabeth had been chairman of the organization for five years before her health began to fail. Their efforts at getting passage of the liquor reform bill continued on without her. They rallied to protect children working in dangerous places or women enslaved to long hours in poor ventilation, leaving children untended and given no rest periods in the factories; rules that put women's health at risk. Elizabeth and Jennie had spoken often of such issues, when her strength allowed it. Jennie could tell that her passion for these causes brought meaning to her life, even as it seemed her life was slipping away.

Old friends brought Christmas cakes, marveled at the garlands of greens that decorated the parlor and draped the hearth. Mr. Chen baked nonstop, the smells of cinnamon and spices permeating the halls. They all prepared for a grand gathering of the Parrish clan on Christmas Day: Norman and Henrietta, Samuel, and his brother and his new wife. It turned out Charles Winn was but a year older than Jennie.

Josiah and Jennie had worked out that half of her salary would go against the debt and the other half she could use to support herself and Douglas. Josiah had resisted putting any toward the debt, but Jennie had insisted, wishing she could put all her earnings toward relieving that weight. But she also wanted to reimburse her parents for her son's care, though they insisted they would simply put the money aside for when—or if—she might need it later.

"Perhaps you'll go to school, become that doctor you always wanted to be," her mother said on Christmas morning when Jennie gave her the latest allotment.

"I'm a mother now. That's not a dream to nurture." Jennie stuffed an orange into Douglas's stocking. It pained her to say that, but it was true, and Jennie was much better now about seeing the world the way it really was, not the way she wanted it to be. The dream of medical school that she rarely admitted even to herself had departed with Charles, along with the wish for a happy marriage, a big family. She'd prayed that her healing gifts would be used, and today, caring for an elderly woman appeared to be the answer.

As the new year came, making way for spring with Elizabeth not improving, Jennie began to question what healing gifts she really had. Josiah had spent a few weeks at a church convention in Chicago, leaving Jennie in charge. His trust in her both encouraged and alarmed.

Jennie thought Elizabeth's lack of energy might be due to the bleeding Dr. Wells insisted on doing. With diplomacy she proposed to the doctor one morning that there were new articles in medical journals that suggested bleeding weakened already compromised bodies.

"Nonsense. Where did you read such scuttle?"

"There's a new journal published right here in Salem by Dr. Shelton. He was trained by the Physio College of Medicine in Cincinnati."

"Jefferson College in Pennsylvania where I

studied is highly regarded and bloodletting is a proven method. If anything, I should do it more, to remove the impurities in her blood."

She'd brought the subject up in the hallway, outside of Elizabeth's hearing. She felt guilty speaking about Elizabeth without her present, but she didn't want her to lose confidence in Dr. Wells. He was her chosen doctor and Jennie barely a self-trained aide. "I've given her burdock to help purify the blood. She especially likes the roots Mr. Chen stir-fries."

"Parrish lets that Chinaman fix her special food? No wonder she's not improving. You should be preparing her meals. And watching for skin irritations. That's your role."

"She responded well to the flaxseed poultices on her one sore. There are no open wounds. I help her walk several times a day, which is how I've come to notice her weaknesses after bleeding. As for her meals, we prepare them together. And burdock is an important treatment. She does seem stronger when she eats it, her face less flushed and she—" Jennie stopped, the delicacy of women's functions always gave her pause when speaking to a man. "Her urinary output is much better after she's consumed burdock. I've been—" She cleared her throat. "I've been keeping a graph."

"You're monitoring my practice?"

"I'm keeping track of my own efforts and

incidentally, yours. Would you like to see my notes?"

"No. What does Parrish say?"

"Reverend Parrish? Why, I haven't discussed it with him. He's just returned from his convention." Josiah had been busy with public events too, including pounding the first stake into the new California Oregon Railroad south of Portland. "Elizabeth knows, of course," Jennie continued, "that I'm making note of when she has the energy to walk versus when she needs to lie in bed and rest more. There's always a risk of bed sores then, when she's less active."

"Her husband should be made aware of what you're doing. I'll speak to him myself."

Jennie bowed to his upset, lifting the edges of her apron-covered dress, then turned, swishing her skirts down the hall back to Elizabeth.

"I shall speak to him this very day," Dr. Wells shouted to her back.

Jennie waved to him without turning around. Her heart pounded. Speaking up to authority wasn't easy.

"What's that about?" Elizabeth said as Jennie entered and opened the curtains to let in the April light. Pink blooms broke through the mass of green, promising a spring and summer of color.

"A little conversation I had with Dr. Wells. About the value of burdock versus bleeding."

"I hate the bleeding." She sighed. "Do you

181

think I'm getting better, Jennie?" She reached for Jennie's hand.

"On many days, yes. When you can be up and walking in the hallway or sitting in the parlor when your sons come by, those days seem hopeful, don't they?" Her fingers were fragile as a child's.

"And you think those days might be related to the bleeding?"

"Dr. Wells is a fine physician, but there are newer practices in every area of medicine. Cobwebs are no longer the only way to stop a cut from bleeding, and carbolizing wounds now shows great promise in reducing infections. Some physicians seem to think looking at options challenges their expertise. If I ever became a doctor I would vow to keep open to new ideas."

That last she said more to herself than to Elizabeth, whose pillow she now fluffed so she could sit up. Josiah had brought home a small red-and-white dog he called a King Charles spaniel. The dog hopped up onto Elizabeth's bed and curled his tail around himself, looking up at Elizabeth with adoring eyes. She stroked his small head. She'd named him Van Dyck after the Flemish painter who placed such a little dog in one of the paintings the Parrishes had hanging in the hall. On labored breathing days, he was simply "Van."

"Have you thought of that, being a doctor?"

"As a child. But not now. No. I'm a mother. I'm a divorced woman. Who would allow me to treat them once they learned about my marital status? You are more than generous to allow me to nurse you, but how would you feel if I was your doctor?"

"The divorce part does not offend me, don't you know? For many women, it is the only option to protect themselves, the laws being as they are." She wore a nightcap and Jennie helped her sit forward to remove it so Jennie could brush her hair and braid it in a twist at the top of her head. Thin. *Is she losing hair?* She liked a lemon powder for her face that Jennie brushed on lightly, handed her lip color. She looked at herself in the mirror Jennie held for her. "All these wrinkles and blotches. And still he says he loves me." She put the mirror down. "He calls me beautiful."

"And so you are. Besides, love has nothing to do with how we look, does it?"

"Not real love fired from years of sharing life and loss, no. Still," she lowered her voice to a whisper, "Josiah has always had an eye for lovely women. Not that he has ever strayed, I know that. But he likes me to look my best. He does so much for me, it's little enough to put a little powder and lip rouge on my cheeks, don't you know?"

"You two still flirt with each other."

She grinned and nodded. "I hope when I'm gone he marries again. He says he's too old now, but I know he'd be happier having someone to love and pamper. It's in his very bones to love like that. I've been so fortunate."

"We're going to get you well so you won't have to think of such things."

"So you say," she said and laughed. For a moment, she heard Charles in the room with his "you say" and felt a wistfulness of longing she'd thought she'd put to rest.

While Elizabeth slept one afternoon, Jennie visited with Ariyah, took her some brews that might assist with Ariyah's hope to become pregnant.

"Being a nurse becomes you." Ariyah took the tin from Jennie and returned to her cross-stitch as the women spoke.

"It's stability that's wiped away some of my wrinkles."

"The latest in women's cosmetics. Too bad it can't be bottled."

They laughed together and Ariyah spoke of the continued honeymoon she lived in.

"I'm so happy for you," Jennie said. "I suspect that's how the Parrishes began, and they've sustained their love even through the loss of a child." Elizabeth had told her of their son Lamberson's death and how Josiah and she had sustained each other rather than been torn apart by the grief. "That's what Charles and I didn't manage to do—care for each other."

"Jennie, you did the best you could and Charles likely did too. He chose a different way and not a good one. But you, you've landed on your feet. I'm proud of you."

Jennie fidgeted and changed the subject. Accepting the help of others hardly deserved praise.

While Dr. Wells did not speak to Jennie again of using the bleeding, Josiah asked her about the procedure and her concerns. Jennie explained and showed him the records of walking days versus days when Elizabeth was simply too weak to rise. Josiah held her notes of big block lettering. "I can see how it corresponds to Wells's procedure."

"I offered to share this with him, and the article was in the *Oregon Physio-Medical Journal* that Dr. Shelton, right here in Salem, writes and edits. He included an entire issue on the treatment of ague. He attacked bloodletting and gave reasons." She took a deep breath. "Now that we have a Willamette Medical Department, Dr. Wells could check with instructors there if he doesn't like Dr. Shelton's advice. I'm sure they'd have the latest information."

"I appreciate your talking with him. I'll tell him I'd prefer he use Shelton's methods."

His decision made Jennie pause. What if the doctor's actions were the very best thing and the information she gathered coincidental to his practice? What if Jennie was wrong? Medicine wasn't a science with perfect outcomes promised. Would she have harmed Elizabeth by speaking out? She didn't always get things straight, even when she read them three or four times. Which she did, rereading Dr. Shelton's article again. He suggested in his piece that baths with tepid water helped and recommended the use of spearmint along with "pure air, sunshine, bathing, sleep, exercise, rest and all the hygienic agencies and innocent vegetable medicines—for their recovery from disease when sick, and for the preservation of health." Tomorrow, weather willing, she would take Elizabeth to the garden in the wheeled chair Josiah had had made. She'd do what she had the power to do and prayed it would be enough.

Ariyah lamented the passing of her first anniversary without the promise of a child.

"It'll happen," Jennie assured her. "Try thinking of other things. How are your music lessons coming?"

"My mother makes better progress," Ariyah said. "Oh, I'm doing all right. I just wish that, well . . ."

"I know. What about doing something with

children? Start a little choir or maybe Peleg would give lessons to children."

"Would having them around make me miss babies more?"

"I don't think so. Maybe they'll send some sort of baby signal to your body."

She laughed and Jennie said, "I've said something funny."

"And I got it!" Ariyah said. Then more thoughtful, "I just might take up voice lessons. That's a good idea."

"It's possible to find a happy life even in the midst of waiting for one."

"Jennie Pickett, you're becoming a philosopher."

That really made the friends laugh.

Jennie's monthly weekends with her parents and Douglas were like small respites when Douglas shared all his new skills. He could ride a pony on his own, had his own bow and arrow he could shoot at a target. He had learned to sound out words and did so with a small book her mother had given him to read. She blinked back tears as he read, so grateful he would not repeat her reading problem.

At each visit, her parents greeted Jennie as a long-lost relative, feeding her and telling her she needed as much rest as she insisted Elizabeth get. "I have a very fine employer," Jennie told them. "I get plenty of rest. And my knitting, too, has improved. It's something Elizabeth can do and she's been guiding me." Her mother's eyes narrowed slightly at her comment. "But she's not as fine a teacher as you, Mother."

Her mother grinned and handed Jennie a taffy from her candy jar.

They didn't chastise her indulging Dougie with candies and simple toys either, though at one point her father did say it wasn't necessary to "purchase" her son's affection.

"Is that what I'm doing?"

"It looks like that at times," he said. "You've no reason to feel guilty, Janie."

She pumped the handle for her father, thrusting clear water into the bucket while he used the calomel soap to scrub his arms and hands and face. On weekends he performed physical work to counter the mind-numbing and endless arguing as a new member of the legislature. He lifted the bucket over his head to rinse his hair. Jennie handed him a towel. "Ah, Janie. We've enjoyed the boy so much. Reminds us both of Mathias when he was a child. Good memories. And Douglas has adjusted well to all the changes, I'd say."

"Does he ask for his father?"

"Sometimes. We tell him that Charles was ill and needed time to heal."

"That's one way of putting it. And of me? How do you explain my absence?"

Her father held the flannel to his nose, wiped his face, then looked over the towel's edge. "He doesn't ask," he said when he lowered the towel from his face. "I think it's because he knows you're doing what you must, that you've arranged for a good place for him, and he knows he'll see you soon. You don't wonder out loud about what you think you know."

Maybe she was no longer needed in her son's life. Her parents adored him, were excellent teachers. Should she even imagine a time when Douglas and she would make their way alone?

"Does he blame me for Charles's absence? He did once. That's why I ask." She washed her own hands beneath the rushing water while her father pumped for her.

"He makes comments not specific to you. That's a greater worry in my book, Janie. That a child of a divorce will write a chapter about his own faults in all the pain and disappointment of his parents."

A child of a divorce. The phrase jabbed like a hatpin.

Her father continued as he handed her a towel. "We work to help him see that hard things happen and it's not always because of something we did or didn't do, not a punishment or lack of faith. I think of Job—oh, not a story I tell Dougie at this point, but it's a reminder that in all the trials, God is with us."

She wasn't comforted by her son's never invoking her name. But her father's words were a good reminder: the divorce wasn't because of something she did or didn't do on her own. It happened inside a relationship, that knot fraying from constant strains against it. And it was now her task to make her life with Douglas move forward as best she could, even if that meant for a time without them together quite as often as she might like.

Chapter 17
No Fury

The Parrishes and Jennie attended the State Fair that fall of 1868. Jennie sat beside Elizabeth in her wheeled-chair while they ate at the restaurant operated by the colonists of Aurora, listened to the music of their Pie and Beer Band. Later that day, friends and family held a harvest gathering at the Parrish house to celebrate Josiah's sheep earning top awards. Van scampered at Jennie's feet as she brought a tray for Elizabeth, his red-and-white fur swirling in excitement. The little dog rarely barked. Elizabeth beamed in the activity of her children's families. Even though she could see Elizabeth was tired, Jennie didn't suggest she lie down. These were moments of sustenance that wouldn't be possible for long. She envied the ease with which this extended family expressed caring for each other.

Christmas came and once again Elizabeth's family swarmed in to tend her, bring her music boxes and new bed jackets, a meat bone for the dog. Grandchildren gave gifts of drawings that made Jennie hope Douglas would present her with something like that too. He did not. Too busy being a growing boy. The Parrish clan remembered her with linen handkerchiefs and gifts for Douglas and gentle words about her care for their mother.

Norman's wife, Henrietta, was especially kind, saying that each time they came, she thought Elizabeth looked better. "We understand you stopped that dreadful bloodletting."

"Not me. Mr. Parrish spoke to Dr. Wells about it."

"He said it was at your impetus. Thank you. I, myself, do not do well with sick people. I so admire those who do." She had a missing tooth near the front. "Meeting the needs of another is a gift not everyone has." Jennie blushed but inhaled her words.

On Epiphany, the twelfth day of Christmas, Jennie took the star from atop the Christmas tree, the crèche from the hearth, and wrapped them both for storage. The wreaths and mistletoe she hauled to the burn pile, the ending of the Advent and Christmas season always leaving her a little sad. That year especially so, as Minnie had married the day after Epiphany and left to make a life with her new husband in Portland. Change. All of life pushed out through that wrapping, no matter how hard one might try to keep the strings from letting loose whatever unknown remained inside.

Through that spring of '69, Chen carried on with his cuisine without Minnie and without missing a clang of his triangle, a device he used to bring Josiah in from the barns for lunch. He clanged it now, and Jennie watched from Elizabeth's bedroom as Josiah began the walk up from the fields, the fresh green of April sprinkled with daffodils and daisies, while white sheep like fluffy clouds dotted the emerald land.

"Father is enamored with his animals."

Jennie startled at the voice. Then realized it was the Parrishes' youngest son, Charles Winn. They always added his middle name when they spoke of him. Jennie was sure that pleased Elizabeth, as Winn was her maiden name.

Jennie had just moved Elizabeth's wheeled chair to the solarium where she soaked in the sun. Van lounged on her lap, and the elderly woman stroked him absently while she spoke with her daughter-in-law, Charles Winn's wife. Jennie pulled bedding, planned to bring in fresh water to the bedside for when Elizabeth tired and she'd be wheeled back inside. Jennie could never be in the room without taking a moment to gaze at the garden and must have been deep in thought, as she hadn't heard Charles Winn come into the room. He stood close. Jennie stepped away to put more distance between them.

"Enamored is a good word," Jennie said.

Charles Winn had his father's good looks, long

face with a wide smile, eyes that took you in and held you, thick well-trimmed hair. She imagined Josiah must have looked like his son when he was younger. She turned back to the view. Josiah walked with Norman and Samuel and a grandchild or two among the sheep, the black-and-white guard dogs lying to the sides, watching as Chen rang the bell again.

"What will you do for employment after my mother dies?"

"What?" His directness startled. His father was always truthful but never blunt. "My efforts are here in this moment, caring for your mother with the absolute hope and prayer that she'll improve."

"She has, actually, under your ministrations. But we all know—and she does as well—that these are her last months. Even Dr. Wells agrees."

"I—I'm sorry, I don't think of my time with your mother in that way."

"Perhaps my father will keep you on now that Minnie's up and married, though Chen should be able to care for him well enough."

"Your father hardly needs tending, especially as long as he has his sheep to monitor. Have you seen the breeding records he keeps? He's a man of science, your father." She stepped away as Charles Winn had moved closer to her, their shoulders almost touching. "Could you pull that end of the sheet there? Thank you." Jennie rolled the linen, held it at her breast. "Or perhaps you and Mrs. Parrish will come live with him."

Charles Winn grunted at that. "We'll soon be heading to Canyon City. Mining towns need attorneys, so I'll be there." He took a pipe from his vest pocket. "I wonder at any claims you might make upon my mother's death."

"Claims?" Jennie frowned. "Your parents have been a godsend to me. I only hope to return their kindness in some small form. But claims against your mother's estate? No." Did the family think she was a treasure hunter? She wondered if the attorney in the family knew of the huge debt she owed to his parents. Maybe that was why he'd broached the subject. "I'm here only as long as needed and I will repay all my debts."

"Good. I wondered." With that, he left the room.

With Elizabeth's family visiting, the decision was made to send Jennie home for an entire two weeks.

"Here our Ladies Commission labors to . . . reduce long working hours for women," Elizabeth said. "We insist their employers give . . . them ample rest time." Breathing had grown more difficult for her. "Then we keep you . . . here night and day. You go. Henrietta and Annie . . . will do just fine looking after me, won't you?" Jennie was tempted to finish her sentences to save her breath but did not, speech being a sign of commitment to living.

"Yes, Mother Parrish." Henrietta took her hand and squeezed it. "I, myself, will relish the time with you."

Annie Parrish smiled. "We can speak of babies," she said, her due date approaching and her condition no longer concealed, now that hoops were going out of style and more slender-izing lines marked high fashion.

Before going home, Jennie stopped to see Ariyah, who knew all her secrets now: divorce, debt, destitution, and new determination to make a new life for Douglas and herself.

Her friend's face glowed as she hugged Jennie and said the strawberry tea had worked this time.

"You've conceived!" Jennie squealed her delight.

"Just," Ariyah said. "April 1870. Our baby will be born in the new decade."

"I'll start knitting booties this afternoon."

Charles Winn's question of what she'd do had stirred future thoughts in her as she rode the stage toward French Prairie. Her father had written that they considered moving to Salem to be nearer to the legislature and other legal work that claimed him there. But he would hate to leave his beloved farm.

Maybe I can keep the farm for them, Douglas and I together. She'd never worked the land, only her garden. Still, the thought comforted. It felt good to have a possible next step.

Annie Parrish's baby was due in August. They planned to stay at the Parrish house until delivery, as Canyon City was still a miner's boomtown with few midwives or doctors not competing with liquor. She'd asked Jennie to serve as midwife. Jennie considered midwifery as an occupation. The women were well-regarded, more than some physicians. She'd need to live in a city though, in order to support herself and Douglas. This time with the Parrishes had lent respectability to her status, but the reality was that Jennie was "damaged goods"—a "grass widow," as divorced women were called—so getting employment even as a midwife might be difficult. And hopes for a second marriage weren't wise. Other women sometimes acted as though she meant to steal their husbands when she nodded to them at church; and single men wanted their own children, not saddled with someone else's child. The truth was, she didn't relish the thought of raising someone else's children either. Unlike caring for ill people, her mothering had never garnered compliments.

For now, as the stagecoach dropped her and her bag at the stop, she would think only of her son and of respite.

"Mama! Mama!" Douglas jumped down from the porch railing. She felt his solid body slam into her, nearly causing her to lose her balance. He'd seen her coming up the lane. There'd been an earlier rainfall, not amounting to much, but just enough to muddy up her shoes and make her watch her footsteps.

"Whoa, goodness, how you've grown." At nearly six years of age, he had shot up, his head nearly to her shoulder. She held him at arm's length, then reached to hold him. He wiggled free.

"Papa came to visit. He brought me a telescope of my very own. I'll show you. Come, hurry, before he leaves."

When it comes to family, nothing is ever really settled. There are pauses of forgiveness and healing, then falling back to that former place a family once thought they'd moved beyond.

After Charles deserted them, she had planned what she would say if she ever saw her husband again—like a lawyer, she'd ask pointed questions of how she might have been different to head off what happened. She'd ask after his health, where he'd been, what had he been doing? Or maybe she'd shout about his having left them in debt, taken everything from them, forced his son to sleep on the floor until she could sell the pearls. Or maybe, after shouts and tears, she'd tell him how great sadness fell upon her as she considered how he'd divorced her without ever giving her a chance, that wound nearly as deep as when Baby Ariyah died, the betrayal a bloodstain that never faded.

Here was reality, staring her in the face, and she was speechless.

"Jennie." Charles's eyes were black holes, the bachelor-button blue long sunk into darkness. A ragged beard scruffed his cheeks, his chin, covering up that cleft. His hand shook when he reached out to take hers, steadying himself with both hands holding tight. "I should not have come. But I am in desperate need."

Her parents stood to the side, both with stiff shoulders.

She felt her stomach lurch. Did he think she had funds to give him, to help feed a habit that still drove him?

"Let's talk outside." He began to pull on her while Douglas returned, having scampered to his bed and back, holding the brass and glass. He shoved it between them.

"See, Mama? It's as nice as yours, the one you lost."

She'd told her son that lie, that she had lost it, when in fact Charles had taken it with him. She saw it was the same one that Douglas now held, that little ding in the brass having been put there when she'd accidentally banged it against a rail. The calla lily painting now chipped.

"Yes, it is."

Douglas's pushing forced Charles to release her hand. "Your mother and I need to speak." Charles barked the words and Douglas cringed.

"Show me." Jennie's father intervened. "Let's look at the potato field, see if there are any deer marauding out there."

"No!" Douglas jerked from her father's gentle hand.

"Go with your grandpa," Charles told him. "Give me that thing before you drop it." He grabbed the telescope and Douglas stumbled back.

"Stop it, Charles, please. You gave it to him. Don't take it back."

He ignored Jennie, grabbed her elbow, and dragged her out onto the porch, the telescope gripped in his other hand. Douglas screamed behind them. She could hear her parents offering comforting words, moving him out of sight.

"What are you doing here?"

"I need money. Buy this and I'll be out of your hair. You'll be done with me. I won't darken your door again. That's what you want, isn't it?"

His clothes hung on him. Cheekbones like jagged rocks jutted out, making the hollows under his eyes more pronounced.

"You're ill. You should see a doctor."

"You say. You're working. You've got money, I know you do." He shook the telescope at her.

"What coins you have in exchange for me getting out of your life. For good."

"I—I don't have coins. What little I have goes to pay off our debt to the Parrish family and to provide for Douglas. My parents aren't rich. None of us are rich, Charles. You'll have to find another buyer for your telescope." Her heart pounded as she saw his eyes narrow, his arm rise with the telescope glinting in the afternoon sun. *He's going to hit me.*

In that moment she knew that she would do whatever it took to stay alive, to be there for her son. As he attempted to lower the brass onto her shoulder, she kicked him in the shin, then pushed his head down when he groaned to grab his leg. He dropped the telescope and Jennie picked it up, holding it to her breast. She could hardly speak. "You. Will. Leave. Now. Don't ever come back. Get help, Charles. But do not come here. Ever. Again."

Charles backed up, a sly grin his way of saving face.

"Papa!" Douglas sprang from inside the house. "Mama hurt you."

"Go." Jennie's voice shook. "Let me deal with the aftermath, once again, of you."

"I'll drive you," her father said as Douglas broke free and grabbed his father's knees.

Please let him spurn Douglas, please.

"Douglas, your mama and grandpa don't see

how much I love you, boy. They don't want me stayin' around. Got to go now. You be good. Enjoy that telescope I gave you."

The child sobbed, clinging to his father. Jennie pulled him away, kicking, screaming, while her father rushed Charles to the barn and the buggy. How long would it take them to harness the horse? *Please let Charles stay in the barn until they can leave.*

That prayer was answered.

She held her son against the wails of disappointment. When they saw the buggy depart, she let him go. He ran after the cloud of dust shielding his father. She knew her son wouldn't return to her for comfort. And he didn't.

Chapter 18
Arrivals and Departures

After his father left, Douglas became a statue to his mother, impeding any effort she made to have their lives sing a shared song. He wasn't interested in looking through the telescope. He never even picked it up. Her effort to engage him in conversation about Quilton or her praise for how he helped his grandfather brought on scowls. He sassed her parents; Jennie sat him in a chair. He kicked at the wall. Douglas missed three meals before snarling, "Sorry." Jennie could not make him mean it.

Jennie had been visiting—and she realized she was indeed the visitor—when she suggested one afternoon that he clean Quilton's cage sitting on the porch. "He doesn't appear to like the meat you've given him. The flies do though. After you do that, we can go together to gather leaves and twigs for him if you like." She watched him comply, grateful he had. When she checked a few minutes later, Douglas stood beside an empty cage, looked up at her, and said, "I set Quilton free."

"But you loved that little rodent." Jennie squatted so she could look into her son's emerald eyes. The flounce of her skirts offered a soft hush. She touched his forehead, pushing back his dark curls.

Douglas shrugged. He'd gone from being distant to hurting himself, deepening his sadness.

"Quilton's better on his own." He stepped back so she couldn't touch him.

"He'll miss you. Maybe he'll come back."

"He wouldn't stay. Papa didn't stay."

"Your father could have if he had been—"

"Welcome. You didn't welcome him. Paw-Paw and Grandma didn't either. He came all that way and brought me a new telescope and you all made him leave."

"He was still here when I arrived, Douglas. They didn't make him leave."

"You did."

She sighed, pushed herself up, and sank onto the wicker chair. She closed her eyes against the sun, not feeling any warmth. "I did ask him to leave after he . . . I was very sad to do that, Douglas, but his behavior—"

"He wanted to stay with us! He came back for me!"

She couldn't tell him that his father had come back for money to feed his addiction. It wouldn't matter. Douglas's broken heart filtered the memory.

"Your father isn't well. He was too sick to take care of you."

"I could take care of him."

And spend your life looking after him, hoping to earn a love that should be freely given from a father to a son. "Maybe when you see him again, when you're older, you can suggest that."

What did one say to the child of an addicted, tortured soul? "I hate to see you give up Quilton. Let's put a bowl of milk out and see if he comes back."

"I don't want to hope for it." He walked toward the barn where Jennie's father readied the buggy that would take her to the stage and back to a place of guilty joy.

The newest Parrish baby arrived on a sultry August morning. Jennie served as midwife, though Dr. Wells was also called at Charles Winn's insistence.

Annie held her newborn, a girl they named Winifred, and whispered to Jennie, who pulled slips over the down pillows, "Thank you for insisting Dr. Wells wash his hands before examining me. Goodness. I could smell Father Parrish's Merino sheep on him the minute he came through the door. I nearly emitted."

"The good news is that he listened, even though he had to tell us that he had 'every intention of doing so without a nagging nurse to remind me.'"

Annie laughed at Jennie's impersonation.

"What's so funny?" Josiah entered the room to see his newest grandchild.

"Jennie does a perfect impression of our Dr. Wells," Annie said before Jennie could shush her. It wasn't polite to make fun of anyone, let alone a doctor.

"Does she?" He grinned at the women. "He told me Jennie did a fine job of assisting, so I hope you aren't too hard on him. We old men stick together, you know."

"I never think of you as old, Father Parrish," Annie said.

"May I?" He asked to hold the baby, and Annie lifted her up into Jennie's arms, the swaddling clothes hanging loose. Jennie placed the bundle in Josiah's arms.

Something in the way he held the baby to his chest, the look of utter love he cast upon her, brought tears to Jennie's eyes. She'd never have another child, never experience that joy again, but she could see it was possible to spread love like the sun, warming any child. All children. Douglas might not be able to accept her love for him right now, but it was there for him, always.

"She's beautiful." Josiah's deep voice was soft as a whip-poor-will's.

"She is," Annie agreed.

"When you're able, Elizabeth will be so happy to see her latest grandchild."

Annie nodded. "In a while."

He handed the baby back to Jennie, who placed the infant in the cradle beside her mother's bed.

"We'll let her rest," Jennie said. "And you too."

Van, the little spaniel, trotted between Josiah and Jennie as they descended the stairs. Charles and Annie used an upstairs bedroom where Charles Winn had spent his growing-up years. Jennie had taken over Minnie's room on the first floor to be closer to Elizabeth, should she call in the night.

"Van's been following me around all morning like I needed herding." Josiah nodded toward the little dog who ran ahead, then waited for them.

"It's odd he's left Elizabeth."

"Maybe all the excitement of the new baby."

But when they entered Elizabeth's room, Jennie could tell that something had changed. Her patient's breathing was more labored. Jennie checked her pulse. Weak. "I'll get a plaster for her chest."

She had prepared beef gall to molasses thickness and only needed to add mustard, pepper, and lobelia. Van jumped up onto the bed, rounded himself against Elizabeth's rib cage.

"Maybe he wanted to herd me back here." Josiah sat and took Elizabeth's hand in his. "Upstairs, new life. Downstairs, new life too. Just one we don't get to be a part of."

• • •

"I believe . . . the plaster helps." Elizabeth awoke with as good a color to her cheeks as Jennie had seen in weeks. Mid-August had come upon them "hot like johnnycake," as Chen put it.

"Maybe we've turned a corner." Jennie put her hand to Elizabeth's forehead. Warm but not feverish. Summer heat rose to ceiling beams and beneath the chemise of every Salem woman.

"I wouldn't go . . . that far. Not a cure, dear Jennie. But I am . . . so grateful for these last days. To be aware. To hold Baby Winifred. To see my children . . . all settled in their lives before leaving mine."

Jennie didn't like to hear her talk like this, as though Elizabeth gave up hope.

"I'll be seeing Lamberson soon."

Lamberson. Their oldest child who had died before I was even born. "Is it wise to speak of such things?" Jennie said. "Would you like some iced tea?"

"Yes and no." She smiled. "Come. Sit. I . . . enjoy your company."

"I can get Josiah for you."

"No. He will want to stay until the end. I want . . . a few words with you . . . before then."

Jennie sat, but not before she smoothed Elizabeth's bed jacket, then took her hand in hers. *Such elegant hands.* Van snored quietly on the bed, the little spaniel stretched out now the length of Elizabeth's narrow rib cage. She waited for Elizabeth to gain strength to speak, prayed she would say the right things, *do* the right things.

I should get Josiah so he can alert the children.

"We've been married . . . thirty-six years. Grand years. I've never stopped loving him . . . nor has he ever stopped loving me. And he won't, I don't believe, unless . . . someone takes him under their wing and helps him see. He still has much to do, much to give. Much to love."

"He will grieve you deeply."

"He will. And I . . ." She closed her eyes.

"You're tired. Why don't you rest while I get Josiah. He'll want to be here."

She opened her eyes. "Not yet. Let me say this. Jennie . . . stay with him. He will want to move to Portland . . . not remain in this house after I'm gone. I don't want him to sell it right away. He will come back here. He must. This is where . . . his life has been the richest. So when he asks . . . agree to stay with him and help take care of him. Please . . . say you'll do that."

She couldn't imagine he'd need any help from her once Elizabeth passed. He'd never mentioned Portland at all. Most of his business interests were in Salem. His Merinos were here, and he talked of breeding rare Angora goats, something that would occupy his time and perhaps distract him from his grief. The land Elizabeth had donated for the new orphanage was her legacy. He'd want to oversee its construction.

But she didn't want to deny a deathbed request. "I could continue to work for him, for a time." *Doing what?* She could bring Douglas with her. Josiah had raised four boys. He'd know how to help bring Douglas around. "I owe so much to you both. It would be a way to repay the debt."

"The debt has already been repaid. In so many ways." She closed her eyes.

Jennie knew the loan was not close to being paid off. Elizabeth's comments were about the philosophy of the debt, not the practical part of it. Jennie quietly stood up.

"I want you to remain . . . with Josiah until his feet are on the ground again," she said. "I hope . . . he'll remarry. He's a loving man and needs . . . someone to love deeply. Someone who can love him back. Would you stay with him . . . until he finds that person?"

Did she want her to continue nursing Josiah, who didn't need it? What Elizabeth asked—on her deathbed—was for someone to shepherd him through the grief. Whether he found another to love in the way Elizabeth imagined was out of her control. It was time to support herself and Douglas and begin that arduous journey to bridge the chasm in their lives. And repay the debt the more typical way, by making payments from her earnings. Her life ought not be wrapped up in whether Josiah Parrish found someone to love.

But this was a deathbed request.

"I will stay for as long as is necessary," Jennie told her.

"That's not exactly . . . the commitment I hoped for." She opened her eyes and grinned this time, and a flush of color rose to her face, and for a moment she was young again, the wrinkles faded into smooth. "But it will do. I only ask that you don't . . . settle for the first time he says you may depart. Offer to stay a little longer. When he says it the second time . . . then, yes, you may leave. Promise me?"

"I promise." *How will she ever know?*

"And don't think I won't know . . . if you renege." She shook a finger at Jennie, who laughed out loud. Elizabeth smiled. Jennie wished she'd known her longer.

"Worse . . . is that *you* will know . . . if you fail to keep that commitment. I know you, Jennie Lichtenthaler Pickett. And not keeping a promise you've made—even one to yourself—is a worse torture . . . for you than losing a friend."

"No." Jennie patted her hand and suppressed a sob. "There's nothing worse than losing a good friend."

Elizabeth's health declined. The family gathered. Henrietta sang sweet hymns standing at the foot of the bed. Samuel, their middle son, came in his Portland police uniform and knelt at his mother's bedside, whispering prayers. Two old Indian women sat outside in the hall, keening a high-pitched strangely soothing tone. A single drummer beat out a rhythm that made Jennie think of ancestors witnessing this woman's life. Josiah welcomed their presence, nodding, offering them food and drink for the vigil.

"She is beloved. The Paiute called her White Dove when I agented at the Malheur reservation," Josiah said when Jennie commented on the Indian women with their calico headscarves, shawls, and faces lined with age. His blue eyes looked far away to another time, a shared memory that only he and Elizabeth had. How the Indians knew of Elizabeth's dying Jennie didn't know. But they honored her and Josiah with their presence.

Baby Winifred slept in a cradle brought into Elizabeth's room, the youngest of the clan there with the oldest. Jennie burned a candle laced with lavender, the scent sweet comfort as they listened to Elizabeth's labored breathing. Jennie kept soothing facecloths as cool as August allowed, replenishing them as needed, moving in and out of the room, hoping to be as silent as a shadow.

"It's not all that different from a birthing, is it?" Annie said. She rocked the cradle as she sat farther back than the Parrish siblings and Josiah, Josiah honoring Indian tradition that a newborn not be too close to one dying, lest the deceased seek out the fragile soul of the young one to go with them.

"The waiting, watching, loving," Jennie agreed. She remembered Ariyah's birth and death, within minutes of each other. To ask to love and grieve at the same moment can only be accomplished with the strength of God's cradling. Charles might have drawn hope from that moment too, if he'd been present. But he hadn't been. It had been one of many losses liquor had begun.

"Would you like a sassafras?" Jennie had served everyone who wished it, and now she approached Josiah, who chewed his lower lip.

He shook his head. He'd been at Elizabeth's bedside for a full day and night, holding her hand. He rubbed his nose now and then with his handkerchief. Jennie could tell he prayed.

And when the moment came, when Elizabeth left this life behind, he laid his head down on the bedsheets and he wept.

Chapter 19
Winnowing

Elizabeth Winn Parrish died August 30, 1869. Peacefully, with her husband and children beside her.

The family and close friends had returned to the Parrish house after the funeral attended by hundreds, and now most had spoken their comforting words to Josiah and the children and left. Jennie tidied up the parlor, taking dishes and dainty teacups to the kitchen where she found Chen sniffling. She opened her arms and he bowed, took her hands, and let her offer comfort. She returned to brush crumbs into the silver pan. Josiah had retired and she could hear a baby crying in the upstairs bedroom.

"I know my mother asked that you remain, at least for a time, to help my father." Charles Winn surprised her in the parlor.

"She did."

"I've talked it over with my father and he says he doesn't think he needs anyone tending him."

"I'm sure he doesn't. I agreed only as a courtesy to your mother, to ease her last days as

214

she worries about your father. She loves him very much."

"Loved him," he corrected.

"And still does. As does your father still love her."

Charles Winn nodded. He had curly brown hair, like his father's. "It wouldn't be seemly to have you remain."

That thought had never occurred to Jennie. Nor did she think Josiah Parrish would care what other people might think. She had been his wife's nurse, a housekeeper of sorts, nothing more.

"Whatever your father wishes."

"It's what we wish."

The Parrishes had been there for her and her family in ways she could never have imagined. She was indebted to them and always would be. "I can leave in the morning."

Am I doing the right thing? After all, she'd promised Elizabeth to wait for two occasions of being told she wasn't needed before accepting Josiah's request that she leave. But Charles Winn was adamant—he was likely the executor of his mother's estate as well—and neither he nor his father needed any challenge from a nurse.

In the morning she served breakfast for the Parrish clan. "We'll see you again, won't we?" Henrietta asked. "You're practically a part of the family."

"The sister we never had," Samuel offered. He

poured honey on his johnnycake. She hadn't had much time with the police-officer-Parrish and she held him at a caution, knowing he was involved in work that might put him in contact with her now former husband while arresting drunks on the streets of Portland. Samuel was always very kind to her. It was a Parrish trait, though Charles Winn modeled directness more than mediation.

"I'm sure we'll have occasion to encounter each other." She filled coffee cups. "My son and I will go to the fair. I have to see how Josiah's Merinos show."

"It might be wise to refer to Father as Reverend Parrish now," Charles Winn corrected.

Norman, his older brother, frowned.

"Oh. Of course. I'll bring more huckleberry jam." Jennie slipped into the kitchen to cauterize the wound sliced by Charles's sharp words. He was right. Things were different. Elizabeth had chinked them all together with her glue of love and acceptance. Now she was gone, so cool winds could blow through space between the logs of this once-solid shelter.

When she returned, Josiah—Mr. Parrish—sat at the head of the table. Jennie asked if he'd like waffles or pancakes and he shook his head. "Just coffee if you please, Jennie. Just coffee."

The table remained silent for a moment or two, and she wondered if his children were thinking he ought to call her Mrs. Pickett now too, or if it was his sallow look and his turning down food that brought them all to silence.

"Jennie." Mr. Parrish cleared his throat. "I know that Charles Winn discussed your status here."

"I'm packed. After breakfast I'll have the livery pick up my trunk."

"I've been thinking. Maybe it would be good for you to remain. I'll need to go through Elizabeth's things and—"

"The girls can assist with that, Father." Charles Winn spoke between bites of waffle.

"We can come back in October and do that while we attend the Harvest fair. Would that work, Father Parrish?" Henrietta made the offer. She always sounded as though she had a cold.

"I appreciate that, Daughter. And last night I thought I'd like to be left alone, close up the house, sell it, move to Portland."

Elizabeth knows him so well.

"But I've decided to go through Elizabeth's things, set aside certain treasures for each of you. I've already given several of her shawls to our Indian singers. I could still smell her perfume—" His voice caught. He blinked and looked down at his hands.

"Too soon to go through her things," Charles Winn said. "Go to Portland. We'll help in October."

"The Indians, they give away the precious

things of the deceased." Josiah paused. "So her spirit can leave and not be held back by the people who love her and don't want her to go. No. I think I shouldn't wait." He looked at Jennie then. "What do you think of that, Jennie?"

"Me? I . . ." It wasn't her place to comment, but her healer heart spoke to him, even though she felt uncomfortable discussing this great loss with his family staring at her. She knew that people "telling" you what to do in time of sorrow only seemed to heighten the powerlessness that death brings. She put the huckleberry jam down and stood without the protection of something in her hands, folded now over her pinafore. She struggled for the right words, spoke a silent prayer. "Grief has many siblings," she said. "It's good to honor all of them—the sadness, emptiness, anger sometimes, a wish to do something of merit on behalf of the person. I don't think it's too soon nor too long to do those things that help us memorialize a life."

"Spoken like a preacher," Samuel mused.

"I didn't mean to—"

"No, no. What you said was perfect." Josiah looked around the table. "I'm asking Jennie to stay to assist me. Elizabeth loved her. She can help divide her jewelry, precious things, without family rancor—" He anticipated the objections, held up his palm. "Oh, I know that can happen in the best of families. Besides, you have your lives to return to, and if Jennie is willing to delay the return to hers for a few weeks, then I'll close up the house and head to Portland after we've sorted things here. Yes, I think that's best. Don't you, Van?"

The spaniel lay with his nose on his paws near the sideboard, his thick ears that dragged the floor jiggled. He raised his head to his name.

There didn't seem to be room for disagreement, or perhaps his children respected their father's steps on his mournful journey.

"Are you agreeable, Jennie? I'm not sure I want to try this without you."

"As you wish, Mr. Parrish." She curtsied. "I'll unpack my things after breakfast."

"Mr. Parrish? Who would that be?" He looked around the room. Charles Winn's eyes moved toward the coffee urn, and he rose to refill his cup, stepping over Van. "Josiah." He spoke to them all. "I've always been Josiah to my friends."

Later, Charles Winn stopped her in the upstairs hall as the livery men carried down the family's trunks. "I'm still wary of your being here, but I do understand that my father has asked for your help. And it does give you a way to continue to pay off your debt. Which, if anyone asks about the 'arrangement' here is what I'll say. That you continue to work to meet your and your former husband's obligations." Almost to himself, he added, "Yes, that's the story I'll tell."

They'd been winnowing, as he called it, for several days now, spending a few hours in the morning and a few more in the afternoon. At dusk he walked out among his sheep, and Jennie read, often removing her glasses to think until the light failed when the clock struck nine chimes. They took breakfast together and other meals that Chen served them, the cook often being asked to join them at the table. Josiah told her stories. But he also asked for hers.

Early one day, he held a fine wool cape of Elizabeth's with a fox collar, and she told him about her fox and the joy she'd had in sharing the inventiveness of that animal with Douglas.

"Plucked wool from the willows, did he? They are clever, those foxes."

"I was impressed that he took care of his problems all by himself."

Josiah frowned. "Perhaps. But he had the help of the sheep leaving wool, the willows, and the river. So he wasn't totally independent."

That hadn't occurred to her. There were always gifts from others if one took the time to look.

Jennie enjoyed the winnowing, the rhythm of sorting and storytelling not unlike the spinning wheel's contentment.

"And what's the story of this?" Jennie held up a gold ring with an eagle imprinted onto it.

"Let's see." Josiah reached for it, showed her

that the eagle lifted, revealing a tiny container. "It's English and supposedly salts went there, for when women fainted from their tight corsets, forgive the liberty of my language."

Jennie laughed. " 'Corset' is hardly a curse. Well, possibly." He laughed then. "But what's the story of Elizabeth having it?"

"You know, I can't remember. She must have liked it. It's in her 'precious box.' "

"I guess you could write a note about the ring, that it was in with her treasures." Jennie still held the jewel in her hand.

"It'll come to me." He leaned back in the Windsor chair, hands restful on his thighs. "Elizabeth often picked things up that I never remember her ever wearing. She liked the story, I think. This ring"—he nodded—"I suspect was one of those. Why do women even wear such things as whale bone corsets, so tight they faint and need smelling salts to revive them?"

"I suspect if you ever broke a rib, being trussed into a good corset could prove a comfort."

"Oh, ho, I like that idea. An everyday solution to a problem. Very inventive." He tapped his temple. "You've a good mind, Jennie Pickett."

She blushed. A man and a woman were having a conversation about women's underthings without the least bit of embarrassment—until he complimented her on her thinking.

"Not to mention the effect on the poor whales

who gave their lives for the stays," she added.

"Yes!" He clapped his hands. "It takes courage to defy the fashion patrollers. Elizabeth did just that. Let's write that story down, about Elizabeth choosing the ring as a reminder to not suffer corsets—unless there's a broken rib in the story. You know, well, of course you know, she rarely wore them, even when she was quite well. I think it might have been as a tribute to the whales. We watched for them when we lived in Clatsop. She loved the coast." He reached for the ring, his hands touching Jennie's for just a moment.

She wrote his words down in her slow and steady pace, her cursive like a child's, not as smooth nor looped as Josiah's. He didn't seem to mind. He watched, deep in thought. "Have you been to the coast, Jennie?"

"I never have."

"Hardy settlers there." He mentioned an Owens family he'd given food to after their arduous journey back in the '40s. "They named a child after me. They had a girl with an interesting name too." He thought. "Bethina. Another bright child." Van wandered in, looking lost. He jumped onto Josiah's lap and waited for the pets he knew would come—and did.

When Jennie finished writing, Josiah said, "I think we should give that ring to Winifred so she'll have something very personal of her grandmother's. I'll tell her when she's older about the stricture of fashion and that the ring can remind her not to be bound by tradition unless absolutely necessary."

It was a bit disconcerting to hear "*we* should give the ring." Perhaps he and Elizabeth had been a "we" for so long he didn't know how to now say "I."

"That would be lovely."

"This is a country that demands courage of even its women. Winifred won't have to live with the hardships Elizabeth did when we first arrived at the coast. But each generation has its own challenge." His eyes closed. "She always wanted a girl, not that she didn't love our sons with the fierceness of a mountain cat. But she missed being reminded of her own growing, her own mother and daughter-ness. A girl would have brought that to her. At least she always thought so. It was our one regret. Your presence helped fill that well for Elizabeth."

Had she seen Jennie as the daughter she never had? She hadn't gotten that impression. They were friends.

"I had a daughter." *Why am I telling him.* "Ariyah."

"Named for your friend?"

Jennie nodded. Of course he would have known, being a friend of her father's. "She . . . she didn't survive her birthing. There were complications. The cord." She swallowed. "No doctor came in time. I always wished I'd been schooled in medicine and perhaps I might have saved my child." She didn't tell him about Charles's betrayal that evening, arriving too late with a doctor, alcohol on both their breaths.

"I think I remember your father saying something about the baby. I'm sorry."

"Elizabeth and I share that regret, of never having a girl to raise and pamper." *I should change this sad subject.*

"You're young yet. You'll remarry."

He handed the ring back to her, and she wrapped it in the foolscap where she'd written the story, with WINIFRED in block letters on the front. She stood to put the paper package in the basket where Josiah had placed other items for Charles Winn and Annie. Other baskets contained treasures for Norman and Henrietta and Samuel too: a locket from England, a penny dreadful she knew Norman would like to read—*Malaeska: The Indian Wife of the White Hunter*—a cross and a lamp from Algiers, dear items Elizabeth had treasured. As she passed by Josiah, he reached up to touch her arm. "I can't thank you enough for staying with me to do this."

"It's been my pleasure."

He held her hand then, rubbed his thumb across her knuckles, her ringless fingers. It was an absent gesture, a desire for human touch, Jennie suspected, but it felt warm and kind. A log rolled in the fireplace. She pulled her fingers free and kept walking toward the baskets as he rose to poke at the flames.

"I feel a little guilty," she said. "Because the stories and your reminiscences are so precious. Your children should really be hearing them, not me."

"They'll have the stories. To read at their leisure." He sounded dismissive, the first negative emotion she'd witnessed from him. But every family had dozens of incidents with tangled memories attached. She wasn't privy to them nor did she want to be. Josiah continued. "I left home at a young age, so I have few family memories past my youth. I think my father was disappointed I became a minister and headed west with Elizabeth. He thought I did well as a blacksmith—and I did, as a blacksmith for God and the Lee Mission here in Oregon. My work with the Indians was profoundly satisfying."

He stood then, still able to stand as a young man without pressing against the arms of a chair. He faced a great loss, but he wasn't beaten down by it. "I doubt my father ever understood that one can combine an occupation with a God-directed purpose and find both challenge and fulfillment there."

"Perhaps the key is seeking that direction."

"It is. And in staying close to always wonder if the work of love we're called to do is what we're actually doing. I've told my sons to do something they loved. Fulfillment will follow." He tugged on his beard, and Jennie wondered if his words could speak to her, to do something that drew her and purpose would appear. "Charles Winn always loved to disagree," he continued, a smile on his face. "Now he argues on behalf of those less fortunate, miners and their widows. He was led to lawyering, the perfect occupation for him."

Despite the goal being to sort the belongings of a loved one, Jennie found the time filled with joy not only in discovering more about Elizabeth and her life but of their lives together. And there were insights into her own grieving, about how to celebrate what had been left behind rather than lament what no longer was. She might never understand the role she played in the dissolution of her marriage. Had she carried resentment too long, been angered by the change in possibilities after Charles fell? Was she too demanding about having things go her way? But she was here now and she'd been given a new path, to help heal others as she allowed others to help heal her. She must forgive both Charles and herself so she'd be free to raise Douglas with gentleness, not the unspent anger meant for his father.

She considered bringing Douglas to the Parrish house until they finished, but she didn't want to disrupt Douglas's life more than necessary.

There'd be another adjustment when she found other employment and worked out where they'd live next.

In between directed efforts of making notes and sorting, Josiah and Jennie continued to share meals. Beneath the dining-room chandelier, they spoke of world affairs; of certain southern states being given representation to the Congress by agreeing to never amend their constitution to deny Negroes the right to vote, hold office, or gain education. She learned that Josiah was an abolitionist who grieved the death of President Lincoln. They talked of the transcontinental railroad, now complete, and how it would change the world. Josiah had driven the first spike in Portland for the tracks between Portland and California the year before. The Fifteenth Amendment passed, giving Negro men the right to vote . . . but not yet women of any color. Jennie expressed her dismay at the delay. They discussed the day's schedule, Chen refilling coffee cups. They laughed at Van's antics as he raised his paws to jump onto Jennie's lap as he'd done to Elizabeth just short weeks before. She was as contented as she had ever been.

Caring for another required taking care of oneself first, and Jennie hadn't always done that. This time of sorting through Elizabeth's things had been a respite. Did Elizabeth know she'd need that time? She didn't think of their readying the house to be closed as "taking care" of Josiah though. Elizabeth might be surprised to see how well Josiah was doing, grieving her with strength and hopefulness but finding moments of joy. At least that was how Jennie saw him. They shared a kind of intimacy in letting go of Elizabeth, an intimacy Jennie began to wonder if Elizabeth had known would take on a new story in the months ahead, an intimacy Elizabeth nurtured before she left this earth.

Chapter 20
Tendrils of Change

Jennie finished putting sheets over the furniture in the upstairs bedroom that had been Samuel's. It was an early December morning in 1869 with the sun shining and a mist rising from the still-unfrozen fields. Josiah left to attend a construction meeting related to the orphanage. Only Josiah's bedroom and the one Jennie used downstairs remained to be gone through. The kitchen was Chen's domain, and it had been decided he'd go to Portland with Josiah when the work here was finished. Aware she had some time before Josiah returned and that it had been weeks since she'd seen Ariyah, Jennie bundled up against the cold, gave Van a pat, and headed out.

"I can't believe your birthday came and went and I did not have a package sent your way. I'm a perfect failure as a friend." Ariyah opened her door with wide arms of acceptance and an apology.

Jennie hadn't thought much about her twenty-sixth birthday passing on November 29. "Hello to you too."

Ariyah took Jennie's cape and muff while Jennie untied the bow at her throat and pulled the hat from her head. Her wool skirt swirled raindrops as she lifted the bustle and sat, grateful that Ariyah's chairs were wide as church pews but much softer.

"No apologies are needed. I'm equally at fault for not coming by, especially not being more faithful in checking on your pregnancy."

"It took us forever, I know. I think the strawberry tea you brought over last spring did it. Peleg listened to your description and he made the tea often after that. I thought I'd float away, or at least a baby would, I drank so much."

"Babies do live in water, you know."

"So I've heard. Here's something else." She patted the braids wrapped around the crown of her head. "My blonde, almost-white hair has darkened, don't you think?" It did appear so. "Why would that be?"

"I don't know. Maybe . . . the changes your body is going through keeping your baby happy."

"All is going well, though. I'm perfectly grateful."

"Will you move to your own place once you have your family started?" If Jennie were her, it would be hard to leave the luxuries, but at the same time living with others could stymie a relationship. She had experience with that.

"I don't think so. Peleg loves being here and my parents love him, and now with the baby coming, why change?"

"There'll be change enough with a child, that's certain."

"How much longer will you stay at the Parrish house?"

"Is there talk?"

"Oh no, at least not around me there isn't. I know it's perfectly innocent, your living there with him."

"I'm not *living with* Mr. Parrish. I'm simply helping him in a time of need, looking after the dog." *So people are gossiping.*

"That's what I tell people. And that his sons are grateful you've stayed to do the mournful work."

"So there's talk." She didn't want to stain the Parrish reputation in any way and especially not do anything that might diminish Elizabeth's legacy. "We're almost finished. Maybe I'll spur things up. I wouldn't want tongues chirping like the crickets."

"Let them. You're helping a friend. That's all that needs to be said."

But was it?

They looked at tiny baby items knitted by friends and Ariyah herself. Peleg's family had sent a lace cap and gown for the baptism one day. Ariyah pulled Jennie into her bedroom to

231

show off her own latest hat and gloves. "The millinery has wonderful new things shipped from back East and the Orient. With the railroad, I wonder if we'll get things from San Francisco sooner."

"We can travel between San Francisco and Council Bluffs, Iowa, faster than we can get from here to San Francisco by rail. It'll be a decade or more before they figure out how to take a track across the Siskiyou Mountains. No, we'll still have to wait for ships bringing what we long for from San Francisco."

"You must come with me sometime soon to that shop. The reticules are beaded with little cut glass, and there are velvet ones as soft as a lamb's nose."

"It would be fun to look," Jennie said.

Ariyah clapped her hands. "Let's go now, could we? I'll have the carriage brought around."

There wasn't anything holding her back. Josiah wouldn't return for several hours. "I won't be purchasing, but I could ogle, as my father would say."

" 'Ogle.' Is that German?"

Jennie nodded. "It means to stare and maybe desire, but nothing else."

"I like it. I'll ogle too, unless I see something I simply have to have. Then I'll tell Peleg to buy it for me." She grinned, then gathered up her cape and hat, tying the latter beneath her already doubling chin.

Jennie remembered how full her face got when she carried her children. Her dimples even disappeared.

Jennie had a pang of longing, then chided herself. It did no good to compare her failed marriage to the joyous one of Ariyah and Peleg, or even Elizabeth and Josiah's loving life together. Her chance for that had passed. She had been blessed with loving parents and siblings, a son, good employment, a future even as a divorced woman, and great friends. She would cling to that.

Millie's Millinery was housed in a brick building not far from Ferry Street, nestled near a hotel. Millie hoped to attract female guests traveling through. Carpenters' hammers pounded in the distance as they worked on a new opera house, and Jennie wondered if Charles might have found work there. If he had, maybe he could make a payment toward the debt. *But he won't, the swindler.* A sign in the window read "Shopkeeper Assistant Wanted, Temporary." The room smelled of lavender and the oak counters looked newly oiled. A fire in an iron stove sizzled in the background. Millie herself approached them as they entered. She had a cold sore at the side of her lip, and Jenny thought to suggest a paste of shooting star leaves, but sometimes helpful healing hints weren't welcomed.

Ariyah's cape camouflaged her pregnancy, but Millie noticed things and apparently wasn't afraid to comment on what she saw. "With child, are we?" Millie wore wax to cover what looked like the residual of the pox on her face.

"We are. Today I'm looking for scarves. Oh, look, Jennie, that perfect hat has a perfect mauve color. It's so divine, don't you think? And there's a yellow scarf that would bring out your green eyes." Both were lovely.

Jennie lifted the silk. Ariyah led her toward a mirror as the door opened, and in walked a woman wearing the duplicate of what Jennie had just wrapped round her neck and tucked in as a hint of yellow at her throat. In the mirror, she saw Millie stiffen at the sight of the woman.

"Someone else loves that scarf," Ariyah leaned in to whisper. "But I think it looks better on you."

"I'm just ogling, remember."

"I'm afraid we have nothing to suit your interests," Millie said to the newcomer, who Jennie peered at more carefully. *But hasn't the woman shopped here before? She owns the yellow scarf.*

"Oh. I was certain my . . . fiancé mentioned where he'd purchased this." She fingered the butter-yellow accessory. "I was looking for a matching reticule."

Jennie noticed a purse meeting that description with yellow sequins next to the display of scarves and started to point to it, but Millie stepped between her and the customer. As she did, Jennie recognized the girl—Miss Priscilla.

"We have nothing like that. I'm sure your *fiancé* is mistaken that he purchased anything here."

She mocked the word "fiancé," and for a moment Jennie wondered if Charles might be the purchasing man. A weight pressed against her breast.

"I think it best if you leave," Millie said.

Miss Priscilla's face blushed the color of a ripe tomato and one of her eyebrows twitched. In the bright light of the shop, compared to the darkness of the house she lived in, Miss Priscilla appeared much younger. A part of Jennie relished ogling this soiled dove who had left tracks over the now cold field of her marriage. She deserved disdain, didn't she?

It isn't Miss Priscilla's fault.

"I think this reticule would be a perfect match." Jennie walked around Millie and held up the beaded purse by its gold chain.

Miss Priscilla's eyes expanded in recognition, her mouth opened to an *O*. "Yes, that would be it," she said as she regained composure and accepted the purse.

Millie grabbed it. "It's not for sale."

Miss Priscilla stepped back as though slapped, and she had been, by words. Jennie knew how that felt.

"Will you sell it—to me?" Jennie said.

Millie straightened her shoulders, glaring as she turned. "Of course." She marched toward the counter, purse in hand.

Miss Priscilla edged toward the door.

"I hadn't planned to purchase," Jennie said, raising her voice, handing Millie coins. In fact, buying the purse put quite a hole in her budget. "But it's the perfect match to Miss Priscilla's scarf."

Miss Priscilla stopped, her back to them. Millie hesitated, looking from Jennie to Ariyah. Then she took the money and thrust the purse toward Jennie, unwrapped.

Jennie fast-walked to touch the shoulder of Miss Priscilla, who turned. "Merry Christmas. And may the spirit of the Christ child bless you today, all year long, and forever."

Tears welled in her brown eyes, the single feather in her small-brimmed hat bobbed. "Thank you." Her eyes met Jennie's, then she fingered the sequins. "Thank you very much."

"Well, I never," Millie huffed after Miss

Priscilla departed. "Do you know what kind of woman she is? She's of a class that shouldn't even be in a fine establishment like mine." Millie twisted her hands as though she washed them without water.

"But why not? Can't you use the sales?" Ariyah nodded to Jennie's question.

"Yes. But she's, well . . ." She leaned into the women. "She's a prostitute. I simply can't condone the behavior of women like her."

"You called her by name, Jennie." Ariyah sounded puzzled.

"Yet you sell to the fiancé, the men these women . . ." Jennie struggled for the right word.

"Who can tell what men do?" Millie brushed her hands as though waving away a fly. "I know of these women. I see the adulterers leaving their . . . house on my way to work. It's sinful, that's exactly right." She dropped her hands to her sides.

"Our Lord was not afraid to be seen with prostitutes," Jennie said. "He made one of them a missionary, sending her out to tell others about him. You could do that here. Who knows what lives you might change for the better." Her heart pounded. She should just keep quiet and leave. If Millie challenged her biblical views, she doubted she could respond.

"It's not in my nature." Millie nodded toward

the scarf Jennie still had loosely wrapped around her neck. "Are you purchasing that?"

Jennie removed it, folded it, and placed it back on the shelf as two other women entered. Millie waved a happy hello to them, then turned back to Jennie and her friend.

"You have good taste." She nodded to Ariyah. "Perhaps a bonnet with a havelock in back might interest you. *Godey's Lady's Book* featured it just last month."

Millie nodded as a mother and daughter entered and the shopkeeper lowered her voice as she returned. "You see my dilemma. I have a reputation as a churchgoing woman to protect. I can't have fallen women here, influencing children." She straightened her shoulders. "Or divorced women either, though those sinners too are difficult to identify."

"Divorce isn't contagious, nor is prostitution," Jennie said. "And for your information—"

"This is the perfect time to leave," Ariyah said and hustled Jennie toward the door.

"You have not been telling me everything going on in your life, my friend." The sky looked like wet hat-felt, dark and gray, though it couldn't be more than three o'clock in the afternoon and the day had begun with the hopeful rays of sun. A duck waddled down the cobbled street, moving out of the way as Ariyah's carriage approached.

238

"Are you consorting with prostitutes?" She said it in jest. When Jennie didn't speak, she added, "I liked what you said, about a biblical woman of negotiable affections being a missionary. And what's contagious or not."

"I'm not sure when I became an evangelist." Jennie lowered her eyes.

"Oh, you've always been that, by your desire to take care of other people, defend them." Her words warmed. They stepped into the closed carriage. "But you need to tell me all of it."

Jennie sighed. Perhaps this was the time. "After Charles left us, I went to see Priscilla. The room was dark and I didn't realize how very young she is. She sounded so confident, but seeing her in the store today, I saw a frightened young woman who might find her way out if someone opened the right door."

Their carriage rolled over a rock. Ariyah jumped as though poked. "I'm jittery these days. I'm not getting a lot of sleep. A very active baby." White gloves made circles on her belly.

"I'll bring you some skullcap tincture. It's a mild sedative. It might help you sleep better."

"Always looking for ways to help, aren't you."

"I guess I am."

"I so hope you can find another nurse position after Mr. Parrish moves to Portland. It's in your blood."

"I'd better find something soon." Jenny thought

she might take a bit of that skullcap herself. She wasn't sure how she'd make up the money she'd spent on a purse for a woman tangled in the dissolution of her marriage.

Jennie returned to her duties scrubbing the linoleum, a new oilcloth product Josiah had ordered in last year. It was really the last of the work to be done before the final closing up. They'd be finished before Christmas. Josiah had already secured a home in Portland, and with Jennie's parents moving to Salem right after Epiphany, she'd have a place to stay until she secured a new position.

"Next Tuesday I'll have additional duties," she told Josiah. "I trust that's acceptable. I'll work on winnowing until then. But we're mostly finished. I'll—I'll miss our time together. Thank you for allowing me to be a part of your family these past months. I can continue to make my payments to you through Bush's new bank if that's acceptable."

"Where?"

"The Ladd and Bush bank, on State Street."

"No, where are your duties starting next Tuesday?"

"Oh—I've taken another position. I can meet my obligations, including my debt to you."

"I see." He stood, sat down again, then stood and walked to the window. "I'm sorry to hear that." His hands were clasped behind his lean back, marking the dividing line between his white blouse and the britches he'd tucked into black boots. His hair curled just above his collar.

His reaction surprised her. He seemed disappointed. Jennie wished she understood subtleties better. Perhaps he thought she wouldn't need to work to support Douglas? "You'll be in Portland. The work here really is complete. The house is closed except for the rooms we use daily. We only have a few boxes remaining of Elizabeth's things I found in the attic to sort through."

"Yes, I see that." He'd sat back down and now drummed his fingers on the table where he'd been drinking the coffee Chen prepared for him. He stroked his beard the color of new snow over soil. "I could pay you more, Jennie, so you wouldn't have to assume additional duties elsewhere."

"It's a temporary position. And I do need to leave once you're gone."

"Will you nurse somewhere else?"

She shook her head. "That would be too soon after Elizabeth, whom I so loved caring for. No, Millie's Millinery needed someone through the season." She thought of Millie herself, tied up in her prejudices, and wondered at what point she would tell her that she was divorced.

"A millinery. Perhaps you can help me choose

gifts for my daughters-in-law. For Christmas."

"I'd be pleased to." Relief flooded over her.

They worked in silence for a time.

"Probably have Christmas in Portland," he said.

"I thought as much. Maybe Chen should precede you."

"Yes. He'll need to prepare the kitchen. I'll hire a housekeeper."

"I'll finish at the end of the week then, when Chen leaves."

"That would be best."

She had known this was coming, had prepared for it. Yet it felt as though she faced another loss. But she was gaining! She'd join her son's life, adapt to her parents' patterns. There'd be a new house they'd all be adjusting to, so perhaps the timing was perfect. And yet . . . she'd found healing here, first as a nurse and then with the privilege to walk beside another, bringing comfort. Hadn't her father once said that the Greek word for *comfort* was translated as "to come along beside"? She had kept a promise to Elizabeth to come along beside Josiah. She'd done her duty. She'd been vulnerable with this man, and he had never wavered in his kindness. She'd miss that. It hadn't been an obligation. She'd miss him.

The two had often shared a room in silence at day's end. Him reading, Jennie knitting, their solitude interrupted by single sentences as though the other had been privy to intimate thoughts. Jennie had seen that happen with her parents now and then, and as a child had always been confused at the words they exchanged that came from nowhere, rarely saying, "What are you talking about?" Somehow they got in step. That had never happened with her and Charles. She would miss that ease that came with Josiah. The thought startled her. She had compared quiet times with Josiah to her parents' loving interactions.

She shook her head, finished the scrubbing, then removed the wrapping around her head. In the parlor now, she pawed through one of Elizabeth's button jars, wanting to make sets for each of Josiah's daughters-in-law's baskets. She marveled at the variety, the smooth ivory, the nubby deer horn, tiny shells. She looked up to find Josiah staring at her. "Is there something you need?"

"No." Then, "Yes." He cleared his voice. "I need to tell you that I will miss you, Jennie Pickett." He spoke it like water warming over her. She swallowed.

"I'll miss you too, Josiah Parrish." She softened her voice, conscious that she needed to. "And Van. I'll miss him too. You mustn't forget to feed him twice a day."

"He'll adopt Chen, I suspect. The rewards are better in the kitchen."

He hesitated, opened his mouth to speak, then didn't. She was grateful. Her own feelings of loss were as mixed up as the dog's food. Her hands shook, her heart beat faster, and the buttons slipped from her fingers. She felt Josiah stand before her. She looked up at him. *He stands so close.* Her world was awash with confusion.

Chapter 21

When Air Becomes Breath

Life changes in a breath, the air distilled to purity, meant for one, then two, alone. Jennie remembered a verse from Ecclesiastes of two being better than one, for if one falters, the other can pick them up. The words pushed through memory as Josiah removed the button jar from her fingers, took her hands in his, and pulled her to stand before him. She had no breath at all.

"Jennie."

She knew what he was going to say before he said it. "It's too soon. It's not—we're not—I'm not . . ."

"Yes. We are."

He kissed her then and all the breath of a thousand angels seemed to swirl about them, their wings fluttering her heart. A wash of bubbling water moved through her. She felt the softness of his lips, then a pressure before release, and he pulled her into his chest, his chin now on her head. She wrapped her arms around his chest, held ribs and spine and sinew. She eased into the comfort of him like an infant settles into her protector. Safe. Secure. Loved.

"What should we do?" she whispered.

"Marry, of course."

She wanted to ask him if he wasn't still mourning Elizabeth and misplaced his deep affection for her as that of love. She wanted to ask if he saw her as that daughter he'd regretted they never had—but his next kiss and its intensity silenced questions. She wanted to ask him if he loved her, but then didn't need to.

"I love you, Jennie. I didn't know it until this moment when I realized I would no longer have you in my life. The ache of it was nearly as deep and profound as losing Elizabeth."

"Perhaps it's that I've been a bridge for you. And you're afraid to cross it without familiar faces. But you'll do well without me. You know you will."

"I don't doubt I would. But I don't want to. I never thought I'd feel this way again." He held her at arm's length. He shook his head in wonder. "You will never find anyone who loves you as much as I do at this moment and will forever. But the question is, how do you feel? About marrying a man some years your senior?"

His age was nothing in her mind. Perhaps it should have been, but she'd had young love, and though she had turned only twenty-six in November, she'd lived a lifetime. Young love had brought her Douglas, yes, but more hard times, betrayal, loss, and pain. She couldn't imagine Josiah cloaking her with such robes. And she had never truly been aware before of the feelings that filled her now. Never.

"I wouldn't be marrying a man 'some years my senior.' I'd be marrying a good man."

He laughed then, a deep, relaxing laugh. "So will you?"

"Yes." He kissed her again as Van barked and jumped at their feet. When he released her, she said, "It's come late, but I love you too, Josiah Parrish. I didn't know it until now."

She heard Chen calling for the dog, charging down the hall. He stopped when he saw them embraced. "Misser Parrish, Miss Jennie, I sorry." He bowed his head, started to back away. Jennie stepped to Josiah's side, picked Van up, and held him close.

"No need, Chen," Josiah said. "You'll be the first to know. I've just asked Mrs. Pickett to be my wife."

"Miss Elizabeth, she tell me look." He pointed to his eyes. "Plan wedding Miss Jennie. Mr. Parrish, she tell me. Bake cake now?"

Elizabeth thought this would happen? "In a while." Jennie laughed, then sobered. What were the implications of them being in this house together now and how would his children feel about them? And Douglas.

Over tea that Chen brought in, they planned.

"You still must go to Portland and I'll stay here in Salem, at Ariyah's, then at my parents' when they move. We must give ourselves time, a few months, to see if this is really what we both want."

"A few months?" He rolled his lower lip out like Douglas did when he pouted.

"Yes." Jennie smiled. Now that both their eyes were clearly set upon each other, everything made her smile. "We'll set a date but wait until after Epiphany to tell people. Maybe marry in June. There'll be roses blooming. It gives us time to discuss it with your children." Charles Winn was only a year older than she was. He might not take this well.

"Nothing to discuss. It will be so."

"But you have to give them pause. They've just lost their mother."

"Who apparently saw this coming."

"They might think something untoward occurred while she was still alive. Or that you're marrying out of grief. Or that . . ." She didn't want to say it out loud, but she knew others would. She inhaled. "They might say that with the loan, I am digging gold in the Parrish household instead of in the mines of Canyon City." It was a mantle worn by divorced women.

"I'll speak to my sons. They know when I make up my mind I'm not easily dissuaded. As for the

248

latter, no. That won't be so. No mining needed to repay a nonexistent debt."

"But Charles Winn was only comfortable with my continuing to work here because he knew I was paying off that loan. He'll think, or he could, that I'm marrying for the financial benefits." She stopped. "There's no more debt?"

"Elizabeth canceled the repayment in her will. She didn't want anything to anchor you to something your former husband began."

"I felt responsible."

"She knew that. Which is why she wanted the loan nullified, not reduced. Debt paid. And my son knows that too, being the executor, but it made him feel better not telling you until after I moved to Portland. He does have a little problem with how things might 'look.' I agreed because I wanted very much for you to stay. I actually asked him to delay, so that you would. I really did think it was to help winnow Elizabeth's things, but I realize now my affection for you ran much deeper. I just didn't see it."

They'd been winnowing more than memories. The generosity of the Parrishes was beyond any Jennie could have imagined.

"We would have forgiven what was left after seven years anyway. It's an Old Testament practice that I see as still having merit. I've always found greater abundance arrives to well cover the lost payments and interest from what one forgives." He took her hands in his. "My sons will come to understand."

Charles came to her mind. She must move forward on that act of forgiveness because harboring resentment took up room in her heart, stole breath from the air of her existence, breath that she wanted now to mingle with Josiah's love. She would tell Charles of the debt forgiveness too, if she saw him again. Perhaps it would relieve him of some suffering, when he sobered and might see himself as worthy, move away from weariness and distance. And what better way to begin another life than relieving the suffering of another, including her own. She took in the sight of this good man before her, and thanked God for keeping her eyes closed when needed and dropping the scales from them now.

Josiah argued against her taking the position at Millie's. "There's no need." The two walked in the Salem dusk, accompanied by the winter mist, her arm through his elbow. She found she could express herself better facing outward rather than looking into his eyes.

"I want to know that I can meet a commitment I've made. And this gives us time to be certain."

"I am certain."

Jennie was as well, but it was happening so quickly. She had made one poor choice in a marriage and didn't want to get swirled like a taffeta skirt into another poor one. "Your children need time to adapt to this. I want them to know I am able to support myself and my son. And paying off my Parrish debt. At least until the executor tells me the debt is freed."

"Oh, he will." Josiah scuffed his boots on the boardwalk, knocking off light snow. "Why not find a position as a nurse, then. Or work for a doctor. To pursue your medical interests."

"You remembered." She stopped and looked at him, elbows entwined, her hands warm inside the muff. They would join Ariyah and Peleg that evening, breaths visible in the night air. Their friends would be the first to hear the news, though they'd be bound in secret until after Christmas, until after Josiah spoke to his sons and their wives; Jennie to her parents and to Douglas.

"Of course I remember. You're a natural healer. You should work, if you insist on proving your independence to my children. But why not do what appeals to you."

"Studying with a doctor, yes, that would be welcomed." She looked into his eyes, found herself lost in the depth of them, in the silver beard he trimmed, rounding it like a clamshell.

"It's not necessary for you to pursue anything."

251

"It is for me." She told him then about the encounter with Miss Priscilla and Millie's reactions. "I thought I might do some good when an undesirable, as Millie calls them, comes in. If they do. And besides, I'll get a discount for my own Christmas purchases." She poked him with her elbow.

"It's temporary?"

She nodded.

"I should stay in Salem then. Why go to Portland at all?"

"Because your children expect it and because we need that time. I do." He was quiet but she felt him tense beside her as they began to walk again. Jennie tried to catch a snowflake with her tongue. Into the silence she said, "I'm not questioning . . . us."

"You knew what I was thinking."

"I want time to prepare Douglas. It will be difficult for him to suddenly have a mother and a father again. I thought if I could ease him back in with me and then introduce you in your new role, it'll be better." She'd seen Douglas with Josiah and she'd seen Josiah's parenting in the goodness of his children. He'd be a good father to Douglas, but it was another adjustment for her son. For them all.

"Will we have children, Jennie?"

Could Douglas adjust to a brother or sister? Her son had awaited Ariyah and was saddened and

252

confused when the baby did not stay in his world. And Jennie had lost a child. Did she wish to face that possibility again? Her stomach tightened with Josiah's question, but she didn't know if from joy or trepidation. She just knew she didn't want to answer it now.

Chapter 22
Weaving New Fabric

Jennie started to tell Ariyah and Peleg that she and Josiah planned to marry in the new decade, but Ariyah stopped her. "We both wondered how long it might be."

"How did you even think that? We didn't know ourselves until earlier today."

"The way you spoke about him. And Peleg ran into Josiah a few days ago, and all you could talk about was how helpful Jennie was being." She shook her finger at Josiah. He started to speak, but she interrupted him. "Perhaps you didn't know. Men are blind, aren't they, Peleg?"

Her husband shook his head and smiled. "Blind. *Sí*. And deaf, as you tell me. But we pay attention." He said the last word like a good Spaniard, *atención*. "I could interest you in a cigar, to cel-e-brate?" Josiah declined and Ariyah took over the conversation again, speaking now of children, of her wanting Jennie to come stay with them when her time got closer. "The *bebé* is to arrive in *abril*," Peleg told them. "After, we will move to new *casa*. I have convinced her."

Ariyah blushed. "He wants our own household, but I like my parents close."

"Your parents, they can visit us any time. You like the house I pick for us, *sí*?" She nodded and he bent to kiss her forehead, brushed the blonde braids with his lips before turning back to Jennie and Josiah wishing them "mucho happiness and many *niños*."

The talk turned to politics and whether Oregon would ratify the Fifteenth Amendment. Oregon citizens had failed to ratify the Fourteenth, giving Negroes citizenship. Oregon had not been kind to people of color. Jennie wondered about Peleg, with his darker Spanish complexion, but it wasn't something to discuss even with friends. Josiah supported ratification, as did Jennie's father. Both even said women ought to vote, but Jennie suspected that was decades away. She might not live to see it.

It was a companionable evening and Jennie realized how pleasurable the interactions were between men and women speaking together where there was no fear of someone overimbibing in liquor or the worry over how to make amends for unintended hurts. She would like being part of this kind of couple.

On the return walk home, snowflakes danced on her fingertip cape, melted on Josiah's hat brim. "Let's do speak of children now," Jennie said.

"Good." Josiah squeezed her arm linked in his. With the other hand he carried a lantern, and the light reflected off her taffeta skirt. A night owl hooted.

"Would you really want another family? I mean—"

"At my age?"

"No, given that you have a family already, and so do I. There are orphans we could help if we wish to hear the sounds of gurgling or manage wet napkins."

"I'll do what you would like. But as for me, I would love to have children with you, hold them in my arms, watch them grow up, with you." He swung the lantern, spreading a sparkle of light against the boardwalk and a shrub of mountain holly, as Lewis and Clark called it. Waxy green, purple berries, it usually grew beside creeks or in the mountains. Someone had transplanted it perhaps for the yellow dye that came from its bark. She wondered how it would fare come spring. Transplants didn't always take.

"It was the very best part of marriage for me, raising a family," Josiah continued.

Jennie thought about the death of his firstborn; of her own loss. With great love of wanting a child came the risk of losing. But that would be so loving an orphan too. Blending a family, like a transplant, didn't always work either and they'd be doing that if they took in an orphan or tried for their own. She did long for another child, had left that wish behind—like so many others—until now.

"And there is that possibility of a girl."

"Let's see what happens," Jennie said. "Let nature take its course. After you've spoken to your children and after I've had time to prepare Douglas for his newest family member, you. Then we'll decide if it's worth the risk."

"Every step forward is."

Jennie nodded. "My father once told me, a carriage is safest in the livery stable, but a carriage isn't built for that sedentary place. It's built to roll upon the roads to unknown places."

"And on to unknown trails, making new ones."

Jennie planned to work at the millinery through Epiphany, staying with Ariyah and Peleg until her parents moved to Salem. Miss Priscilla never came by again and Millie never raised the issue, apparently happy with Jennie's ability to match her clients' interests to accessories in her shop. Jennie was glad for both the money and the work to keep her mind from missing Josiah. Now that she'd opened up this place inside her heart, she worried something might happen to him before they wed. Would he eat well without her there? Yes, Chen would see to that. Josiah was older than Jennie; sixty-three if she calculated correctly. Was he as healthy as he looked, as he acted? Then she'd chastise herself: she wasn't his caretaker. She was his fiancée. She pondered about separating those roles out but let herself live with the uncertainty. They had each other to talk things through when they met together again. She wasn't alone.

Being among Millie's embroidered handker- chiefs with their delicate flowers, the Irish linens, the Belgium lace, were all lovely distractions. New Year's came and went and they did not see each other. She'd forgotten that she could long for someone so much; she was embarrassed that she did. She was a schoolgirl who sent perfumed letters to him to arrive on his birthday, January 14, singing in the rain beneath her umbrella as she walked to the post.

She stayed on longer with Ariyah, her parents delaying their move to a month with "less rain, more sunshine breaks." Their new home had an orchard and a field that needed stumps burned out where her father could work out his frustrations from his legislative time. A large porch with a railing surrounded the board house on three sides. Four large bedrooms, big enough for a family to reside in, marked the second floor on either side of a stairwell. "We'll let Douglas choose which bedroom will be yours," her mother said when the appointed time arrived.

Douglas chose a room that looked out over the orchard. They viewed the apple trees through one of the long windows on either side of the fireplace that harbored a crackling fire.

"This is a good choice."

"I like it, Mother," Douglas said. He sounded so formal. Then, "Did you bring me a candy?"

"I did." She gave him a paper cone he unwrapped and popped the mint into his mouth. Jennie decided to broach the subject of her heart. "Soon I won't be bringing you a candy every time I see you because I'll be seeing you every day. Come, sit beside me." She patted the bed, wondering for the one hundredth time how to tell him. She hadn't yet told her parents, but somehow it seemed best to let Douglas know first of all. "I have news for you. In a little while, we will live in a different house, in Salem, the capital city, where Grandpa does his work in the legislature so you'll still see him from time to time."

"We lived there before."

"We did!" She was surprised he remembered Salem.

"When Papa was with us. Will he be there?"

"In Salem? Maybe, but not in our house."

"Why not?" Douglas was six years old already and full of questions. He lifted those big green eyes to hers.

"Your father decided we would be better off without him living with us. You remember he sometimes consumed alcohol too much?"

259

Douglas nodded. She could smell the peppermint from his candy on his breath. A tiny piece of white had flaked onto his lip. She reached to wipe it with her finger, but he moved his head back so she couldn't. Her finger kissed the air.

"I remember."

"Yes. And when he did that, drank too much, he didn't always make good decisions. He did things he later regretted." *Is that a lie, about his regrets?* "But someone else will be living in that house with us. Do you remember Mr. Parrish?"

Douglas frowned.

"He calls you Mr. Pickett and shakes your hand. It's where I've worked."

"He has a white beard like St. Nicholas?"

"I suppose it is a bit like that. But his hair is dark brown." *Why did I say that?*

"Why will he live in our house?"

"Because he will be my husband and your stepfather."

Douglas pooched his lower lip out. "God won't like it."

"Why would you say that?"

"God likes me living with Paw-Paw."

"Mr. Parrish is a good man, a pastor, like Grandpa."

"He's Paw-Paw's friend?"

"Yes. And mine. And in a few months, he will be my husband and you will get to know him better. He has three sons."

"Do they bob for apples?"

"I'm sure they did once." She hugged him and he allowed it. "They're older now, as you'll be one day. For now, it will be the three of us."

"Will you have a baby?"

"Really, Douglas, you ask so many questions! Let's wait until you meet Mr. Parrish again. I think you'll like him as a stepfather."

"I like Paw-Paw and Grandma."

"Let's go tell them the good news, shall we?"

He shook his head. "I want to stay here."

And then she made the mistake she'd repeat until she saw what it could do; but by then it would be too late. "I'll give you another candy if you come downstairs with me now."

"All right."

And so their world began to change.

Her parents took the news in silence, then, "Josiah is . . . older," her mother said.

"I know. And capable and vibrant and active. He chops wood, tends to the sheep, even holds the rams during shearing."

"I don't doubt his constitution," her mother said. "But you'll end up taking care of him in a few years, a very few years likely. Or widowed. What is he?"

"Sixty-four. Just. In January."

"Was this going on while—?" Her father cleared his throat.

"No, nothing like that. It was in the winnowing, my helping close up the house, write down the stories of his life with Elizabeth, that he realized. And I realized it too. We immediately made steps for me to go to Ariyah's and for him to go to Portland, to give us time."

"It's not settled then." Her mother sounded relieved. She started stirring the soup she'd put on to cook. The onion scent breathed "homey." Jennie looked forward to cooking for Douglas and for Josiah. *Will Chen remain as cook?*

"It's settled. We'll marry in June."

"Why rush? You can stay here for as long as you like. Let the romance take its course." Her father motioned Douglas to come sit beside him. He smelled the peppermint. "Oh, candy before supper? What did I tell you about that?"

"The sugar monsters will eat my teeth." He giggled. "Mommy gave it to me. Two of them." Her father frowned at her. She'd broken a rule.

"You've been so preoccupied with caring for Elizabeth, cooped up in that big house, and haven't gotten out and about to meet other young people." Her mother spoke, hoping to dissuade.

"If I were seventeen as I was when I married Charles, and he was fifty-four, would you be as worried about age?"

"You have so much life ahead of you," her father said. "I hate to see you—"

"I want to spend that life with him. We're both adults, we understand the risks."

"I suppose that's true enough. What do you say, Douglas?" He patted Douglas's head.

"I'll stay here with you."

"We'll have it that way for a while, indeed. A June marriage you say?"

Jennie nodded, weighing mixed emotions of Douglas's answer.

"That gives us time to get used to the idea. Lord knows I admire the man, have great respect for him. And you, of course. But I never imagined our family would be intertwined with his."

"Neither did I."

"I don't want to move again," Douglas said. "I like my room. I like my grandpa. I like *my* daddy."

Her father patted his shoulder.

She hadn't realized how difficult weaving Douglas and Josiah into a new fabric was going to be.

Chapter 23
For Better or For Worse

Josiah's looping yet precise penmanship put Jennie's to shame. At least he knew of her difficulties with reading and writing, but she still thought of asking Ariyah to script her short missives. Once she moved in to assist with the baby, she'd ask her. But for now she persisted in her own writing of her love of music, reading with delight his expression of the same. In one letter, she asked the all-important question: how had his children taken the news?

They like you, Jennie, he wrote. *Charles was grateful we made other living arrangements as soon as we knew of our changed affections. But I do not want to wait until June. How have your parents responded? Should I speak with your father? Could we move the date up?*

They corresponded about where to marry, who could officiate, if they'd take a "honeymoon," as some called that time away after nuptials, and if Douglas would go with them. Always the worry had Douglas's name in it.

She was visiting Ariyah one February day when a knock came at the door. Jennie expected the delivery of groceries Ariyah had ordered for the week. Instead, there stood Josiah. She thought her heart would burst through the sheath that kept it in her breast.

"I've missed you, Jennie."

"And I you."

He picked her up, kissed her, then swirled her around before setting her down light as a hawk's feather drifting to the floor. Doubt of whether this love and marriage was right or warranted disappeared.

"I'm opening up the Salem house. I'm here to spend time with you and Douglas and make this happen come June."

Van barked from the carriage and he was freed to join the reunion.

Josiah's entry into Douglas's life brought new chords to the music of her days. Her parents worked to see Josiah as a potential son-in-law and not only a revered pastor they had known for years. Douglas kept his distance, but he didn't kick or scream when the three of them took a picnic to a stream, nor did he ask Josiah for presents or candy as he did with Jennie.

One day, they had him pick out his room at Josiah's house. He chose the bedroom across from the indoor bathroom. He had a dozen questions about the various washing tubs: the foot bath, the hip bath, plunge bath, the sink and shower bath Josiah told him was called a douche bath too.

"Will I have to take a bath in every one every day?"

"It depends on how dirty you get," Jennie said and was pleased to see him smile.

Douglas and Josiah worked in the barns together, Van hopping up on Douglas's legs until he picked him up and carried him around. She wondered if he still thought of Quilton, but she didn't ask, grateful he'd found a friend.

"It is time." Peleg knocked on Jennie's guest-room door in early April. "The *bebé*, she comes."

Jennie had moved in with Ariyah and Peleg as her time grew near. She rose and met Ariyah's mother in the hallway. "It'll be fine." She patted her arm. "Let's boil the water. Peleg, you'll go for the doctor?"

"Yes, *sí, rápidamente*!" He rushed to the door, returned, grabbed his coat, left, came back for his walking cane, turned about once, came back to Ariyah's side.

"Go!" she ordered. "Take the carriage." He was out the door.

Their maid had already started the water. Earlier, Jennie had prepared soft bandages that were folded and stacked for later use. She was ready.

"It's perfect. Everything is perfect." Ariyah

repeated those words when Peleg brought the doctor back and then again when Peleg insisted he remain despite the doctor's telling him he should leave.

Peleg paced, stopped to hold his wife's hand, grimaced when she cried out with the contractions. The joy when a perfect boy arrived eased the worry from Peleg's face the way a rainstorm drives away insipid heat. Jennie thought then that fathers ought to be allowed to be present when their children were born, if they were capable of seeing their wives in pain while being powerless to stop it.

The happy couple beamed as grandparents fluttered about and the doctor washed his hands and then Jennie walked him to the door.

"I will take you back, Doctor." Peleg stood from his chair beside the bed where Jennie had placed Alexandro into his arms. "It will be difficult to leave." He gazed at his son. "He has long fingers. He will play the piano, Ari."

"Just send the carriage," Ariyah ordered.

"No, no. I must see to this man who brought my son into the world." He handed the baby to his mother-in-law. "Let me get my coat."

The doctor nodded his thanks and told Jennie, "You are a good nurse, anticipating my needs, bringing comfort. Well done, Miss—?"

"Mrs. Pickett," she said. "But soon to be Mrs. Parrish."

"Ah, the widowed marrying the widower." She didn't correct him. "The drink you gave her, when the pains were extreme, what was that again?"

"From beans, Coffea. Her husband had them and said they could be made into a brew like coffee. Real coffee, not that grain potion we drink here."

He chuckled.

"Ariyah drank it often when her ankles swelled and I thought it might assist with pain. And so it did."

"Inventive."

Peleg returned, coat over his arm. He waved to Ariyah, who waved back. "You are perfect, my sweet Ariyah," he said and without embarrassment blew her a kiss. They heard the carriage leave.

Ariyah put her baby to her breast, though her milk had not yet come in. The child's eyes were open and alert, taking in this new world to which he'd been so recently introduced. Jennie watched the grandparents both hold the child. Jennie's thoughts turned to a wish that she might nuzzle another infant in her arms, her child, and if God willed it, that it might be a girl.

She brought out a new nightdress for Ariyah, bathed her first.

"This is the most wonderful day of my life," she said. "After getting married. Maybe even more. Yes, more perfect than that." At last she fell asleep, her baby on her breast where he'd suckled. Jennie stroked Alexandro's dark hair. He had his mother's ivory skin. His life had such promise with two parents who loved him so dearly and doting grandparents who had looked on in awe.

Ariyah's clock struck the quarter hour. Peleg was taking a long time, and Jennie wished now he had simply sent the driver to take the doctor home. Like Ariyah, Jennie dozed and awoke with a start to the front door opening. Sunrise spilled across the room as cool air came in, followed by the doctor and then by sorrow.

Jennie sent word immediately to Josiah, who kept his arm around her narrow shoulders as she told him of Peleg's death. "The doctor had been dropped off, and before Peleg could step back into the carriage, he said he was 'dizzy' and then collapsed. 'Dead before he hit the ground,' the doctor said. He was so young! And a doctor right there beside him within seconds but nothing he could do. Nothing. He told them Peleg likely felt 'no pain.' Oh, Josiah. Life is so short, death an untimely visitor no matter when it comes."

He swept Jennie into his arms and held her while she cried. She had not done so yet, being strong for Ariyah, who sat dazed, the loss so very great at any time but especially for one so young.

"Alexandro will never know his father now. It's so . . . unfair," Jennie said.

"Unfair indeed. Life is. But we trust, Jennie, that Peleg has entered into peace away from this calamitous world."

"I think he would have liked to live with calamity for a while longer," Jennie said. He squeezed her shoulder. She dabbed at her eyes.

"How is Ariyah?"

"Terrible. She has to be strong for her boy and her parents, but she's still in shock. I'm so glad they didn't move to their new home before this, so glad. Timing is everything."

He nodded.

"Which is why once the funeral is over—she wants you to say the words over Peleg—I think we should marry. I want a life with you. And children with you. And truly, I might die tomorrow or you might. We ought to live as fully as we can today."

With Ariyah's blessing, they set their wedding date for April 14, 1870, a week after Peleg's interment. Only later did they realize it was the fifth anniversary of the day President Lincoln was shot. But perhaps that was a perfect day to commemorate, not with mourning, but with new beginnings. DW, Jennie's brother, was on the Republican ticket for prosecuting attorney and the election was the next day, so they didn't expect him to attend. But as Josiah said, they would proceed. Ariyah being still in mourning, planned not to hear the vows.

"Peleg and I—we had a great love for a short time. Don't risk it, waiting, Jennie. Marry now."

Ariyah ordered a dress be made for Jennie, who protested, but Ariyah said it gave her pleasure, something to think about besides the large, empty hole inside her heart.

The dressmaker burned the midnight oil making the taffeta gown. The skirt was a half bell, moving the fullness to the back into the bustle. Smooth and flatter in the front, the beige material flowed over Jennie's narrow hips and emphasized her smallish waist. She made a separate jacket of the same material and wound green embroidered roses at the cuffs, up the arms, and down the V-shaped neckline. It looked like ivy and, as Ariyah knew it would, drew out the color of Jennie's eyes. Her generosity in such a time of sorrow astonished.

"I've found, my friend"—she told Jennie while she twirled in the dress—"that giving to others helps relieve a grief."

Jennie hugged her and the friends cried together yet again.

"Oh, I'll stain your dress," Ariyah said, stepping away.

"No. Those are angel tears."

Jennie had so looked forward to the four of

them with their children growing old together, and truth be told, she imagined Ariyah would be helping Jennie mourn the loss of her older husband long before Jennie was called upon to comfort her. But this was the way of life. Jennie was coming to see that. On that carriage road, there were hills and valleys, sunshine and rain, and the best one could hope for was to share the trail with someone you loved—and pass on the lessons learned along the way.

They married at the large home of JC Thompson in Marion County, formerly of the 12th Regiment, Illinois Cavalry. He also served as witness. His brother, HY Thompson (she never did know what the initials stood for), Salem's esteemed schoolteacher and lawyer and Josiah's friend, was the other witness. Charles Stratton officiated, a Methodist minister and graduate of Willamette University. The Strattons came down from Portland where he pastored and worked on building the Taylor Street Methodist Church. His wife, Julia, looked on with a smiling face, as did Lucinda, Joseph, Jennie's brothers William and DW (Fergus was busy in the Idaho mines, and George, traveling), their wives and parents.

Her father seemed relieved when told that Reverend Stratton would do the official duties, but they attended. Lucinda helped Jennie dress and clasped the jade cross around her neck that

Josiah had given her as a wedding gift. Lucinda looked tired, lines like a half-bell skirt marked either side of her pursed lips, but Jennie didn't comment, instead promising herself that she'd call on her soon after the wedding.

"Charles lives in Forest Grove now." Lucinda spoke, removing pins from her mouth, putting the final touches on the fitting.

"Is he . . ."

"Sober?" She shook her head no, adding, "But Joseph says if that town founded by dozens of missionaries and preachers can't cure him, nothing will."

Jennie allowed herself to feel hopeful that he would go on to have a good life in Forest Grove, no longer begrudging him that he might build it on shared sorrow. Jennie was leaving sadness behind this day, or so she thought.

Before she left the upstairs bedroom where she'd dressed, Jennie gave Nellie and Mary, her nieces, flowers from her bouquet to press. As they descended the steps, Douglas saw they each had a stem and he grabbed at Nellie's.

"Douglas. Here." She handed him his own tulip. "I can help you press it later."

But he trotted off to stand beside his grandmother and gave it to her. She held his hand. A twinge of envy but also of shame passed through Jennie. She ought to have thought of giving her mother a flower. Lucinda too.

Josiah's children attended, and a few of her parents' friends. She supposed there were thoughts expressed beyond her hearing about them—the age difference, the speed with which Josiah was remarrying after Elizabeth's death. But Jennie understood: Elizabeth loved Josiah dearly and she knew that his life was fullest when he loved someone back. She felt so blessed to be that someone.

They spoke the vows, this time before a pastor rather than a judge, and Jennie blinked back tears with the traditional words. "Jane Lichtenthaler, wilt thou have this man to be thy wedded husband, to live together after God's ordinance in the holy estate of matrimony? Wilt thou love him in sickness and in health, and forsaking all others keep thee only unto him so long as ye both shall live?"

"I will."

Josiah's baritone voice rang out strong as he repeated the vows, and people laughed at his enthusiasm when he announced, "I most certainly will!"

He kissed her on each cheek, and then before they could turn around to face the happy faces of their families, Josiah's best man—his son Norman—placed a Hudson's Bay blanket with its red, yellow, and black stripes around the couple in the tradition of the Paiute people. "This is our part"—he swung his hand to include the congregation—"in keeping newlyweds wrapped together."

People applauded as the couple swung toward them, the blanket around their shoulders. Douglas ran over then and nestled into the blanket between them, facing the gathered guests. Everyone laughed and Josiah whispered to him, "Welcome, Mr. Pickett. Glad to see you're with us."

Chapter 24
Ocean Discoveries

Small fluffy clouds like distant sheep bounced across a blue sky, while robins pulled at earthworms on the edges of the Thompson garden. The happy couple spoke their vows under a canopy of vines. The trio of Josiah, Jennie, and Douglas (accompanied by Van) left the following day for their honeymoon to the Oregon coastal town of Astoria where Josiah had once served as missionary to the Clatsop and Chinook.

They traveled up the Willamette by ship. Josiah had many friends in the Clatsop region, and the Indians came out to greet them at the old fort when they visited there one day. Lewis and Clark had wintered at that site. How the Indians knew of their arrival was a mystery to Jennie, but there were gifts of cedar baskets and dried salmon and a necklace of shells for both Douglas and Jennie. Josiah spoke to them in their languages as Jennie watched, their round faces attentive. One man looked at her and grinned, then spoke words that made Josiah's cheeks turn red. *Men talk.*

Clatsop women had carried the gifts, and now they fingered the ribbon on Jennie's hat, pointed at the light blue linen skirt, the belt that lined her narrow waist, giggling as Jennie turned to let them see her bustle. They wore calico dresses and were rounder people than Jennie. A soft pair of moccasins arrived in her hand, but she couldn't see by whom. Jennie smelled the smoked leather, held them to her heart, and thanked them all. She loved the scent of wood smoke carried on the hide and the smiles, oh the welcoming smiles.

Other friends of Josiah's feted them, spoiled them with gifts, and Jennie thought that some of the things of Elizabeth's they'd winnowed might well have come from the generous hearts of people like these. The Owens family, who had named a son after Josiah, asked them to their homestead nestled beside cleared ground where ocean winds had toppled trees, and Jennie was glad she had a wool cape to ward off the bursts of cold. Over steamed sturgeon and an early salmon, spring greens, potatoes, and a berry pie, Mrs. Owens spoke of their daughter Bethina living in southern Oregon.

"She always wanted to be a doctor, but she owns a hat shop in Roseburg. She had to find a way to support her boy."

Jennie waited until their ride back to their boardinghouse for more details from Josiah.

"Bethina's marriage ended in divorce," Josiah said. Douglas slept between them in the livery carriage they'd rented. "She was married at fourteen. Too young." He shook his head. "Married her father's farmhand. Her father picked him. As a family friend and their pastor, I tried to dissuade it. Bethina had a natural talent in the healing arts, not unlike yours, Jennie. And she always wanted to be a doctor."

"It must have been difficult to divorce when her husband had been handpicked by her father."

"It took courage." Jennie hadn't thought of a divorced woman as demonstrating courage. Maybe Charles *had* done her a favor divorcing her, not making Jennie and Douglas live through his downfall. Any claim less than adultery would not have granted a divorce to her, and even then, there'd have been the humiliation of testifying in court about his lapses. She caressed Douglas's sleepy head, felt the ring beneath her gloved hands. Custody would have gone to Charles. Bethina's having custody meant there must have been very hard times with her husband.

People did have to give up dreams. Bethina made hats now. Jennie had a husband and child to take care of, threads of a new life to weave.

Douglas found the ocean beach a great place of joy. He threw rocks, made a fort out of driftwood. Josiah and "Mr. Pickett," as Douglas wanted to be called, got on well enough. Jennie hoped he'd one day let himself be called Douglas by Josiah, maybe even one day "son." They were at the place where the Columbia River met the Pacific. Jennie had Van on a leash and wished she could put Douglas on one too, as Josiah said there were "sneaker waves" at the coast that could rush in so quickly and pull out so fiercely that if one lost their balance they could be taken out to sea.

"Grown men," he said. "If it ever happens, swim parallel to the shore until you're past the pull, then head inland but do so quickly. The water's very cold."

"We'd best stay far away then. Neither Douglas nor I can swim."

"I can, Mama. Paw-Paw taught me."

"Oh. I didn't know." *What must Josiah think of a mother who knows so little of her son?*

They started back from the water, their feet leaving wet imprints in the sand. Jennie had pulled her skirt up into the waistband and carried her shoes. Josiah had his arm around her middle and reached to take her burden. He leaned to kiss her and she blushed even though they were the only three on this section of the shore.

Jennie called for Douglas, who instead of hurrying toward them ran in the opposite direction. Van barked at him. "Van wants to run with you." The wind pushed back against Jennie's words.

Douglas stopped, held his arms out as though to call the dog, and Jennie let him loose to run to Douglas, which he did, dragging the leash behind him. But instead of picking the spaniel up, Douglas kicked him. The little dog yelped and flew toward an incoming wave.

"Douglas!" Jennie shouted.

Josiah left her side and fast-walked toward Douglas, his rolled-up britches revealing his white ankles. He splashed on the way to pluck the drenched dog tumbled forward by an incoming wave. Van's wet tail snuck between his legs and Jennie couldn't hear if he whimpered.

Josiah reached Douglas, who had moved inland, head bowed. Josiah squatted down, and she saw Douglas wince in anticipation of a blow, the way he had when they'd lived with the Sloans, when his father had lived with them. None came.

"The dog did you no harm, Mr. Pickett," Josiah said as Jennie approached, his voice strong but calm. "He means to be your friend. If you're upset, you can speak of it to me or to your mother. But never harm Van again or any sentient being." She wondered if Douglas would remember the fox and when they'd first discussed that "sentient" word.

Without apparent anger, Josiah handed the shivering dog to Jennie. Douglas was fortunate Josiah had reached him before Jennie did. "Nor harm anyone else," Josiah continued. "Not yourself either, and you do harm to yourself when you hurt another."

Douglas lowered his eyes.

"I know you are capable of kindness. That is what I wish to see. Maybe you're cold. We've been on the beach so long. But words are the way to make a change. And look, Van squirms to be with you even when you've hurt him. He forgives."

"What do you have to say for yourself, young man? What you did was—" Jennie tried to think of anything that might have triggered her son's cruel behavior. She couldn't. "You say you're sorry." He reached for Van, but Jennie didn't release him.

"Let him think about it," Josiah said, standing. He touched Jennie's arm and Jennie wondered if that sort of easy manner and calm wisdom had been what the Indians had come to love about this man she'd married. "Let's build a driftwood fire. We'll warm up and I think there might be clams we can dig. Have you ever done that, Mr. Pickett?"

Douglas shook his head.

"I suspect your mother hasn't either. Let's find ourselves a shovel—after we get that fire going." He put his hand out and Douglas took it.

Van wiggled down and Jennie held his leash. The dog trotted ahead, uninjured and once again jumped up against the back of Douglas's legs, then scampered back to Jennie. So forgiving, that dog.

Later that evening they ate the steamed clams

the boardinghouse cook prepared. The clamming had gone well and Jennie had heard Douglas squeal with laughter as the tiny hole in the sand gave way to dinner. He'd worn rubber boots to do the digging, and Jennie watched him run along the beach leaving tracks with Van close behind him. A boy and his dog. Yes, that was what he had needed. Now, Van lay beneath the serving table and Douglas leaned over, patted the spaniel. "I'm sorry."

Relief she didn't know she longed for washed over her.

Chapter 25
Threads of Love

They wove their lives with threads of love, their days a wondrous fabric. They traveled back from their honeymoon on the ship *Moses Taylor*, oblivious to the looks of passengers grinning at their devotion to each other. Back in Salem, Jennie read to Josiah the notice in the newspaper of "the marriage between Miss Jennie Lichtenthaler and Josiah Parrish." The reporter added, "It was an old man and a young woman, but the ill-matched couple were fairly happy." They acknowledged Douglas's presence with an added editorial comment: "Mrs. Parrish gave her whole love to that boy." That wasn't quite true: she gave much to Josiah too.

They formed a family with fits and starts, but isn't that the way of all blending? Josiah returned to business interests, went to meetings. He served as a trustee at Willamette University, which now had a small medical department among others. One evening over one of Chen's rice-infused suppers, Josiah suggested she enroll. "There are fourteen students in the medical program this year."

"I see. Though I understand they did not gradu-ate your first woman student, Mary Sawtelle."

"She failed anatomy."

"Was that it? I heard rumors it had to do with conflict with the faculty, that she 'didn't know her place.'"

"You wouldn't have that problem." They sat beside each other on Elizabeth's red-velvet settee, he with his arms behind his head, elbows out, long legs crossed at the ankle in front of him; Jennie with knitting needles and yarn, working on a cape for Henrietta and Norman's baby, born a week before their wedding.

"Because I'd know my place or because of your influence over the faculty?"

"Neither. You'd work hard and make it on your own, without my influence. And you'd pass anatomy, I have no doubt."

"Your confidence warms me, Husband." Anatomy would be a difficult course and Jennie would have to memorize much. "Do you think I could receive the list of books used?" Even if she never did anything more with it, never went to college, the knowledge would be a gift.

"I don't know why not. I'll see what I can do."

It was such a generous offer, his urging her to school. But it was best to devote her time now to Douglas, to making his world a safe and predictable place. And to Josiah. She wanted this marriage to go right.

She silenced a small voice suggesting she have Josiah make a new distillery. Instead, she planted a kitchen herb garden; she didn't even order in new aromatics. It was a penance, this turning away from something she so loved in order to give Josiah and Douglas full devotion.

Douglas proved a challenge. His ability to pay attention to anything Jennie said was shorter than an eyelash, and in the blink of one he could be out of sight. She tried to make up for years of absence and even for her happiness with Josiah. If Douglas wanted a new toy seen at the mercantile, Jennie paid for it out of the generous allowance Josiah gave her for household and personal needs. Douglas had been known to race through the mercantile, grabbing things from the shelves and dropping them if she told him no. Eventually, she decided not to take him with her but then felt guilty about leaving him behind. Once when she said it was time for bed, he shouted, "I go when I want. You just want me to go away!" If Douglas wanted to visit his Paw-Paw, Jennie drove him in the buggy for the day, sometimes leaving him for the entire weekend. And yes, she felt guilty with relief as she drove away, anticipating a few days with Josiah alone.

Both Josiah and Chen had better luck with managing Douglas. So did her parents. He'd run to them and hug her father and her mother, sometimes looking back at Jennie with a grin as he took her mother's hand and leaned into her aproned body. Did she not love him as much as they did? She loved him more.

Her futility as a parent was a veil over her happiness. But she couldn't make Douglas do anything, just as she hadn't been able to make his father change his ways. She could only change herself.

When Josiah's latest grandchild, Nina, arrived for a first visit late in the summer and Jennie held the baby girl in her arms, the infant's presence made Jennie's heart ache for her own. And then she felt guilty for wanting a baby and perhaps a chance to redeem herself as a mother. Her prayers were to be the kind of mother men wrote about when they got older, mothers who never left their hearts. She wasn't sure she was even in Douglas's heart.

That first fall after their marriage, Douglas started at the East Salem school, at the corner of Center Street and Winter, a building a few blocks from their home. Jennie walked with him every day, Van on a leash trotting along. She liked the chance to talk with him and encourage him to have a good day, and most days, he allowed it, though he would not take her hand.

When he wasn't working with his sheep or goats, wasn't talking with his land manager, Josiah was busy "supervising," as he called it, his "investment" in completing the orphanage and his latest effort, the building of a new Methodist church. The steeple promised to be a beacon for miles around. Sometimes, on the way home from school, Jennie and Douglas detoured to watch the men work on the brick building at Church and State Streets. Jennie was always a bit nervous if Josiah wasn't there, fearing Douglas would dart away and cause havoc among the men.

Ariyah remained her stalwart friend. Alexandro was now a chubby six months old, unaware that his mother still cried herself to sleep at night. "But not for as long," she told Jennie when the women took tea together.

"I know Peleg would not want me to be unhappy," Ariyah said. "He would tell me to remember our perfect life together. At least I'm past the 'why' stage." She wiped at the baby's mouth. "There is no why. Death comes to us all, and while I miss him like I've lost a limb, I also cherish memories that hold no sorrow in them." She blinked back tears, cheered her voice as she said, "I've even hired a new piano teacher. I know Peleg would want me to continue lessons. And Alex needs to hear music, though what I do to that piano can hardly be called music." She laughed and changed the subject. "Why haven't you gotten Josiah to have a distillery made for you?"

"If he did, I'd devote too much time to it. Anyway, the house is big and needs care. Josiah might be able to see a house window out of plumb from thirty feet, but he can't seem to see his underdrawers need to be tossed down the laundry chute. He steps right over them." They both laughed and Jennie said, "Besides, being the wife of a prominent man keeps me occupied, more than it should with Douglas having needs." She sighed. "I've had to limit calling days or I'd do nothing but chat, drink tea, and eat Chen's scones, and then turn around and return those calls to other ladies in Josiah's circle. More scones." She patted her stomach. "I don't want to spend a dime on new clothes—unless they're maternity ones."

Ariyah burped her baby, then put him in the cradle. He slept quietly, lying on his back, his dark eyelashes like tiny feathers on his cheeks. Jennie's lost baby visited in her mind.

"Doing something you love would give you more confidence though, don't you think?"

"I have confidence."

"Not in managing your Dougie though. Am I right?"

Jennie nodded.

"I don't know what I'd do if I didn't have the joy of playing the piano to keep me taking deep breaths of happiness at least sometime during the day. Alex needs that from me. I have to fill up in order to give to him. Maybe Dougie needs that from you as well. He might feel a lot of pressure competing with Josiah for your attention."

She hadn't thought that Douglas might be jealous nor that she might need to replenish her own sustenance to have enough love to shower on both Douglas and Josiah. "I'd give Douglas a lot more attention if he seemed to enjoy my company." *Could she be right?* "He's so good with Josiah. I am grateful for that."

"While he's in school, you could be working in a drying shed, nurturing those plants. Do you still have that tincture you told me about? My lips are dry and so are my—" She motioned to her breasts.

Jennie never understood a woman's reluctance to use words for parts of their created bodies. "You aren't washing your breasts with soap, are you? That can dry your nipples."

"I need to be especially clean for Alex. It has lavender in it."

"I know, but it also has ash in it and that can be harsh no matter how well it smells. Try olive oil, just like the Greeks did. Or butter."

"Perfect."

Jennie paused. "I have some calendula I distilled."

"From those little yellow flowers, marigolds?"

"Yes. I have a cream too. I can't believe I didn't bring some over before. I'm a terrible friend."

"Don't chastise yourself." She leaned into Jennie. "Just go get it. I'm desperate."

Jennie did return and brought the calendula cream and the tincture. "If the skin is open, don't put this on."

"You see, you really need to return to your passion." She held the tincture bottle in both hands like it was precious gold.

The holidays consumed Jennie's days, preparing for this first Christmas as Mrs. Parrish. They exchanged gifts. Jennie gave Josiah a new spring measuring tape in a circular leather case. "It's the latest thing." He grinned as though she'd handed him the moon. Josiah gave her a tome called *Gray's Anatomy, Descriptive and Surgical*. It had been published first in 1858, but Jennie now held the latest edition. She gushed with gratitude.

"You must keep it from Douglas's prying eyes, though" he warned, a twinkle in his eye. "There are drawings of humans without clothing in that book."

"As when we were born. Thank you. I will cherish this forever—if I can carry it."

For Douglas, Josiah made a Lallement's velocipede from a patent he had his lawyer get so he could make it himself, his old blacksmithing skills put to good use. Douglas was genuinely pleased and insisted on taking it outside in the

December mist to give it a try. "He'll get hurt," Jennie protested, but the two of them, Josiah and Douglas, gave her no mind. Douglas didn't even whine the numerous times he fell trying to manage the two-wheeled thing. Jennie watched through the window. He was a persistent child. He had whittled out of pine a little dog, a gift he gave to Josiah. But when Josiah asked what he'd done with the gift he had for Jennie, he said, "I broke it, Joe." Josiah turned to Jennie. "He bought you a lovely vase. I'm so sorry."

"Me too." She didn't try to relieve Douglas of his guilt—not sure he felt any.

New Year's Eve took them to a party at a colleague's home; fireworks exploded through the spray of stars, the night sky clear, a rarity in that season. On Epiphany, Jennie and Josiah took down the tree. With each ornament, Jennie tucked away into a box filled with down, she prayed for blessings on Douglas, on the entire family, on all the world in this new and extraordinary year.

Chapter 26

Collaboration

O h!" The young woman stood at the door and said her name was Lizzie Hampton. "Mr. Parrish didn't say there was a maid already." She looked Jennie in the eye without embarrassment or challenge, bending to do it. "We'll work it out, I'm sure." She straightened. "I'm here to see Mrs. Parrish. Mr. Parrish hired me." She held out her hand for Jennie to shake it as a man might. "Could you please call the mistress of the house?"

Jennie invited her in out of the February cold as she kept talking.

"I'm to clean and change bed linens and look after their son, if he'll have me. That's what Mr. Parrish said—'If he'll have you.' I've five brothers all younger than me." The latter was perhaps her highest recommendation for a potential *Kindermädchen*. "I can stay or go, as you please, as my family doesn't live too far away, but I didn't know there was another here. Is the house large enough for two maids? Maybe there's a nanny quarters. I'm eighteen, if you're wondering."

A year older than Jennie when she'd married Charles.

"Could you please let Mrs. Parrish know I'm here?"

"Are any of your brothers nine years old? That's how old Douglas is." Jennie could hardly believe that they'd held their second Christmas at the Winter and Center Street home, sponsored the New Year's Eve party in the parlor with the fireworks over their fields. Jennie had prayed that same prayer of blessings with each ornament she put away at Epiphany.

Lizzie nodded. "A little scamp he is too, but I can handle my brother. We have fun together."

"Douglas is a fine boy. I'm sure you'll get along." It was Jennie whom Douglas took issue with.

"Thank you, miss. Ma'am. Now if you'll please let Mrs. Parrish know I'm here, I'll hope to please her." She curtsied. "You can show me later what best needs for me to do, aside from the child, of course. That would be the most important."

"I'm Mrs. Parrish." Jennie held back a grin. It wasn't the first time the mistaken identity had been made and wouldn't be the last.

Lizzie put her hand to her mouth as though to stifle a scream. "Oh, la." She sank to the settee. "I am so sorry I mistook you for the—I've ruined it now." She almost wailed.

"You haven't ruined a thing. You were kind

and respectful to whom you thought was the help, and that's exactly how we want everyone here to be treated—with kindness and respect."

Lizzie shook her head. "I should have kept words to myself until I knew who I was talking with. My ma always said my mouth is like a river, it just keeps flowing."

"I think I'd like your mother."

"You would, ma'am."

"What did Mr. Parrish tell you would be your duties here?"

"The usual. Cleaning, serving, helping the cook, and most of all looking after his son when he's not in school or with either of you."

Jennie had a few more queries about where Josiah knew her from (her parents attended the church where he used to preach; they'd known him a very long time); what she liked best about being an older sister (her brothers made her laugh, and she had a sister older than she was too, so she knew about the pecking order); what special interests she had (music—she liked to sing and had been known to dance around the parlor while she cleaned; she hoped that wouldn't be a problem—tending children was her calling). She had earth-brown hair with natural waves that framed her round face, brown eyes, and pink cheeks. She wore a brown full-bell skirt and cream-colored blouse with a single purple ribbon at her throat. A brown hat sat at an angle on her head where a brown feather bobbed with her enthusiastic chatter. Her personality brought needed color to the room.

"Why didn't you tell me you were interviewing young women for household help and to be a *Kindermädchen*?"

"Nanny, you mean?"

Jennie nodded. Her parents used that word, but "nanny" was the English equivalent. "Yes, nanny. The household is really my purview, I think."

"Why?"

"Why is the house my responsibility?"

He nodded.

"Because—" It was a good question.

"I thought you could use the help, that's all, Jennie. Elizabeth always had assistance when we could afford it and we can now. I like to think we do this together. Collaborate."

"I like having some say in who is in my home each day. We might have interviewed together rather than have you spring it on me."

He cleared his throat, a nervous tic. "I hoped . . . that is, that, well, that you might consider going to medical school if you had help."

She gasped. "That's . . . not likely. I mean, not while Douglas is young." *Is he trying to divert my upset over his not including me in this decision?* For a fleeting moment she wondered—was he like Charles, cutting off her thread shorter than she liked in order to control what she chose to knit? No, this man had her interests at heart. Still, being told something would happen unless she objected wasn't quite the same as a collaboration.

"It's totally your choice, of course. That's why I had her come by to meet you."

"You might have warned me. I had my apron on and had been polishing the silver."

"I might have. But I was afraid you'd overrule me."

Jennie laughed at that. "I only have veto power. But you—"

"You could veto me. Will you?"

"I'll see how she gets on with Douglas. You've known her family for a long time?"

He sipped his tea that he'd cooled by pouring it onto a saucer. She'd seen the Irish do that. "I have. They've barely a farthing to their name, but they brought flowers to the church each meeting time. Her father works in the woods. Her older sister nearly died a few years back in childbirth. Needed a good doctor." He looked pointedly at his wife.

Lizzie's meeting with Douglas took place that afternoon. Jennie and Lizzie walked to Douglas's school, where Jennie introduced him to his new nanny. She didn't say it that way, because Jennie suspected he might want to be consulted, collaborated with at least. He didn't have a vote.

"This is Lizzie Hampton, Douglas."

She reached out to shake his hand and he shook it as she said, "It's nice to meet you, Douglas. Or do you want to be called Mr. Parrish?"

Jennie winced. *No one told her.*

"Douglas is all right." He didn't even flinch. "Why are you walking with us?"

"Your parents are considering hiring me to help in the household, and when I'm not cleaning and polishing—so you won't have to, Mr. Douglas"— she grinned—"then I get to do important things like teach you how to play the ukulele—if you don't already know. Do you?" Douglas shook his head no. "La! You'll have a good time learning that. And singing. Do you sing?" Again Douglas shook his head no. "I do. We can sing together if you'd like. I'll teach you. What *do* you like to do?"

"Ride my velocipede Papa made for me."

A stab of hope shot through Jennie. *He called Josiah Papa.*

"Can you ride one?" Douglas asked her.

"Ride one . . . La! I don't even know what that is. Will you show me?"

Douglas nodded and then went on to chatter like a chipmunk about all he knew of bicycles, which was quite a lot for a nine-year-old. Lizzie seemed genuinely interested. Douglas and she were absorbed in conversation. Lizzie had a companion on her river trip, their words flowing like two streams blending together. Jennie wished she was on that river with them, but there seemed only room for two.

"You will consider going to Willamette now, won't you?" Josiah stood with his arm around her on the wide porch, watching Douglas run beside Lizzie on his velocipede, an iron streak across the green grass. Her whoops and hollers of "La!" rang through the unseasonably warm February afternoon. The usually short sun break had already lasted an hour.

"I promise, I will. I have been reading the anatomy book. It's going to take a long time to get through that."

"The cadaver work would make it more real. Does the thought of that make you ill at all? The professors have said some people get sick."

"I have an iron stomach. Once my brother made me eat a frog leg. Raw. He wouldn't take me to the fair unless I did. I succumbed. I nearly emitted, but I held it, chewed, and swallowed."

"Which brother? I'll have him flogged."

"Fergus."

"Have I even met him?"

She thought back. "Not yet. He worked the mines in Idaho. My father said he'd moved to Portland. He has a butcher shop with a partner." Jennie laughed then. "Maybe his interest started by dissecting frogs. My father says he's applying for police work. At least the frog he made me eat was dead." Then the strangest thing happened: saliva formed in her mouth, she felt a lurching from her iron stomach.

"Excuse me." She peeled away from Josiah's arms and lifted her skirts, running up the stairs to the washroom. There she deposited her noonday meal into a bucket. Her face felt hot, her forehead moist. *Goodness, I've quite an imagination to bring this on. The frog?* No, it wasn't memory reaching into this new time: it was the growing of a new memory. At that moment, she knew she was with child.

Chapter 27

Gingerly

On hot spring days as her body changed, Jennie gave up her corset and instead wore loose wrappers. She cooled herself with thin wooden fans boasting "Smith Furniture and Undertaking" written on the side. "Nine months seems excessive," she told Ariyah as the two sat in the shade.

"At least you'll have greens to eat, fresh peaches and apples, rhubarb pies and berries. Lots of berries."

"If this baby arrives looking like a blueberry, I'll know why."

Lizzie's presence proved a blessing, as the morning sickness didn't stay to morning alone and it didn't cease at three months. The doctor Josiah hired, Dr. Joseph Wythe, had once been the dean at Willamette Medical College and taught classes. He'd been "let go" when he was found smoking outside the building, a violation of the university's strict code of ethics. His private practice was mostly in Portland, where he'd returned to serve as pastor at Portland's Taylor Street Methodist Church.

"I'm not sure it's necessary to have a doctor of such renown," Jennie told Josiah. The man had written a book on the use of the microscope, and Jennie remembered her simple glass and brass and vowed to show it to him the next time he visited. He had also trained in Philadelphia and was one of the first to perform an ovariectomy to remove a tumor on a woman's ovary. She'd read about it.

"He's my friend and a very good doctor."

"Even though he got fired for smoking?" she teased.

"The trustees made those rules. We had to follow them." Josiah brushed at his tie. It seemed to need straightening.

"If he can stop this morning sickness, I'll be grateful!" She'd lost weight and began to worry over the baby's health.

Jennie had used a small amount of nux vomica, or strychnine, to halt the vomiting, but it had not helped. It was a poison, of course, used to kill rats, but very tiny amounts extracted from the seeds could aid digestion and help with nausea. She kept it among her aromatics and oils in a small glass vial clearly marked with the universal sign of danger, the skull and crossbones.

"Compresses." Dr. Wythe asked, "I suspect it's worse in cold, windy weather?" He'd made the trek from Portland, for which Jennie was eternally grateful. She nodded. "And between three and four in the morning?"

She was surprised. "And with spicy foods. I've given up any seasoning."

"Don't give up ginger," he said. "That may do the trick." He sat beside her bed.

"Ginger?"

He patted her hand, then stood. "I expect your Chinese cook will have some. Chew on it now and then. Try to get up to exercise a bit, even when you think you might vomit."

"I will. Thank you." He had a nice bedside manner. She wanted to ask him about some itching in a private place, but didn't. She thought then how nice it would be to have a woman physician to confer with. He and Josiah left to have coffee in the parlor and discuss politics.

Jennie closed her eyes. "Ginger. How could I not have known that, Van?" It was such a simple remedy. Van lay at the foot of her bed, his little brown spots for eyebrows lifting at her voice.

"How could you not have known what?" Ariyah said as she entered. She sat her son down on the Persian carpet of many knots and colors.

"That ginger might help this nausea. I should have thought of that."

"You're being much too hard on yourself."

"I'm trying to do everything right this time. The last pregnancy—" It was a sorrow seven years in the past that still reached out to pluck her breath.

302

"I'm sure you didn't do anything wrong and you won't this time. 'He will wipe every tear from their eyes. There will be no more death or mourning or crying or pain.' There's the promise."

Jennie thanked her for the uplifting verse from Revelation. She liked thinking of that time when there would be no more death.

"That's what I pray for you, Jennie. That there'll be no more death for either of us in our lives for a very, very, very long time."

Ariyah allowed Alex to wobble from the bed to the chair to the table and back again, making an unsteady circle of the room. It was April and the friends both had anniversaries to celebrate (Jennie's wedding and little Alex's arrival); but there were sad dates too. Peleg had been gone two years already. He'd left Ariyah with sufficient funds, so she didn't have to wonder over finances the way Jennie once had to. Unbeknownst to Josiah, Jennie still made payments out of the household accounts, as Charles Winn had yet to release her from the loan. It was a bit strange—using Josiah's money to pay off a loan to him, but Jennie didn't want his sons thinking she didn't remember her obligation. Jennie knew all she needed to do was ask Josiah for a bit more if she needed something for the baby; or tell him about the loan payments being made to the estate through Charles Winn. But she didn't like asking for money. From anyone. Josiah had recently donated a full block of lots he owned for a school for the deaf and feebleminded. The paper had speculated that it was worth $2000, so money wasn't a worry for Josiah.

"How are your piano lessons going?" Jennie asked.

"Wonderful. He's not the instructor Peleg was, of course, but he's reliable and I know I'll be totally absorbed for at least an hour that day, my mind not wandering to Peleg memories. It's very refreshing, the piano. And practicing in between, I love that time too." She fiddled with the lace at her bodice, turned to see Alex had plopped on his bottom and now reached for Van, who darted toward him, then backed up, darted forward, then danced back to Alex's giggle, his tail sweeping the floor. The dog's rear was high in the air, his front paws and face near the carpet, a position of play.

"What does Douglas think about the baby?"

"So far, he's been happy about it. I think Lizzie's devotion to him really makes a difference. He'll be almost ten when the baby is born, so we've been talking about how important he'll be to his little brother or sister in growing up."

"You don't think he'll be jealous?"

"He worried over Baby Ariyah, and when she died, he wondered if he'd go to heaven too. I decided after that to never refer to death as 'God took his angel home.' It's frightening for some children."

Ariyah looked away, drummed her fingers together, then tugged at the strings of her hat she'd removed and kept on her lap, almost like a barrier between the two of them. That in itself was rare. "Jennie—"

"Doctor man say give you ginger, right away."

"Thank you, Chen." The small man step-stepped into the room then, his black eyes holding worry. Jennie took a bite from the root he'd handed her. Bitter, but if it helped she would not complain. "This is perfect, Chen. Thank you." He nodded. "What were you going to say, Ariyah?"

"Oh, nothing. We can talk about it later. Right now I need to get Chen's recipe for that mango sauce he served at Easter." The small man beamed. "Mangos shipped from San Francisco, I imagine. It was perfectly delicious."

"I haven't eaten anything but hard tack and tea. Josiah even made up pemmican, hoping that would ease the discomfort."

"He's attentive the way Peleg was." Ariyah sighed.

Lizzie, along with Douglas, joined Jennie and Ariyah as Chen left. "Mrs. P, would you like to sit in the chair for a while?"

"What's this?" Douglas picked up the vial of nux vomica.

"It's a medicine." He was close enough that Jennie put her hand out, and he put the vial into her palm. "Thank you. It's very dangerous. You mustn't pick up any of Mommy's vials and potions. I wouldn't want you to get sick from taking them by mistake."

"All right," he said. He stood back while Lizzie helped her up, and she suggested that they walk the hallway both for exercise and to see if the ginger helped. Douglas led Alex by one chubby hand, walking him slowly down the hall, and then found the library where Josiah and Dr. Wythe talked, and there Douglas abandoned his younger charge.

"He's no longer acting the older brother," Ariyah said, lifting Alex.

"He's still young and has no practice." He'd been appropriate. She wasn't sure why Ariyah's comment had upset her.

"Are these the same paintings that were here when Elizabeth was alive?" Ariyah asked.

Jennie nodded.

Ariyah paused before an oil landscape of green fields and mountains with a sunset behind them casting a yellow glow. She bounced her son on her hip. "Maybe you should bring in some of your style to the house. I bet Josiah would allow that."

It hadn't occurred to Jennie to suggest to Josiah that they engage in furnishing changes.

She liked Elizabeth's taste, and the settee and bedsteads and vases and paintings were familiar to him—and to her now too. She wasn't preoccupied with her surroundings. Her medical books Josiah had sent for lured her into their world, so what hung in the halls or the furniture they sat on were not places she thought to change. It was the interior world that captured her and the universe of relationships that spun their webs. These were the accoutrements she fussed over: Douglas's response to a younger child, Josiah's encouragement of her medical interests, Ariyah's observation left unfinished.

"But you're a society woman now, married to Josiah Parrish, soon to have his child. You have to look the part."

"None of those society women will see the upstairs hall," Jennie said. "Though they could. Lizzie keeps it sparkling."

"Thank you, Mrs. P." Lizzie held her elbow. "They might like seeing the indoor bathing room. All those tubs!"

"I can imagine a tour of that room. Should we plan it for Christmas? Hang mistletoe in the shower?"

The women laughed with Jennie and she warmed to their presence. They were a hundred times more relaxing than the society women who brought their calling cards to take tea and ogle.

"Josiah's really a simple man with simple tastes. I'm not much interested in style or fashion. That's one reason I need you to remind me now and then." Jennie looked at the table in the wide hall below the painting. It held a spray of wheat that picked up the color of the yellow sunset. It was lovely. "I might not need to change my surroundings, but noticing them now and then might be wise."

"Did I tell you I've taken up artistry?" Ariyah hadn't. "It's another place I find relief. Art and music," she mused. "They help fill this empty hole I wonder how I'll ever fill."

The three women finished the afternoon before Jennie realized she'd gone a full two hours before she needed the emesis bowl. But afterward, she didn't continue into spasms. Perhaps the ginger really would work. She sipped water and it stayed down. Jennie even felt well enough to get up on her own and walked Ariyah to the door where sunlight poured through the glass panel. Jennie didn't try to lift Alex but touched his head, thanked him for being such a good boy. To Ariyah she said, "I needed this visit."

Ariyah hesitated but said only, "Thank Douglas for his walking Alex." Then she hugged Jennie and swished out the door.

Jennie made her way back up the stairs, wondering what Ariyah had planned to say before Chen's interruption and then before she left. She let it go when Douglas came into the room, dragging Lizzie by the hand. "We're going to plant the garden tomorrow, can we, Mama?"

"I don't see why not."

"I love carrots. The seeds are teeny tiny. Lizzie showed me."

He turned to Lizzie with adoring eyes and Jennie felt that familiar twinge of regret that her son had never looked that way at her. Perhaps one day this child she carried would.

Chapter 28
The Education of Jennie

Josiah kept busy with his college board, lamented greatly the burning of the old Institute building that had housed the first school in the territory. University Hall now contained the entire college, with expanding music and theology and biblical classes and offering degrees in medicine, a business school, and music. Jennie labored through a textbook from the 1820s titled *Women's Concerns*. The author was somewhat condescending and Jennie hoped one day a woman physician would write another. Maybe Bethina Owens would. Josiah had learned that Bethina no longer had her hat shop but had instead placed her son with Abigail Scott Duniway, a friend and women's rights activist, then left for medical school in Pennsylvania, the same one Dr. Wythe had attended. She would become a doctor, sacrificing time with her son to do it.

"You can do that too," Josiah told her. They strolled the boardwalk on a sunny afternoon, Douglas and Van running in front, but the dog at least coming back to check on their slow pace.

No longer hampered by morning sickness, Jennie felt whole again and joyous in the summer day. Josiah tipped his hat to Mr. Gill, owner of the new bookstore building and Jennie thanked him for ordering in her medical books. Women's skirts took up the walkway so the men had to step out onto the cobbled street while the women chattered about the weather, and Jennie kept her eye on Douglas poking a stick at the horse manure in the street. Josiah signaled Douglas that they were turning back.

"I wonder why Mrs. Owens didn't come to Willamette's medical program." A flock of birds rose before them, became a black garland sweeping across the sky.

"Perhaps the reputation of Mrs. Sawtelle spreads," said Josiah, "that we aren't fair to women—who don't pass anatomy." He was a little sensitive about Willamette's not graduating Mrs. Sawtelle, even though he made light of the attack of unfairness.

"I suspect it was more the faculty dissension that caused her to depart," Jennie offered. "I'm plowing through this book of *Women's Concerns*, and the general tone is one of women being frail, needy creatures and the doctor required to bounce between pampering and dogmatically telling women what to do."

"It's an older text, isn't it?"

"Yes, but I suspect little has changed about the

male attitude toward women. 'Bouncing' isn't the correct word, but you get my meaning."

Josiah nodded.

"Women, I've found, are neither in need of pampering nor parenting," Jennie said. "We bear children every other year while still cooking, cleaning, plowing fields, sewing, harvesting, drying foods, quilting, milking cows, tending horses, chopping wood, making deals, selling wheat and buying beans, teaching children, wiping runny noses, all while often suffering from boils and bruises and childbirth and acting the perfect wife." She sounded annoyed even to herself and she wasn't sure why.

"Her husband and children praise that Proverbs 31 woman you've just described," Josiah reminded her.

"I suspect she might have preferred a little help."

He laughed. "One day you'll be a doctor and you'll treat your female patients differently."

"If that ever happens, I'll ask their opinion and not assume they don't have one." Her dream of becoming a doctor was like looking through the glass and brass the wrong way: instead of bringing an object closer to her, it got smaller and farther away.

"Mrs. Sawtelle did get her degree, by the way. In New York." Josiah broke into her reverie. "Her husband is entering Willamette Medical this fall and she's opened a practice here in Salem." They dodged fat slugs squiggling on the boardwalk as they strolled.

"She has? It would be much more practical to have her tend me than Dr. Wythe. He'll have to stay with us because it'll be so difficult to come from Portland. And what if the baby comes early?"

"I think we should stay on the course we've started," Josiah said. "I want the best for you and that's Wythe. He has the degree, has written a specialty book, practiced and taught."

"And apparently passed anatomy."

"The medical curriculum does have demands, Mrs. Parrish."

"Why don't you go to medical school, Mr. Parrish?"

"At my age?"

"Didn't Tabitha Brown start Pacific University when she was even older than you? And imagine how you could combine your native healing with science."

"I'll pass it on to you and you can use it. When you have your degree." He squeezed her arm. "But if you think it would help, I'd be pleased to read the texts while you take notes."

"Or I could knit while I memorize. I'd like that." His confidence both warmed and warned: that someone who loved her thought she could achieve a childhood dream brought on the warming; the warning came from the risk involved in pursuing that dream. If she actually committed to doing it, there'd be no one else to blame if she failed.

"I'd glean wisdom from everywhere," Jennie continued. "Even Mrs. Sawtelle—Dr. Sawtelle. Imagine being her colleague."

Josiah said nothing and she thought it might be awkward for him to have this first female medical student at his university—one who had been asked to leave—now be his wife's colleague, let alone her patient. But Jennie vowed she'd seek her out after the baby was born. She'd be her doctor if Jennie liked her bedside manner. And maybe Jennie would find in that relationship the encouragement to do what Mary Sawtelle and Bethina Owens did.

That fall, they enrolled Douglas in the new elementary school at Willamette. A few weeks later, they met to discuss Douglas's needs.

"He's bright but . . . a scamp. He teases other students. He's bigger than many of his classmates and isn't always aware that he is, shall we say, rough at times." The teacher fidgeted as he spoke of his concerns. Jennie imagined it wasn't easy to tell a trustee that his child was known less for his academic achievements than for his less-than-stellar behavior. "But we'll manage. He seems quite taken with science and with the

314

construction of things, though nothing seems to interest him for long."

"What can we do to assist you?" Jennie said. They were in the teacher's office on a warm September day.

"Oh, I think you've done quite enough in that realm, Mrs. Parrish." Jennie frowned. "Some punishments don't seem to work with troubled boys like Douglas."

He went from scamp to troubled? *And what does he mean that I've done enough already?*

Jennie was too stunned to ask, but Josiah did. "Your meaning?"

"His broken home, of course." The teacher had gained his voice, no longer intimidated by a trustee's family before him, and he spoke now to Josiah, not to her. "Divorce casts such a terrible pall over a child. I've only had one or two such children in my teaching positions, but they are almost always troubled, conflicted, and sadly, it does not seem to improve with a stepfather, no matter how loving. Forgive me for speaking frankly, Mr. Parrish. These children often create problems at school, have a hard time applying themselves to tasks, are known to run away at a young age or take up drink. It would have been so much better if his mother had not divorced regardless of the issues." He talked as though Jennie weren't even in the room. "But of course, that can't be undone." He finished with a cheery,

"We'll do our best, I can assure you, Mr. Parrish, despite the challenge." He smiled and adjusted his glasses over his beak of a nose. Jennie didn't know what Josiah said next because her fury had closed off her ears.

"We need to move him from that classroom," she told Josiah as they exited the room. He had her elbow and had found a bench in the hallway for them to sit on while she took deep breaths. "The man has made a dozen assumptions, all of them wrong, and I fear he'll promote them rather than face the possibility he might be in error. The university fires people for smoking, but they keep on teachers who demean?"

"He is said to be one of the best instructors."

"He didn't even speak to me except to chastise me for 'having done enough already.' He can't possibly know what my life is like or the circumstances of my divorce." She turned to Josiah. "What if he suggests those things to Dougie, makes him think the divorce was all my fault? I didn't even want it. I tried to work things out." She brushed at tears, annoyed they came when she was angry. Or perhaps it was the powerlessness. Again. "I only hoped to protect Douglas from the truth about his father. And give him a good life. Oh, Josiah . . ."

"I know that. It'll be all right. It will. We'll work harder to catch Douglas 'being good,' as the instructor suggested. And maybe one day tell

316

him about the circumstances of your marriage and divorce." He helped her stand up.

She retied her bonnet at her throat, smoothed her skirt over her burgeoning belly well-camouflaged by the hoop. "You know I did my best."

He nodded. "And because of something happening beyond your control, a good thing came about, and I will be forever grateful that I have both you and Douglas in my life."

She had to believe that this path was somehow a part of a divine plan for her life and for Douglas's too. If she lost that sense of direction, or if she failed to learn the lessons from what had gone before, Jennie feared she'd repeat them and in the process lose herself. And where would that leave Douglas, Josiah, and this new life she carried?

Chapter 29

Grace

The contractions came mild at first and far apart. It was a week after their meeting with Douglas's teacher. Dr. Wythe had moved into the guest room down the hall the week before, prepared to stay until her delivery, his presence a luxury of "society" Jennie was willing to accept. She had plodded through the house that morning like an old, aching horse across a stony field seeking the oat bag at the paddock. Now she sat reading in her room, as she imagined Dr. Wythe did in his, and Van snored in sniffles at her feet. Some questions arose and Jennie pushed to stand and planned to call on Dr. Wythe when she felt her water break. She called out to Lizzie instead.

"Get Josiah and Ariyah. This baby is arriving!"

"Shan't I tell Dr. Wythe too?" Lizzie said from the doorway.

"Yes, yes. Then come help me don clean dry clothes."

The rains had arrived, pelting the window-panes like an anxious percussionist at the concert hall. Then they'd stop like a hand

318

had silenced the cymbal. A ray of sunshine would pour through the trees, causing ground fog like steam to rise between the shrubs and drift into the firs and dogwoods. Jennie let herself be distracted by the weather while she waited.

Soon the room bustled with people as Dr. Wythe told Josiah what to do. The carriage was sent for Ariyah, who arrived shortly, she and Lizzie throwing open the curtains to let shy sunshine peek in.

"Boil the usual water," Dr. Wythe told Lizzie. "I'll put my instruments in it. Papa"—he pointed to Josiah—"you'd best wait outside."

"Can't he stay?" If something went wrong as it had with her last child, she didn't want to face that tragedy without her husband at her side. She thought then this was something she should have discussed previously with the doctor. Somehow Josiah's presence had never been questioned in her mind.

"It's best if he doesn't. Even stalwart men tend to faint when their wives face the pain of childbirth."

"I intend to hold my wife's hand through it all. I missed my sons' births. I don't want to miss this one. Besides, it might be a longed-for daughter." He squeezed Jennie's hand. "What kind of father would I be if I wasn't there for her first look at the world?"

The doctor frowned, started to speak, but decided against it, pursing his lips instead. Jennie vowed that if she ever was a physician attending a woman's birth, she'd claim the promise that two are better than one. She remembered the night Peleg witnessed his son's birth just moments before he died. How grateful they all were for Alex's sake that Peleg had met his son.

"Thank you." She squeezed Josiah's hand.

A part of her wanted to remember all the details, seeing through the eyes of a physician, being objective about what Dr. Wythe did or didn't do, but very soon, not soon enough, all Jennie's focus went to pain and pushing. She barely heard Josiah's voice of encouragement, Lizzie's humming as she fluffed a pillow, Ariyah's telling funny stories. She squeezed Josiah's hand. She'd heard women cry out and scream their husband's name as though tortured. She had no desire to curse her husband until he began to tell her of the practices of Indian women, how they squatted or took long baths, often giving birth right in the bathing tub, "or so I'm told."

"I don't need your—your anthropological explanations at this moment, Mr. Parrish. I would have you keep such musings to yourself. At this time—Oh, oh, oh!" This was followed by both Ariyah and Lizzie halting for a moment what they were doing and a look exchanged and then Jennie's louder cry.

She prayed that this baby would be born whole and healthy and come into a world where she knew always and forever that she was loved.

And so Gertrude Grace Parrish greeted her parents within seconds of her arrival on October 1, 1872, at three in the afternoon: their daughter, who took up as much room as a bouquet of flowers in Jennie's arms, and within minutes brought a thousand times the joy. Lizzie went out to bring Douglas in. He'd been at school and wore his uniform of brown pants and coat and gray tie. "Meet your sister, Douglas," Jennie said. "She'll fall in love with her big brother."

"She's so little." Douglas gently pushed the receiving blanket she'd knitted away from Gracie's chin. The baby stared at him, eyes so wide, tiny lips pinching. "She's the size of one of Mr. Chen's hams."

Josiah laughed and pressed his hand to Douglas's shoulder as he stood behind him. "Almost as pink too."

"Perfect. Absolutely perfect," Ariyah sighed.

"We Methodists have godparents at the baptism. Will you do our honors in a few days, Ariyah?" Josiah made the invitation.

"I'd love that."

"And maybe Douglas, would you like to stand

with us too? I'm sure you don't remember your baptism," Jennie said. "That would make two of you as godparents."

"Better than one," Josiah added and looked at Jennie with such sweet joy that one would have thought she'd changed the world. In fact, she had. They had.

Later, Josiah told her he'd had a chat with Charles Winn and the matter of Elizabeth's will canceling the debt had been "resolved."

"How did you know?"

"I didn't. I simply asked him if the estate was resolved and he said something about the matter of the outstanding loan still pending. Until then I hadn't known. You ought to have told me." He didn't sound angry, only hurt.

"I didn't want anything to come between you and your children, especially money. It can say so much more than it ought to."

He nodded. "It's settled now, as well it should be. We have new things to consider." He touched their daughter's tiny nose.

On the Sunday following Gracie's birth, the little family with Ariyah, Douglas, and the newest addition stood at the baptismal font of the Salem First Methodist Church. Jennie's father baptized their daughter, and Jennie heard the words of those agreeing to help raise her in the faith, tears sliding down her cheeks.

Gracie wore a long white lace dress that had

been Jennie's, her mother having brought it across the plains. Jennie imagined how she'd have lovingly wrapped precious paper in between the layers of the delicate lace and folded it among the few clothing items she could bring. She had anticipated that one day there might be an infant granddaughter to wear it as Jennie had once worn it. Jennie looked out toward the congregation, then back to her gathered family, breathing a prayer of gratitude.

Norman and Henrietta Parrish had come; so had Samuel. And her brothers George and DW. *I should have asked my brothers to be godfathers.* Still, she knew they'd be there for Gracie even without the formal words of "godfather" applied to them. She even expressed a word of thanks to Charles who had left her and again forgave him, forgiveness being a journey rather than a destination. He had forced her to leave behind an old path; she'd had the courage to take the next steps onto a new one. If only she could remember that nothing could separate her from God's love, even when she wandered in those wilderness places.

Jennie urged Josiah to spend even more time with Douglas, taking him with him when he went to the barns to look after the Angora Cashmere goats. Josiah had purchased them out of California, the entire transaction written up in *The Weekly Enterprise*, the animals were so rare. He'd gotten them not long before Gracie was born, and Douglas had initially shown interest and had even gone with Josiah to the fair in October, taking with them the chickens the *Enterprise* reported as "a good display, embracing the finest breeds." Douglas had paid attention to Quilton those early years, and Jennie thought an interest in animal husbandry might be his future. There'd been no repetition of harming Van after that episode at the coast. But Douglas shrugged his shoulders when Josiah thanked him for his help with the chickens and the goats. "We got written up in the paper, Douglas. You helped do that."

"Who cares about that old newspaper."

Douglas was good with Gracie, though. He liked holding her, and when they had the photographer come to the house, Douglas insisted she be placed in his arms for at least one of the family portraits. Jennie had high hopes for this family woven into a strong fiber. And truly, who had time to consider medical school?

By January, Jennie knew she was pregnant again. She'd been breastfeeding so hadn't thought she could conceive and made a mental note to never tell any patient that breastfeeding was a way to space births. Two babies in so short a time? Was her body ready? Josiah was elated. He took the well-wishes from his friends with good spirit, though Jennie admitted to embarrassment.

"Goodness," her mother had said. "Will you be as rabbits?"

What could Jennie say to her except that she loved her husband and didn't relish the morning sickness or the challenge of feeding her baby while keeping her body strong for this second child. But she did love Josiah, more than she had ever imagined possible. And he loved her back, allowing her to express worries to him while sharing the joys.

"What about a wet nurse?" Josiah raised the issue. "Or mix cow's milk with flour or even try the new Leibig's Soluable Food for Babies."

"You've been reading up."

He shrugged. "I like knowing what's new."

Formula hadn't been available when Douglas was an infant. And neither her doctor then nor Charles had wanted to discuss ways to help the baby thrive. Her sister suggested trying the Pratt device, a hard rubber nipple. With cow's milk and flour mixed, Douglas began to gain weight, but still she wondered if that change might have contributed to his problems now, separation from vital nurture begun at such an early age.

But the nipple was cumbersome for Gracie's tiny mouth and lips to suck on, and besides, Jennie liked nursing her babies. She'd felt a failure using it for Douglas, and she could imagine herself nursing Gracie while another baby kicked from her belly. That image became so comforting she decided to keep nursing, then nurse in tandem once the second child arrived.

She called on Mrs. Sawtelle—Dr. Sawtelle— in February. She was a gangly woman, tall with a narrow face, big teeth that showed often as she smiled. Her blonde hair curled in a cluster at the top of her head. Her eyes stared and she rarely blinked. She had a loud voice that startled Gracie, whom Jennie held in her arms. They met in her home office on Main Street, a few blocks from Willamette where Dr. Sawtelle's husband was finishing his degree. Rosebushes lined the path that split off from the main house to a side entrance Jennie entered.

"I'd like you to attend my birthing," Jennie told her when the doctor brought her into the examining room.

"Ha. Looks like it's already been attended to." She nodded with her chin toward Gracie.

"I have another due in September."

"Breast-feeding?"

Jennie nodded.

"An old wives' tale proven once again to be a poor story. I have some options for you to keep that from happening. Are you able to care for a second child? Do you need assistance with food or shelter?"

"I'm fine. Truly. I have a loving husband—"

"Well, I can see that."

"A loving husband and a good home. You may know of him. Josiah Parrish?"

"Ah, *that* Parrish you're from. But he's an . . . older man. I met his wife, Elizabeth, at Willamette before they sacked me."

"Elizabeth passed a few years back." Jennie took a deep breath. "I heard of your dismissal at Willamette."

"Did you? For failing anatomy, they said. Of course I had to fail it, my favorite subject. They didn't allow the female students to do dissection, something about our 'tender sensibilities.' Ha. I've since informed them that I passed my tests at The New York Medical College and Hospital for Women, not that it mattered to Chase, my old professor." She washed her hands in a bowl, dried them on a towel. "But let's not wander that path. We have a new one. A baby. How did your delivery go and who attended you? A midwife?"

"No, Dr. Wythe."

She nodded approval.

"But I'd prefer a woman and one in Salem. I—I have an interest in medicine myself. I've done some reading and applied homeopathic cures." *Why did I mention that?*

"Have you? It doesn't get the status it deserves, given that it was Hippocrates himself who began the homeopathic study. I find a blend of it with surgery and modern chemicals might be the future. Presently, my homeopathic interest has kept doors closed in some so-called medical institutions and societies as well. Ha."

She held a sausage-shaped stethoscope to Gracie's chest and listened. "Isn't it grand," she said, "that this item was invented because a French doctor felt uncomfortable putting his ear against a woman's breast to diagnose chest problems." She listened to Jennie's heart next. "You'd attend Willamette, of course. I wonder what Old Chase would do with the wife of a trustee wishing to perform dissections. I'd like to be there for that."

"I have an interest, but college? That's not likely." She changed the subject. "My delivery was classic. An easy birth, only six hours of labor. I have another child, a son who is nine, and that birth too went well. But I lost a child, Ariyah, at birth. The cord—it—"

"Ah. I'm very sorry." She patted Jennie's shoulder as she rewrapped the blanket around Gracie, then put the stethoscope onto the table. After a moment she said, "But good to know. Was the physician aware of the infant's distress?"

"He—my husband then did not go for the attending doctor and instead brought a physician too late, too . . . unprepared to make a difficult delivery." The memory seared like the touch of a hot poker from the fireplace.

"Unprepared by drink. That was it, wasn't it?"

Jennie nodded.

"Liquor destroys more people than the mosquito, though it takes longer for the victim to die." She shook her head. "We'll be aware then. I have no doubt that Josiah Parrish will call for me well ahead of time."

"Dr. Wythe stayed with us. I'd welcome that."

"I'm a short carriage ride away, so not necessary. Now, let's examine you and see where things are. What's your baby's name?"

Jennie told her.

"Grace. Lovely. My husband has little time for religion, but I think the concept of grace is the apple of religion's eyes. Come along then, Grace." She lifted her daughter from Jennie's arms, held her like a cherished vase, fragile and precious, then laid her on a blanket on a table with a little fence around it so if she rolled over she wouldn't fall off. Jennie watched with interest the way this woman doctor examined her child, the quiet chatter, large hands gentle on Gracie's tender skin. "You have a healthy baby. You're doing a fine job of mothering, Mrs. Parrish." She handed Gracie back, and Jennie sighed deeply, wearing a contentment she hadn't known for months, perhaps since Baby Ariyah's death. "You keep this up and your second child will thrive just as well."

Jennie felt light as a butterfly. And meeting a very pregnant woman in the waiting room, a woman from Jennie's past, didn't bring back sad memories. Her eyes met Jennie's and she nodded. Yes, Dr. Sawtelle was just what Salem needed: a doctor to all women. Jennie heard her greet Miss Priscilla warmly as she welcomed her into the examining room.

Chapter 30
Family Wisdom

D r. Sawtelle said to call her Mary. Jennie— and Gracie—progressed well. Both kept their weight where Mary felt it mattered. Jennie ate fresh vegetables and apples from the Smith Family Orchards owned by early founders of Salem. Baby conversations would blend into doctoring and Mary's experiences.

"We really need a medical society in this state to address the charlatans who claim they're doctors while offering hot peppers and salt as a cure for catarrh and even gonorrhea or sell pure liquor put up in medicine bottles." Dr. Sawtelle put a fresh apron on over her dress. "Of course, as a woman I'd have to fight my way in. Eclectics tend to dismiss homeopathic doctors. Men will find any number of ways to keep a woman from achieving her highest goals."

"Your husband is supportive."

"He is."

"Mr. Parrish wants me to go to medical school."

Mary narrowed her eyes as though assessing

Jennie's capability. Jennie hurried on. "He always has. It's very endearing and I did once tell him I wanted to do that, but now, with babies, I couldn't be more content." Gracie was already seven months old and a diamond in her father's chest of feminine jewels. He delighted in Gracie's one dimple on her right cheek, her serious frown, and how the child could focus on a single toy, not be distracted by other shiny things until she was ready.

"Ha. You may find in time that your interest makes gains, weaving through the blooms of motherhood, being a wife, a good citizen. I know any number of women who have chosen that profession later in life. Bethina Owens did. Gave her child to the care of a friend and headed off. "

"You know her?"

"I do indeed. She'll graduate next year. Does that hurt?" She pressed Jennie's abdomen. "One day medical school will be six or even seven years long, as long as it takes to become a preacher. But for now, two to three years and we have our diploma. Baby moving well?" Jennie nodded. "But she'll want further study in surgery, I suspect. Now, how are your bowels moving?"

Mary seemingly held several thoughts at once. Perhaps Jennie's own flightiness as a child could be honed into the ability to keep many subjects in her mind at once, as Mary did. It might be a requirement of a physician.

She pushed Gracie in a perambulator down Winter Street, pinecones crunching underfoot and squirrels scampering. The azaleas bloomed bright red, and once or twice yellow petals invited notice, bobbing toward the street. Lilac perfume wafted over their heads as Alex pointed to a rodent with a walnut in his mouth, its eyes still and staring at the little boy.

"You're an only child, Ariyah. How did you get so wise?" She had just told Jennie that having a sister—and maybe two—was good for Douglas, that larger families help children learn they aren't the only note in the symphony.

"My mother," Ariyah answered. "She made sure I had lots of friends. Maybe that's what Douglas is missing."

Jennie thought back. "Douglas really hasn't had many friends. He had such a good time with Quilton. I think that porcupine was his best friend." She bent down to make sure seven-month-old Gracie was still asleep in the May sunshine.

"Whatever happened to that pet?"

"Charles visited at my parents', and after that terrible encounter with me, Douglas let him go. He told me of Quilton's leaving without much affect, like he'd seen a squirrel with a walnut in its mouth, staring. It was almost . . . eerie, like he punished himself without showing pain." Jennie shivered with the memory.

"Were you there? Did you see him release it?"

Jennie shook her head.

Ariyah let Alex walk beside her then, holding his hand while he helped push his own perambulator. "I shouldn't say anything. I mean, I don't really know, of course."

"What?"

"Douglas, well, this has happened a couple of times. He, Douglas, doesn't always tell the truth, Jennie. Once when I watched him for you, I found him in the cupboard where we keep the medicines. I asked him what he was doing and he said he was 'ogling.' But he had the laudanum in his hand and the cap was off. I . . . took it from him, of course, and he didn't act as though he'd had any but . . . he insisted he was just looking with the bottle still in his hand." The women had stopped. "I could see he lied. He was old enough he should have known he wasn't telling me the truth. And there were other times I questioned his veracity. I'm sorry." She looked away. "I didn't know how to tell you."

Jennie hadn't seen him be untruthful, had she? When they'd spoken to Douglas about his teacher's concerns, he'd said the teacher didn't really like him, that he treated him differently than the other children, called on him more often to make him look bad. Jennie confessed that she thought the teacher made erroneous assumptions too. He might have been accurate about Douglas being a scamp, but he hadn't said he lied. Honesty was such an important virtue. How could her son have drifted past it?

"I'm glad you've told me. I'll watch for it."

"Maybe invite some friends for him. Or cousins. Take him out to your brother's farm more often. He could ride horses there."

"Yes, that would be good."

Instead she decided to watch Douglas and to ask Lizzie if she ever questioned Douglas's truthfulness.

"Oh, la, Mrs. P. I do wonder at times. But my brothers told tall tales too, to get themselves out of trouble. They weren't very good at it and neither is Douglas. I don't think you need to worry."

Their second baby had a plan of her own. Jennie's contractions began the evening of August 19, a full month earlier than expected. Josiah went immediately for Mary and Jennie heard them mumbling in the hall.

"If that's your wish," Mary said. Jennie suspected it was the "father in the birthing room" conversation, and this time it lasted only a moment and occurred early in the process, as Jennie had spoken with Mary about it months before.

Because Jennie wasn't dilating, she and Mary discussed ways to move the birthing forward and agreed to try physical things before offering tinctures. Jennie was up and waddling, Josiah at her side. Then Lizzie filled the clawfoot tub with warm water—as the Tillamook women might do it, Josiah reminded her. The steaming water eased Jennie's back but did nothing to bring on the awaited arrival of a baby.

"I don't detect infant distress," Mary said. She set the stethoscope tube, like a fat sausage, down on the tray beside the bed, and so Jennie got up and walked again.

"You didn't say anything about mother distress," Jennie chided her.

"I worry over mothers when they aren't distressed."

Jennie actually laughed in between gasps and pants. Mary was almost as good as having Ariyah with her, who wasn't there because this baby was coming early and Ariyah and Alex had gone to the coast.

But in the early morning of August 21, Josephine Lunalilo Parrish was born. They named her for Josiah, called her Josie and then JoJo as she grew. Her middle name came from the king of the Sandwich Islands and honored Josiah's many coastal friends who had been brought to the territory by the Astorians. The name meant "generous and benevolent," and so she was, her presence a noble gift.

Josie had her father's thick, dark hair and Jennie's green eyes, and both parents couldn't have been more pleased.

"Where's Douglas?" Jennie asked as she held Josie in her arms. Lizzie rocked Gracie's cradle. She'd turn one in less than two months. The nanny looked as exhausted as Jennie, as she and Josiah had carried all those tubs of steaming water up the stairs.

"Lizzie, go see if he's in his room. In all the excitement I never saw him."

Lizzie rushed out and returned with a puzzled look on her face. "He's resting, Mrs. P. Sleeping like a baby, as they say. But—"

"But what?"

She held up a bottle of laudanum. "I was sure it had some left in it and, la, it's missing much."

They kept no liquor in their home, but that afternoon, Jennie wondered if they even ought to keep laudanum around. Douglas denied he'd taken it, didn't know how it was the bottle could have gotten into his room. "Lizzie musta left it."

Jennie assured him that was not the case and

337

they would have to think of some consequence, which then aroused him to howling about how unfair she was, which woke Josie and caused Gracie to cry. She vowed to deal with Douglas when she was more rested, but then the babies needed feeding. She sent him back to his room to "think about what you've done."

"He claims it was already empty and he was just being curious of what was in the cabinet that might ease your discomfort." Josiah returned after escorting Douglas out.

"He was worried about me?"

"It's possible that medicine was used up before," Josiah said. "You'll never win an argument with a child on the facts." He held Gracie in his arms, wiped her little face of mother's milk.

"I don't want to be unfair, but he ought not to have had it in his room."

"Maybe Lizzie did leave it there by mistake. Or I did. I've been known to have a lapse now and then."

That was true. Jennie had noticed that Josiah sometimes repeated a question she'd just answered for him. At sixty-seven, he wasn't old, but with many things on his mind, one could be forgetful at any age. "I doubt that you'd forget that."

"Parents seek fairness and justice when a

behavior is in need of reprimand while the child has nothing else to do but plot adventures. There were occasions with my boys—"

"So what do I do? We can't let him slip by us." Jennie raised her voice. "Ariyah said once she caught him in her medicine cabinet."

"We'll keep it locked, get a different key and hide it."

It was a lapse on her part, her nose in an anatomy book rather than tending her son. The nux vomica hadn't been secured either. What woman of medicine would be so careless? More evidence that her place was here, in this home, paying better attention.

They celebrated Gracie's first birthday, then Douglas's tenth that October. Jennie had asked Josiah to buy Douglas a pony of his own to ride. She hoped giving him an animal to enjoy and be responsible for would interest him. He walked around the gray horse with an almost white mane and tail, patted his neck.

"Did you get me a gun too, Papa?"

"Douglas. Please. Don't be rude. This is an exceptional gift."

"Would you like to ride him?" Josiah asked. "His name is Biscuit. The white mane apparently reminded the owner of good bread dough."

"I guess." Douglas let Josiah help him mount the animal, take the reins, and trot around the paddock. Lizzie held JoJo and Jennie carried Gracie on her hip and they watched her son. Dust followed the horse around the fenced circle. When he finished, he trotted right up to the collection of women, a little too close. They all stepped back as he slid off. "Will I have to take care of him?"

"Yes, of course." Jennie's face burned with embarrassment. "Your papa has brought you a lovely gift, but such an animal needs attention to be maintained."

"I guess."

When it came to Douglas, guessing was what they all did.

Raising three children consumed them that year: loving them all, trying to anticipate what they needed to be healthy and strong and grow wise, matching discipline to acts and age. It was Jennie's hardest year.

So, when Douglas turned eleven and Josiah suggested he attend the boarding school part of Willamette, Jennie considered it.

"He'll make new friends there," Josiah said. "Perhaps it'll help him realize that the girls need your attention now and that Lizzie's time too is taken by the little ones. Maybe he'll develop some interest in a team activity."

He could make friends his own age; and she was tired. Every day seemed to have some new challenge, a negotiation over whether he had fed Biscuit or whether he'd left Van's leash out in the rain. It was often easier to do things herself rather than struggle with getting Douglas to do it. But a boarding school? When they lived in the same town? Wasn't that admitting failure?

The turning point came a year later when Charles showed up with his new wife.

Thankfully, Douglas was at school. She would always be grateful for that divine timing. Josiah was working at the barns, so it was Jennie who saw her former husband to the parlor.

"Meet Felicity Kellog Pickett." She was a short woman, Jennie's height but heavier. She wore a bonnet with new ribbons, the burgundy matched her dress, the ribbon bunched tight at her throat. Charles looked better than he had that day at her parents' farm, less gaunt, his eyes clearer.

"I work with her brother at *our* store on Main and Second."

She didn't comment about his having a penchant for working with his wife's family and instead congratulated him on his store ownership and his new marriage.

"We have hats for sale and other doodads for ladies," Felicity said. "Charles thought you should know, as you like nice things, he says." Her eyes gazed around the room that was still furnished with most of Elizabeth's furniture.

"I know I gave you full custody of Douglas when we separated."

"When you divorced me."

"But now I'm a family man and thought it would be good to have my son with me."

She didn't blink an eye, but her heart lurched and she heard a silent "No!" scream in her head.

"Douglas should have a say," Felicity said, "his being almost fourteen and all? He'd be a good worker for the store." She added that last under her breath, answering an unspoken question Jennie had of "why now?"

"We could do it legal-like or you hand him over."

"He's just twelve. Still a child."

"Why, I was working for my da when I was eight. It's good for a lad or lassie, isn't that so, Charley?"

"I'd need to confer with my husband."

"Old Man Parrish? What's he got to say about my son?"

"He's helped raise your son, fed and clothed him, is educating him at Willamette." Lizzie had brought in a tea tray and Jennie served as her hands shook.

"It's a father's choice about how his son is raised."

"Josiah's been a father to him when you were . . . indisposed."

"I'm not now."

"So you say."

"Let the boy decide," Felicity insisted. "He's of an age."

Jennie sat up straighter, heard feet in the nursery overhead, breathed a prayer of gratitude for provision. "I'll not ask Douglas's preference and neither will you. But I will speak with Mr. Parrish. Some decisions are best left to the adults."

She wanted to say, *You take him and see how hard it is to raise a child affected by grief and abandonment and liquor.* Did she worry that Douglas would do well with his father and it was she who had created the problems in Douglas's life? Yes, a little. But it was out of protection she hesitated, her son's safety and his father's history ruling her thoughts.

"If you care to check back in a week or so, I'll have had time to talk with Mr. Parrish." She had nothing more to say to Charles. Gray swept his temples, washed-out white speckled his beard. She tried not to judge the woman he'd married. Charles's decision to leave them had brought newness to their lives, so why should she begrudge his having a new life too? And maybe Douglas would be happier with his father. She did wonder what Felicity had that kept Charles happy; what held the two together and what was the lack in her?

A police report in the *Enterprise* the next

morning answered her question. They'd both been arrested for disorderly conduct outside a saloon in Salem. Felicity must have gone drinking with him, something Jennie never would have done.

Chapter 31

A Carousel

Their lives moved like horses on a carousel, ups and downs, circling a center. Yes, they had daily troubles with spilled milk or bumps and bruises, but they knew the moments of down would soon be replaced by a rise above. Jennie had found wisdom in the lower places, discovering that even there she was not alone. A divine spirit walked beside her and she learned to trust that those dark places would not last. A fox would trot into her life when she most needed a reminder about healing grace.

Gracie's focus turned to music. JoJo scribbled pictures and had a flair for colors and relished it when her antics brought on adult laughter. They both loved books and Josiah read to them with animation, making sounds of animals and creating suspense with his voice. Jennie loved seeing her husband enjoy his girls.

Jennie hated to admit it, but Douglas being in the boarding school helped enormously. He came home on weekends, and they all walked on pebbled trails then, ignoring little discomforts. He was respectful to adults, appeared to enjoy being with the little girls, who adored his attention. The time when he was at school gave them respite to prepare for the uncertainties of when he was with them. She felt justified in not telling him that his father had come calling.

Then came the dreaded school conference. That unpleasant man had left—and his physics teacher said, "Douglas neither works nor spins. His charm will get him through though."

"What did he mean by Douglas not spinning?" Jennie asked as Josiah helped her into the carriage. "Was he talking about him not doing even light work, like spinning yarn?"

"He's a physics teacher, so I took it to mean he lacks a kind of momentum, what's needed to keep a top upright so it keeps spinning."

Both characterizations worried her for his future: indolent and purposeless. But there were no reports of minor thefts of laudanum and the school rules prohibited smoking or drinking. If he was going to learn to work and spin, he was in the best place to make that happen.

Their lives were excruciatingly normal. Josiah worked on completing the transfer of the thirty-three acres of land and to begin building the state school for the deaf, mute, and now blind students too. A small work building went up and Josiah was ready with his hammer, his mechanical tape measure, and his enthusiasm at the site. It was one of those carousel-up days until Jennie answered the door.

"Reverend Parrish, he has fallen, Missus. It's real bad." The workman rubbed his cap in his hands, didn't want to look at her as he stood in the hallway of their home.

"What happened? Is he at the doctor's?"

"He is, Missus. Closest was Dr. Sawtelle, that woman one."

"Excellent. I'll get the carriage and be there."

The workman's shoulders sagged in relief. He must have worried over a woman doctor being asked to treat a man. Jennie thought that by 1875 such attitudes would be adjusted. "You come with me, Missus. It be faster."

She grabbed her hat and reticule. "Lizzie, I'm going with the workman." She breathed a prayer, "Help, help."

"Yes, missus, I'll help ye." He reached for her hand so she could sit beside him.

The horse clip-clopped at a fast pace. What had Josiah been doing on that ladder? He'd turn seventy in January, though his hair had less gray than Charles's, and except for his white beard, one wouldn't think he'd met fifty. He was a vibrant man, active, his mind always working on some problem to solve. She supposed she had no right to try to keep him from ladders.

They sped past Willamette, where she looked to see if Douglas was outside playing rounders or maybe sitting beneath an oak, reading. The horse trotted to Dr. Sawtelle's office, where a few men meandered around outside, some leaning on the wagon that must have brought Josiah, as blankets marked the bed.

"Mrs. Parrish, we're so sorry." This from a man wearing a top hat he removed. "I tried to suggest that he let me or others make the climb, but he insisted. I've sent for a real doctor. A surgeon. She"—he nodded toward Mary's office—"was the closest. Mr. Parrish said he knew of her."

So he was conscious. *Thank you.* "Thank you. Let me through, please."

She rushed into the examining room. Sunshine poured through the transom over the door, casting colored prism light from the glass jars that lined Dr. Sawtelle's shelves.

"Broken ribs. And you can see the leg wound. Can you assist? My nurse is ill."

Jennie spied the white of a femur bone when Mary cut off Josiah's pant leg. Blood. Her stomach lurched. She'd never had a problem witnessing blood, but there was something different about knowing it belonged to someone she dearly loved.

"I'm all right, Jennie." His voice was raspy. *Lung damage from the broken ribs?* "Just a little nick." He took a breath, winced.

"Minimizing does no good, Josiah." She held his hand. "This looks serious to me."

He squeezed back with good strength.

Good. She pressed her fingers to his wrist. His heart raced but it was steady and strong.

"He apparently fell off a ladder. Looks like two broken ribs, leg fracture, and then something metal jabbed into his thigh. See here." Mary moved him, gentle as a baby. "Missed the artery. Ha! I'll need to set the bone. Infection is our worst problem."

The top-hat man had followed her in. "The surgeon will be here soon. Don't start anything until he's here."

"Dr. Sawtelle will do fine." She leaned over Josiah. "Does that meet with your approval?"

"Whatever you think best, Dr. Parrish." He winced.

Mary shooed Top Hat from the room, motioned Jennie toward the steaming water and soap, then advised her on how to deliver the chloroform to make certain she didn't put herself to sleep while taking Josiah under. Josiah drifted off as the called-for surgeon burst through the door.

The doctor from the night of Ariyah's birth.

"I can take it from here, ladies."

"I don't want you near my husband." Jennie's surge of courage made her voice boom in the room. "He has an attending physician. Leave. Now."

"But has she set bones? Managed compound

fractures? Delivering a baby is one thing, but this is serious surgery."

"While I feel no need to defend myself to you," Mary said, "I will say, for Mrs. Parrish's sake, that I have trained in New York and seen and assisted with my share of wounds and broken bones. It is Mrs. Parrish's wish that I continue. Now you, please leave. Or stay in silence if you care to assist. A decent doctor never turns down the wisdom of another. I shall proceed."

"Mrs. . . . Parrish?" He looked at her, recognized her, Jennie thought perhaps remembering his liquored late arrival at Ariyah's birth. And death.

"Two assistants will be better than one," he said.

Jennie managed the chloroform; he washed his hands and Mary did her work. She was meticulous with the cleaning of the wound, said that dirt carried bacteria that could harm. The surgeon grunted, but they were a team.

Mary set the bone and bound it but noted that the puncture wound on his thigh would "heal better with open air to it. But we'll have to watch for infection, change the dressings twice a day at least, and put honey on the bandage and a little oil. I've packed this cotton into it with zinc. Ferrum phosphoricum powder will address the fever that will surely come. I'll let Mr. Parrish recuperate here, Jennie, if you approve. At least

350

for a few days. Then you can take him home and nurse him there."

The nearest hospital was miles away in Portland, and many saw it as a place to die rather than heal.

"Such nonsense, those tinctures and powders." The surgeon spoke, but Jennie thought she detected a begrudging admiration in his voice.

The healing proved long and arduous, with many consultations with Mary. Jennie had a cane made for Josiah with a gold fox head. He'd need it when he began to walk again.

"We're moving to Portland after the first of the year," Mary told her one morning when Jennie stopped by to pick up more powders. "Cheston has finished his degree and I can do much more in Portland than here. I like treating women, but it's surgeries and a wider range of medical problems that most intrigue me."

"But women here need you."

"Truth is, we can't make a living here, Jennie. We need a wider population, women physicians do. It's something I have to think about with a child. You're fortunate that money isn't a part of your struggle."

"It was once. That's why having treatment for women is so important."

"Then you go to medical school. You become their doctor."

"Have you been conspiring with Josiah?"

She looked puzzled. "I remember what you told me a long time ago. And when I saw you assist with Josiah's injuries, I knew you'd do well as a physician, though it's too bad that you aren't hungry enough to pursue it."

"A different kind of hunger drives people toward their passions and can keep them from them. I have a family now, children. Money has nothing to do with it." Jennie sighed. "And the real barrier? Reading and writing. I have to memorize and work so hard to decipher texts."

"You'd never know that, Jennie. You've compensated well. Don't let that stop you. As you know, neither Cheston nor I are religious sorts of people, but we do believe that we're created with a spirit that drives one forward for the good of others. You listen to yours."

They were interrupted then by a woman with a small child.

"Callie Charlton, meet Jennie Parrish." She used their Christian names. "Jennie here has an interest in medicine and I know you do as well." She turned to Jennie, holding out the powders Jennie had come for. "Callie's studying in Portland with a well-known physician to prepare herself for entrance to Willamette in the next few years. How is that progressing?"

"Well. I teach at Hollady Addition during the day and study with Dr. Rafferty one evening a week. Lorena here gets the rest of my time." She stroked the child's blonde hair. "Widows make do."

Callie stood tall like Mary, with a wide face, high forehead, and serious hazel eyes behind round glasses. She wore a silver collar pin polished to a shine. Side by side, the women were formidable. Jennie wondered if women interested in medicine had to be larger than life to be taken seriously or even noticed. Her small frame would be one more disadvantage.

"Perhaps the three of us could gather for tea," Jennie offered. She longed for female companions who put healing as their cause and missed Mary already.

"I'd like that," Callie said.

"Ha. We can plot how to get you into Willamette and be able to take dissection."

"Every one of us has cut up a deer or two, so it isn't like we haven't seen blood and guts." Callie's frankness sealed her charm for Jennie. She'd like having her as her physician. Callie said, "When Lorena is four or five, I'll attend Willamette. If they'll have me."

"They'll have you or my name isn't Dr. Mary Sawtelle."

"Perhaps with two of us wanting to enroll, they'd have a more difficult time saying no." *Did I really say that?*

"That's the spirit," Mary said. She waved her

stethoscope like a wand in the air. "I'll see you both one day in the Medical Society!"

Josiah came down the steps, the *thump-thump* of the cane announcing his arrival. It was Advent, the season of waiting. "I've wrapped the girls' presents. Should we put them under the tree?"

His family tradition meant exchanging gifts on the Eve of Christmas, with Christmas morning a time of worship, followed by a huge meal and children playing with their treasures. Neighbors often joined them, and Ariyah and Alex would on Christmas Day. Douglas would be home that afternoon for the Christmas recess.

Jennie pondered what Chen had told her about Douglas a few days before. She knew it had taken great courage for him to come forward, saying, "Mister Douglas, he at Chinatown, play cards and smoke."

"Douglas? My Douglas? Oh, Chen, surely not. He's a child. It must have been his father. They do bear a striking resemblance."

"Just tell what see, Missus."

"I appreciate that." But he had to be wrong.

"Jennie? About the presents? Under the tree or hidden away?"

"Oh, sorry, my mind took a detour." She didn't share the news with Josiah. No need to worry him over a mistaken identity. He was already despondent over the slow pace of his recovery. It bothered Jennie too.

"Under the tree. We'll have to watch Josie. She'll want to pull the paper off right now! But it's fun to anticipate the possibilities, don't you think?"

"Maybe the mantel. They can see them and anticipate, as you suggest, but not reach them."

"Except for Douglas. We'll have to make sure he doesn't conspire with Gracie to get them down for her."

Josiah nodded. How she longed to hear his deep-throated laugh, the one she thought she might not hear again after his terrible fall. Infection had strained them. At least now he was up and using the cane to move around. He suffered from a chronic leg pain Mary thought was nerve related, but he rarely complained. Jennie witnessed his wincing and he occasionally asked for laudanum when it became too much to bear. She ached for him and for not being able to relieve his suffering. Still, he was upright and loving his daughters and his wife.

She finished baking her famous apple pie, forcing Chen out of the kitchen for her Christmas cooking. He'd spend the day in Chinatown off Liberty Street. Van huddled at her feet, hoping for a crumb or two to drop. His black ears swept the floor as he scampered for a piece of apple she put in his dish. Josiah came in and eased into a rocker, Josie tugging at his beard as she sat in his lap.

"You have a surgeon's hands, Jennie."

"My baking makes you think of surgery?"

"I'm recalling how many times those hands have brought relief to me and others."

"And I didn't even need to go to school to offer such curative ways." She hadn't healed him though, nor her son's deep troubles. She blew hair from her forehead, tightened the bow at her waist where her pinafore tied. Water bubbled in the pot and she offered Josiah a cup of tea. He declined.

"You change the subject," he said. "But one day—"

"We'll see one day."

Douglas bounded into the kitchen then, and Gracie raced to hug his legs. Josie sat on Josiah's lap, the shy one, seeking quiet sunshine; Gracie faced the wind. At twelve, Douglas was nearly six feet tall and sometimes Jennie caught her breath when she saw him and the resemblance to his father. He towered over her and came to the table, holding Gracie in his arms. He leaned over and grabbed a bunch of dough Jennie had filled with cinnamon, sugar, and butter and popped it into his mouth.

"Don't you want to wait until it's baked?" Jennie moved to peck his cheek but he turned.

"Huh-uh. Takes too long." He bent to put Gracie down.

Jennie grabbed his hand then and kissed it. He let her and smiled. "I'll take seconds when the dough is browned. You always make the best."

They'd turned the corner, Chen's message set aside; his teacher's too. They were a Currier and Ives lithograph. Just perfect, as Ariyah would say. That's the holiday picture she hung in her mind.

Chapter 32
"In All Things, Be Content"

For Christmas that year, Josiah gave Jennie a gift she could not have imagined. Nothing sparkling or fashionable but the *perfect* gift, as Ariyah described it when she showed her friend.

"He's an amazing man," she said.

"Yes, he is that." She fingered the envelope that he'd had wrapped inside a basket he said came from a Clatsop woman's weaving of cedar bark and grasses. It contained a deed to thirty-three acres of land in Salem and the payments from a contract with a man named Pittock who had built a mansion on property once owned by Josiah. "So you will have land of your own should something happen to me," he'd said. "You can sell it or keep it or give it away, whatever you wish. It's yours. In your name."

"Thank you" was all she could muster. They both assumed that she'd outlive him. Having land was the best kind of investment in this Oregon country. It was a safety net for her and the children. Along with her trust in Providence, she needed nothing more.

Douglas spent that next summer with them rather than staying at the boarding school. A big celebration for the one hundredth anniversary of the nation's independence meant speeches by Josiah as he felt up to it; parades and parties. Douglas seemed to enjoy himself. He worked with Josiah and the husbandman they'd had to hire, tending the Cashmere goats and the sheep. Josiah had added hogs and there were the chickens, of course. Douglas took special interest in the chickens. It all seemed to be going so well. Even Josiah's spirits had raised with Douglas's presence.

"Stacys are interested in having their daughter get one of the goat kids to raise, maybe show at the fair next year. Would you like to come with us and help her pick one out?" Josiah put his fork down and looked at Douglas.

Douglas shoveled one of Chen's noodle dishes with beef and vegetables into his mouth. The child could consume a garden by himself, as Jennie's father would say. But he was a tall boy and still growing. "Sure. I like the goats. Any one of them would be good."

Josiah nodded, finished drinking his coffee. He picked up his cane. "They'll be here around 3:00 p.m. Bring them over when they come, if you will, Douglas. I need to see if we've cured the rat problem."

"Did you need nux vomica?" Jennie asked.

"I think I have plenty of strychnine at the barn."

Josiah headed out in his now-familiar hesitating step with his cane. Douglas tossed a stick for Van to chase while they waited for the Stacy family. "We'll serve tea when they arrive." She checked in the nursery, where JoJo sat on Lizzie's lap, a book before her. "We'll have visitors at 3:00 p.m. Bring the girls down then, would you?" She was back downstairs mending a tear in Josiah's wool pants when Douglas came in panting.

"What is it?"

"Let me catch my breath."

"Is Josiah all right?"

"Of course." He bent over, hands on thighs, breathing hard. "I ran all the way back. Whew!" He stood up, brushed his brown curls, shiny with sweat, away from his eyes. "He wants your strychnine. He ran out."

"The key's . . . in the bottom desk drawer, in an envelope near the back. Be sure to bring back whatever he doesn't use."

She had a slight twinge telling him of the key, knowing the nux vomica bottle was right next to the laudanum. But he had matured, was no longer a little boy challenging everything or seeking notice in troubling ways. He was a young man. She could trust him.

The Stacys arrived and Chen served tea while Jennie cradled JoJo on her hip. She sent Lizzie to the barn to tell Josiah and Douglas their guests had arrived.

The couple were the spitting image of the Mother Goose rhyme about Jack Sprat who could eat no fat and his wife who "could eat no lean." Their daughter Nora, the same age as Douglas, was a blend between the two. She fidgeted on the chair, her eyes darting to the mantel, then the vases on the table, stopping at the paintings before smiling at Jennie, then Gracie, then looking away. She reminded Jennie of Douglas in younger years with always-busy hands and eyes. Josiah had walked back and the men discussed goats and breeding while Nora's short legs rocked her back and forth on her chair.

"Douglas, why don't you take Nora to the barns? We can follow, but I'm sure you've already penned the goats you have in mind for her to choose from."

"Good idea, Mother." The two headed off and the adults lingered, talking. The Stacys soon brought their wagon around the house to stop before the barn while Josiah and Jennie watched the girls scamper before them. The day was decidedly spring, with birds flitting and the fragrance of irises and yellow daffodils marking their way. By the time they arrived, helped Mrs. Stacy from her wagon seat, and entered the barn, Nora sat beside a kid in fresh straw, petting it, stroking it methodically. Douglas had put a halter on the animal and placed the others back in with their mothers, as it was the two children and the goat in the pen. The kid bleated and flicked its tail. Nora looked up.

"He's so soft." Her gaze was languid, so different from her agitated state when she'd been in the parlor. The kid brought her comfort, reminding Jennie of the way that Quilton had once given such calm to Douglas. Jennie looked at her son. His eyes drooped as though tired too. He moved his hands slowly so as not to startle the kid, leaning over the short wall to scratch the animal's ears.

"Looks like you've found your show animal." Josiah went on to describe the pedigree, answer questions. The Stacys nodded, said "*Ja, ja*" often, agreeing in their German.

"Time to go, Daughter."

Nora nodded, moved ever so slowly. She stood up, grimaced a little, darting eyes returning.

"Are you all right?" Jennie's doctor/mother instinct on alert.

"My stomach feels upset." She looked at the

kid. "I think I'll name her Penelope because she had to wait so long for me to find her. Oh"—she clutched her stomach—"I don't feel well."

"Our girl loves the classics, especially Odysseus." Her father beamed.

Anxiety? "I have licorice root tea I could send with you. It might make your stomach feel better."

"She be alright when we get home."

They loaded the kid into the wagon. By now, Nora's eyes were darting again. She massaged her hands as though she had a ball of dough in her palms.

"Just excitement," Mrs. Stacy said. "She'll be fine, we get her kid into its own pen. Right on the porch."

Douglas looked sleepy too as they sent them on their way. Josiah put his arm around Douglas's shoulder and they walked back to the house. Jennie carried Josie on her hip, held Gracie's hand as she skipped and tugged her toward every wind-dancing daffodil she could find.

"Going to my room," Douglas said, lengthening his stride.

Jennie met Josiah's eyes over the top of the girls' heads.

Douglas had left them, moved on ahead and out of sight.

• • •

The knock on the door came not long after the Stacys had left. Jennie and Josiah had just started up the stairs to the girls' playroom.

"She's taken real ill, Missus," Mr. Stacy said. "Thought we'd check with you."

"Nora? Could she have a reaction to something we served here?" Jennie tried to remember what was in the tea cakes, but it was nothing out of the ordinary. "I'll come, see if I can help. You sent for the doctor?"

He nodded. "You work with herbs and oils. You can help her?"

"Is she vomiting?"

He nodded. "She's so sick, Missus. Sweating and shaking all over." He shivered and Jennie watched fear spread through his body like a snake slithering from head to toe.

"I'll get licorice root." She ran to her medicine cabinet, grateful to have a remedy. It was unlocked. She remembered then that Douglas had taken the nux vomica down to the barn. She did a quick scan for the licorice root, grateful the plant grew wild and she had harvested some last summer. "Chop into warm water and see if you can get her to drink it, like a tea." She handed the paper package to Nora's father. "Go home. We'll come shortly."

He nodded, mounted his horse, and was gone.

364

Douglas snored a contented sleep, so she closed his door and she and Josiah rushed to the Stacys', Lizzie tending the girls. Once there, the kid bleated on the front porch in its pen.

The doctor shook his head as they entered to Mrs. Stacy's wails. "We're too late. Strychnine poisoning."

Strychnine. "Poor child. How?" *My suggestion of licorice root tea would have made it worse, if she'd been able to keep it down.*

"She was comatose when I arrived. The symptoms, white foam."

"I don't know where she gets it. None here." Her father's eyes pooled with tears.

Coldness washed over her. "Josiah, the nux vomica. Did you use it all?"

He frowned. "I didn't need it. I had crystals for the rats, a small amount and in the corner, far away from the pens. It couldn't have been that."

"But you sent Douglas for it?"

"I didn't."

She gripped his arm. "He—Douglas said you needed it. We need to go. Find out if Douglas—"

Guilt, regret, anger rode in the carriage. She set those emotions aside. She knew what it was like to outlive your child. She prayed she wouldn't outlive another.

"I didn't mean to! I only wanted a taste of laudanum, just a little. I took both bottles. I

365

thought she only had some of the sleep stuff. Did she drink the nux?"

"Yes, she did." Jennie shook. "And she's dead. She's dead, Douglas."

"Dead?" His color faded. "I said it would calm her down, but she was drinking the laudanum. She drank—the bottles look alike. I didn't . . . I didn't know she took it. I didn't, Mama, I didn't."

He covered his head with his hands as though to ward off blows.

"Oh, Douglas. I'm so, so very sad. What made you think you had to have laudanum in the first place? And why take the other bottle at all? To cover your lie that Josiah had sent you for it?"

He cried now. "It makes me feel better. I thought it would help her. I didn't know she took the other."

The bottles did look similar; such a fatal error. Jennie's own mistake in letting him use the key without rising and going there for him.

"She must have consumed what was left in the bottle." Josiah's voice carried the defeat Jennie felt.

There was blame enough to go around and surely the Stacys, if they chose to, could win a lawsuit. They would find a way to grieve and do what they could to serve the Stacys in theirs.

Nora's parents took the information in silence,

remorse the cape they wore as they spoke of the two children—for they were still children at twelve—drinking what they thought would make them calm, not knowing that what Nora took would do great harm, given the amount. Douglas told them of his lie, sobbing his regrets. Mrs. Stacy kept a handkerchief to her nose, her eyes as red as beets. Mr. Stacy shook his head. "You are children, making childish choices. We know you did not intend. It was an accident." The kid bleated and he asked Josiah if he could give the animal back.

"Of course, of course. And we will provide all you need for the funeral."

"*Ja*, that would be good then. Like the apostle Paul, we seek to rejoice in all things, be content, he says. But this, it takes some time for." He caressed Nora's doll.

The *Statesman* reported on the death of Nora, saying she'd been playing at "the Parrish household and got into strychnine and died at home before anyone knew what had happened." Jennie hated that Josiah's name—his name—was associated with death, when always before his reputation carried the highest standards of compassion, good judgment, and generosity. His name appeared in articles about a pioneer picnic he spoke at or his good citizenship in giving land for public uses, even his marrying

Jennie, "an old man and a young woman" looking happy. Now it would be forever tainted. Worse was the great loss of a child because of carelessness—Jennie's—in not overseeing what was taken from the medicine cabinet, in not supervising carefully her own son.

But blame and accusation can only stall one on the road to healing and hope. One had to return to the commitment, to love and to life.

Josiah and Jennie spent the following days discussing Douglas's penchant for escape. Perhaps there was something genetic in his struggle, his father having had that same thirst. When Jennie thought of Charles, she cringed, as there seemed no hope, reports of his drinking coming from many sources. But some blame must be with her, she decided. She'd gotten caught up in her world of a loving husband and babies and had not participated in the anti-saloon efforts. She hadn't attended city meetings dealing with beer and its effects; she hadn't spoken up when she'd seen children carrying home their pails of beer lined with lard to keep the foam down so more brew could be brought to their parents. She hadn't once signed a petition to pass a prohibition liquor law as her father and brother had.

She'd barely paid attention to Mary Hunt's work either, letting anti-drinking information into textbooks or Frances Willard's passion with the Women's Christian Temperance Union. What had she done with her own passion of seeking medicine to stave off that thirst? After Charles left, she had turned her thoughts to her world, her life.

Like Douglas, she had hid from painful things, found sham contentment in the mind's escape.

"Do you think that asylum doctor, Hawthorne, could help Douglas?" She knitted a sweater for Gracie.

Josiah was thoughtful. "It's worth the effort. People get crazy after liquor. Laudanum, spirits, even beer, despite the brewers calling it 'liquid bread.' I'll make a contact."

"No, let me. It's something I should do."

"It's only for a short time, Douglas. They think they can help you stay away from . . . well, you know."

"Liquor, laudanum, Mother. You can say them." They sat in the parlor, Jennie across from him. "Let's add opium. Yes, I saw Chen in Chinatown. And then there's the white powder of cocaine. Lovely stuff."

"Oh, Douglas. Please don't mock this. What you're doing, it's killing you. And us too. The heart can only take so much."

"My heart or yours?"

"Please. Give Dr. Hawthorne a chance. His hospital . . . it will be a good thing. We'll visit.

369

I've spoken with him. He's a good man. The hospital is clean and—"

His eyes watered. He was just a child. She reached for him. He jerked away. Would she ever find again that happy boy who had lived behind such grand green eyes? Could medicine offer any silence for those tragic siren calls?

Chapter 33

Forcing the Fiend Away

Y ou need to silence the fiend," Ariyah said. They were in her parlor, the heavy brocade drapes pulled back to expose the sun.

Jennie frowned.

"Nicholas Rowe, the English writer. He said that guilt was 'the avenging fiend that follows us behind with whips and stings.' You've whipped yourself enough about Charles and Douglas and now dear little Nora. It's time you looked through a new lens."

"I no longer know how."

"When I feel guilty, I have this practice." Ariyah set her teacup down. "I first confess to my wrongdoing. That could take some time."

"I've confessed so loud and long I think the Lord might have gotten clouds to stuff in his ears."

"Then I seek forgiveness and accept it. The hardest part. But it lets me consider what sort of personal change I'm being called to make, to address whatever it was that made me feel guilty in the first place. I put my focus there, then set

371

my heart on what I can do, instead of on what I can't." She patted her friend's hand. "I know this is difficult, but the Greeks say wisdom comes from suffering."

"Has anyone ever told you how wise you are?"

Ariyah laughed. "It's one of the things I miss most about dear Peleg. He thought I was the smartest woman he'd ever met. He told me often." She sighed. "I miss that."

Jennie took her words to heart. What personal change could she make? What new lens might she see her world through?

The curriculum at Willamette included "Scientific Temperance Instruction" from the work of Mary Hunt, a former chemistry teacher turned reformer. Jennie was grateful the school took drinking seriously—as had school boards across the country. The drinking on the streets of Salem was so pervasive, one could smell the mash while walking by a saloon, and it did not mask the scent of vomit in the gutters. Jennie had ignored that as much as she could until now.

But the school primer "facts" concerned Jennie when she read them. "The majority of beer drinkers die of dropsy." *They do not.* "When alcohol passes down the throat, it burns off the skin, leaving it bare and burning." *There's no evidence for that.* These "facts" were efforts at intimidation rather than science, and she couldn't imagine that such miseducation would stop someone like Douglas from drinking.

They'd had him admitted to the Hawthorne hospital. He had gone without complaint, perhaps as defeated as Jennie felt. She had visited, conferred with the doctor. She so hoped this psychiatry field would offer him release.

After church one fall morning several months after the death of Nora, Josiah helped Jennie into the carriage, newly arrived from around the Horn. The service had spoken to her, or the one Charles Wesley hymn at least. *Forth in Thy Name, O Lord.* It was the second verse that struck her.

> The task thy wisdom hath assigned,
> O let me cheerfully fulfill;
> in all my works thy presence find,
> and prove thy good and perfect will.

The door lock clicked with a firm sound, reminding her of the day they'd left Douglas at the Hawthorne hospital. He was back with them now, in school, no warmer to Josiah or her, but he was pleasant with the girls, and Van still curled in his lap. There'd been no incidents at Willamette. She hoped he was truly better. But she wondered, did her works reflect "thy good and perfect will"?

The driver chirped to the team and they *clop-clopped* down State Street, the scent of horse droppings on the road strong in the summer heat. The girls were dressed in their "Sunday best," sitting on either side of Jennie, Josiah across from them all. She put her arms out to protect instinctively as the carriage hit a bump.

"You saved us, Mama," Gracie said, straightening her straw hat.

"Yes, if I hadn't held you, you'd have fallen right into your papa's arms."

Josiah grinned.

In that unexpected moment warmed with love, perhaps because her spirit had been opened from the hymn, Jennie felt an *Einsicht*. "I want to go to medical school."

"I'd say it was about time." He grinned at her as though he'd just discovered fire. Perhaps he had. Her fire.

"I'll have to find a doctor to read with first. When he thinks I'm ready, if he does, I'll try to enroll."

"When *he* thinks you're ready? Why not study with a female physician? Bethina Owens now has her degree and is back in Oregon."

"She is? Is she in Portland?"

"Southern Oregon." He leaned against the padded back, straightened his hat still grinning like a man just learning he had fathered a child.

"You're not the least surprised?"

"I knew the time would come."

She shook her head, smiling. Then, "It does feel a bit like a betrayal, not reading with a woman, but a male doctor will lend legitimacy when I apply or try to join a medical society."

"First a preceptorship, then medical school, then president of the medical society." He clapped his hands and the girls did too, with no idea of what they cheered.

"I'll need a certain kind of physician." The memories of her learning to read with her brother's patience rushed back; the long hours of deciphering texts Josiah had bought her before the girls were born. Maybe she couldn't do this. Maybe she was already too old at thirty-three or too set on an arc of a wife and mother to now find a way to serve beyond. And yet her whole life had taken her to this decision. Her gifts with oils and herbs; a family who encouraged her despite her challenges; friends who turned to her for nurture and who gave back; and a husband who had both the means and intention to seek and trust and model that for her. "It'll take time."

Josiah nodded agreement. "Somehow we think we must be large enough to finish before we first begin. You'll make a gain by just beginning."

"Yes. Just begin."

"I can make inquiries."

"No, I want to do this myself, without your influence. Now, don't pout." He'd rolled his lower lip out like a child. Both girls giggled, Josie first. He exaggerated the gesture, wiggled his graying eyebrows at them.

"Papa's funny," Gracie said. She pointed her finger. She'd be four soon. They'd just celebrated Josie's third birthday.

"Your papa is funny." Jennie smoothed the ruffles on her dress.

"I only want to help in any way I can." His hands crossed over on the cane's top to hold hers. "What's the benefit of being president of the board of trustees if I can't assist my own wife?"

"You do contribute, greatly. Being there for the children, offering me a space to work and the time. And letting me cry on your shoulder when I'm frustrated." He kissed her gloved hand and released it. "It took me nearly a year to get through *Women's Concerns*. Douglas's trials have my name written beside his. Maybe I can find a way to alleviate the degradation that comes from consumption, though Prohibition laws may be the best defense."

"There will always be home brews and distilleries and 'medicinal uses.' There's a little alcohol in sauerkraut, you know," he teased.

376

Jennie couldn't see the lightness. She was already planning how to find a physician. Josiah softened his voice. "Some things are worth doing, Jennie, regardless of how they turn out. I'm so pleased you finally believe that."

Chapter 34
Reading Life

T he girls can come here for piano lessons. Alex would love the company." Ariyah took to the idea of Jennie's reading and added to it. "JoJo's a little young, but Gracie's the perfect age for piano. Maybe Josiah will order one for them to have at the house, so they can practice in between lessons."

"Let's see how they like it first. Gracie enjoys the bands in the park but sitting for practice, well, I guess we'll see. I think the hardest part about this will be worrying over the children getting enough attention. Lizzie's so good with them, but . . . I'll miss them."

"They'll want *your* attention, but it won't be forever that they have to share you with texts. School is only for two years, isn't it? It takes longer to become a preacher than a doctor, didn't you say?"

That Josiah had studied more years than she would did seem odd, but then he had trained to help the soul and she sought ways to heal the body, the latter less complicated. She pushed the girls in the swing that Alex's grandfather had hung in Ariyah's big oak trees. Each child had their own and didn't have to wait.

"Again, Mama." JoJo kicked her legs up high, her striped stockings like a rainbow against the blue sky.

She'd miss these moments, savored them all the more for beginning to transform her guilt into something good.

Jennie sought the proper practitioner. She wanted a "regular," as nonhomeopathic doctors were called. Josiah gave her suggestions from his contacts at the university, and one of the earliest graduates appealed to her. She found him in Gervais, a small town on the French Prairie north of Salem and near where her parents had lived. William Cusick had a background in farming and botany, then the military, which gave him surgery experience. He also consulted with Dr. Hawthorne's asylum in Portland. *Perfect.*

"Dr. Cusick has agreed to interview me," she told Josiah. "Anyone who has an interest in plants must be patient, and that's what he'll need with this student."

They stood at the barn, where Josiah shoed a horse. Jennie held the halter rope and rubbed the horse's nose. She'd forgotten Josiah had been trained as a blacksmith until she saw him work. She hoped his bad leg would allow him to finish what he'd started with this animal. He was always challenging himself to do more. His arms were a sinew of muscle. He'd exercised even while lying on his back in his recovery. His handshake, her father told her once, was the grip of a man in his forties. Sometimes it seemed he had more energy than she did. Aging invited people to its dance in peculiar ways.

"You have to interview him as well," Josiah said into the horse's hock. He pounded with his hammer. "There are others you could study with, so if there are tensions, look elsewhere." He stood and stretched, patting the horse's rump.

"I hadn't thought about my choosing him so much as finding a doctor who would accept me." She needed to "adjust her lens," as Ariyah would say. And so she did.

Dr. Cusick had reddish hair that he said came from his Irish mother. His rounded belly was a German influence. He sat across from Jennie behind a wide desk stacked with orderly folders on either end, so she looked at him through a tunnel of paper.

As she had when she interviewed Lizzie, she condensed answers so she could remember them. She asked him questions about homeopathy (excellent area of study); asked whether he considered himself a "regular" doctor (he did; surgery and pharmaceuticals can do great good to the human body). He asked her how long

380

she'd been interested in medicine, and she told him since a child (always good to have a child's passion for it, he'd replied). But because of her reading problems, she had let the dream drift away like a wayward kite. Now she hoped to tug it back.

"What are your reading problems?"

"Words don't appear to me as they might to you, so I have to translate as though they were a foreign language. At least that's how my brother described it to me. I had to learn the letters a different way to get their sounds and sight matched up."

"But you are able to do this?"

She nodded. "I've read several texts already. Where would you have me begin?" She needed to know if he thought her capable of the more difficult texts: anatomy, physiology, others.

"What texts have you read already?"

"*Women's Concerns* for one. I read Dr. Glisan's article, the Portland physician, on 'Climate and Diseases of Oregon' in the *American Medical Journal of Sciences*." She listed several other texts and journal articles. Josiah had purchased a subscription to the journal for her. She told the doctor of *Gray's Anatomy*.

"A special concern of yours would be?"

"Liquor. How it affects the brain but also how it affects the rest of us, all society, especially women." He blinked. "I remember telling my sister once, 'How can someone in their right mind keep drinking when it causes them to lose employment, family, friends, their health.' Now I see the error in that question. I had assumed the person was in their right mind—but after all that consumption of spirits, very likely they aren't. Mere living can cause brain illness. Sadness, constant stress, watching someone you love die, being abandoned—those events, not only infection or trauma—affect the brain and heart. I'd like to know how liquor touches both."

"I'm not sure there are scholarly works written by physicians that can address that, Mrs. Par ish. Autopsy is how we discover much about the brain and the liver, other organs. But how that person lived while they consumed such toxins, that's likely another field of study. Perhaps with Dr. Hawthorne. You know of his work?"

He needed to know about Douglas and Jennie's story of living with a husband who imbibed too much.

"Yes." She looked at her gloved hands. "My son struggles. His father, Charles Pickett, you may have read about him in the paper now and then. He . . . abandoned us for his love of liquor. Now my son seems drawn to its siren call. He's spent time with Dr. Hawthorne. We are hopeful that cure will hold. I've had an interest in oils and aromatics, homeopathy. I look for natural healing, but they did not seem to prevent the cravings or bring about a balance in the system of my former husband or my son. I'm turning now to allopathy—regular doctoring."

"It's a challenging . . . effort."

"What interests me, too, is the stress of lost paychecks, empty cupboards, sick children, mothers who can't afford medicine for their own worn-down bodies, illness caused by venereal diseases, internal damage to organs from drunkard husbands. And then there are the trials of pregnancy, many children, and the very risk of childbirth. I know those may not seem like issues related to alcohol and other addictions, but I think they are. I would like to read to find out if I'm close to being correct."

"You forget violent behaviors and even death of women and children because of drink. And prostitution and its evils related to the demon. You're not suggesting that only men consume?"

"Not at all." Jennie was thoughtful. "Maybe I'll study women's diseases and the effect of alcohol on them both when they consume it and when they have to live with it around them." Miss Priscilla's yellow beaded reticule and scarf flashed through her memory; her pregnancy. Did she drink? How would that affect her child? At least she had Mary Sawtelle to treat her. But Mary had left town.

"It's a large order, addiction and women's

health. Very well, how do you propose to do the reading?"

His asking her was both respectful and frightening. It would be up to her to establish her own study. "I thought we could discuss various texts you think I should be exposed to. And then we could delve into them a chapter at a time, perhaps two texts at once?"

"You can come weekly then? Perhaps twice?"

She nodded.

"We'll discuss what you've read and you can sit in with some of my patients, if they agree. We can explore questions and ways to pursue answers."

"I was hoping you could give me the answers."

He smiled, which helped slow the beating of her anxious heart.

"I know that knowledge comes more from questions than from answers, and I appreciate your willingness to let me ask and search and find my way."

"So you'll have me as your preceptor?" He looked over the top of his glasses.

"Yes, of course. Shall we discuss fees?"

"I usually read with two students," Dr. Cusick said. "And take on at least one *pro bono*, as my lawyer friends would say."

"It ought not to be me. Josiah and I can afford this. Would we study together, your other student and me?"

"Yes. I've a widow with a young child who wishes to matriculate eventually. She's saved her money as a teacher but still needs financial support. Callie Charlton."

Jennie gasped.

"You know her?"

"We met in Dr. Mary Sawtelle's office."

"Ah, Mrs. Sawtelle, who flunked anatomy, they say."

Would she ever be known as just a good doctor? "She says she was refused a graduate degree because of politics."

"I fear she's right. You'll face your share of it, Mrs. Parrish, despite your husband's influences."

"Perhaps because of them."

"Perhaps. Medicine itself struggles with seeing the female as strong enough to complete a degree, despite the many women doctors back East who have. Others feel a woman ought to keep the home fires burning, put herself into doing social good, Christian reaching out. Nothing wrong with that view." He tapped a pencil on the pad before him, leaned back into his chair. The springs creaked as he did. "But I am of the opinion that we're created with desires, and one's gender ought not get in the way of what-ever purpose has been planned. I'm in the minority. Even after reading with me, there is no guarantee you will be allowed entrance or that you'll find patients if you do."

"I understand. It's worth the effort regardless of how it turns out."

"A great definition of hope, I might say." He stood to shake her hand. "That understood, bring me a list of what you've already read and let's take a look at my texts. You can order your reference books once you've graduated. Until then, you'll have the loan of these."

Once I've graduated.

He spread his hand around the room, floor to ceiling with books. Textbooks. Medical books. Books with questions and answers. Books to guide her path.

Chapter 35
Grace Dancing

When they met in his office, Callie and she, Dr. Cusick led the discussion, asking questions and telling stories. Jennie created a way to make notes that highlighted the major points, drawing pictures from the texts and Dr. Cusick's lectures. She even wrote down the bad puns he was fond of using suggesting that the "orthopedic lecturers were riddled with bones of contention" or that people taking advantage of free surgeries to provide experience for students at the college had become "epidemic," not to mention how the politics of medicine threatened to "rupture the organ–ization." He'd grin.

His gentle teaching built her confidence that she had the ability to take in the information and use it for good. She learned from Callie's questions too. Dr. Cusick added texts to their lists. The Scripture speaking of being "fearfully and wonderfully made" held new meaning for Jennie as she learned of the intricacies of bone and blood. Medicine was more than knowing how organs functioned or nerves wove their way through the body; it was also about disease and countering it with potions and surgeries to oppose its ravaging of body and spirit. But most of all, being a doctor was about human warmth and understanding, about healing. Her medical book spoke of *incarn*, a word that meant "the growing of new flesh." That referred not just to the human body but to a person's soul. Listening with the heart grew new flesh; being present for another's pain, even if one couldn't stop it, brought healing. Healing also meant admitting that sometimes allopathic and homeopathic answers stood beyond their reach. Then a practitioner must create paths toward acceptance of mortality and do it with grace. It was the perfect venue for a woman's place. Women ought not be left behind.

She read each text through the lens of addictions and how they wove their way into one's body. She was a student now, studying, doing what she could to stave off that fiend of guilt sporting "whips and stings."

She loved the days when she and Callie met with his patients, one a woman very pregnant whom Dr. Cusick had tried to dissuade from drink.

"It helps me sleep, Doctor. A little brandy in the evening."

"It's not good for you. We three doctors sitting here believe so."

Her eyes looked at each of theirs. Jennie had smelled the liquor on her when she entered.

"Are you mothers?" The women both nodded. "Did you take a snort now and then?" Both shook their heads. "Well, you ain't living with my husband and six kids or you would have." She had a few of them with her, and one had facial features that didn't reflect the family resemblance. Narrow eyes with little folds at the edges, a flat nose with smoothness below and ears closer to his jaw than his eyes.

"Did you use brandy when pregnant with each of your children?"

"Yes, ma'am. They turned out all right."

Dr. Cusick asked her to take a walk down the lane before bed instead of brandy.

"I'll try."

Later the students peppered him with questions. Jennie commented on the child's interesting appearance and Callie spoke of those same features present with some children she had taught. "I never put them together with liquor consumption."

"Maybe they don't go at all," Jennie said. "Still, it's best to not imbibe, that's the main point, right, Dr. Cusick?"

"Indeed. It might make an interesting study, Mrs. Parrish, but I'm not sure how you'd formulate your hypothesis."

"We must ask more questions of our patients'

daily lives," Callie said. "With this woman we could smell the alcohol. But with others we might not."

"Perhaps you could prepare a series of questions a family doctor might ask, in general, to find out more about his patients. Her patients," he corrected.

And so they did.

Callie's presence and perseverance as a young widow encouraged Jennie; her persistence with reading and observations inspired Callie. When they met in Salem, in between reading instructions, they shared stories of husbands, of children's antics, of mothering, and of parents, the purview of a daughter's life. Callie's daughter, Lenora, often came with her, and the girls played side by side while their mothers "boned up" on orthopedic topics. Lizzie brought them tea. Josiah listened in, always a smile on his face.

"You're a good team," he said once after Callie had left.

"Two are better than one."

Jennie was disappointed, though, that none of the readings gave real insights into alcohol and addictions. Dr. Cusick said people had become more interested in punishment and shame as poisons to quench the thirst of addiction.

"Personally," Jennie told Josiah after they put the girls to bed, "I think such tactics only serve to push the person further into their destruction. I don't believe they can stop imbibing. Something within the brain and body makes that so. One day pathologists will tell us what. I think it's a disease like ovarian cysts or appendicitis. The fearmongering of so-called educators like Mary Hunt and even the WCTU may get the laws changed, but it will not stop the cravings. We'll have more people in jail for drunkenness, with nothing to offer them when they sober up."

The textbooks on obstetrics and gynecology fed her desire for learning. In between her studies, she devoted time to Josiah and the girls, drawing with them, settling disputes, treasuring their existence. She took packages of cookies to Douglas at Willamette, did not address his reddish eyes (had he been crying or drinking?) nor his furtive glances. She visited with Ariyah and her sister, her parents too. Jennie had no hobbies that consumed her. All was family and medicine washed with prayers of gratitude that she was allowed to pursue a dream and had a family that supported it.

She'd been reading about six months. They'd seen Mrs. Harvey's newborn (who had none of the strange features); assessed Mr. Johnson's swollen hand (infected from lack of treatment after he cut it with a butcher knife); and little Bessie William's swallowing a BB. "It'll shoot right through her, if you get my meaning," Dr. Cusick told Bessie's mom. The woman blushed.

Later he said to his precepts, "It'll be a shot fired in the dark when that BB comes forth." The women rolled their eyes.

"So now," he continued, "I'm going to recommend you both for membership in the Marion County Medical Society." It was March 1877.

"Not yet!" both Callie and Jennie said.

"I realize this is a new organization and that neither of you are physicians. But at the recommendation of a preceptor, I'm hoping they'll let you join. It'll expand the ranks and give legitimacy to the organization and certainly to each of you. It allows you access to presentations, the reading room, and museum. You can borrow microscopes, crutches, other equipment. You'll rub elbows with some of the professors. Get you ready for a bit of politicking. Medical societies are a great place for that." He rubbed his hands together like a man over a fire.

The women sat before a crackling flame in his study while March winds blew dead leaves past the window.

"There's all that talk of moving the medical college to Portland, lots of politics. If you indicate your intention to apply to Willamette's Medical School, it will enhance your chances of being accepted into the society. They're lobbying to keep the college here. The Ford sisters have graduated now, the first women from Willamette. You two could be next."

"What lectures are likely?" Callie asked.

"The diseases of women and children is scheduled next month. You might discuss your women's survey questions. Could be instructive for members. Women are more likely to express their complaints to one of their own sex. It's usually the husbands who object, thinking women will conspire against them. They like the assurance of a man-to-man diagnosis. Truth is, I think you're ready, both of you."

Callie's gasp expressed Jennie's awe. "For the society," Callie said.

"And to enroll," Dr. Cusick said. "The new term starts next month. Within two years, you could be having 'Doctor' before your names and dancing up the stairs to your own office. Here is the invitation. Now is the time to dance."

He winked as he handed them the next texts, and Jennie realized he received as much from their dancing as she and Callie did.

Jennie was accepted as a member of the Marion Society, but Callie was not.

"Pure politics," Dr. Cusick said. He thumped his desk. "Deplorable." It bothered Jennie too. Likely it was Josiah's influence that allowed her acceptance. She invited Callie as her guest and they presented their questionnaire together. It might have helped Callie, as the following month both were accepted into the Willamette medical program with five other women and seven men. They would graduate as doctors in 1879, two years away.

"I'm so proud of you." Lucinda hugged her when Jennie told her sister. The Sloans had moved to Portland, where the sisters met at a tearoom near the railroad station, the scent of mint fresh in the air. "I wish Rebecca and Mathias were alive to know you're in medical school."

"They taught me how to read."

"And I dismissed your interest in medicine." She picked her napkin up, then replaced it on her lap. "I'm sorry."

"You were realistic, Lucinda. It's a miracle that I'm about to enter school."

"The world needs healers, Jennie. All kinds. You were willing to dream."

"Josiah really pushed me."

"Some husbands motivate." She looked at Jennie, stared at a tea cake. "You were right about Joseph, he was pushing the foam. He quit the prison and is back to being a carpenter now and so much happier."

"If only my Douglas finds a stable path."

"He's young." She reached for Jennie's hand and patted it. "He will."

Jennie hoped her sister's lens would be truth and not a hoped-for fiction.

Beginning in April, Jennie sat in lectures for six hours a day. Twice a week students gowned up with aprons and masks for simple surgeries performed in a cramped room. The equipment was sparse, nothing compared to hospitals like St. Vincent's in Portland. Jennie suspected the lack of a hospital in Salem was one impetus for a separate medical college in Portland.

"Why not start a hospital here?" Jennie asked her husband. They each fixed a child's hair with ribbons and bows while the girls sat before Jennie's dresser mirror. They pointed at each other and laughed. Sometimes Jennie thought they might have a secret language between them. She was glad Ariyah taught them weekly with Alex and two other children she'd enlisted for piano lessons. She'd added art.

"Too expensive to open their own hospital. Salem only has 1,200 people. Portland has 15,000 to draw on, perhaps more as those wagon trains keep bringing people west. They can support two hospitals plus Hawthorne's Asylum. Speaking as a trustee, I'm concerned." He was even more chagrined when that fall a formal agreement was signed between the Portland area Medical College boosters and Willamette's medical faculty. In it, the Portland group agreed to disband and the Willamette group agreed to move the college to Portland—but Jennie's class would graduate from Salem before that.

Note-taking, reading, and remembering took her time. And dealing with the often not-so-subtle efforts by the male staff and students trying to discourage the three women still enrolled. Their cadre—made up of Esther Yeargain, Callie, and Jennie—was committed to withstand those efforts to dissipate their dreams.

At least none of the men tried to keep them from working on cadavers nor did they surprise them with the autopsy of a man. The affronts were mostly based on a belief that women were not as intellectually up to men's standards. Jennie likely wasn't, with her reading issues.

"That has nothing to do with your intelligence," Esther Yeargain retorted when Jennie made her observation. "They're simply not accustomed to women knowing as much as they do and being better able to integrate the material with actual practice. Unlike the men, we're not in competition with each other. We're looking for cures, not to win a game."

Cures, yes, that's what had led Jennie to this place. That and finally listening to her heart's leading.

• • •

"Of course you'll go," Jennie said. Josiah had come into the room Jennie had turned into her study on the second floor, down the hall from the girls' rooms. The Seth Thomas clock on the mantel over the fireplace struck the hour.

"I hate leaving you and the girls." Gracie would be six in October and Josie five in August. Josiah was asked to negotiate a serious problem with the Bannock tribe in far eastern Oregon on the Malheur Reservation. Josiah's health had continued to improve, and his regard by the Indians and his ability to speak native languages made his services valuable to the military. She could see how much he wanted to still be of service.

"There'll be a school recess soon. Douglas will be here."

"I'm not sure that makes me less concerned about leaving you."

"You'll be back by the time I return to class."

"I hope." He hesitated, then said, "It occurs to me that one should consider, that is . . ." He cleared his throat. "Jennie, this is about war. I won't only be talking. Something could happen."

He'd always discounted her concerns about his mortality early in their marriage when he'd been at the barns alone or traveled away. In the past eight years she hadn't allowed such fears to come to the surface. Maybe because she had confidence that her children were secure; that God was present even in loss. Still, Josiah was being asked to go into a war, to quell it if possible. And people died in wars.

"I'm sure you could decline the request. You are seventy-two."

"If I can help, I should. It's just—" He lifted the book she read, set it down, and pulled her to him. "I miss you, Jennie Parrish."

"I'm right here."

"But you are also inside those books, engaged in your heart's desire. I want to be sure I stay in your heart until I return."

Did the vocation she loved take her from the people she loved? *Yes.* Did they all know how grateful she was that they allowed her this passion that had made her life complete? *Probably not.*

"There is always room for you." She kissed him and marveled at the thrill that still worked its way from her lips to toes. Breathless, she said, "And some said it wouldn't last." She brushed his hair behind his ear.

"They had no idea what love can bridge: age, time, loss."

"You're a poet, Mr. Parrish."

"If so, you're my muse, Mrs. Parrish. What say you finish that chapter tomorrow." He kissed her again and they walked arm in arm to the girls' rooms, settling them into bed, and then found respite and peace in each other's arms.

• • •

Their good-bye two days later lingered. The girls hugged Josiah's legs and he picked up each child in turn, hugging them and kissing their foreheads. "JoJo, you work on that loose tooth." She nodded. "And Gracie, will you keep teaching Van how to roll over?"

"Yes, Papa." They chirped it together.

He pulled Jennie to him, his hands wide and firm at her waist. "Study hard, Dr. Parrish."

"I will. You come back."

"I will." He kissed her one last time and she knew then she would never be held by another with as much love as that of Josiah Parrish. He mounted up, turned the rein against his horse's neck, doffed his hat to her one last time, and rode off to meet Colonel Nesmith. She had admired her future husband from a distance, and in time, loved her husband close. That day she felt him both with her and away, but love bridged the distance.

She pressed any concerns aside, spoiled her daughters, and indulged her son, giving him spending money for a planned climb on Mt. Hood with a few other Willamette students once school was out in July. She hired private tutors for both girls at home. Lizzie and Ariyah remained the other consistent women in their lives. She doubted she could have stayed in school without this army of people.

If the three female medical students continued as planned, they would graduate next July. "I don't think I'll be ready," Esther Yeargain said. They often studied together and met for their noontime meals, that day sitting on a low brick wall surrounding a fountain that burbled in the background. Robins chirped in the nearby oaks, shadowed by tall fir. Jennie wanted to talk with her colleagues about missing Josiah, but both were widows—they knew about longing and hers was temporary, or so she hoped.

Jennie began to think about post-diploma work at a university that had a hospital attached. To land in San Francisco or maybe New York for surgical experiences. She was anxious to discuss it with Josiah. As students, they had very little exposure to appendectomies or, more important to Jennie, women's surgical needs such as hysterectomies or removal of ovarian cysts. She'd need postgraduate work for that. Esther and Callie planned postgraduate studies as well.

"I'll choose Portland." Callie ate her jerky, a supply of which she had prepared at the beginning of the term, mixing berries and nuts with the venison, nutrition to get her through her school days cheaply. She wore the silver collar pin. Jennie wondered if it was her good-luck charm. "The Medical College will be open by then. It's where I want to practice anyway."

Jennie vowed to talk with Dr. Cusick to get

his suggestions for her postgraduate work. *Postgraduate work.* She was going to be a doctor.

The Portland faction had chosen a building at the corner of Yamhill and Morrison, and the dissecting room would be over a livery at Park and Jefferson. New students would have access to Dr. Hawthorne's asylum, St. Vincent's and Good Samaritan Hospitals, but Jennie's class would not.

"We'll have a big party," Ariyah said when Jennie picked up the girls that next day.

"We'll have a party?" Gracie chimed in. "I love parties, Mama." JoJo pressed between them, wanting to show her mother her latest painting. "Aunt Ariyah says parties should happen every day."

"Not every day, exactly," Ariyah corrected. "But each day we're given something to celebrate. And on some occasions, the perfect party must be held. Like a birthday or graduation. Let's see, what can we serve?" She tapped her finger on her lips.

"Chocolate éclairs!"

"Cinnamon candy!"

"You'll have help with your planning." Jennie laughed and took her budding artists home. The girls chatted about their tutor. "He has very tiny shoes, Mama." They praised Chen's noodles while Van snored under the table. Jennie let them read to her, then tucked them into bed. She gave herself a half hour to sit and knit, a relaxation to quell tumbling thoughts that included assisting at an emergency Caesarean. People didn't go to hospitals until they were ready to die, so she loved that she had witnessed this procedure in the doctor's office. She'd been in awe. The human body was amazing; a healthy child, a gift. She could hardly wait to share the details of the surgery with Josiah. She missed him so.

She slept.

When she heard the door latch open, she stood, wiped sleep from her eyes. "Josiah, are you back?" She straightened her glasses, threw the knitting into the basket. Van barked as she raced down the hall. It was late, very late. He must have ridden through the day and into this night, as anxious to see her as she was to see him.

Chapter 36

The O'er Wrought Heart

It wasn't Josiah at all. It was a very drunk Douglas she faced.

He was fifteen now, a good-looking boy. He was never mentioned in the *Collegian*, the campus newspaper, as having passed his semi-term grades at any significant level, but he was also not listed as being in trouble. Their conversations were often awkward and usually ended with his request for a few extra coins for this and that. But she had never seen him like this, words slurred, scowling. Anger pressed out through his pores.

"Why didn't you tell me my father wanted me to live with him?"

"I—we considered it, but then he got arrested and—"

"And the dignified Mrs. Parrish couldn't have her son be seen with a drunk, even if he is his father." He belched. "But it was all right to leave him in an insane asylum."

"We didn't think it would be wise. And we thought you did well at the hospital."

"*We* didn't think it would be wise. *We*," he

mocked. "That *we* never included me though, did it? Or my father. Just you and the old man."

"Douglas, don't. Josiah rescued us."

"*We* were rescued, is that what you're saying, Mother? *We* were rescued so *we* could live a privileged life, go to Willamette. Who's happier there, do you suppose, you or me? Or are *we?*"

She wasn't sure why she'd said "we." Josiah and Jennie hadn't actually discussed Douglas going to live with his father. She'd made that decision on her own. Funny how even when under the influence as Douglas was, he could bore into her own layers of guilt, mine the cavern of her grief-laden heart with his words.

"How do you even know your father came by? He never returned, never heard my answer. Walked away from us as he did the first time."

"He came to see me. Today." He wobbled and Jennie motioned for him to precede her into the parlor where she'd been knitting. He stood for a moment, glaring, and then he moved down the hall, flopped onto the settee.

"Your father's responsible for your state, then."

"No, I tipped the brew up to my lips all by myself." He made a gesture of a mug to his mouth. He closed his eyes. "I'm a big boy now, Mother."

"We can discuss it in the morning. Can you make the stairs? You need to go to bed. We can return to Willamette together tomorrow."

"Don't you always say 'everything in God's time'? Hmm? Well, his visit was timely because I was expelled today."

"Expelled? For what? Why?"

He opened one eye, grinned almost. "Cheating, they said. There'll be a letter coming. Maybe now's the time for me to go live with my papa. His new wife left him like you did, so he's all alone."

"I never left—" She stopped. Hadn't she learned with his father to never argue with a man under the influence? "Go to bed, Douglas . . . Douglas?" His snores had already begun.

She laid a Log Cabin quilt over him, opened the door that led to the garden. The new screen Josiah had installed before he left would keep creatures out but the stench of drink could leave. Jennie shivered, less from the cool air. She didn't want the girls to find him like this in the morning. She'd wake him early. Frogs serenaded at the pond but couldn't erase her despair. No, great discouragement, not despair.

Lantern light bounced before her on the stairs. She undressed for bed but didn't sleep. Maybe Charles could stay sober with his son's presence. Maybe he was a lonely man. Maybe his battle—and Douglas's battle—with the bottle was so overwhelming that he needed others to stake him like a fragile garden plant, to keep him from falling over in the slightest wind. With the help of others, she had moved on, made her own life, tried to give Douglas every advantage so he wouldn't suffer, yet he did.

A verse from Second Chronicles came to her in that moment, about not being discouraged, as not every battle belonged to her. Her stomach burned. She got up to take cayenne powder, wishing she had some of the new pharmaceuticals her instructors had discussed. She remembered that cayenne was used by the Indians to treat intoxication and grimaced at the irony.

"Everything all right, Mrs. P?"

"Fine, Lizzie. Douglas is . . . indisposed in the parlor. Let him sleep."

He's been expelled. She'd have to deal with that in the morning too. She had her own exams in physics from a text she'd plodded through by Balford Stewart said to be an "elementary work." Nothing about it had been elementary. Each student had to present a paper in front of their peers in a second class. She was almost as worried over that as when she'd been examined before the dean preceding her admission.

She tossed and turned, going over the presentation in her head, memorizing all the sentences because she knew she could not read it under duress. But did it even make sense, her paper? Was it medicine to merely wonder about addiction when there was so little science to explain it? She offered no conjecture about cures except abstinence. Her son sleeping off a drunk in the parlor suggested that such a cure could not be brought about by a mother's love nor by the most ardent prayers of a physician-in-training. There was only so much she could do for Douglas, and it had already been done. Perhaps it really was no longer her battle.

A carousel is predictable. A rider knows how far they'll rise and how far they'll dip below. The only uncertainty is when to get off. Life isn't predictable at all, and Jennie wondered why she'd even made the comparison once. The psalmist proclaimed that each person is brought to a "place of abundance," and if Jennie looked around, as she did that morning, preparing her hair with the curling iron, managing the clasp on the jade cross she wore beneath her blouse each day, hearing the girls rise and laugh with Lizzie down the hall, how could she not see abundance? And yet, this morning her eyes were red from lack of sleep and crying, her stomach still presenting pain. Was it hypocritical to present a paper to the class, one that suggested links between alcohol and how a chronic user's thinking could be affected even when they were sober? The links were all anecdotal, more in the new field of psychiatry than in physical medicine. And what treatment in the allopathy field could be recommended? What pharmaceuticals or surgical treatments might be suggested? She had no answers. She could be laughed out of the room.

But Dr. Cusick had said medicine made gains by the mere offering of an alternative diagnosis or idea, something to be studied in more detail. "An innovative perspective forces physicians to look through a different lens and that's good. Anecdotal information is weighty. People tell us stories for a reason. We're all made up of stories. It's how we best come to know another person, and that's critical if we are to help them heal." He said it all without one single pun.

Jennie held on to that view to quell her queasy stomach.

She met her girls in the hall, and holding each other's hands, they descended the stairs, Josie skipping as Jennie lifted her from step to step. "Your brother came to visit last evening." They approached the dining room. "You go on in to breakfast and I'll see if he's awake."

"He isn't in his room?" JoJo asked.

"He slept in the parlor last evening."

"That settee has lumps in it, Mama," Gracie noted. "Unless you're little. Douglas's feet will hang over the end."

"Like a sleepy scarecrow." JoJo offered floppy arms and the girls giggled.

Lizzie followed and took her daughters to the table where Chen already had their barley bowls steaming. *Barley. Also good for stomach pain.* Jennie took a deep breath and headed into the parlor.

Douglas wasn't there. Her knitting basket sat undisturbed. Van slept beside it. The quilt was folded, neatly left on the settee, the only evidence he'd been there at all. Should she look for him? She checked the watch pinned to her bodice. *Try to track him down? Or make my class? What would a good mother do?*

She chose the class. Forever after she would wonder, was she selfish? Had the barnacles of motherhood been worn smooth, reshaped who she was? Did repeated bouts of alcohol affect those who did not imbibe but who stood in the vortex of the addicted person's swirl? But that, too, was a part of who she was: the worrier fighting off the fiend, the person who struggles leaving "this is over" behind, reworking it like a cow chewing her cud.

She presented her memorized paper, adding on the spot that additional exploration was needed on how a bystander's life might well be changed by repeated exposure to a loved one's drinking. "Alcohol Consumption Repercussions" is what she named it. Her original title, "The Bystander Brain," seemed too light for the weight of this

409

subject. She recalled her wedding dance and Charles's fall. Maybe the changes in who he became started with that moment and the alcohol was simply his way of treating a longstanding pain. That didn't change its impact on their family.

Callie came up after she finished, whispered in her ear, "You look terrible but that was fabulous."

"Quite inventive a theory," one of the male students said. "A bystander brain. I suspect you'll receive a high score for it, though how one can apply it in practice I fail to see."

She allowed him to "fail to see," too fatigued to explain that she sometimes questioned her own saneness in trying to affect the behavior of an addict.

After the class, Jennie told Callie about Douglas's visit as the women walked to Willamette's secondary section. Jennie asked for an appointment with the dean. She was granted immediate entrance. How she wished Josiah was with her, but she was a grown-up now. She wouldn't always have Josiah with her to help fight her battles.

"Do you want me to stay? I will," Callie offered.

"No. You go home to Lorena. I'll be all right."

Callie hugged her, and Jennie was ushered in, sweet tea served. "I understand there is an issue with my son, Douglas Pickett."

"An issue?" the dean said. "Several."

"Why am I just now learning of them? And through my son."

"We try to handle problems in-house." He handed her a copy of the letter he said had been sent out the day before. "It's his drinking that is the primary issue. We've had demerits. We've punished him with refusal to allow him to participate in desired experiences such as climbing Mt. Hood this summer. We've put him on kitchen duty for more than a week. Nothing. We've tried rewards for his attendance, for remaining sober. We've gone further than with any other student because of his—well, your husband's position here. He's the last remaining trustee who began this institute, saved it from financial ruin. That's worth something, we all felt."

Her face burned with the humiliation of so many people knowing of Douglas's behavior and that even Josiah's reputation had not been enough.

"Is the expulsion permanent?"

"Yes. His cheating was the final stroke. He broke into the office where the tests were kept, took one, and of course managed an excellent score, even though he had shown little accomplishment in the course throughout the term."

"Could you tell me of his friends?" Shame

411

accompanied her having to ask about who her son spent time with. She should have known. Or was that fiend rising up again?

"They aren't students here. People he's met elsewhere. Not the best crowd, I'm afraid. I don't really know their names."

"His father was here, I understand?"

"We asked him to leave. He was . . . under the influence."

But coherent enough to tell his son that he had asked for him to live with him and that his mother had refused.

She walked to Ariyah's, thinking he might have gone there. She was his auntie.

"He'll return. He knows a good thing, Jennie. He's probably embarrassed. Didn't you say that was part of the pattern people told you of: shame, remorse, renewed effort?"

"Until the next craving. Maybe he's at my parents'."

"Go home. You look exhausted yourself. Get some rest if you can."

"All my efforts of study, my whole idea of becoming a doctor, was to help him." *Is that true?* "And I've failed even as I get a sterling grade for my paper. What's the point?"

"The point is that you are pursuing what you believe to be the best path toward loving your son and your fellow man. And woman. There aren't any promises that all will be well, but what's the alternative? God's timing, remember."

"Douglas mocked me with that phrase last night."

"He's hurting and you may not be able to relieve that, Jennie. Shakespeare said to 'Give sorrow words; The grief that does not speak whispers the o'er-fraught heart and bids it break.' He has to find his own words."

She heard the sound before she realized what it was. Someone chopping wood. Jennie rushed to the shed, hoping Josiah had returned. But it was Douglas there, sweat beaded on his bare chest, his brown curls wet, his hand on the axe.

"Douglas?"

He put the axe down. "I'm so sorry, Mother. I am."

"I know you are." He looked as vulnerable as a newborn lamb, his head hung down, breathing hard from the exertion. She opened her arms to him and he let her hold him, sobbing.

"I'm such a disappointment to everyone, to myself."

"Shh, shh. We are all disappointments to ourselves. But we are loved nonetheless."

"What will I do?"

"You'll come here. Be tutored. Or work on one of Josiah's projects. You'll grow and change, like we all do. We'll keep praying."

"Why would God listen to someone who keeps doing the same hateful things?"

"Oh, Douglas, God knows we're frail and needy and loves us anyway."

Jennie vowed to be the example of such love.

Chapter 37

Through the Rapids

Josiah arrived home the following week. He looked tanned and younger than when he'd left. There is something about discovering your passion and being allowed to pursue it that is invigorating. At least that was how it affected her husband. He scooped her into his arms and said, "I missed you so, Jennie, my girl." He rubbed his whiskers across her cheeks and she giggled like her daughters. He set her down, looked up and saw Douglas. He reached his hand out to shake Douglas's. "Doug, how's your summer been?"

"Good. I, uh, Mother'll fill you in about things. I repaired the back fence. Under Tom's direction. And we harvested the wheat."

"Good, good. Tom needs good help. I hope it didn't take you away from your studies."

"We can speak of that later, husband. You must be exhausted. Douglas, will you take care of Josiah's horse for him and then come join us?"

It was October and leaves fell, a colorful rainbow marking the paths. Douglas led the horse away, and Josiah and Jennie entered the house.

"I'll get the girls shortly. They'll be so happy to see you. As am I!"

"So what is it Douglas referred to that you'll fill me in about?" He set the saddlebags down.

Jennie began the latest saga and told him how she'd chosen to attend the class rather than seek Douglas and even mentioned her theory of consumption repercussions. "We all act crazy at times trying to figure out what to do to help the addicted person. I mean, it isn't normal to lock up cooking sherry or in my case laudanum when they're on the top shelves well out of reach of children. But that's what we do and deride ourselves because we think it's our fault, that we prompted another person to choose that behavior. But I think now more than ever that it isn't even a choice for them." She called to Chen to bring in coffee for Mr. Parrish, then continued. "We don't choose an infection or a cancer. Oh, maybe there are things we do that expose us to the problem—not cleaning that wound so it gets infected. But what about a cancer? And what about an addiction? I think some of us are prone to it and some not."

"We are fearfully and wonderfully made." He motioned for her to sit beside him on the lumpy settee. His words reminded her of what she'd witnessed while he was gone that had given her such joy.

"There was an emergency Caesarean, and

oh, Josiah, it was . . . divine." Her eyes started to tear. "To know that life was plucked from death with both mother and child surviving is to see the hand of God." She was quiet, then, "I want to do surgical work in Portland after I graduate. If you approve. With Douglas no longer at Willamette, maybe we should all move to Portland."

"Doug's not at Willamette?"

"It's a long story. Too many demerits, drinking, cheating. Not spinning." She recalled that physics teacher's observation. "And we need to talk about what to do when he drinks again, which I believe he will. Like his father, I don't think he can help it. He doesn't know how to spin."

"A man goes away for four months and the world shifts."

"The world shifts whether a man goes away or not. But it's so much easier to manage the wobble when there's a good woman by his side."

"Indeed," he said and kissed her soundly.

Douglas remained with them until he didn't, one day leaving a note saying he was going to live with his father. Jennie did not attempt to change his mind.

Graduation, July 29, 1879, was a day of celebration. Six men and the three friends received diplomas and permission to call themselves "doctors." Almost everyone came. Her parents, brothers, Lucinda, and Joseph attended. Lucinda looked thin and pale, but she brushed Jennie's observation off. "Working too hard is all." Nellie and Mary arrived, wearing wide-brimmed hats with pins nearly a foot long. "Nellie's working at Millie's Millinery." Jennie hadn't known, her world taken up with her family and studies and not much with her nieces. "We're so proud of you, Jennie. We surely are," Lucinda said. "It's like we're a tiny part of it getting to watch someone fulfill a childhood dream."

Josiah's family attended, except for Charles Winn as they resided several days away, or so Jennie told herself. Ariyah and Alex and even her parents fanned themselves in the pews of the Taylor Street Methodist Episcopal Church, where the commencement was held. They had all contributed to this day. Lizzie sat between the girls in the row with Josiah. Even Tom Winston, the farm manager, and his wife attended, on her lap a basket of bread so fresh Jennie could smell it several pews behind the graduates.

Dr. Cusick ushered in his wife and daughter, Ethel. Callie's Lenora sat with Esther's family, and they would later sip sarsaparilla and savor sweets at their parties.

At the reception, her brothers "the twins" brought gifts for her and the girls too. "You shouldn't be the only one getting raves," DW told her, and the girls squealed in delight with their new lockets as Jennie fingered a hat with a yellow ribbon. Such good brothers she had.

And Douglas appeared, late and saying he wasn't drunk but under the influence. Josiah walked him away, called a carriage, and sent him back to his father's. Jennie didn't know any of that had transpired until later. She thought he hadn't come at all. But she determined not to allow his lack of presence to mar the joy of this day so long hoped for.

Van's death marred her packing, but she supposed their grief over the little dog set the tone for a melancholy she fought against. One morning he was running about slower than usual and the next day he didn't wake up. They held a funeral for him in the garden, Gracie sobbing and JoJo's realistic words bringing a smile to Jennie's lips. "We all have to go sometime." Yes, they did.

Jennie knew her sadness over Van mingled with the impending separation and her departure for a year. Josiah was very supportive and a part of Jennie wished he had said she couldn't go. But he would never do that, and Jennie knew she would have defied him if he had. She needed this special instruction in surgeries, and New York was the best place to get it. Josiah had been approached by a group of Portland men thinking of starting a homeopathic college. Why they didn't ask a woman doctor didn't surprise her; that Josiah agreed, did. "It'll be something to occupy my time while you're gone. Now that Willamette Medical has moved to Portland, a homeopathic college might offer a solid alternative, if not competition."

"You're much more political than I thought."

He grinned. "Was I not present at the Champoeg vote choosing our territory to be American over the British? Politics must be in my blood."

She left immediately after graduation for New York. She wanted at least one term focused solely on surgery. Josiah and Jennie had agreed to place the girls in Willamette's elementary boarding school for the fall term. She didn't say it out loud, but she wanted to keep them away from Douglas for fear of his bingeing and them having to see their brother that way. She doubted he'd appear at Willamette, but he might show up at the house.

She boarded the ship to San Francisco, then caught the train across the continent to Chicago and on to New York. That Jennie Lichtenthaler Parrish had the courage to travel and be so far from home, on her own, amazed her. How far she'd come from the timid child afraid to stand in front of a class because she could not read.

The bustle of the city with its omnibus and cable cars mingling many bodies going from here to there surprised her. But so did the degree of sickness and poverty she saw in the women's clinics. They talked of difficult pregnancies, their aches and pains soaked in the stories of drink and abuse. "I don't know why I stay, Doctor," they lamented and yet were too frightened of what would happen if they left. Jennie followed up on surgeries, walking past community houses teaching English to new immigrants, and climbed the steps, dipping past fresh clothes drying in the smoke of factories making fabric.

But she took pleasures too. One weekend while summer lingered, she rode the train to Philadelphia to see firsthand Dentzel's "flying horses," the carousel she'd read about, a steam engine in the middle pushing the horses around while a band played off to the side. She even rode on it beside the children, wishing Gracie and JoJo were there to share the joy.

Several of her instructors were women who also had private practices. They were more open about the trials of doctoring alone in a city. "You'll be businessmen," one told the men and women. "And have all the trials of that—collections, hiring and firing, renting space. Find someone who can help you with that so you can care about your patients."

A supervising physician complimented Jennie, a rarity. "You're good with the women and children. They don't flinch when you tell them about a tonsillectomy or discuss a terminal illness like cancer. You were excellent. They trust you."

"I suppose I can relate to what they tell me."

He frowned.

"No, I haven't had a cancer, but I'm not only Dr. Parrish, wife of a prominent Oregonian, mother of three. I'm also Jennie, divorced wife of an alcoholic and mother of one as well. For a great number of these women, their troubles began with their family member's decline. Perhaps they trust that I've walked where they walked."

"Empathy and not just sympathy." He grunted. "You'll need to distance yourself, however, or you'll take on their pains."

"Perhaps. But wouldn't it be better to take on a wound rather than let the patient feel they were abandoned by a too-distant physician?"

He didn't reply.

And so she wore the gown and put on the mask and assisted with a Caesarean surgery, the thrill of doing greater than watching. At another delivery, the umbilical cord had wrapped around the child's throat but the newborn lived. Baby Ariyah was in her heart more that day. She helped repair a botched abortion; assisted when a clumsy surgeon removed an ovarian cyst and the woman nearly bled to death. Knives could heal and then might not. It was an art as much as a science. With her instructor's guidance, she completed a sterilization of a woman already mothering eleven children and she was Jennie's age, thirty-six.

Christmas came and went. She visited the community center in the tenement and helped serve a meal, her hands so busy dishing out the potatoes she barely had time to look each person in the eye as they said "thank you." She'd remain until the following summer, completing a rotation at the asylum in New York while Josiah looked for an apartment in Portland so she could begin doctoring close to a hospital.

And then the carousel stopped.

The telegram read:

LUCINDA PASSED. STOP. SLOAN DEVASTATED. STOP. COME HOME. STOP. LOVE, J.

Life hands out wounds that need healing whether one is ready or not. Jennie missed Lucinda's funeral, taking several days to return after receiving the news. And once she arrived, family needed her. Lucinda's girls, her parents, Sloan. Jennie had noticed Lucinda's paleness at the graduation but had not pursued it. It was cancer, she was told. Jennie took little time for her own grief. She was the healer who must grow new flesh.

Not having Lucinda to share the opening of her practice in Portland proved to be a new sadness, another "missing" of her sisters. But between Samuel, Josiah's policeman son, and Jennie's policeman brother Fergus, Josiah had learned of an empty apartment at Fourth and Harrison, number 403. Police officers often knew of empty places.

Josiah, Jennie, and a weeping Nellie took a carriage to the apartment where they'd all be staying. Lizzie had remained in Salem to tend the house there; Chen was with them, stir-frying venison at that moment.

They decided to keep the girls in the academy in Salem. Ariyah was close to them and the train ran daily between Portland and Salem now. They'd be with the girls on weekends and in summers. She didn't say it out loud, but she was still cautious about Douglas. Josiah said he'd help Nellie find a job in Portland, which he did. Mary, her sister, lived in Illinois for now.

"Mom was very proud of you, you know," Nellie said.

"I know. She was proud of you as well."

"She wants us—wanted us—to do things like that too, go on to school."

"We'll help you, Nellie." It was the least they could do for Lucinda and Sloan.

Callie—Dr. Charlton now—had chosen Portland too, and with a bit of irony, she pursued a homeopathic program while Jennie chose "regular" doctoring. Jennie located a surgeon she could continue studying with, one who had a special interest in women patients. To add to their continued friendship, Callie's apartment and office were on the same street as the Parrish apartment. They often walked together to the hospital when they had admitted patients.

Josiah bought Jennie a medical bag with her initials worked into the leather. Together they ordered cards with JENNIE PARRISH, M.D. on them and a series of books she wanted to have on hand. They'd be shipped from San Francisco.

A building on First Street had five large rooms on the second floor that housed her fledgling practice. A waiting room, two for examinations, a library, and an office. Jennie wandered through the empty space, marveling that this was hers to tend. She must get Ariyah to come furnish it.

On the day she moved in, a sign graced the door. Josiah had had it painted.

Jennie Parrish, M.D.
Office hours
9:00 AM–11:30
2:00 PM–4:00
6:30 PM–8:00

She wished she had a camera to take a picture. How grateful she was that he understood the small pleasures that indicate someone supports a dream, opens his heart to that cloud of faith, believing none will fall through.

"You got a good rent." Jennie looked at the contract.

"We own the building."

"We do?"

"The downstairs will be the pharmacy. EG Jones and I are partnering."

"No more homeopathic college work?"

Josiah smiled. "You're a regular doctor now, Jennie. You'll need a pharmacy. Without it, I might never see you. With it, I'm a part of all the good you're doing. I'm not so old I don't want to have a way to keep serving."

She took on the accoutrements of a small-business woman. She acquired a post office box, kept office hours, referred people as needed for pharmaceuticals, got admitting privileges at Good Samaritan Hospital. An accounting firm kept her books and made collections, though Jennie screened who she felt could pay and who couldn't. She hired a nurse who also greeted patients when they came in and kept their records. Jennie placed ads in *The Oregonian*.

Mrs. J. L. Parrish MD (late of New York), physician and surgeon makes diseases of women and children a specialty.

She added her address and office hours. Her ten volumes of medical texts arrived to line the bookshelves Josiah had made. He'd also made her desk. She flapped the newspaper at Josiah, then read with her usual hesitation under "Business Women in Portland" of her practice opening where they added "Late of New York." Though not a full year of surgery experience, her time back East brought not only new skills but apparently prominence. West Coasters were enthralled by the aura of the East.

A few men came to Jennie's practice, mostly to protest their wife's wish to use a contraceptive after seven or eight children, occasionally lecturing her on her distorted role of womanhood. "You need to be home with your husband and children. Widowed women doctors are fine, but married ones? Appalling."

Most of her patients were women and children, and she listened to their stories, encouraged them to do whatever they must to keep themselves and their children safe from a spouse or uncle or father who became a different person when they drank. And she always encouraged them to dream.

Obstetrics allowed Jennie to see women excited about their babies, rejoice with a mother who had had three previous miscarriages now carry her infant to term. She taught classes about nutrition and spoke of ways to increase the chance of a successful delivery. No one ever asked her for an abortion, but more than once she repaired damage done by self-inflicted efforts to terminate a pregnancy. She had to tell one woman she would likely not conceive again; to others she spoke of pacing births even with the Comstock Law in place prohibiting the mailing of materials about contraception. They were deemed "obscene." Women needed information and there was nothing obscene about the way a woman's body worked. She never mentioned her distributing such material to the police officers in her families. Some things were better left unsaid.

Chapter 38
Racing Time

Where's that pewter hat pin I so love?" Jennie bustled about the apartment as Josiah and she prepared to take the train to Willamette to hear a concert where Grace and Dr. Cusick's daughter Ethel were going to play. They'd treat the girls to éclairs after the concert and spend the night in Salem.

"In your hand," Josiah said.

"Oh." She pushed it through the felt and into the twist of hair, took one last look in the mirror to check on the seams of the jacket she wore over the olive skirt. She'd had the skirt taken in; she kept forgetting to eat.

The girls played "Wedding Reception Polka" by A. S. Sweet. Later a reviewer wrote, "The duet was rendered in a way that reflected credit upon them, Miss Parrish being one of the youngest members of the conservatory." She was ten already. The girls spent summers with their parents in Portland, but they missed their friends in Salem. Jennie began to think about moving back, but her practice grew. She pondered what to do while listening to that duet.

The music had been composed the year Jennie graduated. It was funny how she equated events with "the year I graduated" or "two years after I graduated," as though that was a new marker in her life. She knew that great joys like marriages and when children were born made markers on stories. So did longed-for accomplishments achieved.

Thankfully, the girls thrived at Willamette and the *Collegian* reported on paintings the girls had done in oil of Mt. Hood. "They are engaged now in flower plaques," the reporter wrote. Ariyah had inspired their artistic ventures. Douglas . . . well, Douglas continued to challenge. He had reappeared briefly about the same time Nellie went to New York, something the Parrishes arranged for her when she told them she was being harassed by a man at her work. Douglas stayed a fortnight, keeping sober. Then he disappeared again. Between Samuel Parrish and Jennie's brother Fergus, who was a municipal police officer, they learned *about* him. He'd taken a job as a carpenter. "With Charley Pickett, his dad," her brother told her.

"With Charles? Oh, Fergus. Are they, I mean, do they drink together?"

" 'Fraid so, Sister. The department gets calls about drunken behavior of them both."

"Can't you put him in jail, get him sober so he can try again?"

"Oh, we do. Sometimes he's in the hospital with a cut or bruise from a brawl. Such a handsome boy." He shook his head.

All they could do for him now was to pray, but perhaps that was always the only real thing that could change his behavior. That and change her own sooner, refusing to give him money if he asked, assuming it would go for liquor and not whatever he told her it was for, like for climbing Mt. Hood.

Chen remained with them, but otherwise, it was Josiah and Jennie in the apartment and often just Jennie, as Josiah spent time in Salem getting their new home built on the thirty-three acres Jennie owned. Once finished, they planned to return to Salem. It had grown enough, it could support her practice. Josiah took Chen with him. Jennie wanted to be sure he and the girls had plenty of good food. Her own appetite wasn't much these days.

The practice kept her occupied, but alone in the apartment, listening to the street sounds of horses and delivery wagons, carriages and carts, she missed Josiah and wondered how much longer she'd have the love of her life. He'd turned seventy-six in January and she noted his steps had become a little slower. His response when she asked him a question took longer. Sometimes she had to repeat what she said. But at night he still held her tight, kissed her with the fierceness of a man in love. Sometimes they danced together. She would cling to those moments and not think about his growing older.

On a winter's day in 1882, Callie and Jennie were asked to present papers at the newly organized Oregon Medical Society. Jennie's was on "Diseases Incident to Pregnancy" and Callie's on "Typho-Malaria Fever." They were both elected into the group this time. Mary Sawtelle clapped Jennie's back, called her "colleague" as she offered congratulations, and added, "You're looking a little piqued. Don't overdo." The chairman suggested Jennie run for office.

"That isn't of my interest." She thought of the politics still rumbling about the move of the medical program to Portland, dealing with those disappointed in the transition. She'd stayed out of that politics and planned to continue.

Dr. Ford-Warren, a first female Willamette graduate, had given an address at the meeting and she pointedly told Jennie afterward, "You must do your part to assist other women in their medical pursuits." Jennie wondered why she didn't run herself, but then she was likely still grieving over the death of her sister in Jacksonville. She'd died in childbirth, as so many women did.

"Perhaps I could offer to take on one reader, maybe more."

"That takes care of one, but if you were active in the society, more women would see the possibility of becoming physicians. Run for vice president. See how things operate for a few years."

"But why me?"

"You're bright, well-studied with New York recommendations. And you've taken on the task of educating women to reduce problems of childbirth. We've needed that in Portland."

"I'll consider it after I've been in practice longer."

"There's never any time like the present."

"It was astonishing," Jennie told Josiah, waking him at dawn when she returned after a delivery that turned into a Caesarean she had to perform on her own. "I remembered everything, could see the drawings from those texts, gave direction to the midwife. It was . . . spiritual, as though I wasn't alone there holding the scalpel."

"I've had moments like that. Hard to explain."

"Yes. The midwife was a great nurse. I told her she ought to think about becoming a doctor. She said it had always been her dream but she didn't see how that could happen. I told her not to give up hope."

"Maybe the medical society could offer scholarships," Josiah said as he plumped up the pillow and patted the bedside to have her sit.

"Yes. Maybe." She hadn't thought of that.

"A scholarship might be something an officer of that association could champion."

"I'd do more good trying to repeal Comstock's Law or passing Prohibition."

Josiah laughed. "I thought you weren't interested in politics."

"I'm not. Oh, Josiah, the siblings at that delivery grinned at the sound of their baby sister. It was as though we were all part of something larger, while the midwife cleaned the baby and I stitched the mother's wounds. This is what I went to school for, dreamed about, distilled those herbs for, even tried to understand the brain for. That one day, my hands would bring joy into the world."

"It's all been worth it then? Even with Douglas not responding as we hoped?"

"Yes. It's worth it." She cuddled up closer to him. "I like the scholarship idea. I might even be able to enlist other women doctors in the cause. Bethina Owens. Ford-Warren. Callie. Esther." She thought of several others.

"Don't exclude the men. They could contribute too." He coughed.

"Are you all right?"

"Morning catarrh. Don't you worry."

"Maybe I will let my name be put into contention as vice president. But I'll tell them why and propose the scholarship at the same time." Politics can be used for good. She leaned her head against his chest, listened to his beating heart. She'd need to change and go to the office in a few hours, but she might catch thirty minutes of sleep. First, she wanted to hold him who kept coming up with ways to enhance her life. *A scholarship.* To any medical school a woman might prefer. "Josiah Parrish, you're a treasure I can't imagine being without."

Both Callie and Jennie advanced their causes: Callie became a member of the board and Jennie let her name be put in as vice president. She was sure there'd be someone she'd run against, but on the actual day, she was the only nominee. They elected her unanimously, the first woman doctor to serve in an office of the Oregon State Medical Association.

She'd discouraged Josiah from attending— family members could join them for tea and cakes at the end—but he slipped in the back to see her make her acceptance speech and introduce the scholarship effort. She missed her sister at that moment more than she'd allowed before. Lucinda would have applauded—and baked fine cakes for the occasion. Callie and Jennie had brought all the refreshments. It was what women did.

"You're beaming," Josiah told her at the tea table, his head lowered to hers in a whisper.

"I am."

"That dimple is as deep as an ocean when you smile. I'm so proud of you, Madam Vice President." His eyes watered and she squeezed his hand.

Back at their apartment she placed her hat in the box, fluffed up her hair with her fingers.

"Here you go then." Josiah handed her a package.

"Is it a new vase?"

It was a foot tall.

"Guess again."

She pulled off the wrapping. "A new microscope!"

"Used to be I bought you necklaces and now it's doctor supplies," he said wistfully.

"And one day a new home." She kissed him.

"If I ever get it finished. I can't do as much hammering as I used to, Jennie. Sorry it's taken so long."

"You're a meticulous man. And stubborn, I

might add. Let the builders do the work now."

Adding on an office space had delayed the Salem project, but it would offer the option of having a practice in both cities. She'd begun attracting the daughters of prominent families in Portland and Salem, women taking the train. She allowed Josiah and the girls to have their say in design and furnishings and actually felt relief that they had activities to do together when her own kept her focused on her patients and her practice. It was as though she ran a race against time, watching the girls grow up, seeing Josiah's fading years. And yet it was in being a doctor where she found the great joy that fed her love for all around.

"I don't mind the wait for the house except for not having you close by. It's harder to keep my eye on you. You aren't climbing any ladders, are you?" He shook his head. "Good. Recovery would take much longer if you fell now."

Callie, her medical confidante and friend, surprised Jennie by announcing she would take a year of study in Chicago at the homeopathic Hahnemann Medical College there.

"Who will I complain to? You talked me into running for office and then desert me? What about our scholarship program?"

Callie laughed. "It's only a short study. I'll be back by '84."

Jennie felt a sense of loss she didn't understand. She'd been her colleague, her encouragement, and now she wasn't going to be there for her to consult with, tell her stories to.

"We'll write and I'll likely be back by the time we've raised sufficient endowment for the scholarship. I can help you make final choices." She reached out for Jennie and hugged her. "Come on. You'll be fine. You spent months in New York on your own."

"I know. You go." She made her words light and teasing. "Breathe in the aroma of frankincense and explore the Pulsatilla plant's healing properties. I once thought I might be a Pulsatilla type. Homeopathy has much psychology to merit it."

"And a long history."

Jennie nodded.

"You needn't turn your back on what you know of it because of what happened to Nora. That wasn't your fault."

"Oh, I think I've grieved that."

Callie clucked her tongue. "You never get over a death, accidental or otherwise. And you've had your share of them. We have to find a way to take wisdom from the loss. And you did. You have. You're maybe even a doctor because of it."

"See. I'll miss your insights."

"You'll do fine without me. You have your

438

girls and Josiah, better champions you could not find, isn't that right?"

She knew it was. Her carousel would move up and down in a predictable way. The only thing uncertain now was when she'd step off.

Chapter 39
Women's Ways of Knowing

A grand piano arrived by ship under skies that wept rain. But the squeals when the girls saw the Steinway drowned out the rare January thunderclaps and the steady patter of raindrops against the roof. He had surprised them with the piano. After all these years, she could tell by his eyes that he still loved to surprise her. The girls each played a piece for him and teased him when he tried to sing along.

With Ariyah's help, Jennie planned an eightieth birthday party for Josiah, inviting her parents, his children, as many brothers and sisters of hers as could come, old friends from his Indian agent years and missionary times and young ones who worked on the house and the orphanage and the schools for the deaf and blind and mute children. Josiah's children had come to the party, and Charles Winn didn't wince when his father told him that this new house was in Jennie's name and that they planned to sell the house he and Elizabeth had lived in.

"No sense having two homes," Jennie overheard him say to Josiah.

440

"Dr. Jennie is taking good care of you." It was the first time he had referred to her as "doctor" or acknowledged that she was good for his father.

"We take care of each other."

Without knowing, the gathering became a funeral preparation for Jennie's father. He was three years older than Josiah and died of a heart attack the afternoon of the party. Jennie learned that day that her mother had been born in the same year as Josiah. She seemed much older than Josiah, especially on that day of great loss.

The funeral was barely passed before they learned that Fergus's wife suffered with a fast-acting cancer. It felt as though her family was disappearing. She'd already lost sisters and a brother, a daughter. And Douglas to drink. She vowed to cut back her work efforts and be with the girls and Josiah more—and did for a time. But she couldn't seem to set aside her sense of urgency to accomplish all she could for her patients, her family, her late-in-life response to choose joy.

As though called to it, Jennie volunteered to meet with patients at the new state asylum, Hawthorne's hospital at last moved to Salem. A new doctor, Fraser, was a specialist in diseases of the brain among other things and was now the dean at the medical college. Jennie moved back and forth between the two cities but mostly lived in Portland. They let the apartment go when Jennie learned that Charles Pickett had taken one in a building on the same street. They might have seen Douglas in passing if they'd stayed, but it didn't seem wise to be in that proximity to Charles Pickett, and who knew if Douglas was still with him or not?

Instead of the apartment, they stayed in one room of the office above the pharmacy when Josiah came to town. Jennie kept a supply of herbs and oils in her office, but the dosages of the purchased powders and pharmaceuticals were already measured out and more convenient. They still needed to keep them safe. Break-ins and thefts were a common concern for pharmacies and doctors' offices.

"I want you to have a gun when you stay here alone." Josiah had taken her to the back of the farm where he'd posted a target. "Hold the Pepperbox like this."

She was uncomfortable with the revolver, but it comforted Josiah to know that she could fire t, so she practiced. "I'd probably faint if I ever had to use it and the would-be robber would take it away and use it on me."

"With a little confidence you'll be fine." He stood behind her, arms around her shoulders, over her hands. "Your arms are thin as knitting sticks. Are you losing weight?"

"Just tell me what I'm supposed to be doing."

She had moved the buttons on her waistbands and vowed to take more time to eat a midday meal she often skipped to make notes before her afternoon patients.

She'd paid her $300 medical society membership fees for that year and the next, and to her great joy, Callie returned and reopened her Portland practice. They talked through the night about her coursework, and her enthusiasm for healing and helping women. "It's so good to have you back," Jennie said. "I've missed you."

"I missed you too. The camaraderie of women can't be spoken of highly enough. Even when we have to catch it in snatches. There's an intuitive quality to a woman's world, don't you think?"

They gabbed on about that until Jennie literally fell asleep on Callie's shoulder. She woke Jennie to tell her to rest on her daybed rather than making her way back to her room. She had never slept like that before, simply nodding off and staying that way.

A few nights later, she was alone in the office-apartment when she heard the window to her office door break. She reached for the weapon but could barely hold it. She knew the person was in the office and might not even make his way to her room at the back. He'd be looking for morphine or laudanum. She kept a very small supply in the locked cabinet. *I'll stay huddled here, use the gun only to defend myself.* She pointed it toward the door.

She heard voices. *There must be two.*

Even before she could distinguish the second, she knew it would be Douglas. *After all this time, it comes to this.*

"What are you doing?" She'd gotten courage to stand in the doorway.

"Mama, I didn't think you'd be here. It's my mother."

The second person responded with inebriated mumbling. Neither was armed as far as she could tell.

"I repeat. What are you doing here?"

"Getting drugs, Mother, what else?"

"Oh, Douglas."

" 'Oh, Douglas,' " he mocked. "Go back to bed or take care of your patients or whatever it is that consumes you. We'll be gone in a minute."

"I—I can't let you take that. It's harmful."

"But useful. Makes you feel any better, I won't imbibe, I'll sell it to buy my liquor."

His accomplice laughed again. "I'll take it and so will you, you liar."

"We'll be out of here and you can report it as a robbery. You're not going to use that gun and you know it. That old man made you get it, didn't he?"

She lowered the weapon, could barely breathe as she watched them smash the cabinet glass

444

and grab the laudanum and morphine. They overlooked the opium tincture. They left and Jennie crumpled to her knees. *What could I do? What have I not done?* This was the mantra of a mother with an addicted son.

In the morning she notified Fergus of the robbery. She hesitated to say it was Douglas who had done it, but in the end she told him and gave him Dougie's last known address. Fergus told her after checking that it was an empty apartment. No one there.

"Put your time into things you can affect now," Josiah advised when she lamented this latest encounter. "I know your heart is breaking, but you've done all you could for Douglas, a long time ago."

"And I failed."

"But you turned that failure into improving the lives of others. Maybe one day someone will get through to him when we couldn't."

"Thank you for sharing the blame, but it's all mine."

"It belongs to Douglas and his choices." He patted her back. "Work on those scholarships. Maybe one of them will find a cure for drink and drugs. But now come sit with me and we'll gaze out onto the garden while our girls play duets."

It was good advice. When feeling powerless, rest; then return to your passion, to whatever first inspired your dreams. Plunge in. Life is so short.

They held additional teas and events for the scholarship account, opening their Salem home for the fetes. Ariyah proved the "perfect" party planner for their endeavors and helped the Society reach its goal of one thousand dollars. Callie and Jennie began the process of accepting applications and interviewing interested parties. Most of their applicants were married, and Jennie wondered how many of them, like her, had once dreamed of being a doctor before they became wives and mothers. How many of them looked to bring solace as a way to mitigate a family member's untreatable wounds.

"We need to set a date for personal interviews for the scholarship," Jennie told Callie one mid-January morning in 1887. They were at the association's reading room, the applications spread before them. "We could grant three this first year." The price for a term was $50 and they hoped that the interest on the endowment would continue to allow offering at least two more each year. They'd continue to fund-raise as well.

The smell of dusty books and a freshly oiled table made Jennie cough, and she stood to move farther from Callie in case she was catching a cold. Rain drizzled outside and their umbrellas sat like red and yellow tents in the foyer, drying off before the next foray into the mist.

"Why are you holding your stomach?"

"Am I? Habit, I guess." She sat back down. "I have a pain now and then. Nothing significant." She looked at the papers. "Let's set the date and ask the Association secretary to send them out."

"Excellent. We'll choose the candidates and set the appointment times. I'll take the list to the Association."

"Good." She coughed and sighed. "For some reason, I'm tired today."

"Today." Callie laughed. "I marvel that you aren't always tired, changing hats from mother to wife to doctor."

"You do the same thing."

"Not the wife part. And I take more time off. I'm not consulting at the asylum nor teaching classes nor helping with the annual bazaar each year at First Methodist Church. That event alone would wear me out and you do it every year."

"You volunteer at the women's prison and the women's suffrage gatherings."

She ignored Jennie. "Nor do I have evening hours every night of the week. You might consider cutting back to one evening a week. You don't need the money."

"But those are the times when poor and working women can come in, the washerwomen and the shopkeepers. Otherwise it means taking time away from work and they need that pay."

"Well, it's no wonder you're tired. You've

barely time for yourself. You encourage that in your classes, don't you? You should listen to your own advice."

"The classes are for expectant mothers, of which I am not."

"Are you sure?" They both laughed at that.

"Actually, I've entered the transition, I think." Jennie hesitated, then said, "I'm having some spotting."

Callie leaned back in her chair. "Young for that, don't you think?"

"I'll be forty-four this November."

"Still. Any other symptoms?"

She shrugged. "I haven't checked whether an aching back and a constant feeling as though I've eaten a watermelon are indicative of the change. Maybe a little bladder pausing. No chills or feelings of skin-heat though."

Callie frowned. "Who do you see for your own doctoring again?"

"I haven't been to a doctor since Josie was born."

"What?"

"I haven't been ill, so why would I? Don't bully me now, Callie Charlton. I've taken herbs and whatnot."

"What's that old adage, 'A doctor who treats herself has a fool for a patient'?"

"It's not that bad. I just haven't had time nor the need."

"We should have a look though, don't you think?"

"Not really. When would I find the time?"

"I'm serious, Jennie. You've lost weight since I've been back and you didn't have any to spare. Now these symptoms, for how long?"

She held up one finger.

"A month?"

"A year."

"You come to my office next Tuesday." She already had her appointment book out. "Between your last appointment and those evening hours. I'll see you at 5:00 p.m. Don't forget."

Jennie didn't forget. She also didn't tell Josiah. Sometimes a person knows without knowing.

"Dr. Cook in San Francisco. You could write to her. But Dr. Fraser agrees with the diagnosis."

"Yes, I've heard about Dr. Cook. Specializes in uterine cancer."

Jennie's mind swirled with what Callie had told her, though she had suspected. Still, cancer wasn't a word anyone wanted to hear in connection with their own bodies, nor someone they loved.

"Do you want me with you when you talk to Josiah?"

"No. No, I'll tell him." Though she didn't know how. "How much time do you think?"

Callie's voice cracked. "Six months."

"Six months." She took in a deep breath. "Not much time at all. I'll need to make up a will. Arrange for the girls. Josiah—he'll be devastated." She halted in her race of words. "We always thought I'd outlive him. We joked about it." She felt nauseous, the rush of reality surging through her from her abdomen to her throat.

"Are you all right?"

"Yes. Oh, that's an odd answer, isn't it, given the diagnosis?"

"Worse question," Callie said. She put her hand on Jennie's. She'd been sitting next to her to tell her. *I'll remember to do that when I must give bad news to a patient.* Callie's presence felt warm as fresh bread. She looked at her through tears and nodded. Speechless.

She gave a little more information about how the diagnosis was made; being technical helped bring Jennie back from the puddle of emotion. They arranged for when they'd meet again so she could write her will.

"Will you have Charles Winn draw it up?"

"No. I'll draw it up, have it witnessed, and I'll have my brother manage it."

Callie agreed to witness it and said she'd talk with Dr. Fraser as well.

"February 1. Good. That gives me a week to talk with Josiah."

"I really will go with you."

Jennie shook her head. "No. I can do this. We'll go through this together. Two have always been better than one."

"Which is why I'm more than willing to be there. He'll have questions."

"Maybe later." She straightened in her chair, tugged her skirt over her bony knees, crossed her ankles, and leaned back, hands clasped in her lap. "Now let's look at those applicants and do what we need to do to prepare for their interviews."

"Jennie, maybe you should—"

"No, now. I want to do this. I have to do this before I die."

Chapter 40
Two Are Better Than One

They planned to interview three women and no more, hoping each would be a recipient and they wouldn't need to tell two or three no after they'd gotten that far, having filled out applications, provided references and their essays of why they wanted to be a doctor. Two had already found physicians to read with, but one, Mrs. Melvin, had not. Her reference was Jennie's brother Fergus, who had been in business with her husband, owning a butcher shop, all before Fergus became a police officer. He praised her kindness, her good business sense, how neighbors came to her for healing potions and pastes she made herself. Her essay of why she wanted to be a physician had impressed both Callie and Jennie with her line "to heal a broken world, broken spirits, broken bodies, and bring them back to health." She'd added a line that made them curious too. "And once, a woman helped me in a difficult time and I want to pass that on."

"I wanted to heal broken spirits and broken bodies too. I didn't think that doing that would heal the universe," Callie said.

"It helps knit the fruits of the Spirit into the fabric of the world," Jennie offered. ' "Love, joy, peace, longsuffering, gentleness, goodness, faith, meekness, and temperance.' That's what we try to bring to the profession, isn't it?" *Temperance. Something Douglas lacked.* But maybe she did too, always pushing, always busy. Perhaps she spun too much.

They would interview the applicants on a Friday, the second week in February. But first Jennie needed to talk with Josiah and the girls. And then, write her will. She hoped Josiah would agree to what she wanted to do.

"We need to talk." The girls would be home on the weekend, so Jennie had time to think of what she'd say to them. She needed Josiah to help with telling them. She picked up her knitting needles as they sat in the parlor, Jennie across from him as he sat on Elizabeth's settee that, like other furnishings, fit perfectly in their new home.

"So . . . I talked with Callie a few weeks ago. I told her about the bloating and inflammation. Some other issues."

"Like your coughing and losing weight."

"I think that's a cold coming on. Or I thought that."

"You've worked yourself to a frazzle, Jennie girl." He leaned back, his arms behind his head, elbows out, ankles crossed before him as his long legs stretched into the parlor. He was still a handsome man, at this moment trying to look relaxed, but she could see by the tension in his eyes that he knew something was coming.

"I know. Well, that'll be changing."

"Good."

"Not good."

He narrowed his eyes. "You're a very successful businesswoman in addition to being a fine, fine physician, Jennie. Taking time off will be good for you."

"I had a little physical exam with Callie a few weeks ago and she referred me to Dr. Fraser, you remember him?"

"Dean, isn't he?"

She nodded. "A very good doctor across the board and his most recent interest has been in diseases of the uteri. He's a surgeon as well. And . . ."

"Come over here where I can hear you better." He patted the spot on the settee next to him. She complied, but she kept the knitting with her. Something about the soft feel of the yarn and the grip of the bamboo needles was comforting and she needed comfort.

"And . . ." She took a deep breath. "I have cancer, Josiah. I—they give me six months, maybe. I've apparently had it for a while."

"What are you saying? Six months? Surely not."

"I'm going to beat you to the pearly gates." She kept her voice light, for him, for her. Tears spilled.

He took his handkerchief, a big farm one the size of a table napkin from his pocket, and wiped her eyes. He no longer leaned back lounging. His arms were now around her. "Can this be true? Are they sure?"

She nodded.

"We can get another opinion? Treat it."

"I've written to Dr. Cook in San Francisco. I haven't heard back. There isn't much hope, I'm afraid. Or time for treatment if one were available."

He sat stunned for a time. "What about the girls? What do we tell them?"

"I've been thinking about that. I—I want you to hear this in just the right way, Josiah. I think I should ask my brothers, David and George, to act as their guardians until they're of age."

"George travels so much. He's in France now, isn't he?"

"Yes, but he corresponds. David's a lawyer and a judge accustomed to managing these sorts of things." *I'm speaking of the aftermath of my death as "these sorts of things."* "You'd still be their heart holder, their father. I want to save you from the details of the estate and all."

He chewed his lower lip.

"You, you're already eighty-one and the girls

are just thirteen and fourteen . . ." *I won't see my babies grow up.*

"Always looking after me, aren't you, Jennie?"

"We have the resources to send them on to school and you have your own income, still, of course. I'd like to leave this house to them, and property. Just the thirty-three acres in my name, maybe the Bush contract and the bank account, as I close up the practice."

"Yes, of course about the property, the money. But I'm their father. The guardianship . . ."

"You are their father whom they love dearly, as do I." She had to keep racing through this. "I haven't spoken with my brothers yet, but they could . . . manage things. It would relieve you of that responsibility and free you to be with Gracie and Josie, to love them and be their rock, as you've been mine. They'll need that of you, more than ever."

His eyes filled with tears. "I know I've been a burden of late."

"Not at all. No. Not that." She hugged him. *Don't fall apart. Don't fall apart.* "You've been everything I could ever ask for. Divine light on this earth for me, illuminating a world I could never have imagined." And he had been. "Selfishly, I'm glad I'm going first because I don't know how I would go on without you. But you will go on without me. I know that." She wiped at her eyes. His. "Maybe even remarry."

456

He could barely speak. "At my age?" His voice broke. "Oh, Jennie. I love you so." He held her chin in his fingers as he faced her. "So very much." They put their foreheads together. "At this moment it's so hard to see the Lord's plan in this."

"Reverend Parrish," Jennie chided, afraid she'd succumb. "We've had a wonderful life together and now—"

"It isn't fair, Jennie. You're so young. I've lived so long already."

"Fair has nothing to do with it. Our lives are filled with abundance unimaginable to me those years before I met you."

"Yes, I know. But I don't feel blessed at this moment."

They both cried then, the knitting pushed aside as he held her once again. The Seth Thomas clock chimed the hour. She was relieved that the girls weren't there, that she could gather herself before she had to tell them.

"What will I do without you?"

"You'll go on until you don't. And then we'll be together again."

"What about Douglas?" Josiah's concern made her love her husband more.

"Make a space for him, when he's sober, if you can. My brothers will help if he's trouble to you or the girls."

Josiah nodded. "He'll grieve when he learns of

it. But you must not spend time there, Jennie. Let those who know how to show that they love you do that now."

"I'll leave a small amount of my funds for him, a very small amount. I'm afraid it will support his downfall otherwise and I can't do that to him. I so hoped to find a cure."

For a time, they simply held each other and then began to mention moments in their marriage that they treasured, memories he'd have and Jennie would cherish for as long as she could. The soft talk turned into hopefulness. For there is always hope. "Maybe the San Francisco doctor will have something to say. Are you up for the trip?"

"Maybe. You'll be with me when I tell the girls?"

"Absolutely. Haven't I always said that two are better than one."

What was left? To tell the girls first and, foremost, to let her brothers know. And her mother. Jennie hated her having to face the death of another child. Jennie had lived that journey and it wasn't easy. She would have to tell Ariyah. Maybe she could see patients right up until that moment of transition and tell the girls then? But what if she waited too long? And Josiah said to allow those who knew how to show their love to her to do that. "It would give a gift to them to be able to comfort you."

She made her way to Ariyah, inhaled deeply before she shared the news. Ariyah's tears mingled with her own. Then Jennie began a song of regret, but Ariyah interrupted her.

"Douglas loves you," Ariyah said. "He just can't show it. Addiction gets in the way of love's expression, and one day, when he's sober, he will have to face the fact that he was not there for his mother's passing. But for now, you must let us love you into your next life."

Even in exiting the carousel of life, there were choices she could make.

Callie opened the door and invited the last scholarship applicant into the room. Mrs. Melvin wore a large-brimmed hat with a small yellow flower as decoration. Around her neck was a glorious silk scarf and she carried a matching yellow reticule.

"Miss Priscilla?" The shock must have been evident in Jennie's voice.

"Mrs. Priscilla Melvin," she corrected as she took Jennie's hand, looked Jennie in the eye, nodded. "Mrs. Parrish."

"Have you two met?" Callie showed her to the chair.

"Years ago. She wasn't Mrs. Melvin then and I wasn't Mrs. Parrish."

"But you were the kindest of women and I never forgot that."

"We barely spoke." Jennie tried to remember what she could have said to her that was memorable. Mostly she'd judged her when she confronted her about being with Charles, envied her that Charles had spoken of their lives to her; Jennie blamed her. "I can't imagine what I might have done or said that was kind."

"As I left Millie's Millinery with this purse you gave me"—she held up her reticule—"you said, 'May the spirit of the Christ child bless you today, all year long, and forever.' I know you meant it as a simple Christmas blessing, but it turned me to wonder what drove such kindness, who this Christ child was. I met Mr. Melvin after that and he helped me find another life where I could serve others. As you do."

"I—I'm speechless."

"Then I'll begin the interview," Callie said. "I haven't been able to follow your conversation, so I'll start one of my own. Tell us about yourself, Mrs. Melvin. Why do you want to be a doctor?"

Epilogue

"A re you up to this?"

Jennie nodded. "I always loved this path to the creek. I once showed Douglas a fox here." The girls walked arm in arm ahead of the group, Ariyah beside them while Lizzie pushed the wheeled chair behind. Josiah held her up as she took slow, labored steps. He used his cane to help balance and the two were like a drunken sailor walking. She told him that and he laughed. Dr. Cook had said she might have something to offer, but Jennie would need to come to San Francisco to see her, and by May when Jennie heard back from her, she knew she could not do that. She was too weak and it was too late. It was as though having once admitted that something was wrong, the disease sped up, but of course it had its own timing.

She'd completed her will. Her brothers agreed to be named executors and guardians. Both Dr. Fraser and Callie were her witnesses that day. And with Josiah's help they told the girls and vowed to make this a good summer for them. They had each other and Josiah. It was August and she'd made it this far. She hoped to be there for JoJo's birthday.

461

Lizzie had returned to their lives more fully, taking care of Jennie so Josiah didn't have to do those messy things. He read to Jennie, who dozed off and on. Not the textbooks anymore but the Psalms and poetry of Wordsworth and Emerson, in whose words Josiah heard his own "loss of a great love."

Ariyah had said she'd have the perfect funeral and "you'll be here to help plan it." She dabbed at her eyes, hugged Alex a little closer. But plan they did and it was a strange joy to Jennie that she had time and awareness to say the good-byes and dictate the letters, saying things she'd always thought but had not taken the time to scribe. Letters came to her as well, from those she'd touched in her life. Patients. Friends. Her daughters. *Abundance* was the word that comforted.

"There! That's where we saw the fox." She pointed to her girls. *Has it only been twenty-one years?* "He took tufts from the willow. Oh, now I see there are fences, but they still have wool stuck to them."

"And he'd pull them off and jump into the creek?" Gracie asked.

Jennie nodded. "Fleas and bugs jumped off him onto those tufts. Smart fox."

"He washed away his troubles," Josiah said.

"Of course there were daffodils then," Jennie

remembered. "It was spring and they popped up between the willows."

"'And then my heart with pleasure fills, And dances with the daffodils.' You know, Wordsworth said he could recall those blooms in times of solitude," Josiah said. "They'll remind me of you when I see them now each spring." His voice cracked.

"Think of me when you see a fox too. Oh, look! Girls. See—?" She bent over with a gasp of pain.

"Jennie?" Josiah held her as she leaned into him.

The chair was behind her in seconds. "La, Mrs. P, you rest now."

Jennie sank into it. "Pushing a little too hard," she said. "Might be time for the blessed morphine. Just haven't wanted . . . to disappear yet."

Callie would stay with them soon to administer the drug. This would be her last outing. As when she'd waited for the arrival of Gracie, a doctor would "live in" with her. Josiah squeezed her shoulder while Lizzie wrapped the knitted wool across Jennie's lap.

"We're heading back," he shouted to the girls, who had moved down the stream. "Your mother's tired. Come when you're ready."

"We'll come with you now, Papa." JoJo waved her arms, swinging them like a windmill. Gracie

463

followed behind, holding her linen skirt above her white shoes. The girls passed them, went on ahead, their beautiful girls holding hands; kind and loving people. Strong. They had each other.

Josiah pushed Jennie in the chair, his gold-handled cane hooked over the back, clanking. Ariyah and Lizzie walked behind. Only Douglas was missing, though he lived in their hearts.

Jennie reached up to pat Josiah's hand. Together, they had given the world these strong, faithful young women. And despite her wish to have it last longer, to have achieved more, she had truly been given riches and prayed she had passed some of them on.

Author's Acknowledgments and Notes

With the publication some years ago of *Love to Water My Soul*, Portlander Audrey Slater sent me a letter writing that it was her family who descended from the Indian agent Josiah Parrish mentioned in that book. "His wife became one of the first doctors in Portland working with women and children." That letter began a friendship that twenty years later has resulted in *All She Left Behind*. I am deeply indebted to Audrey and her daughter, Dianne Gregoire, for sharing stories of "Grandma Josie" and Josiah Parrish, for sending me a copy of Jennie's diploma from Willamette Medical College in 1879, and for inspiring this story. I'm grateful too that the family allowed me to pursue where the facts might lead (to new information they never had) and to bring Jennie's story of faith and perseverance to others.

My friendship with CarolAnne Tsai is another treasure that also began with a letter to me expressing an appreciation for my stories and offering to help in any way she could. Discovering her experience as a social worker (just like me!) who loves stories (just like me!)

and that her expertise was in medical research (not like me at all!) opened doors to a variety of research sites.

The Methodist Archives in Philadelphia unlocked Jennie's will, details of a house fire that took Jennie's Salem house shortly after she died, copies of invoices for medical books she ordered, newspaper accounts and letters from her children to their father, details about a piano and programs from concerts attended. The Oregon Historical Society archives and Marion County Historical Society gave us obituaries and newspaper accounts of events, city directories and the addresses of Jennie's office in Portland, details of their lives in Salem, and old photographs to bring the cities to life.

From Jennie's will we learned of her previous marriage, of the son she'd had and his struggles, and how she intended to care for her children after her death. CarolAnne also located newspaper accounts verifying the addiction problems of the Pickett men.

CarolAnne was a constant voice of encouragement, a wise confidante about the story and Jennie's possible motivations and where the story might end. I'm grateful beyond words. That we've shared family moments has been an added gift of abundance, including a handtooled pen made by her husband Stan and a drawing on our refrigerator made by their daughter Annelise. Research ought to be fun and CarolAnne made it so. She also read versions and gave advice.

Janet Meranda is another faithful friend who is a master copyeditor, but all errors or omissions belong to me.

I'm grateful to the team at Baker/Revell: Andrea Doering, Michele Misiak, Barb Barnes, Karen Steele, and so many others whom I've never met. Thank you for your confidence and professionalism in bringing Jennie's story to readers. To my agent, Joyce Hart of Hartline Literary: we've had twenty-six years together in this publishing world and I am grateful for your care, vision, and grace. Leah Apineru of Impact Author has kept my social media life alive— I'm so grateful; Paul Schumacher keeps my website fresh and up-to-date. Thank you for your patience. Carol Tedder, my events coordinator, has helped me say both yes and no. I'd be lost without her.

Thank you as well to my prayer team across North America—Loris Webb, Judy Schumacher, Judy Card, Susan Parrish, Carol Tedder, Gabby Sprenger—and faithful friends like Marea Stone, Jill Dyer, Blair Fredstrom (who died during the final phases of this book), Melinda Stanfield (who offered insights as a retired physician), Sandy Maynard, Kay Krall, my sister-in-law Barb Rutschow, stepdaughter Katy

Larsen; family and friends at First Presbyterian Bend and around the country, too numerous to mention, who offered encouragement and who are held in my heart. Thank you.

A special thanks to the unnamed photographer from the United Kingdom whom I met on a cruise who told me the story of the fox and the fleas that he outsmarted with wool.

And to Jerry, who listens patiently while I lament my chosen field of endeavor, and who helps me celebrate too. Thank you for enthusiastically cheering me on until I begin to believe what you have all along: that the stories are like prayers taking me to where I'm meant to go.

Jennie's story unfolded with that one line from Audrey Slater's letter years ago. From that I learned first of Josiah, an icon of Oregon history, and with much more digging, Jennie's history of her first marriage, Charles and Douglas's addiction issues, the marriage status, loss of a baby girl, her marriage to Josiah, their age difference, newspaper accounts of "the old man and the young woman" looking happy, the birth of Grace and Josie, the strychnine poisoning, Jennie's enrollment and graduation, her election, Josiah's operating the pharmacy and interest in the homeopathic society, professions of Jennie's siblings, their deaths, and both her brother and Josiah's son as Portland police officers. The generosity of Elizabeth and Josiah

Parrish, their faithful Chinese cook, Charley Chen, and "Lizzie" are all from the historical records, as is Josiah's giving Jennie thirty-three acres in Salem. Quilton the porcupine and Van the spaniel are not historical, though my husband did once have a friend with a pet porcupine that held up its bowl for milk.

Neither is Ariyah based on history. She is the result of a high bid to name a character at the Authors for Education event of the Gresham Barlow Education Foundation. Bess Wills was the high bidder and she gifted the win to Sue Piazza. Ariyah is Sue's granddaughter's name. It does mean "Pure Music" and Jennie needed the kind of friend Ariyah became.

At eighty-two, Josiah did remarry following Jennie's death. He died of complications of a stroke in 1895 at the age of eighty-nine. Both Gracie and Josie—often known as JoJo—completed college and married doctors. Shortly after Jennie's death, her house in Salem, along with valuables and precious letters that might have unveiled more about Jennie's life, was destroyed by fire. The girls' letters to their father lament the loss of so much but express gratitude that the piano was saved.

According to his obituary, Douglas died at the age of thirty-six, in jail as a result of "excessive indulgence in alcohol, cocaine and morphine to which habits he has been addicted for a number of years." Was Jennie motivated to understand the impact of alcohol scientifically? We do know she was an allopath or "regular" doctor in her studies and practice. Did she hope for a cure? We don't know. But given the obituary for both Charles and Douglas, the terrible waste of life addictions cause, and the overwhelming presence of alcohol abuse in the society of Salem and Portland at the time, it seems feasible that Jennie would have tried to find a way to rescue her family and, lacking that, find a way to forgive herself.

Women physicians were rare in the West, but Bethina Owens was a friend of the Parrishes and she did become the first woman physician in Oregon. The Ford sisters were the first to graduate from Willamette Medical College as physicians. Jennie, Callie Charlton, and Esther Yeargain followed. Mary Sawtelle's experience with Willamette is as described. She went on to acquire her degree and worked while her husband finished his degree at Willamette. Find out more about her at www.oregonencyclopedia.org. Callie Charlton and more of Mary Sawtelle's experiences have been blogged about at http://kimberlyjensenblog.blogspot.com/. Callie was the witness to Jennie's will. Dr. Cook was a female specialist in San Francisco.

Women often chose homeopathic colleges back East where they were more likely to be treated as equals. Many women were taught home remedies as ways to treat their family illnesses, so homeopathic study was a natural direction. Those studying allopathic or "regular" medicine were more inclined toward pharmaceuticals and surgery to treat disease. Their study required access to hospitals and surgery opportunities, "reading" with physicians before matriculating, and as with Willamette, fewer women were accepted, making Jennie's enrollment as a wife and mother unique for her time.

Jennie did not find the cures she sought. Her observations of the physical uniqueness of a child born to a mother who drank did not become known as Fetal Alcohol Syndrome until the 1980s. It must have been a deep grief that she could neither save her husband nor her son from the ravages of addiction. But she saw the value in treating women and children and making it a specialty and educating through the Medical Society other physicians.

She was indeed elected unanimously as vice president of the Oregon Medical Society and might well have become president had her life's trajectory taken her a different way. She was forty-three years old when she died August 10, 1887. She is buried in the Lee Cemetery in Salem.

Jennie's Herbs and Oils

These oils and aromatics were used during Jennie's lifetime by homeopathic physicians for the treatments listed; they should not be used today without proper education and instruction.

Arnica—aches and muscle pain

Barley—stomachaches

Belladonna—poisonous; with care, used for scarlet fever, acute fevers, infection with inflammation; relieves ear infections and boils and assists with breastfeeding

Black currant seeds—oil; Blackfeet Indians used to stave off cravings of liquor

Calendula cream—(marigold) treatment of breast during breast-feeding; tincture and cream

Cayenne—abdominal pain and stomach pain; Aztec treatment for intoxication

Chamomile—liver cleansing and calming bruised muscles

Dogwood root tea—substitute for quinine for malarial fever (Tillamook)

Elderberry—expectorant (Blackfeet/Blackfoot)

Ferrum phosphoricum—fevers from infections

Lavender—hives, insomnia, blisters, boils, bug and spider bites, burns

Licorice root—induce vomiting

Marjoram—bruised muscles

Nux vomica (*Strychnos nux vomica*)—poisonous in certain dosages; sedative, pregnancy cramping, labor pain, indigestion

Pasqueflower—an expectorant for treatment of poisons (Blackfeet remedy); speeds labor; treats syphilis (Shawnee)

Peppermint—spider and bug bites

Periwinkle—headaches

Pulsatilla—treating cataracts, ulcers, tooth decay, depression, gynecological complaints

Quinine—malaria, ague (also cedar root tea)

Rosemary—liver cleansing, muscle cramps, spasms

Rose ointment—blisters

Saleratus—leavening agent; treating stomach upset

Shooting star leaves—treatment of cold sores

Skullcap tincture—mild sedative

Sulfate of cinchona—substitute for quinine treating malaria, ague

Violet root—liver; bringing on milk for nursing mothers; roots act as expectorant when poison swallowing is suspected

Reader's Guide

1. Jennie says, "Some things are worth doing regardless of how they turn out." Do you share that view? Did Jennie's life portray that philosophy?

2. What were the supports Jennie found that enabled her to pursue her dream? What were the barriers? Did she achieve her dream? Why or why not? How have friends or colleagues assisted you on your journey?

3. Was Jennie responsible for her son's addiction? Were there steps Jennie could have taken that she didn't to stave off the disaster of Douglas's and his father's lives?

4. Jennie says that spending time blaming others for tragedy takes one from their purpose. Do you agree with that? Why or why not?

5. Ariyah tells Jennie that guilt "is a fiend" and urges her to make a personal change to ward it off. Has there been a time when guilt held

you back? How did you find a path through it to a new hope?

6. How did Josiah support his wives on their journeys? How did Elizabeth and Jennie support him? Was Jennie justified in the arrangements she made in her will for guardianship?

7. Jennie returned often to the image of the fox. What meaning did she ascribe to that encounter? Do you share her *Einsicht*, her insight?

8. "Pleasure disappoints, possibility never," writes Kierkegaard. Did Jennie discover this? Do you agree?

9. Jennie notes that carriages are safest in the barn, but they are built for the unknown roads. Think of a time when you took a risk. Was the result what you had imagined? Did the possibility give you hope?

10. The author wanted to show that our inability to bring healing and peace to the lives of those we love does not mean we should deny the joys of pursuing our own calling to make a difference in the world. Did she succeed?

Bibliography

Apothecary Society. *Little Lookbook*. Utah: Young Living, 2015.

Cornell, Virginia. *Doc Suzie: The True Story of a Country Physician in the Colorado Rockies*. California: Carpinteria Publications, 1991.

Fuller, Tom, Christy Van Heukelem, and the Mission Mill Museum. *Images of America: Salem*. South Carolina: Arcadia Publishing, 2009.

Gladstar, Rosemary. *Medicinal Herbs: A Beginner's Guide*. Massachusetts: Storey Publishing, 2012.

Harris, Sharon M. *Dr. Mary Walker: An American Radical, 1832–1919*. New Jersey: Rutgers University Press, 2009.

Kirschmann, Anne Taylor. *A Vital Force: Women in American Homeopathy*. New Jersey: Rutgers University Press, 2004.

Larsell, O. *The Doctor in Oregon*. Portland, OR: Binford & Mort for Oregon Historical Society, 1947.

Lockie, Andrew, and Nicola Geddes. *Homeopathy: The Principles & Practices of Treatment*. New York: Dorling Kindersley, 1995.

Okrent, Daniel. *Last Call: The Rise and Fall of Prohibition*. New York: Scribner, 2010.

Tilford, Gregory L. *Edible and Medicinal Plants of the West*. Montana: Mountain Press Publishing Company, 1997.

About the author

Jane Kirkpatrick is the *New York Times* and CBA bestselling author of more than thirty books, including *A Sweetness to the Soul*, which won the prestigious Wrangler Award from the Western Heritage Center. Her works have been finalists for the Christy Award, Spur Award, Oregon Book Award, and Reader's Choice awards, and have won the WILLA Literary Award, USABestBooks Award, and Carol Award for Historical Fiction. Many of her titles have been Book of the Month and Literary Guild selections, with more than 1.5 million books in print. You may read her work in more than fifty publications, including *Decision*, *Private Pilot*, and *Daily Guideposts*. Jane lives in Central Oregon with her husband, Jerry. Learn more at www.jkbooks .com and sign up for her newsletter *Story Sparks*.

Books are produced in the United States using U.S.-based materials	Books are printed using a revolutionary new process called THINKtech™ that lowers energy usage by 70% and increases overall quality	Books are durable and flexible because of smythe-sewing	Paper is sourced using environmentally responsible foresting methods and the paper is acid-free

Center Point Large Print
600 Brooks Road / PO Box 1
Thorndike, ME 04986-0001 USA

(207) 568-3717

US & Canada:
1 800 929-9108
www.centerpointlargeprint.com